PUNK

NEIL ROWLAND

STORY

ACORN BOOKS

Published in 2017 by
Acorn Books
www.acornbooks.co.uk

Acorn Books is an imprint of
Andrews UK Limited
www.andrewsuk.com

to Paul Hewson

Not necessarily in the right order…

Thanks to Sian Pickard for proofreading
Love to my daughter Anastasia
Special thanks to my dad for telling me to finish this book
Friends and family
All our music heroes past, present and beyond

1. Smells Like Teen Spirit

This a celebration of friendship, a punk band and the thrill ride of music.

Who, where, what was I in 1977? I was eighteen year old Paul Bottle, just about to graduate from the local arts college, still living at home, in our town of Nulton. Shock waves proved something seismic was about to happen in the UK. The situation would change, for the nation, for rock music and for youth, even if we didn't recognize advance notices.

There were arguments, but they called this movement 'punk rock'. It was a brat-pop tendency launched during the Queen's Silver Jubilee Year. We were considered a nightmare for the royal family, the government and the establishment. Or most obviously it was The Sex Pistols. How could you ever forgive or forget them?

Punk exploded all my previous ideas about life, everything I'd ever listened to, thought or watched. Music and style, arts and rebellion, identity and growing up, that's where it began. Soon I was knocking around with fantastic new people who could cuss and play a guitar at the same time. The punks strutted around in their glory, like kings and queens of the street, with hardly a King's shilling in their ripped pockets. These were tough times for young people, before social media – for good or evil – mostly in terms of jobs. For many of us a 'career' was like spotting a unicorn waiting at the bus stop. Eventually I got the idea to become a 'pretentious music critic'.

Until punk came along school friends would drag me into town on Saturday nights to bad clubs with terrible soundtracks. I'd put on my check sports jacket and flared trousers (chosen for me out of the Co-operative Super Store). Local girls in home-sewn hot pants would either ignore me or give a jump of alarm. They left me under a plastic palm tree at the edge of the floor, incinerated with embarrassment. I'd turn into a snow man if any girl so much as breathed on my neck; which didn't happen very often. Invisibility didn't make me feel more comfortable under the flashing hot lights of *The Flamingo*.

The revolution started when my fellow student Jon got into punk. He went on to form his own band and I was invited to one of the mad gigs. In fact Jon Whitmore was my next door neighbour, who created amazement by emerging in early punk costume. He chose to make a big art school statement, shocking society and changing popular music.

'You'll never guess what I'm looking at,' dad declared. He was peering around the edge of the curtains and nets into our suburban road. '*Bloody Nora!*'

'What's aggravating you now, Pete?' said our mother.

Our dad laughed in baffled fury. 'Come and look at this, will you,' he told us. 'It's the weedy little kid of them next door. Wearing a bloody dustbin liner. Safety pins through his ears.' Without unsticking his eyes from the glass, dad gestured for my brother Charles and me to come over. 'I've never seen the like of this. Take a look yourselves, you lads. What's that little freak up to?'

My family lined up to watch, as if our bay window was turned into the royal box. Jon was strolling about, trying not to notice twitching curtains going along the road. He had a self-conscious yet defiant attitude, with his arms and legs sticking out of that black dustbin liner. Sure enough there were safety pins stuck around his person. Even most babies had stopped wearing safety pins by then.

For me, I was fascinated by what he was trying to say. There had to be a point behind the stunt. I knew it was some kind of ironic provocation. Of course it was working a treat with my family.

'What's the problem? He's got a friggin' screw loose, that's what. Stupid little berk,' dad was saying. Dad – who was big and physically strong from factory work – itched to unbuckle his belt and give Jon a good thrashing. He wanted to teach him a hard lesson of life too.

Satisfied with the bafflement and shock he'd caused, Jon eventually ducked back in doors – probably to get warmed up. Soon a group of neighbours (the Jubilee Street Party organisers) came out and gathered to discuss the possible meaning of the bizarre exhibition they'd witnessed.

* * *

That evening I got my courage up to call next door, intending to find out the reasons for Jon's parade. This was radical because I hadn't even set foot in Jon's house for ages. This was on account of us taking a boyish, competitive dislike to each other. The fact we studied in different departments at college didn't completely explain our coolness.

The street was calm again and my family had lost interest in the anti-fashion scandal. Mrs Whitmore let me in to their semi, all surprised smiles and calling to her adored son, 'Jon, love, you got visitor!'

There was a pregnant silence from above, until a half-hearted grunt finally reached us. So I clumped up the staircase and, edging forward, found myself sat with the provocateur in his pad. 'Oh, you. A rare pleasure,' he told me.

Surprisingly his bedroom was still filled with boyhood stuff. My own space had been cleared of toys, games and comics long before. My parents considered him to be a spoiled brat, because he was 'crippled' as they put it and his mum and dad (called soft foreigners from Cyprus and Italy) were soft on him. There was some truth to the argument of Jon being spoiled, at least until punk rock came along. I immediately noticed a stack of new 45 records and a new 'music centre' in his room. There was also a black cabinet with a cloth fronted speaker and a panel of little knobs. Only later did he explain that this was a little Marshall 'Master Model' fifty-watt practice amp. Something was going on, so what was it?

Jon had changed out of the plastic garbage chic, but his hair was aggressively tangled up and there were piercings, including a ring through a nostril. No way would my parents have allowed that.

There was a knowing arrogant look in his big melancholy brown eyes. When he spoke his voice had a curious sarcastic whine to it. I sat nervously on the edge of his bed, taking in these changes and waiting for clarity.

What did I understand about the term 'punk'? Jon brought the subject up challengingly. I'd heard the word in a lot of American movies, used by a macho cop or a cowboy. It was generally understood to be a term of abuse for the scum of society. Who wanted to be considered like that?

'Even better,' he told me. 'The word comes from being a prostitute.' Jon spread himself out in lazy comfort, in black jeans and ripped tee-shirt, over the embroidered spread.

'So you're… you know… going on "the game"… or something?' I barely knew what selling your body consisted of.

He looked shifty as he worked out whether I was deserving of his attention or contempt or pity. 'Didn't you hear nothing about The Pistols?' he asked, with a sneer.

'*Pistols*? Oh right. Course I have.'

'No, Paul, I don't mean weapons. I mean the band.'

'What you on about, Jon?'

'Shit, Bottle, where have you been?'

'This got anything to do with… your provocative event today?'

He scoffed. 'Amazing the reaction from standing in your own bloody street,' he mocked.

'Yeah, sure Jon… I see… like…'

'And don't call me 'Jon' anymore, right?'

I stared back disorientated, stunned.

'Nowadays I go by the name of Snot. Stan Snot,' he explained.

'How'd you work that out?' The old boyhood rivalry and animosity had returned, like the point of a plastic Roman sword under my chin.

'Stan Snot' continued to recline on the bed. He was showing off a pair new boots. He hadn't bothered to take them off in doors. This was one punk sponsored by indulgent parents.

'Punk's kicking the establishment,' he stated, in a deep droll voice.

I shuffled and puzzled. 'The *establishment*? Is it?'

'This country's nauseatingly complacent.' His baleful golden eyes turned back to me, in the too large head, under thick black curls.

His bedroom felt uncomfortably small. 'Sorry, I still don't get it.'

Snot gave a dry snort. 'You don't get it! We're going to destroy this tedious way of life.'

'Destroy it? What with?'

'Noise. *Anarchy*.'

I puzzled over it. 'What for?'

'You wanna work in that Vacuum Factory?'

'Nah… No, not really.'

'We're invisible as a generation. We're just fodder and scum. You want to stay that way?' he asked. 'Invisible?'

'Nobody wants to be invisible.'

'Yeah, we want to make our mark. Say "we exist. We got ideas. We're creative. Listen to us too."'

'I can see the point…'

'They are going to notice us for sure, Bottle. Whether they like us or they don't like us,' he warned. 'They are not going to destroy us, we are going to destroy them.'

'So when did you get all these ideas?'

'What does it matter?'

'What exactly are punks going to do?'

'Don't you read the music papers?' Snot challenged.

The back of my eyes searched the front of my brain.

'Take careful note, Bottle. It's about the music scene. I've been down to London. Up on the train to Sheffield and Nottingham as well.' He put his hands behind his head. 'I've been going to gigs by the Sex Pistols. And great bands like the Damned. These groups are the bollocks, my friend. These lads are the godfathers and mothers of punk rock. The bass player, Glenn Matlock, writes the tunes. Johnny Rotten writes most of the lyrics. Rotten's got amazing stage presence.'

'So are they going to be a big hit?'

Jon sniggered at my naivety. '*Big hit*? They're subversive, Bottle. The gigs are like one big fight.'

'A fight? *During a concert*?'

5

'You don't know what could happen. Then the guitar is jacking up behind Rotten and everybody's pogo-ing, trying to smash everything. You can feel the whole venue jolting.'

'Well, right, sounds amazing,' I admitted. Some of the tension between us lifted.

'Punk's going to shake up this whole society. We're gonna make them choke on their cake… during that stupid street party.'

'Do the Pistols wear bin liners as well?' I wondered.

He smiled with sarcastic insight. 'Not any more. The punk scene's changing constantly. It's volatile and shifting. Which is the whole point. Maybe punk will end as quickly as it's started. Who can tell?' he speculated.

'Where did this punk scene start? I haven't heard anything,' I complained.

'Who can say exactly? It could've been in New York, like the clubs. Or maybe from the underground scene,' Snot told me, as if he jetted around the world.

'Somebody must have started it off,' I said, 'or thought about calling it 'punk'.'

Jon spiked up his thick hair (it wasn't yet dyed). 'Where does any anarchistic youth rebellion begin?' he countered – an insider to an outsider.

'Well, I don't know. I don't have a clue.' I didn't.

'You'd look at the *Sex* boutique in Chelsea.'

'Would I?' I felt the heat in my cheeks, like blobs in an oil lamp.

'Yeah.'

'In *Chelsea*? Sex?'

'Why not? The Pistols are all hard London lads.'

'Oh, but… Do they *need* to be hard?' I said, perplexed.

'First of all they tricked the big music companies. Smashed up their offices.'

'Why they do that for?' I was literally on the edge of my seat – Snot's bed – waiting to find out. There was a pile of loud board games behind his shoulder.

'Punk is a focus for alienation. We're part of the rebellion,' he argued.

'Are we? What are we alienated from?'

'Open your eyes. Look around.'

'All right, but what are *you* rebelling against?'

'Society. Power. Authority,' he checked off.

At this moment his Mum called from downstairs. 'Jon, love, your dinner is on the table soon,' she called up, with a croon.

'Always the same ritual,' he remarked. 'It's fucking torture.'

'Maybe I'd better go soon anyway.'

'How is it for you, Bottle?'

I nodded glumly. But I didn't comment on my situation. Anyway I was still thinking about this punk thing.

'Don't be long, Jon, love. I got such lovely dessert tonight!'

Stan Snot jumped up and dug around in his wardrobe. He pulled out the offending black bin liner.

'Want to try it? Put it on,' he teased.

'No, thanks, it'd be stupid on me.'

He explained that the bin bag was already passé. His mum and dad though, as ever, had looked on benignly at his punk pranks. They were about the only parents in Britain not shocked or offended by anything punks could say or do.

'We're the dogs from hell,' Snot informed me.

'You definitely shook 'em up today.'

'To destroy is the ultimate creative statement.'

That type of argument looked good in a college essay, but it startled me, and the implications would reverberate over the following months.

'Jon, love, *dinner!*'

* * *

Over the following weeks 'Stan Snot' played me his entire punk record collection. There was no danger of exhausting it because he was always buying new vinyl – 45s or EPs. Some of the bands were starting to release LPs as well (you didn't call them 'albums' any more). Before long the records came out in picture sleeves. The inventive graphics of the artefacts was fascinating. Later the music came out on twelve inch singles; a format borrowed from the New York disco scene.

As well as The Sex Pistols and The Clash, it was The Damned, The Stranglers and the Adverts, for starters. I realised that The Clash were more radical, political; and had emerged from the London squat scene, as explained to me. The Adverts came out with weird, unsettling songs that intrigued. That song of theirs, *Gary Gilmore's Eyes*, was about the American killer condemned to the electric chair and, apparently, he anticipated the day. The monotonous melody played constantly in our students' common room. Gilmore, refusing the quicker end of a firing squad, finally fried and turned into a punk anti-hero.

Punk bands could record cheaply and roughly, self-producing on small independent labels. That was the whole DIY point. Stan insisted that kids didn't need to be good musicians. I was never interested in playing an instrument. I was desperate to get involved, even if I didn't know how.

My cousin Kevin, ten years older, had showed off his record collection to me. Some of these 'classic' albums made an impact, to be honest, but the artists' image and sound felt very remote from us. Suddenly kids our age were starting their own garage groups, playing small gigs and recording fast and cheap.

Obviously punk had other influences. It had a definite 'glam rock' feel, which linked us to those groups we'd idolised at school – bands that had often been rough and vulgar too under their glitz campery. Then there was the huge and varied influence of David Bowie, collected in cassettes. British punks had taken in the New York scene, even though that city could have been Mars. Reaching back there was the Velvet Underground, Warhol and the Factory; I only knew about it years later. To me everything was completely and radically new to experience.

The punks created a furious, repulsive crash and thrash; and fashions to go along with it. The punks were the garbage of society. And I was soon among them.

* * *

It started like this – during our regular play of new records – Stan dropped a second cultural bomb. 'Hey, Bottle, how'd you wanna come and hear *my* band?'

8

Stunned, confused, impressed, I could only react. '*Your* band?'

'We've got a gig at the college,' he explained.

'Really? At Nulton Arts?'

'Yeah, the principle gave permission. We have to give the money to charity. Maybe there's a charity for punks, I don't know.'

'Does he know about punk? The type of music?'

''course he fucking doesn't, Bottle. He thinks we're the New Seekers, doesn't he. He reckons I look like Leo Sayer. It'll be too late before he knows what we sound like.'

I fell back on his bed laughing. When I'd recovered, I said, 'I don't know what you sound like either.'

'You can come and hear us, Bottle.'

'Amazing. No problem.'

'We're not as good as The Sex Pistols. That is, we're not as bad.'

'So what instrument do you play?' I wondered.

Finally he explained to me what that little black box did – the amp. He went over to the built-in wardrobe, rummaged and finally pulled out a bashed-about blue guitar. At this stage it didn't even have a case.

'Amazing.'

'Mum got me this second hand. Mum's going to ask my uncle Luigi if I can have his old guitar. Not that I play well or want to,' he warned.

'So you're not going to learn?'

'This band's punk and we don't need to play any good.'

'What's your band's name?' Every band's got to have a name, even a punk group.

'It's Mortal Wound,' he announced.

Most likely my eyebrows joined at the middle. '*Mortal Wound*?'

'Yeah.'

I tried to get my head around the idea.

They sounded like a right bunch of stiffs.

2. White Riot

So I accepted Jon's invitation to Mortal Wound's next gig. What was I letting myself in for? We'll see!

The band's first ever gig was at the *Dragon* (our favoured student public house) which turned into a mass brawl (only avoided when an older biker crowd stepped in). The up-coming gig was being promoted by the Principle as a treat for students' graduation. Convinced by Stan's bullshit he was impressed that profits were going to charity. Stan and I had sat exams in the very same hall as the 'concert' would be held. We still waited nervously for our final grades; particularly Stan who'd been offered a tasty design job: an apprenticeship. Nulton Arts College and was about to part company with a talented student.

We'd all enjoyed the experience for three years. I'd spent that period kneading lumps of clay, sketching middle-aged perverts, chipping away at lumps of rock. Sculpture was my speciality and particular passion. I still had the cuts and bruises, lumps and swelling to show for it.

During that summer, rough haircuts, rude cosmetics and safety pins broke out like acne. While the Queen's Silver Jubilee celebrations approached some studios were decked out with the bunting of punk. That classic poster of The Clash was put up in my room. Somehow the college Principle missed these signs of change in culture and fashion. To parents and many teachers (even our trendy art teachers) the punk thing was a hole through the head. To us it dynamited a space in the mind, allowing our passions, energies and imagination to break free.

The original line-up of Mortal Wound was as follows:

Jon Whitmore – lead guitar and vocals
Paul Blumen – lead vocals
Simon Moore – bass
Henrietta Harris – rhythm guitar
Billy Kelly – drums

Otherwise known as:

Stan Snot – lead guitar and vocals
Nutcase – lead vocals
Herb – bass
Anna-kissed – rhythm guitar
Billy Urine – drums

Like sucking arsenic up a straw, I got my first taste of live punk.

Scores of punks (or proto-punks) were hanging about in our college hall, along with an alarming mix of outside cults, hooligans and extremists. Most of them were swigging take-away alcohol, smoking like the *Flying Scotsman*, looking self-consciously bored to the point of mindless violence. Only a minority were or had been students at the college. The 'charity concert' was open to non-residents, in expectation of raising extra cash. Advance notice about a punk gig had spread far and wide; to every town and village in the county it seemed. Luckily the Principle had another appointment that evening and didn't attend in person.

Many teenagers still had only a patchy idea of what 'punk' music and fashion was. Many of them came to Mortal's gig from curiosity, or just for something to do. This was the right spirit. And if you were below voting age you had to get involved with punk, like getting mugged on the top deck of the last bus.

I always hated my appearance. It was hard to fit in. In my opinion I looked awkward and strange, and it was hard not to live up to that very negative self-image. That's the way I was shot out of the womb, I reckon. Paul Bottle, a lanky, awkward, oddball boy. With a long nose, a receding chin and boggly looking eyes. The punk movement took negativity and turned it into a powerful energy; as it did all the pain and discomfort of the misfits and outsiders of society. We didn't analyse it at the time, yet it was bloody true.

As a mate of Snot I got the honour of hanging about with his group 'back stage'. There wasn't a support act that night. It was hard to think what kind of support you'd offer Mortal Wound, beyond a straight-jacket.

Pre-gig we were exposed to a barrage of new punk records through the PA. This came courtesy of a significant local DJ, and a former student at the college too (several years above us) by the name of Marty Gorran. Marty was a passionate early champion of punk rock sounds and groups. Despite holding down a regular job he was heavily involved (and invested) with the local music scene. We didn't know him that well, except by reputation.

Marty regularly visited big independent record shops on the UK network. He had a massive influence by finding new punk releases and even bootleg tapes from America. Not only a successful commercial artist and designer – following graduation from Nulton Arts – he was a promoter, manager and hustler. Marty was a brilliant guy. Like a lot of the people I met during that era – as we'll see.

That night he was spinning a lot of exciting records from new British bands, along with The New York Dolls (a clear influence) back to Iggy Pop and the Stooges. He even had a recording of Television and The Ramones from the CBGB club.

Stan sneaked a gloating look at the dangerous audience. A raucous and simmering mob had turned up to watch his band. Already the gig had been delayed by fights, provoked by rival political extremists, the long-hairs and the suede-heads, the football 'casuals' and gangs from rival towns. Art students were definitely in a minority. The head college steward (or Buildings Officer) along with his gang of assistants, were pressed into service. These guys didn't look pleased to be at a rock concert anyway. When was Leo Sayer going to turn up? There was a tidal wave of illegal alcohol and more weed than North and South Vietnam combined.

Far from being angered by this hooligan hijack, Stan had a smirk and conniving look. Snot was prepared to 'up the ante' of punk with his band's reputation for chaos. The Age of Aquarius, the hippie message of peace and love (as ciphered down to us) was going toes up with a name tag. Sadly for Snot the college Principle would later call his bluff.

'Do we get to hear your band, or what?'

'Lots of time yet. Anna-kissed is learning another chord,' Stan explained. 'It's her second. I gave her a D.'

'You need more practice!'

He turned big dark sad eyes on me. 'Punk bands don't practice, Bottle.'

'You'd better get on. Unless you want 'em to rip this place up.'

'Sounds good. If you'll excuse that horrible pun,' he quipped.

'This is looking ominous.'

'Why don't you come out with us, Bottle?'

'What you on about? To play on stage, you mean?'

'Join us.'

'Now you're really taking the piss.'

'You'd be great, Bottle. You've got ideas, haven't you?'

Snot hardly paid attention to that mob. He was completely relaxed as if waiting for the bus.

'Anna-kissed only joined because she's going out with Herb... You know, that *Simon*. She doesn't realise that Herb only fancies himself,' he commented.

'You mean Simon Moore, who's doing fashion design?'

'Yeah, that tosser. He plays bass.'

'So it isn't harmonious?'

'Any more than the Velvet Underground.'

I'd seen that lad Simon in the refectory, a big show off, laughing loudly – aware of his good looks, swishing his fringe, holding court, waving a French ciggie.

'Someone told me he can play a bit,' I said.

'Yeah, *a bit*. Any fancy work and he's definitely out,' Snot insisted. 'Why don't you play some rhythm guitar? You'd be no worse than Anna-kissed. I'll teach you a couple of chords.'

'No way... that's final. It's not my thing.' What was? There was time to find out.

13

'It's a piece of fucking iced cake, Bottle. What's the matter?' he pursued.

'I'm happy with a chisel… not a guitar.'

Modern sculpture was my specialist subject. Obviously I was preparing myself for future employment: I could have been the Damien Hurst of rock.

'Your funeral,' he told me – eyes still on the unruly audience. 'Or ours,' he quipped. 'You can stay and watch the mayhem… as the rhino shit hits the fan.'

'Yeah, amazing. I'm going to do that,' I said.

Stan slouched back to the changing room. He cut a diminutive, stooped, fragile-framed figure, with piratical ringlets. Yet despite physical disabilities, and other health problems, he was a charismatic lad; somehow a thinker and a romantic. Girls adored him at college, even if he had a 'handicap'. Certainly his female fan club had turned up.

But Stan wasn't completely up himself, as Herb was. Not a bit.

* * *

In that aggressive atmosphere rumours spread, that the gig was cancelled. Most likely the grumpy Buildings Officer had put in an emergency call to the Principle, warning him. Unfortunately it was too late to stop the 'charity pop concert'.

While the band hung back (as engineered by Stan), fuelling frustration and tension, a big fight broke out. This was a signal for the head caretaker, Mr Wheatcroft, to dive in. Wheatcroft was a familiar character around college, with wardrobe shoulders and a ruff of stiff silver hair. On a daily basis Wheatcroft reserved a psychotic look for students. He didn't like lazy and arty tossers such as students. When pushed on the topic he'd openly describe these scholars as 'sheep under my feet'. As they strutted the corridors Mr Wheatcroft and his team gave off the attitude that they had more useful work to do. They only enjoyed making mocking comments about our final art shows.

Wheatcroft was ignorant of recent changes in pop music. His team of porters were the same way.

Stage lights were flashing like last orders for the nuclear holocaust. The PA crackled and popped and drenched the crowd in satanic feedback. Marty Gorran had cleared his decks and found a safer corner. Youths surged forward over the floor stage-front, thrusting beer cans and lighted ciggies above. In that mêlée a lad called Mick Dove came to my notice. Mick was a fellow student and we had begun Infants' School together. But there he was at the centre, lashing out, and wearing a swastika adorned tee-shirt.

Stage lighting was operated by Herb's little brother, Allan. He was no older than eleven and perched perilously in the rigging, surrounded by a devil's nest of electrical cables, switches and hot bulbs. Allan was trying to be creative with buttons and sliders, and it was bad news for migraine sufferers. If he survived he intended to make a future career as a lighting technician.

The presence of a drum kit suggested a musical event of some type. Herb jumped out with Anna-kissed and they unfurled a banner at the rear of the stage. They had created this painted backdrop for the group at college. This featured the legend of 'Mortal Wound' over the image of a severed torso, cut out of a Sunday supplement. It was a very punk shock statement. But I didn't see much shock in that crowd.

This was the cue for the rest of Mortal Wound to appear, with Snot slouching on last, as if going to his final period of the college day. The 'musicians' slowly took their places and fumbled about with sockets and knobs, trying to plug in and tune up, like Bill Gates with his first fuse.

'What you spotty wankers studying?' Stan shouted out. He soaked up a volume of jeers and waving fists. 'This is gonna wipe the fucking cobwebs out of your ears!'

At this, finally, the group launched into their opening 'song'. The audience was blown back by force of jagged, angry, electrical noise. It was absolutely thrilling. That was my first reaction – like running through a hard hail storm to reach a hot room. Immediately those lads at the front began to mosh and fight again. Through these fireworks I gained my first view of the band,

15

which was effectively my first experience of punk and of live rock 'n' roll.

There was Stan Snot hunched over his battered blue guitar (he still needed to concentrate hard) somehow enigmatic in this fury. On drums – bludgeoning his skins like a ship yard worker – was the more experienced Billy 'Urine' Kelly. Billy was a seasoned musician and a good mate of Stan's. The thundering backdrop was a good disguise for the group's chronic musical shortcomings.

Simon – AKA Herb – was the only lad who could really play. Stage right, wearing an authentic 'Sex' tee-shirt, he was on bass. There was something of the 'soul boy' in him, which caused tensions. His well-curated fringe danced along to slapping bass lines. There was a slash flare to his trousers and he was wearing eye-shadow and lipstick. In those days, in our town, that could be a radical statement, despite Glam Rock. He obviously fancied himself a bit, although I admired his guts. The Mods were partial to touches of cosmetics and Herb was into their style.

Anna-kissed focused hard over her rhythm guitar. She forced fingers over the frets, down the neck, to locate a sub-dominant chord or, really, *any* chord. To begin with she struck some petulant poses, to add to the show. Her stage costume was a minimal black plastic skirt, ripped up the sides and held in place by safety pins, with yards of hospital bandage wrapped around her chest.

So that early version of Mortal Wound crashed out a wall of noise. No matter how painful the process, this was the beginning of something.

Any atom of doubt about Mortal's punk cred was burst by their 'singer'. This character bestrode the stage like a bare-chested colossus. His name was Paul Blumen – AKA Nutcase – a man mountain, complete with tree cover. In a pair of ripped tartan trousers with chains attached, he stomped and bellowed over the boards. Taking advantage of an SFX from the college's drama department, he had poured a bucket of fake blood over bare chest and shoulders. That was dramatic and alarming, and he'd glued up a huge green Mohican cut as well.

Flashing lights painted his contorted features, as he squeezed to an even greater decibel. The lad was definitely a shouter, a 'gate mouth' style of vocalist, if you want to push it a bit and say he had a singing style.

After two and a half minutes of this racket – as if pretending to be a three minute pop song – 'Teenage Playground' came to an end. Hardly waiting for a reaction, the group threw itself into the next 'song'. Afterwards I was able to confirm this tune as 'Toast the Bourgeoisie' – in its earliest version. As I remember, the cack-handed musicians set off in different times, then caught up with each other at varying speeds. They all had their own ideas about tempi, despite the drummer's thundering. Simon was trying to play something fancy but, aware of the turmoil, he had a look of blind panic.

The final chord lingered, thunderous and echoing, and was as disturbing as a Seventies airliner taking off.

The band jumped into a third number called 'Punk Spunk'. I witnessed the new phenomenon of spitting. When the musicians dared to approach front stage, that mosh of youths showered them with phlegm. For a split second it put the band off – fingers were slipping on strings – yet they squinted their eyes, shrugged and continued. I was shocked by this storm of disgusting gob. Herb was trying to keep out at the back; swinging his bass from side to side, as if with Kool and the Gang.

There was absolute uproar, pandemonium, in that college hall. It created hell for Wheatcroft and his intrepid porters. Whatever sort of anti-social behaviour they spotted – and it was as case of 'take your pick' – it wasn't smart to jump in. The whole squad of them – what was the cream of caretaking and maintenance – vanished into a scrum of psychotic adolescents.

After a couple of songs somebody had thrown a half-full beer can towards the stage. This encouraged the others and one struck Billy full on the nose. Being a tough lad he played on as if he didn't notice. This time the blood was real and pooled into one of his side drums. Nutcase fobbed off the beer cans and thrust out his Red Wood ribcage; pogo-ed from one side of the stage to the other, snarling out the lyrics:

Bored, bored
Fucking repressed
Your social worker's pissed

Anna-kissed was playing hunt the lost chord, when a beer can hit her. Fortunately it was a nearly empty one. Still, she wasn't much amused; she dropped her arms and glared out at the audience. She was screaming back at them like an abused Billy Holiday. You didn't need to hear what she was saying – you could read her lips. Herb decided to turn his back on it all, flicking his hair, wiggling his tight bum and giving plenty of vibratos with his thumb.

What was Stan doing under this vicious bombardment? He was enjoying himself, that's what he was doing. With an ironical smile he concentrated on getting out even more feedback and reverb effects, to give impact to Nutcase's vocal howls.

The hard life, the hard life
Caught in the urban wars
Kill your social worker

During the second chorus Herb and Anna-kissed lost it with the crowd – those lads hurling abuse and other things. They decided to lose face to keep their good looks. According to their point of view, if you asked them, they were the best looking people in town. Anna whipped out the power cord from her guitar and exited in a huff. Herb followed on her heels. For a minute Stan and Billy ground to a halt, lacking a rhythm section. Nutcase concluded *Kill Your Social Worker* in a type of rasping Capella.

Realising that the gig was ending, the crowd was infuriated. Snot savoured the situation for a few minutes. He even had time to twist knobs on his amp, before at last padding away. Apart from being the smartest lad in town, he was also a cunning artistic *provocateur*.

Unfortunately he also had a bitter enemy and rival from college days. During the gig I had seen Mick Dove in the thick of it. He was also hurling missiles, any type of projectile, with particular venom, at Stan.

I didn't let this ruin the gig for me. I'd never experienced anything like it. We'd unleashed this monster punk. It had torn a hole through our boring and tedious lives.

You had to face the world with some defiance during those times.

* * *

Following the pandemonium I was nervous about meeting them afterwards. It was easy to assume that Stan was humiliated. Even worse, his new band's credibility was ruined, wasn't it? What did *I* know?

I was hanging about, watching as the rag tag crowd left. Mr Wheatcroft and his team gathered by the exits to shepherd them. I'd never seen a more bruised and dispirited lot of college porters in my life. The matter didn't end there. There was no chance Wheatcroft was going to write a rave gig review for the Principle. Any money raised for charity (potentially) would have to go on repair work. Talented student, Master Jon Whitmore, was set to leave college that summer, requiring a reference to begin his apprenticeship.

Crossing the stage I kicked through heaps of spilling beer cans. The boards of the stage were slippery with spit as well. Recently this very stage had produced a student version of *Oklahoma*, getting rave reviews in *The Nulton Chronicle*. Stan Snot wasn't involved in that show of course. That type of musical theatre wasn't his scene at all.

Unknown to any of us there was a cub reporter from the *Chronicle* present at the gig. This lad would put in a review for that week's edition of the newspaper.

In years ahead lads would claim to have been there, as with the Pistols at the 100 Club, the Clash at the Kilburn Ballroom or even the New York Dolls at CBGBs (believe it or not).

Anna-kissed and Herb were all lovey-dovey. She was doing a belly dance and he was swinging a towel above his head. No sign of being down in the dumps. Even a bump on the forehead didn't concern her. Their confidence felt a universe away from me.

The drummer, Billy Urine, was the most hardened musician. Fortunately his nose wasn't broken, just very sore. He'd played in an impressive variety of local bands, including show bands, Fifties rock 'n' roll and even heavy metal groups. So you could say he was versatile, even accomplished, though he didn't brag about it.

'Right then, lads, was I feckin' loud enough?' He had a big grin.

'Deafenin',' Nutcase told him. 'I ad to struggle to get 'eard.'

'Ai, nuttin' bothers me bay! Let the fuckers throw what they want.'

Stan kept himself to himself, minding his words, but no less smug about the gig's impact.

'Feckin' *a-mazin'* so it was!' Billy continued to celebrate, wiping his face and biceps with a beach towel.

'It was World War Free,' Nut commented.

'I've never had so much fun,' Anna-kissed said, giving a skip. 'Let's do it all again soon.'

'Did you notice the way I stuck my arse out?' Herb said. 'Come on your bastards, try to hit this with a can!'

'Ya nob!'

'Not my knob, my *arse*, you dick.'

'You stormed off stage. *Boat* of yer!'

'They chucked the ole off licence at me,' Nutcase recalled. He ran a huge rough palm over the green blade of his Mohican cut. Everyone in the band knew he was a gentle type of giant. And he was a brilliant dad to his toddler.

'You sang good and loud,' Anna-kissed assured him.

'You frightened the life out of them, Nut,' Herb agreed. 'Where does that high pitched scream come from? Honest I really thought my ears would burst.'

'I didn' get all the 'igh notes,' Nutcase recalled – like he was Pavarotti or somebody.

'Fair play now, neither did anybody else,' Billy assured him.

'Just the dogs,' Herb remarked.

'You played some feckin' crackin' guitar there, Stan bay.'

Stan didn't bother to look up from the frets. 'I just filled in the gaps.' Which gaps?

'You've got talent, Stan, honest.' This was Nutcase.

'Talent? I don't want to catch nothing like that.' Yet, even during these early days, he couldn't keep his hands away from a guitar.

'You wanna take yer music more seriously now, bay,' Billy Urine advised. They all seemed to have the same opinion.

'Nah.'

'If you do that Stan, you could go places so you could,' the drummer argued, holding up a forefinger. 'You wanna listen to me now cos I've been around a bit.'

'When we take this disgusting racket seriously, that's the time we break up,' Snot muttered.

The rest of the band gave him a look. The idea of breaking up was a real downer. Despite which he continued to tinker about with the instrument. As a matter of fact a guitar was stuck to him for the rest of his life. Music was his inspiration during times of loneliness, confusion and despair. Though I never played three notes together, music came to have a similar power for me.

Stan had a self-rolled funny cigarette on the go, bobbing along on his bottom lip. Sweet smelling smoke formed an ambient fug in the room, while he adjusted and corrected finger placements, groping towards a new riff.

'How are you feeling then Stan?' I shuffled closer to him trying to make my presence felt.

'Feeling? How should I know?'

'Whacked by beer cans… all that spit flying around.'

'You have to go to the next Pistols gig,' he advised.

'Are their gigs like yours?'

'Worse!'

'Incredible,' I replied.

'So, you know, what did you think to *Mortal*?' Even without looking at me, he wanted to check my opinion for the first time ever.

'I thought you were brilliant!'

Snot nodded with total calm.

'Yeah, but I didn't like the violence directed at you… personally. I've got to talk to you about that.'

'It's *anarchy*,' he retorted.

3. Enter 'The Gorran'

In the aftermath of this war zone, there came a rap on the 'dressing room' door. Who would even bother to *knock*? The police?

Luckily it wasn't the cops. Their surprise visitor was none other than star DJ Marty Gorran, who'd come round to congratulate them. Not only the best alternative club jock in town, he had established himself as a local rock raconteur. And if Gorran came knocking on any band's door they knew their gig had been a proper event.

Marty had all the positive energy, full-beam optimism and supra-confidence necessary for a Pop impresario. He also had a medley of anxious tics and a great talent to stir up a PR hurricane in a media tea cup. Bearing a set of impressive teeth, a striking coiffure of puffy hair, Mick Jagger-like sexy 'tyre tread' lips, a post-midnight pallor and snake hips, the DJ cut a striking figure on the music scene.

'Hello, *hello*, you lot. Fantastic to see everybody gathered together! How all you lads doing then? Great, great. It's Marty. Marty *Gorran*. Yeah, amazing, well I'm blinkin glad to meet you after that cracking performance!'

Apart from Stan the band was dazzled.

The pop *meister* moved among them, shaking hands. 'How are you blinkin doing now you'd touched up your cuts and bruises? Yeah, I mean that was a bloomin brilliant noise and a fantastic show. Or I'm Inglebert Umpledink,' he told them, enthused.

Marty was an 'authority' on punk fashions and styles, due to his day time job as an artist and designer. Gorran was rigged up in the fashions of the Ramones' rent-boy chic. There were Joey Ramone's signature skin-tight ripped jeans and a Warhol tee-shirt, with just a black linen jacket over the top, to indicate his serious business credentials. The playlist at the *Dragon* and for his 'Pink Pants' Disco Nights – as part of his DJ residency - had propelled punk into our neighbourhood, along with the underground disco scene.

Snot was mistrustful of Gorran's hype, as our parents mistrusted PM Uncle Jim Callaghan, or Chancellor Dennis Healey, when they invited the IMF to reduce our national pocket money. Then again Marty Gorran had zero interest in conventional politics or economics. If his aim was to break his groups nationally and internationally, to win them (and himself) acclaim, fame and fortune in the music business, his overriding motivation was musical passion.

'Right, definitely you punks, that was the most amazing blinkin gig I've got to this side of the fucking Pistols' surprise gig at the Duncehead Ballroom,' Marty eulogised.

'It was disgusting,' Stan remarked.

'I fort it was all right,' Nutcase said.

'Brilliant,' Herb said. 'Were you watching me, Marty? Did you see my moves? How my bass lines stand out?'

'Ai lads, what a nob this lad is!' Billy complained.

'Don't talk to my boyfriend like that!' Anna-kissed warned him. 'Why not?'

'You're all jealous of him, that's why.'

'Feckin jealous of this lad? This one here? Me arse.'

Such droll dressing room banter continued, while our big name local DJ tried to make his mark on their egos.

'No bullshit, I was stood out there in the blinkin hall tonight watching Mortal and I an't been so impressed with a new punk outfit since I got into Penetration,' he admitted, looking in raptures.

'So did you fink we was any good?' Nutcase wondered.

'Fair play, Marty, but are you serious now?' Billy replied.

'He says he was impressed,' Herb said, 'and I'll take that.'

'Penetration. Now they are a brilliant group,' Snot conceded.

'No bullshit, I an't seen a better punk rock group this side of fucking Pauline or the blinkin Damned gig at the Rock Garden last month,' Gorran confessed, spreading his hands. He smiled broadly, pale eyes aglow, knobbly inky hands appealing, and spinning a full circle on his heels to include everybody. Strobe lighting came through the infinite filaments of his barnet.

'Ace'

'Did you hear what he just said now?'

'That's complete bollocks,' argued the lead guitarist.

'Amazing. Cheers Marty, mate,' Nut said regardless.

The pop magnate had big snaggle teeth and wasn't afraid to deploy them for effect. 'Straight up lads, something bloomin' special happened here in Nulton Arts College this evening. You completely blew me away to be totally blinkin truthful with you,' he argued, revealing both rows of those rectangular teeth, like yellow icebergs.

'You need to get out more,' Stan suggested.

'Straight up, Jon mate, nobody gets out of the blinkin house more than I do to catch these new punk bands!' he objected, dipping his shoulders dramatically and grinning in amazement at such a misunderstanding.

'It's Stan. Not Jon. *Stan Snot.*'

The burly drummer needed more convincing. 'Fair's fair, Marty bay, ya sure we're good as you say? There's a bit of competition out there now.'

'For once that brute on sticks has a point. There's plenty of new bands on the circuit,' Herb noted.

'Right, definitely, I take your blinkin point on the number of bloomin bands sprouting up like fucking cabbages. But fair play, Mortal's gig was even more bloomin gob-smacking than the first time me and Rob caught the fucking Dolls at the Garden,' the DJ enthused.

'*New York* Dolls, you mean?' said Stan.

Gorran reacted in startled fashion. 'Right, definitely Snot, the blinkin New York Dolls, who else could I mean?' he said, with a wince of anxiety.

'Our band's only been together three weeks,' Anna-kissed said.

'We could break up next week,' Snot pointed out.

24

'Fair play Snot, what you blinkin talking about? Breaking up? Where can your group be next blinkin year, if you put your fucking energies behind it? Cos, straight up, Mortal can have a fucking massive impact on the UK music scene,' Marty suggested, before his grin could shatter under the stress. 'Or I'm Barbara Strident.'

'More bullshit than bum notes,' Snot sneered.

'We don't need you to tell us how good I am,' Herb argued. He was now changed back into a billowy shirt and 'Rupert Bear' style, yellow and black checked trousers.

'The band got to put in a lot of rehearsin' time yet so,' Billy reminded.

'We're a hot band… or we *can* be,' Anna-kissed added. She was remembering her own tortuous guitar practice.

Gorran raised his large blotted artist's palms, like some Aztec chief at the top of his pyramid. 'Right, definitely lads, you already know how blinkin fantastic you are. No bullshit, cos self-confidence is important as fucking sex in this industry,' he argued. The DJ began dragging on a fresh ciggie, exhaling the noxious fog, teeth emerging like the battlements of Leeds Castle.

'We're crap,' Stan disagreed. 'We're the dregs of society and a bunch of losers.'

'Straight up Snot, tell me something blinkin new, or you'll never get on in this business. Fair play, like some nervous donkey running up the blinkin beach, after some kid smacked its fucking arse,' Marty objected.

'What are you offering to the band?' Anna-kissed wondered, cradling her chin as she leant forward.

'Right, definitely, a good question, what can I blinkin offer to this great little punk band? No bullshit lads, how can I promote you in this fucking cut throat bloomin business? So how bloomin hungry is this talented little fucking punk band to reach the top of the indie charts?'

'Fair play, let's hear sometin' feckin' concrete, Marty,' Billy suggested.

Stan looked up from his frets a moment. 'Well expressed, by our friend on a drum stool.'

'Right, definitely, with total bloomin respect and no offence fucking intended, what do you know about the cuts and blinkin thrusts of the music industry?' Marty asked. His facial muscles turned into over-strung strings on the point of snapping under the strain.

'What do we know?' Anna-kissed considered, gazing around.

'Not sure what he's offering,' Herb told her. 'That we couldn't do for ourselves.'

'On the button, that man,' Stan declared.

'Right, no bullshit, all those fucking big shot London managers and music agents'll be waiting for you down in the bloomin smoke. No bullshit, take my advice, cos they'll be fucking swarming around your gigs like a bunch of starving sharks after their blinkin meal tickets.'

'Is that right?' Nutcase asked – impressed.

'OK, so we don't play any more gigs. We break up. This was a farewell gig,' Snot added. He gave a definitive twang.

The impresario gave an ironic laugh and hunch of the shoulders: 'Right, definitely Snot mate, get yourself into the blinkin picture, cos any good new band has to know how to blinkin promote itself and fucking sell its music.'

Mortal was more or less flattered and impressed. They were up for it.

'What's the proposal?' Snot pressed. All the same, he didn't interrupt his after-gig tunings.

'Can you get us some more gigs?' Anna-kissed asked.

'Right, definitely, can I get you some more fucking gigs?' Marty wondered, treating her to five-octave optimism, as he squeaked about on his baseball boots' rubber heels. 'Fair play, *can I* get you some more gigs?' The grin was cranked up to full volume – he was the Motorhead of schmooze.

'We're a punk group. We're *meant* to break up.'

'It's really only a college joke, you know?' Herb – unusually – agreed.

'It's like for charity,' Anna reminded him.

'Yeah, anarchist charity.'

'Right, definitely, very clever Snot,' Marty objected. He froze his ironical expression of disgust, to shock them back to reality. 'Straight up, that's the height of all your blinkin ambition? You've no more faith in your own fucking abilities than that? No bullshit, tell me I got blinkin hearing problems, cos it seems like you don't want to find any more big gigs?' he stated, looking appalled.

'So can we make an impact?' Anna-kissed asked, hopefully.

'We're going to vanish. Overnight,' Snot predicted.

'Maybe this night,' Herb joked, laughing too loudly.

The DJ promoter blenched with pain at this. 'Right, definitely Simon mate, enjoy your bloomin joke. But, no bullshit lads, punk's why I got into this business in the first place. If you want success as a punk band, get me in as your blinkin manager. Cos with the right attitude you lot can go up the fucking charts quicker'n a fucking nuclear rocket,' he argued, keeping up the ends of his sensual Jagger mouth. 'I'm the type of big thinking blinkin promoter and agent, with the kind of push and contacts, that you're gonna need in this bloomin business. Or I must be Des O'fucking Connor.'

'Des has got more talent than us,' Snot jibed.

'I'm the only real musician here,' Herb pointed out.

'You're a nob, so you are!'

'Leave him alone, will you?' Anna-kissed challenged.

'What's your offer Marty? We play gigs and you make money from it?' Stan wondered.

'Let Marty speak 'is mind,' Nutcase appealed.

'Right, definitely, it's appreciated, because we want these high profile gigs in the biggest blinkin venues in the fucking UK. I can find you more top gigs here in Nulton and down in London as well, to put you up in the blinkin glare of the national music press.' Marty's positive grin switched up to three bars on full power, before a wire snapped.

Mortal sprawled about the room, listening and absorbing, in various post-gig postures.

'You truly offer to be our manager? Get us more gigs and even a deal? That's what you're offering here?' Herb concluded.

Stan was playing a kind of sarcastic rock opera, although thankfully without amplification.

Gorran would launch the band from his artist's workshop in Nulton, just as MacLaren had launched his group from the 'Sex' boutique in Chelsea.

The band members were looking at each other, doubtful about the necessary commitment and hard work. The band really did begin as a type of art school dare and provocation, hatched by Snot in the canteen one lunch time.

'I don't want to take my group to that level,' Stan explained.

'Straight up, we can pop down to my workshop in a minute or two and get your first bloomin contract inked up and ready to sign,' Marty clarified.

'We don't need fucking contracts.'

'Right, definitely Snot, but you don't want to fall victim to some smooth talking blinkin alley cat, trying to cheat you out of millions of quid in royalties, and strip you down to your bloomin plectrum,' he said. Marty put a hand over the place where his heart was.

'We need to talk this over,' Anna-kissed suggested.

'Fucking talk.'

At this delicate point Gorran was prepared to be diplomatic and step back. While the band went into a discussion he held his peace, leaving only the aura of that toothy grin.

'I fink he's talkin' our kinda language,' Nutcase said.

'You're not serious.'

'Bays, honest to goodness, I'm not sure if we're ready for a manager. 'Never had a feckin' manager. But I've seen what feckin' managers can do, so.'

'If he can make this group a success. If he makes us very rich, I'm in favour,' Herb said.

'Knock me over,' Stan told him.

'If yer get a manager he'll rip yer off,' Billy insisted. 'That's what most so-called managers do, in this business! After they cut their slice there's nuttin but crumbs left for the group, mind.' He held up his huge spark-covered arms.

'Good point, Billy mate.'

'We're going to need somebody to arrange gigs,' Anna-kissed said.

'Do we need *Mickey the Mostest* here?'

'If the band continues we're gonna need a manager,' she insisted.

'I dunt wanna give it up,' Nutcase explained. 'Whatever the missus says.'

'Let's go as far as we can,' Herb decided.

'*Then* we split up,' Snot argued.

'Me voice as got in its stride,' Nutcase said.

'We need somebody trustworthy to look after us. Somebody who really likes us,' Herb put in.

'You mean this big cheese?'

'Sounds like Marty *does* rate us. I don't listen to flattery… but it's nice. Maybe he *can* negotiate for us, if we want to play bigger venues. The college won't let us play here again, not after tonight's trouble.'

'Don't worry about it,' Stan advised.

'Herb's right. I don't want to give up,' Anna-kissed argued.

'Why not?' Billy said.

'You're only our drummer,' she shouted, rounding on him.

'Yeah, remember Pete Best,' Herb warned.

'Yeah, roight, the best lookin' lad in the group!'

'Nobody mentions The Beatles again,' Snot told them.

'Marty's resident DJ at the *Mad Hatter* and he could get you regular gigs,' I suggested.

'Come on now, Stan bay, you started this group, so what do you fink so?'

'Yeah, Stan, it's your band, so you what do you fink?' Nutcase agreed.

Edgy glances shifted around the circle of non-musicians while the tension and agony of decision mounted.

There were nerve jangling notes and discords from the little guitarist. 'All right. On your fucking heads be it. If you've got to have him.'

'Right, definitely, no bullshit everyone, fucking *congratulations*!' Marty cut back into the action.

4. The Nulton Night Life

Formal contract negotiations were to be suspended overnight, while we went to celebrate at the town's top music club, The *Mad Hatter*.

In those days the town centre was so shadowy and deserted (after pub closing) that even a dead man wouldn't be caught out. But if that unfortunate 'Everyman' did find himself in such a lonely place, most likely he'd pop into the *Mad Hatter* for a nightcap.

For youth (that was us) the place was a sanctuary from early bedtimes, frustration, boredom and restlessness. After '76, thanks to hustling lads like Marty Gorran things were really happening. The DJ got an exciting playlist together and began to promote live music with his local bands.

Gorran pulled his little Austin car into a make-shift car park, over rubble of a demolished block, behind the town's new East Berlin style concrete and glass shopping centre. He worked successfully for himself as a commercial artist, sign writer and designer. And he could afford to buy an Austin *Sunbeam* Deluxe car – '*Bring a little sunshine into your life*' as Petula Clarke sung in the TV ads. In the boot of the car he kept a heap of his artist's tools and materials, besides clip boxes containing records.

Marty took on freelance jobs for the big Co-operative Store, including window and shop floor displays. I often noticed him dashing about the store, because I was also employed by them. I was a 'Saturday lad', working part-time in groceries, handling top quality fruit and veg. The excitement, buzz, enthusiasm and friendship of the local music scene lured Marty, as it did me, as Jane attracted Tarzan. In many ways he was the person who started it all. Gorran's boyfriend Rob was vocalist for a heavy rock band too, which gave him the push to become their manager. Then the punk rock thing came along, he heard Mortal Wound at college and, like Joe Frazier with his jab against Ali, opportunity struck.

So that night, after Mortal Wound's infamous gig, he was desperate to sign them up. We clambered out of his solid little car – yellow as a New York taxi – and strode out through litter and stones towards rock 'n' roll destiny. Marty's thoughts focussed on platinum discs and world tours already, as he loped across that bombsite of thuggish and corrupt Seventies development.

The rock impresario headed towards that alluring bright light, his legs as long and knobbly as a kangaroo's. With that big hair and skinny frame, distinctive in tight-fitting Ramones jeans, and a Johnny Rotten type fluffy jumper over the top, he was unmistakeable. Stan was a much shorter figure scrambling behind, thick set in body shape, swarthy and with a hook nose. In fact he dragged a foot and there was a bump between his shoulders. Putting aside this disability, which was never an issue with him, Snot didn't show any inclination towards health or fitness. Any thought of doing exercise would have killed him off and definitely spoiled the taste of tobacco and marijuana (from a friend's basement).

I noticed that Herb's white Polo car was already parked, like a cubic igloo. Anna-kissed and Nutcase had gone along with him. Excluding street lighting, Nulton was locked down in a paranoid blackout. The down-town area was disturbed only by the whistle of a mail train, rumbling through the shadowy station, passing through the town's valley. Just mixed in with stray shouts and jeers from those drunks out and about, with no interest in music or socialising.

Certainly the *Hatter* was the only establishment with any sign of life. It advertised itself with a neon light over the entrance. As students we'd enter full of youthful hope and optimism, only to become bitterly disappointed with the place. Typically we would find a terrible MOR band playing comatose rock standards, ignored by a room of menacing misogynist drunks. Only at the next weekend, with short memories, we'd repeat the whole dismal scenario. It was enough to turn Captain Sensible into Nick Drake.

When the punk scene developed it changed all that depressing stuff. It ended the regular let downs and sense of time-wasting, the moment Gorran turned up with his decks and music collection.

The club's notorious bouncers were snazzy in dinner suits, resembling tight-arsed snooker players. They'd gaze out in boredom from the entrance, across that rocky baize of desolation. All the same they would grin with pleasure and recognition whenever Marty came along. Our local rock guru could charm the back legs off a herd of asses. He sprinkled music biz fairy dust wherever he went in town, and even those psychotic hard men were flattered by his attention. They were chuffed merely to spot his big blonde afro and blocky teeth, as he came bobbing along the broken pavement to greet them.

'Evening Marty!' These gorillas even touched their forelocks (if they had one) and squeezed buttocks together in respect.

The other Mortal members hadn't received such a courteous welcome. The snooker men had frisked them all on the entrance steps. We heard how Nutcase's trademark Mohican head style had set thuggish nerves jangling. They padded down his massive bulk (still sweaty from the gig) suspicious that he was trying to smuggle in tomahawks or scalps. It was a mark of Nut's gentle nature that he hadn't reacted to this manhandling prejudice.

As mates of the DJ, Stan and I got into the venue free of charge. Another pair of tuxedoed apes pointed us in the direction of the saloon bar. This was the starting point of The *Mad Hatter* offer. The club was located over several floors, with a long bar in each, serving watered down lager at double price. There was a regular upstairs disco, while live music was in a basement area, usually starting after midnight.

Gorran started to confetti banknotes at the bar. 'Straight up lads, I reckon this calls for a bit of a blinkin celebration,' he told us. He was ready to schmooze.

Stan was complaining. 'What we doing in this dump?'

'Come on, give it a chance. Let's stick around,' I advised.

Marty was responsible for the club's *Alice in Wonderland* themed decor. The club owner had tasked him to come up with a decorative concept. Lewis Carrol fantasy characters were painted across walls and free areas. Marty had also created a set of giant playing cards, cut outs from stiff card, which were suspended from ceiling hooks. These garish creations span and dangled ominously (I thought) over our heads. But, as I hinted, many of the customers were more grotesque.

* * *

The owner of the club was a bloke called Dave Crock. In a previous life Crock was a long serving centre-half with Nulton Athletic Football Club. He'd worn that legendary No. 5 shirt through a decade of seasons, including the 1960/61 campaign when Nulton had won promotion to the old First Division. If it hadn't been for his personal problems (and an unrelated armed robbery and GBH conviction back in 1965) he might have gone into football management, rather than pub management. He was a legendary centre-half who'd succeeded in ending the playing careers of several top strikers, including a potential England international.

A bruised toe had forced him into an early testimonial match. That same year he bought his first public house, in partnership with former Nulton Athletic club mate, the dribbly winger Graham Gross. The duo soon had a chain of pubs together, in prime spots around the town and the county. Sadly, Graham Gross (a talented player) was mysteriously eliminated by a sawn-off shot gun, during the middle of the night, while he had been asleep. Despite this tragic setback Dave Crock had soldiered on and even prospered. The *Mad Hatter* nightclub was created in the shell of a derelict Victorian gin palace and became his centre-piece.

That evening we found Crock dominating his lower bar area. He was built like a warehouse, darkly complexioned, hirsute and conky. I heard him above the din of the saloon, laughing very loudly and backslapping his cronies. These blokes were old mates from the worlds of sport, leisure, government and law enforcement.

Gorran was considered 'tight' with Crock, since he knew how to attract the punters with his disco nights. There was gratitude for that *Alice in Wonderland* theme. Marty sensed that Crock owed him a favour for those illustrations, which he was intending to call it in. The idea was to get the publican to offer Mortal Wound their first big club gig. Marty regularly recommended acts for the venue, but required the ex-footballer's approval. Fresh from signing them up Gorran was eager to introduce his new punk talent to Nulton's significant players.

'Right Mortal, look sharp, cos here comes that blinkin Dave Crock,' Marty warned, arranging his stringy limbs. He began to limber up another shit eating grin, if only to keep the club owner at a safe distance.

'Where's Johnny Cash to protect us?'

'Fair play, keep quiet Snot, look harmless and let me do all the blinkin talking. Old Crock's making over towards us now, wanting to know who you are. Straight up, I know how to handle him, so don't say anything until I give you the bloomin signal.'

'*It's Marty!*'

'Dave mate.'

'*Marty boy!* My *moosic* man! Match fit, mate,' Crock barked, steadying himself. 'Match fit and commandin' the centre. 'Preciate you askin', but match fit.' He had an arm around the pop mogul's shoulders, having a feel of that mohair jumper soft as a baby's new blanket. Crock's pink bleary eyes narrowed at us, in a mottled drinker's face, through the bar's smoke-filled, alcohol fuelled atmosphere.

'Dave mate, *Mortal Wound*. Mortal Wound, *Dave Crock*,' Marty declared, with a waft of his arm and a fag in the other hand.

'*Mortal what?*' Dave blurted.

'Wound,' Snot volunteered.

'Fuckin *Wound!*'

'That's it.'

Suddenly the former central defender had Stan in his range. 'Ain't I seen your fuckin face somewhere, son?'

'Right, definitely, Dave mate, maybe you've spotted our friend here and thereabouts. No bullshit, familiar friendly faces apart, you're stood next to the next big rock group in this blinkin town or anywhere, Dave mate. Straight up, that's going to break fucking massive in the UK this summer.'

'Fuck me, that so?'

'No bullshit, cos these blinkin talented, bloomin good looking boys and girls here, are set to be the most exciting new band the public have heard this end of the fucking Seventies. Or I'm Rat Scabies on the blinkin wagon, Dave mate,' Marty claimed. He made an ironic noise while embracing Herb, without touching him, on account of his ciggie.

'And this big fucker stood ere, with the spiky fuckin 'ead? *'Oo's ee?'*

'Straight up, Dave, this big lad's their blinkin vocalist,' Gorran explained. 'He's Nutcase.'

'*Blumen*,' I clarified.

'Fair play, why don't you mind your language, Bottle,' the DJ suggested.

'Me stage name,' said Nutcase.

'Fuck me. What a giant. Well, Marty boy knows is moosic,' Crock agreed, tearing his eyes off Nutcase and getting the crick out of his thick neck.

The publican began to squeeze hands, including mine, even though I could only handle a chisel. Crock was wobbling about, woozy, going in and out of consciousness. His knees had gone and alcohol didn't help them.

'Delighted,' the club owner shouted at us. 'Welcome to the Mad 'Atter. How you lads fixed for a drink? I 'ope Marty's lookin after yer.' He gestured and silently mouthed at the barmaid, as if signalling for a bucket and sponge from the dugout.

Crock had to bawl through the hubbub. *'Bring em over ere Reena sweet'eart!'*

His girth had inflated since the glory days, putting strings and buttons under threat. That once famous shock of black curls was reduced to a silvery shower curtain. But he still had 'none shall pass' presence in the space.

'Right, definitely Dave, that's very kind of you, so me and the band just popped down to the club to say hello and get introduced.

Straight up Dave, I thought you'd better know, after the group just played the most amazing gig I've seen since this side of the Dolls.'

'*Dolls?*' Crock was bamboozled by music biz lingo. 'That's your business, Marty boy. *The moosic!*' A port complexion darkened, as if he was pumping 'Black Velvet' through his veins.

'Straight up Dave, I was so blinkin impressed with tonight's performance I had to get backstage to 'em fast and offer to be their bloomin manager,' Gorran explained, working his shoulders, beaming humbly. He'd had more chasers that Epsom Downs.

'Good for you, Marty boy... So did they accept?'

'After a lot of haggling and long negotiations,' Marty said, grinning and shrugging modestly.

'Well done, Marty boy,' Crock told him, giving him a whack on the back. 'You always fuckin do it.'

Gorran slipped out another ciggie. Lighting up with a flourish, with a snap from a chunky lighter, he finished the wrap. 'Right, definitely Dave mate, lucky they accepted the contract, cos they're gonna need all the fucking inside expertise and advice available to 'em in this hard blinkin business.'

'Listen to this crap,' Snot muttered towards me.

However, I wasn't cynical about the talk, I was fascinated.

The other Mortal musicians stood about dazed and confused. Despite radical punk appearances they were out of their comfort zone.

'Fuckin brilliant, Marty boy. This calls for a big celebration. *Reena! Reena darlin!* This way! Just fuckin *pour*, love.'

Anna-kissed had to look away. 'He's charming, isn't he,' she remarked.

'So that my skin crawls,' Herb agreed.

Mortal continued to swap uneasy looks, even Nutcase, while Dave was flagging emergency orders to the bench. Only Billy Urine had the presence of mind to shout 'Cheers!' Billy could handle himself, but he knew that Crock was the gaffer for a lot of dodgy local construction sites.

'What a dive this is,' Snot remarked.

'Better'n being at home,' I suggested.

'Yeah?'

'I don't fancy playing any gig here,' Herb said.

'Imagine the changing rooms,' Anna-kissed suggested.

'It's a gig though. Give it a chance, lads.' This from Nutcase. Like a privet hedge his green brush-cut ran between the painted figures of the Duchess and the Griffin. For a split second or two Crock had the illusion of being sober, every time he noticed the mammoth singer among us.

'Right, definitely Dave mate, I'm giving you the head's up on Mortal playing select blinkin prestige gigs around Nulton and Duncehead.' Gorran took a moment to suck down the other half of his *B&H*. He winced with pleasure at the intake and blew exhaust over his shoulder.

The club owner staggered a few steps nearer. 'What you *after*, Marty boy?'

'Right, definitely Dave, now you're asking, I've got to negotiate with some more blinkin top quality local venues,' he argued. 'Fair play, you can't expect this group to headline at the Albert Hall without any bloomin extra practice. No bullshit Dave, before they play their headline London gigs and pull in those top A and R men down there in the bloomin smoke. Cos after that they can get signed up to one of the big fucking record labels and think about their first bloomin hit album.'

'Fucking brilliant, Marty. You're on the ball,' Crock told him, rubbing his rough purple nose.

But you could tell that the club owner was on a different planet.

'Wait a minute Mr DJ,' Stan cut in. 'When did we agree to all this?'

'Right definitely, Stan mate, no blinkin sweat if you leave the detailed negotiations to me. No bullshit, there's no big bloomin national tour 'til you get signed up to a serious fucking indie label. Straight up, an't you got any blinkin ambition?' he objected. The body language was hunching up, moderating the grin.

'I'm supposed to be starting a job soon,' Snot explained. 'This band's only a laugh. We're breaking up.'

Crock grew sentimental. 'Marty boy knows is moosic! E's a talented boy. Anyfin' that lights Marty's fire is good wiv me. I've never known Marty to back a loser. I'm backin' this fuckin band.' He stuffed a fresh cigar into his mouth and tried to clip the end of it. For the first few attempts he was snatching at the air.

'Cheers Dave. All the best t'ya now.' Billy was enjoying his free pint.

'You're fuckin welcome son. *Everybody*! Ave another drink! On the 'ouse. *Reena*!'

In disgust Herb and Anna-kissed broke away into a private lovers' conversation. Stan began to study his long gifted fingers. What had he got himself into, just by starting up that band for fun at college?

'Honest, Marty? You fink Mortal can make it?' Nutcase said, pressing him. 'Do you really rate us that much?'

'Straight up, Nut, *do I really fucking rate you*?' Marty replied, nodding his chin and turning a toothy grin of disbelief on the vocalist.

Nutcase's slitty eyes shifted from side to side. 'Yeah, what d'you fink?'

'Fair play Nutcase, do I believe a blinkin word of what I'm fucking telling you? No bullshit, am I going to put all my fucking money where my bloomin mouth is and support this great little kick arse punk group of yours?' Gorran wondered. He looked aghast around the room and back at the vocalist.

'So d'you really fink we're any good?' Nut persisted. He began looking around at the rest of us for help.

'Straight up, no bullshit, Nut, are you any fucking good? Mortal's the smartest fucking little band in town, since Strummer and Simeon first turned up at the bloomin *Stag's Head* without any instruments or even the Kilburns,' the rock guru argued persuasively. Gorran boggled at the wonder of the rock world, waving around another ciggie like Simon Rattle with a baton.

'You reckon?'

'Straight up Nut, don't you remember when Joe and the boys turned up in fucking Duncehead for a surprise gig that time, after missing their bloomin train back to London? Topper without his blinkin drum kit and only a fucking empty instrument case on 'im?'

Nutcase was stunned. 'Honest?'

'*Bollocks*,' Snot said.

'No bullshit, Stan, cos I was the one who blinkin persuaded them to stay and blinkin play,' the pop guru told us.

Dave Crock was impressed, even though pop music was all Greek to him. 'Cheers! All the best, everybody!' The club owner raised his pint pot, like the FA Cup on wobbly extra-time legs. 'Marty knows is moosic,' he added, having drained it in one. 'What do I know about fuckin moosic? *Tom tit*,' he admitted, flushing claret. The booze flamed in his veins. He was roasting alive in a velvet tux and frilly shirt. 'Marty boy looks after me bands. I never fuckin interfere. 'E plays all the 'it records.'

'Right, definitely, that's what I wanted to bloomin talk to you about, Dave mate.'

'Marty's me moosic man. What do I know? What do I fuckin care? S'long as I dunt get no complaints. I trust Marty boy with is bands. E's got a safe pair ov ands. S'long as punters is 'appy. If those kids 'and over their five quid on the fuckin door.' He took a monographic hanky from his top pocket and mopped his eyes, cheeks and brow, breathing heavily.

'Straight up Dave, before we get them out on their first blinkin national tour we'll have to play a few more bloomin showcase gigs a'tome here in Nulton,' Gorran said, wincing.

'You're on the ball Marty. No sneaky moves.' Crock bent his knees to pour down another pint. An unflappable Reena lined up substitutes along the bar.

'Fair play Dave mate, cos there's a big blinkin punk night organised for the Lyceum ballroom off the Strand next month. Straight up, and I can get Mortal on the same bill as the blinkin Buzzcocks, Ruts and UK Subs, if we can back them up with quality local gigs at recognised venues.'

'Marty's knows is moosic. He's always a safe pair of fuckin ands. I don't interfere. Nah, nah, only if I 'ave to kick some fuckers out the back fuckin door,' he recalled.

'Right, definitely Dave mate, so what do you say to my bloomin proposal?'

Crock brought his large mauve face nearer to the impresario's. 'What you *pullin'* Marty?'

Gorran held the winning smile at four octaves. 'Fair play, Dave mate, what I'm politely blinkin asking here is that you offer Mortal a couple of big gigs downstairs at the bloomin *Hatter's Music Box* venue.'

The club owner was stunned. His eyes popped at this impudent genius. '*At the Atter?*'

'Straight up, and we can get the *Hatter* known as a bloomin important venue on the fucking national music circuit, Dave mate. No bullshit and we can get the whole fucking town talking and buzzing about the bands in this place,' the promoter promised.

'What you sayin'? You want em to play 'ere? At the Atter?'

'Right, definitely Dave mate, so we can put 'em on and promote 'em at the *Music Box* down in the blinkin basement,' Gorran enthused, radiating and squinting through more smoke. 'No worries Dave, you'll be pulling in the big crowds of local kids and making a bloomin fortune out of it all.'

'Ten quid on the door. Late bar extension.'

'Fair play, Dave, you can't blinkin lose. No bullshit you'll have the best gig in years. I promise you'll go hop skip and blinkin jumping all the way to the fucking bank.'

'You're sellin' it, Marty boy,' Crock agreed. 'So what's your fuckin cut?'

'Right, definitely, fair play, fifty quid and ten percent of the door.'

'My shout, Marty boy. Call it five.'

Crock's head always cleared at talk of profit.

'Right, definitely, I want to be bloomin flexible on the terms, but Mortal's already in big fucking demand. I've been speaking to Dougal down at the *Dragon* and he's expressed a lot of blinkin interest in putting on a few gigs with 'em.'

'Sixty quid, Marty boy.'

That was a reasonable amount of money then – or so it sounded to us.

'Right, definitely, it's a fair offer Dave, we can blinkin agree between us, ten percent at the door.'

Menace deepened the bass voice. 'That's what I fuckin said. That's what we fuckin agreed.'

'Right, fair play, that all sounds blinkin straight up and narrow as your trousers Dave, so I'll just have a quick flip through my fucking diary, true as I'm talking to you now,' Gorran suggested.

'First Saturdee night next month, Marty boy. No support. Take it or fuckin leave it.'

'Right, definitely, looks here like it's free with us, so let's call it a bloomin deal shall we?' Mortal's manager concluded.

The publican took a few seconds to calculate. 'Cheers everybody!' Crock finally bellowed. 'Listen to Marty boy. 'E knows is moosic.' He steadied himself. '*Reena!* Where the fuck yer got to! Drinks all rarnd. Make yourselves at 'ome. Dave Crock knows ow to look after is mates. Dave Crock 'asn't ad to buy a fuckin drink in twenty two years. Cheers everybody!'

5. Phoenix, Betsy and the contest

Snot apart, the group was mesmerised by such success. If Gorran could clinch a headline gig at the *Hatter* maybe he knew his way around the rock 'n' roll jungle after all.

As the midnight hour passed Mortal nerves began to shred. The saloon area was crowded out with drunks who had no interest in listening to music or to each other.

Above our heads the ceiling was shuddering and juddering from the nightclub stampede. *British Home Stores* lamps and chandeliers in the saloon bar shook and swung, as if the entire floor above was about to crash on our heads. One time I'd gone up into the 'Looking Glass' disco to watch the dancers. While pummelled by the Amazonian vocal style of (the incomparable) Donna Summer, or the squeezed balls falsettos of the Bee Gees, I lost my bearings completely. Marty had fitted huge mirrors along every wall, including the ceiling. Disco dancers were reflected into multiple infinity. For a couple of hours I was looking for an escape route. Even the keenest dancers were prone to smashing into surfaces, or into each other. Despite this the 'Looking Glass' was the most popular club in town. Well, beats me.

'Right, definitely, I'm getting itchy feet here playing statues at the bloomin bar,' Marty argued. 'So why don't we find out who's playing down in the *Music Box*? Straight up, I only gave it a fresh lick of blinkin paint yesterday morning.'

'Fair play, I'm up for it!' Billy agreed.

'*Is* there a band tonight?' Herb asked.

'I can see The Damned playin,' Nutcase argued.

'The Damned in this armpit? No chance, just the usual buncha no hopers,' Stan argued, tongue in cheek.

Gorran flinched amiably, but sustained the HM good mood music: this was the night he'd signed Mortal and it was worth celebrating. For him it was down in legend like Warhol finding the Velvets. 'Right, definitely, Stan, you need to keep your bloomin ears pinned back like that Prince Charles tonight. Fair play, meet some blinkin influential people in the business and form vital bloomin contacts,' he argued.

'Don't be negative Stan. A gig's a gig, bay, an' Mortal's gonna play here next month so,' Billy argued.

'Well lads, I oughta go home 'fore long,' Nutcase told us.

'What for?' I wondered.

The gargantuan shouter looked glum. 'The wife's expectin' me. About an hour ago.'

'Ah come on Nut man, that isn't very rock n roll!'

'Get it straight,' Stan retorted.

'You won't moan if we get that gig at the Lyceum,' Herb pointed out.

'In panto,' Snot cut back.

'Supporting the Buzzcocks!'

'You're too fucking gullible, listening to the big cheese.'

'I can't keep my Janet up too fuckin late. She'll 'ave me for breakfast, wunt she.'

'Well, I don't fancy going home yet,' I argued.

'Right, definitely, if you've finished with all your dirty blinkin laundry in public,' Marty objected ironically. 'No bullshit, it's time we got down there so I can introduce you to these influential music business movers and bloomin shakers. No bullshit, before all you blinkin babies go and fall asleep on me.'

'Who exactly are you expecting to see in here?' Anna-kissed wondered. 'David Bowie or what?'

'Straight up, I heard on the grapevine that Bowie's in Berlin agen with bloomin Eno, cutting another fucking record. No bullshit, in a few years Brian'll be too fucking busy cutting Mortal Wound's LPs. No disrespect but Brian'll be more interested in working with you, instead of hanging around with Iggy and Bowie all the fucking time. And Gord 'elp us all, he's probably sick of looking at that bloomin horrible great fucking wall in Germany now.' Gorran offered a knowing grin, leading us down rickety stairs to the basement.

'It's bollocks,' Snot assured us. 'Don't listen to him.'

'About Bowie?' Anna-kissed marvelled.

Mortal Wound – or most of it – was pissed and disoriented enough to enjoy celebrity status.

The *Music Box* resembled a toxic swamp by then. They had a late bar going, if you could make it so far. You had to wade through lager, vomit and overflow from blocked toilets, topped by a flotilla of discarded cigarette butts and exhausted spliffs. There were inland lakes in communist Romania healthier than this place.

Marty's design concept was to daub everything black. It was like being thrown into a cave of hell, albeit with a record player. Every sense was deprived; apart from the hearing; which was overloaded. To be fair similar clubs were in business all over the country. The legendary Marquee Club along Wardour Street was cramped and claustrophobic. Stan and I assumed that CBGBs had to be some fantastic glamorous glittery club in New York. When we eventually saw photos of CBGBs, we realised that the venue was not any superior to ours. I suppose that grot 'n' grime was rock 'n' roll, and it was definitely punk.

The emergence of punk created this excitingly edgy live scene. Any Mortal appearance would already be a draw to all punk rock fans in Nulton. The group's first club gig was anticipated, even before the date was set.

Marty worked the hype like a hamster in a wheel. Mortal were introduced to his mates and associates – most of them in bands or on the scene – as if the Beach Boys were out socialising with the Monkees.

Gorran shepherded us. 'Guess what band they got on in the *Box* tonight,' he grimaced. 'It's Betsy Dandie and the Screamers.'

We were baffled by the name. 'Never heard of them,' Herb admitted.

'Me neither,' Anna-kissed said.

'I caught them once in the pub,' Stan admitted. 'Crap.'

'Fair play Snot, maybe they an't to everyone's taste, but Betsy's established and starting to make a bloomin name for herself. No bullshit, you have to meet her blinkin manager, Les Phoenix.

Fair play, he's handling little Betsy and the boys this side of the Atlantic. Bet's gigging hard to make it big here in the UK like Jimi Hendrix, after all the American rock fans have got fucking hearing problems,' Marty informed us. Excitement, anticipation and rivalry set off nervous tremors in his volcanic features.

House lights dipped – adding to a murky and confused atmosphere. There was a menacing buzz and crackle as the PA came live. My eye caught a small, yet formidable and busty blonde in the shadows, as she jumped on stage. She had sucked herself up into a black leather bodysuit, lazily zippered. Then a trio of imposing blokes, in leather jackets and black jeans, joined her on the warped boards. In contrast to Mortal's first fumblings, they were strumming and twiddling purposefully. Well, they say the Americans are always one step ahead.

Striking a posture, snatching the mic, 'Hey Nulton! How ya doin guys!' Betsy yelled. At this her band blasted into an opening chord and the first number. As well as being lead singer Betsy had a white guitar, though she mostly filled. They were a tight 'power pop' band, who'd been together for a while, going by how the sound meshed.

Betsy projected herself, every curvaceous rocking inch. She was a sexy macho blonde and knew how to handle herself. She threw her truck-stop voice as if already playing to stadiums. The wheels and hammers of my ears went crazy as Belgium clocks in a freak electrical storm. Later on, when I knew more about music, I'd place her between Chrissie Hynde and Bonnie Raitt. She wrote a lot of her own material, mixed in with cover versions such as 'Try a Little Tenderness' or (appropriately for The *Mad Hatter*) 'Eve of Destruction'.

This was all 'top dollar' for Nulton town, as if Dolly Parton had turned up at a TUC barn dance. The Screamers came back for several encores – they were great value – going off after striking a last reverberating power chord. They waved thanks to a raucous crowd.

The Screamers didn't excite Stan or Marty, judging by their expressions; any more than Johnny Rotten was bowled over by the Queen's Silver Jubilee celebrations.

* * *

High from the show, Betsy and her Screamers pushed through an admiring crush, back to the bar. Marty had the chance to step in to PR overdrive, among her friends and supporters. Apart from the day job Marty was CEO of his *Star Materials* music management corporation. The organisation was based in a spare corner of his workshop/studio, off a Nulton back alley. Unfortunately *Star Materials'* corporate hospitality budget had been overspent. But the *words* still flowed.

'Mortal Wound meet *Betsy and the Screamers*. Betsy and the Screamers meet *Mortal Wound*,' he expostulated, opening up the crevices in his spongy features.

'*Phew*! Like, *wooh*, pleased to meet all you guys!' Betsy said in greeting, still buzzing and breathless from the show.

Betsy turned out to be a genuine American. 'Like I'm pooped,' she admitted, with a big modest shrug. She was drenched in fresh sweat, under the leather, forced to pull down the zip of her body suit. Betsy knew the effect she had on local youth. 'So like what did you guys think of the show?' she wondered. She actually wanted the opinion of a local punk band.

'You was great!' Billy declared.

'Sounded all right,' Nutcase admitted.

'Like we definitely lost energy…during the middle?. Like, fuck man, I felt like I was almost singin to my Mom there. I couldn't believe what my voice was soundin like. Next time I should really, like, invite my Mom!'

'Is your Mum fucking deaf?' Stan said.

Even if she was a fading rock megastar, everyone instantly liked her. She was popular in the town – she had a following. Betsy had been adopted by the local music scene. She was a genuine American export. Just by settling in Nulton she had an instant pop celebrity. They hadn't seen the like of her in the flesh.

'Mortal Wound, *Les Phoenix*. Les Phoenix, *Mortal Wound*.' With gyrations and open palms, Gorran pulled strings and held his charm A/C at full setting.

So we were introduced to Mister Les Phoenix. In truth I'd seen him about town. Les was hard to miss this side of Houston. A lofty fifty-something bloke in a bulky fur coat with a Texan style ten-gallon hat, he was distinctive. Phoenix was the biggest Elvis Presley fan south of Memphis or, come to that, Manchester.

'Hi you guys,' he greeted us, in that cold and aloof style. 'Real happy you enjoyed the show tonight with Betsy and the guys. Yeah, far out, guys. Welcome to the future of rock 'n' roll.'

His Lone Star accent was as mid-Atlantic as some volcanic atoll. Cue much interlacing of fingers and jolting of joints, however. The lights of the Nulton glitterati fused.

'No bullshit, because our Les has been handling Betsy and the bloomin boys ever since they first stepped off the fucking aeroplane,' Marty informed us, grinning at the historic memory. 'Fair play, it seems like a long time ago now, when they had to duck their fucking heads to avoid the blinkin propellers,' he suggested.

'Marty, it's down in the annals of rock history,' insisted Les. 'Down in the hall of freakin fame. Man it must be over a decade back,' Les recalled. He was up in the ceiling and preferred to look right over our heads, as if missing us completely. Under the hat he gave a particular look; he was squinting down an endless highway over the plains of Idaho.

'Les and me kinda bump along together,' Betsy teased, sweetly, giving an affectionate dig into her manager.

The American eagle had a fond twinkle in its acute eye. 'A great gal to handle, my Betsy. She's no freakin trouble at all,' he enthused dryly.

She was trying to touch on an English accent. 'Yeah, and Les heard our first gig, at Peter-borough, and kinda liked the way me and the boys kicked it out. Did you guys, like, ever get to play Peter-borough yet? So when Les offered to handle our careers over here in England, man, I just had to leap at the offer. Les is such a sweetie and he knows his way around England.'

'Straight up Betsy, he ought to,' Gorran remarked.

'Right!' she exclaimed. She showed the perfect pearls and didn't hide them away.

'It's a pleasure to work with this little gal,' Les told us, evenly. 'What a great artist. And let me tell y'all, she's gonna be a freakin huge star in little old England. Period.'

Betsy's dazzling greenish blue eyes shined perfectly. She was definitely a 'sweet' kind of person, you could tell that, whatever we thought about her music – which was obviously, as Stan said, 'complete bollocks'.

'No shit Marty, so tell us what kinda noise does this Mortal outfit of yours make?' Phoenix asked.

'We make a really horrible noise,' Stan told him, adopting plummy tones. 'It's disgusting.'

The ten-gallon hat swivelled a degree as, a bald eagle from a cliff top, Les scrutinised Snot from an American altitude. 'Sure enough man, I can believe that.'

'Right, definitely Les, don't mind Snot's rock 'n' roll bloomin rebel attitude. No bullshit, we shot down to the *Hatter*, hot-foot from the band's fantastic headline gig at Nulton Arts College.'

'They still playin college gigs, man?'

'Straight up, Les, these boys and girls are the best little in-your-face bloomin punk group you'll ever get to hear. Definitely, and if their blinkin live dates go to plan they'll be up there on stage at the Lyceum ballroom, Jubilee year out.' Gorran was set up nicely to put over the hype. 'Or I must be Tammy Why-not,' he insisted, sagely.

Les Phoenix refused to be easily impressed. He dabbed long thin lips into a tumbler of original American malt whisky. Somehow he didn't sweat under that thick coat and big hat. Keeping cool was part of being an American.

'Sure man, so is it heavy rock, blues, country or *what the freakin hell is it* these guys play?' he wondered levelly. However, he didn't object to piss weakened beer soaking into his Cuban heels.

'Straight up Les, Mortal is a new British *punk* band. Fair play, Les, where you been blinkin hiding out these past months? An't you been watching what's been going on musically in the bloomin UK or what?' he objected, with a helpful smirk of being fully in touch.

'Shoot, we already had our 'punks' in the US of A, Marty, baby. Like, are these guys ever gonna sell any rec'rds?' Phoenix croaked.

'This band's not gonna make any records,' Snot argued.

'Right, definitely Les, don't take any blinkin notice of this herbert. Straight up, did the Sex Pistols' debut go to number one in the bloomin charts and right up the nostrils of the fucking establishment? Or have I got my musical nose up my own blinkin arse, Les mate?' Gorran said, grinning in disbelief at the ridiculous idea.

'That your pitch, Marty baby? You're gonna try'n break these buncha hoe-fingered freakin British punk kids?' Phoenix dismissed Snot as any kind of rock star or guitar god. Of course he hadn't heard him play yet.

'No bullshit Les, I'm inviting you, Betsy and the Screamers and all the blinkin *Red Rooster* crew, back down to the *Hatter*, Saturday week, to catch Mortal's premier fucking club gig,' Marty offered.

'Sure man, if our travellin' show's back in town,' Phoenix replied, standoffishly.

'Right, definitely, but…'

'Yeah Marty, you know we're kinda gigging regular now around England. So only if there's a slot in my gal's ske-dule,' Les said, peevishly.

'Fair play, Les mate, you don't want to miss out on the blinkin British punk scene that's exploding all around us.'

'Gee Marty, thanks for the tip, man. God bless, but I don't need your advice about freakin popular music.' He took down some more whisky and his pale narrow eyes scanned the packed venue for alternative interest.

'Rock music's out of style,' Snot commented.

Les turned his gaze down scornfully. '*Money* ain't out of style, son.'

'I hate commercial rock,' Stan added.

'Gee, Marty, where you find this buncha losers from?'

'Straight up Les, you're getting out of touch with the bloomin latest vital music scene in the UK.'

'Look man, maybe I don't wanna be in touch. Cos, shoot, the dollars are in the freakin adult market. Period. Like, if you try to promote these rough Brit kids, you're gonna frighten away your mature consumers. They'll put their dollars into sports or the stock market. Then you've lost your freakin purse,' Les warned. 'Period.'

'Right, definitely, but it's blinkin exciting to witness this music... and the kids in the UK are all getting into this fucking scene now and they're definitely buying all the records,' Marty pointed out, showing his impressive crags of teeth.

'You shittin me? Here in your little old England?' Phoenix said. 'They got any spare dollars in this shoe box?'

The DJ gave a shrug. 'Right, definitely, why not Les mate?'

'Doesn't sound very sexy or rock 'n' roll to me, Marty baby. Like it's Elvis without the wiggle, man.'

'Fair play, how can you write off punk rock, Les mate? Straight up, you could find yourself out of pocket, like some streaker who's lost his fucking trousers down at the bloomin laundry.'

Phoenix puzzled over the risk. 'How's this Mortal outfit goin down in Blue Ridge Montana, Marty? Or at Syrup Creek, Ohio? On the level with you, man, if you're sellin rec'rds from NYC to LA, then come back and talk to me about your hit group, Marty,' he suggested, pinching his long narrow pointy nose.

'Right, definitely, but you're gonna look like a right Nancy Sinatra, with blinkin holes in her fucking walking boots. Straight up Les, take notice of what's happening, or you'll be left with bloomin ostrich egg on your face,' Marty predicted, winking at us all with a little knowing laugh.

'Gee, Marty, I've never had anything on my goddamn face, except *shaving foam*,' Phoenix retorted, pulling up the back of his fur collar.

'Right, definitely Les, you didn't stand at the back of the blinkin hall at Nulton Arts tonight getting a load of this fantastic little punk band here, flooring the whole fucking venue. Fair play, being totally fucking blown away by what we heard,' he raved.

'Like I appreciate your dedication to the little guy, Marty baby. Gee, it's really British of you. But, in the words of that classic Brit rock group, The Who, you don't wanna be a freakin fashion victim, baby.'

'Right, definitely, but…'

'Listen man, I've had more hit acts over the years than you've had maple syrup pancakes,' Les told him. He directed a thinly pitying smile at Mortal. Apart from Snot and me they'd all wandered off, sick of being put down.

'Where d'you come from in America?' Stan asked.

'Beverly Hills,' Les replied. 'What of it?'

'*Beverly Hills*?'

'So why you living here in Nulton?'

'What's the goddamn big deal, son?'

'How long you lived here?'

'Several decades,' Marty commented.

'Ain't no moss gatherin' on this freakin rollin' stone.'

'Fair play, Les, mainstream rock's gone all blinkin Bing Crosby, ever since this punk rock thing exploded,' Marty insisted. 'In the UK and in the blinkin States.'

'Gee baby, I hate to see you disappointed,' Les told him, savouring the warm spices of his drink.

'Straight up, I signed up Mortal Wound to *Star Materials*. Fair play, and the sky an't the limit with this kick-arse little group. Or I must be Dust Springfield.'

'Well, *shoot* Marty, if you're so confident about these punk rock losers of yours, why ain't you enterin' em in for this Nulton 'Battle of the Bands' contest?'

Phoenix took a final finger of his whisky. He wasn't self-conscious about living under a cowboy hat. He pulled off the whole routine with conviction.

'Right, definitely Les mate, what 'Battle of the Bands' competition we talking about?' For once Marty hadn't heard about it. He was alarmed to feel that he wasn't in the know.

The Texan music manager had one up. 'Hey man, don't you ever read your freakin noospapers?'

'Right, definitely, when I get the blinkin time,' Gorran cringed.

'Gee man, you gotta keep up with the media. Didn't you hear about the Battle of the Bands? These politician guys… this local Nulton congress is gonna hold a talent show.'

'You mean those blinkin bastards on the council?' Marty pushed.

'Whatever those politicians call 'emselves these days, man.'

'Fair play, what kinda contest might you be blinkin talking about?'

'Like, the freakin congress is gonna hold a moosic contest, Marty. You gotta put your goddam name forward, man. I've already entered Betsy and the boys. We're gonna kick ass, man,' he predicted. 'What the hell you afraid of, baby?'

Marty blenched and cringed. 'How did all this come about? I never heard a bloomin word about no talent contest?'

'Gee, you need to get up to speed. You ain't up to first base, on this big gig, Marty. Like, the local congress got some juice from your little British department of health and social security,' Les informed us.

The punk guru had a hand on his forehead. 'Straight up, I have to enter my bands.'

The Texan mogul grinned slyly. 'Well, shoot Marty baby, no harm tryin to slug it out with the best.'

Gorran found an inch to scratch in his frizzy birds' nest thatch. 'Fair play, Les mate, what sort of prizes they offering?'

'Like there's this A&R guy from the EMI corporation. He's comin up to this little town from London, to be one of the judges? No bull, he's offerin the winner a freakin rec'rd contract. And EMI are gonna put the new act on a national tour of England. In support of a major act, yet to be lined up.'

'Straight up, Les, no bullshit, that sounds blinkin tempting.'

'OK man, so if you reckon these punk boys a yours got a freakin chance… What have you got to lose, man? Like, only your freakin pride and your Premium Bonds, man,' Les laughed dryly. 'Do you have enough juice for the entrance fees or what?'

'Right, definitely Les mate, so I'm gonna take you up on all that.'

'Gee, this could be my big break.'

6. Mortal on the Run

Mortal's gig at Nulton Arts certainly lives on in the mental record collection. But there was fallout from that fracas. There was even front page coverage in the local press, which got Stan's family door stepped. The experience was uncomfortable, even if his parents protected him and refused to make any comment other than positive ones.

If Snot thought it was just a hilarious stunt, he was definitely mistaken. When the Principle called him back into his office, it wasn't to thank him for raising money for charity. That cheque had been large enough to cover all the damage. Sketchley was appalled by all that negative publicity, which didn't reflect well on the image of art students.

Snot left the Principal's office expelled. He realised there was no such thing as a free riot. Even if he was never mistaken for Leo Sayer again, he wasn't gloating about it. We'd finished our final exams and were expecting the results. Stan needed an academic reference to begin his apprenticeship. As plain Jon Whitmore he'd been offered a career with Drew Spiro's industrial design company. The economic situation of the country wasn't great (understatement), so Snot had done well to get it. The Principle wasn't in any mood to write Snot love letters.

Sketchley wasn't the only one to target us. It was risky to emerge a punk, to make a statement, despite the aggressive media stereotype. We were far from the tolerant atmosphere of the King's Road or Camden Lock. As soon as we punks got a bad image, we were generally feared and loathed. All of a sudden we were vilified and became legitimate targets for 'normal' and 'ordinary' people. Especially when they considered us to be unpatriotic, trying to wreck the Jubilee celebrations. Of course the Sex Pistols were as British as fish 'n' chips.

You can see there was more deference in British society then. Certainly we had to tread carefully on Saturday nights out, any place outside the *Dragon* or the *Hatter*. You'd get a crowd of menacing 'casuals' strolling back home, in deceptively stylish sports shirts and tuck trousers, who just wanted to put their brogues into our ribs. All of a sudden you had to keep your wits about you, just living your life. Even Johnny Rotten/Lydon couldn't relax in his favourite pub any more. It was necessary for him to escape an angry mob by scarpering through the rear car park. That was the effect of the publicity. It was hard for those lads to enjoy all the fame and notoriety.

Fortunately for Snot he was not known beyond the local scene. Incredibly a positive review of the Mortal gig was printed in the *Nulton Chronicle*. The reviewer was a lad called Paulie Wellington. Stan wasn't impressed by the article, but we'll come to all that palaver later.

Mortal Wound went into rehearsals in Snot's garage. Garage Land was a way to hide without giving up the group altogether. There was still a missing element to their sound and line-up, even considering the amateur punk ethos. Despite getting expelled and losing a potential career, Stan was getting to know his guitar. On the sly he was learning about song writing. If he was shocked or upset by events he didn't show it. He kept all his troubles to his dented chest, saving them for his songs, like any true artist. Arguably it was through getting expelled that he fully evolved into the Stan Snot character. It was impossible to go back to being plain Jon Whitmore.

Stan was always an assured and confident individual. He wouldn't let anything or anyone deflect his curiosity or intelligence, about identity, life or art. Call it quiet arrogance, if you want. In this way I admired and learnt from him.

Growing up in the same street, Jon Whitmore and I had been antagonistic. Maybe childhood rivalries are petty, yet they stick in the memory and can mark a relationship. Somehow the punk thing brought us together. We'd found common cause. Even though punks posed as completely juvenile, we were growing up.

Snot was became his own man, as any lead guitarist should be. Then one evening:

'What did you think of the band, Bottle?'

'What'd I think? You got to take it further. It's more than just a laugh now.'

Snot took my comment shrewdly. Even if he kept up the diffident front, I don't believe he disregarded it. Suddenly we experienced a surge of sympathy, like John Cale playing a deafening chord during his 'terrorist' period.

Even our families were surprised by this new camaraderie. Not that our parents ever mixed, just nodding at each other across driveways. Stan coming out as a punk was the big event, like Masai kids with lions or Laurie Lee walking off to Spain.

Nulton Arts didn't have a rehearsal room available. Stan couldn't fully explain why a punk group had to rehearse. Whatever sounds came out of that garage, the neighbours heard too clearly. One Sunday, in response to complaints, the 'musicians' were forced to play without any amplification. It was ridiculous, after a police patrol had come to imposed restrictions. Even without amplification residents were alarmed by Nutcase's howls, reaching them over the Sunday dinner table. The cops had already served Stan with an official caution after his college concert. The Principle wanker had considered it generous not to press charges. A ban was imposed on Mortal Wound 'performances'.

Even Dougal at the *Dragon* was concerned about his licence, and therefore afraid to promote the lads.

Marty went into overdrive to organise secret gigs, under the disguised moniker of The Jon Whitmore Group – or the JWG as they became known. Marty's cunning plan was to change their style to evade the local live ban. He argued that publicans were ready to hire groups because the live scene was taking off. After the little controversy had died down, according to Gorran, the group could emerge as Mortal again to much acclaim. Sadly this didn't turn out to be one of Marty's greatest brainwaves.

Marty instructed Nutcase to arrive late for the JWG gigs. The vocalist refused to shave off his Mohican cut; and he didn't have the technique to change his singing style. The way around was for the vocalist to arrive last moment, even joining the others after they had started playing. We knew that he was a gentle Mohican, but the punters didn't. He'd never want to put a tomahawk into anybody's skull. But people out enjoying a few drinks were not to understand that. When that massive bloke, with an enormous green Mohican sprouting from his head, jumped up on the improvised stage and began to leap about, they usually panicked.

So Marty's plan was for JWG to play small gigs, build a reputation and make money for new equipment. After that they could triumphantly return to the circuit as Mortal Wound. The punk-meister's plan was to play cover versions and keep the volume down. This was the punk era. It was never going to work. Of course publicans read the local paper and knew about Mortal, even if JWG was designed to be as lifeless as the snooker table.

The band sat with Marty to agree on a set list in advance, consisting of old glam rock numbers and a few classic hits for stiffs. *Desperado*, *Bridge Over Troubled Water*, or *Money, Money, Money*, stick in my head as the most alarming examples. Some nights the band smuggled a few old Mortal favourites into the repertoire – engineered down. Few punters ears could endure Nutcase's version of the pop archive. Hardly anyone could get through Nut's interpretation of Sweet's *Ballroom Blitz*. At first people were laughing into their beers or Babyshams. Within a couple of minutes they were more uncomfortable, even hot and bothered. After a couple of songs people were fully intimidated and began running out to the car park. For pub owners that wasn't the idea of a successful 'live music' night.

JWG never got a repeat booking. Eventually their reputation went before them. No venue would touch them. When punks began to turn up as well, knowing it was really Mortal doing secret gigs (however bland the style) that was the final coffin nail. JWG wasn't able to keep any audience happy or even, crucially, the group itself.

Stan had a family baptism, a wedding and two funerals to go to. His parents suggested that he get his 'nice group' to play at his cousin's wedding reception. We didn't think that was a good idea.

Marty soon realised how dire it was. All that promotional hype didn't go down well. There was no sign of a PR breakthrough for JWG. On top of this, Marty hated the music. There was that complex pain and regret on his expressive mug. He'd be propped on a stool at the bar, smirking out with intense discomfort at the sound, wincing and squinting through dense cigarette smoke.

Therefore he had to intervene again to change the course of rock n roll history.

7. Enter the Heroine

Word on the grapevine was that Mortal had split. Not even the thought of winning Nulton's first ever 'Battle of the Bands' competition, with a massive prize and tour, could hold them together.

Marty proved his mettle by finding the group a new rehearsal space. The mogul booked them a block at Crock Sound Studios. This music facility was owned by Dave's son, Troy, based in a row of converted old houses. It offered the facilities of an eighteen track recording studio; handy if Mortal should ever cut a debut 45.

Asking a favour from Troy Crock was always a risky dice throw. Junior Crock owned a portfolio of small enterprises in the town. Like his dad these were focussed around the entertainment industry, including a mucky magazine outlet. Troy was doing all right, going by the big family house he'd purchased recently; in a nice new suburb, more like a suburb of the suburbs. His wife ran a growing chain of ladies' hairdressing salons. It was a method of money laundering, or giving it a shampoo and blow-dry. Troy taught his missus the tricks of running businesses.

In appearance Crock junior was this fleshy, heavy-set, raw-wired thug, dripping in gold and silver, and sports watches the price of the average semi. His low-angled forehead ended between his eyebrows and you could have driven a golf ball from the top of his shaven head. We're going to bump into him later in the story.

Our Mortal musicians assembled that Sunday for a first proper band practice. They were relieved to resume their real moniker, after dropping JWG and that short-lived career as an inept covers band. Billy Urine was the only lad who'd ever been in a studio or a rehearsal room. They benefited from having a trained engineer on hand, to set them up. This long-fringed guy put them on track, when faced with a jungle of dials, sockets and sliders, not to mention windows, wires and microphones.

Not standing on ceremony Herb and Stan were late. Herb took ages at home to prepare his costume and coiffure, fancying himself as Bowie or Ronson or Ferry. On the best of days Stan had problems waking up 'early'. He was non-aggressive character, except with alarm clocks. This developed after he'd been expelled and lost his job; aggravated by a new rock 'n' roll lifestyle. Over the Saturday night he'd been down to London, for a punk night at the Rock Garden. So Stan only returned to Nulton in the small hours by sneaking on the post train. In those days rail services halted before midnight. And there was only a *Wimpy* bar still open, offering a piss-weak tea and a greasy burger 'til dawn. Consequently he rolled up bleary eyed, dishevelled and moody, and having to borrow a guitar.

Anna-kissed had brought a girlfriend of hers to the session. It wasn't so unusual, I later realised, for musicians to bring groups of hangers-on and admirers. The tendency was all part of the general ambience of self-absorption and congratulation. This particular friend though – who'd attended the same girls-only school – was a musician; a real one that is. After introducing herself, with deep blushes even through pancake makeup, she showed them an expensive *Fender* guitar and even a new little *Roland* keyboard and created artistic panic.

'What're you gonna do with that thing?' Snot demanded.

The girl took in the enigmatic hunched lad, for the first time. 'What do you want me to do with it?'

There was unrestrained laughter and horse-play between the others.

'Whatever, you're not playing that thing.'

'You got something against keyboards?' she challenged him.

'Too right, we do. Get it straight.'

'Maybe some keyboards will fit into your sound.'

'Bollocks. Put it away.'

'All right, don't blow up.'

'Blow up that *keyboard*,' Snot suggested.

'Great attitude!'

What an introduction. In fact Gina – Gina Watson – had been taking piano lessons from the moment her chin got over the keys. Rather than twiddling and pinging about, like the other punks, she'd passed bona fide music exams to a high level. This put the tiger among the flying rats.

Gina looked as sharp as a razor blade too – glassy blonde hair starched up into an angel's wing, black lipstick and crusts of black circling glimmering grey-blue eyes.

Yeah, she was really nice looking, cool and tall as a Wimpy milkshake, and so trendy and interesting. When she first spoke to me, I got this strangled feeling, as if somebody was making a bow-tie out of my vocal cords. I tried to sort this out, but a Rubik's Cube was simpler than to find the right words. For weeks this happened to me every time I opened my mouth. It was so bloody embarrassing.

Apparently she'd wriggled out of respectable clothes into her punk gear, on the top deck of the bus over. Her parents were vehemently opposed to her being in any type of rock band. She left her house by the rear, as normally dad was her taxi service. They didn't get an image of Gina playing rhythm guitar in a punk group. No, they visualised her with the Royal Philharmonic and them watching her proudly from a private box.

Neither Marty nor Stan was impressed by musical accomplishment. Both of them were arch punk propagandists. Inspired incompetence was their bench mark. Any talk about 'classical' music produced spasms. The best qualification was not to recognise one end of a guitar from the other. Then you got a band with your mates and just tried to work it out. Joe Strummer didn't take a voice coach, did he – according to Snot. The only way Mick Jones or Rat Scabies used sheet music was to light up their reefers at an all-night squat party.

'What are you going to study at music college?' Herb asked.

'How to get drunk and enjoy myself,' Gina replied.

All was not lost. Gina's attitude, style and punk fashion sense made an impact. Despite dropping her guitar and tripping over wires, she wasn't going to take any shit off anybody called Snot.

She was definitely punk, regardless. She was honest to admit to having lessons and aspirations for a career as a pianist. Of course Marty dreamed of making his fortune from music, albeit without playing anything other than the media. The other band members liked her. And that was before she picked up the guitar or began singing.

Gorran sensed genuine musical talent and gold discs and better. Despite being filling out Crock's timesheet (suggesting he was paying for these rehearsals) the new girl caught his pop eye. Like the characters in a fruit-machine during a power surge, pound signs were revolving in his eyes. His flexible grin became more fixed, as he took her in.

'Right, definitely, Gina, come on and string up that bloomin beautiful guitar of yours. Straight up, lower the mic to the right fucking height. Gord 'elp us, if it an't a breath of fresh blinkin air to have a gifted girl around this studio complex. Or I must be Perry Coma.'

'I'll follow you and see how I get on,' she told the others.

'We're still a punk group,' Stan reminded her.

'Yeah, don't worry. Rock needed a kick up the arse, didn't it? It's exciting,' she added nervously.

She came from a nicer social background than we did. She was a bad middle-class girl and she wasn't the only one. She wanted to see what it was like to go wrong.

'I've heard a lot of punk down in London,' Gina said.

She went through the roll-call of the times. She'd heard all the best new bands, and some of the most eye-catchingly terrible. Stan didn't comment but I could tell he was impressed. She was written all over with street-cred like a Berlin subway.

'My songs are too moronic for a trained musician,' Snot sneered.

'Maybe you can give me lessons?'

Stan huffed and shuffled. 'You don't need any taste in music.'

'I already got a taste of yours,' she joked.

'So you resign?'

Gina fumbled with her guitar lead as if she'd never plugged in before. Soon I'd realise this was just nerves, although the others were giving wary looks.

'The orchestra's waiting,' Stan pointed out.

'Okay, I'm not familiar with this…'

'Maybe you only play the fucking piano.'

'Give her a chance now, Stan bay!'

'I don't want any fucking harpsichordists in this group.'

'Give me the tunings, will you? For the first song?' Gina said. Her hand was trembling as she turned things.

'Never mind tunings. This isn't the last night of the fucking Proms, is it?'

The thing was, when Gina began to strum she sounded fantastic.

Billy called out from the drum stool, 'She can sing a bit too, lads!'

'Nutcase is vocals,' Stan cut back. He pretended to stay unimpressed. Owing to his lateness Snot stooped and crouched over an unfamiliar guitar, which was giving him trouble.

'Nutcase and me are mates already,' Gina insisted. 'Aren't we, Nut? I don't know what his singing's like… but he's a top lad.'

'He is definitely top note,' Herb said.

'You'll soon fucking find out,' Snot predicted.

'All right Gina?' Nutcase greeted her. The giant vocalist stalked the floor in preparation, like some sea monster on the sands.

'Let's address our fucking instruments,' Snot suggested.

'Right, definitely you lot, stop pissing about, let's get a blinkin move on? Straight up, I an't playing no game of bloomin statues with you lot. No bullshit, I can hear the fucking meter going round. Right, so I got a discount from Troy, but this is still costing a truckload of money.' Marty held up a chunky wristwatch, tapping the glass – the drips of paint did not hide the rising tariff.

Everyone agreed that they were ready. Snot awkwardly called out *one two three four*. Somehow missing the obvious cue, they rattled and stumbled into an awkward first number. There was an awful lot of chugging and chopping, sudden tempi changes, intensifying stalls and dramatic accelerations. Even so, when Gina began playing it was a bit of a revelation.

Once the 'tune' had finished, Snot, after a delay, fiddling with knobs, gave his verdict. 'That was fucking terrible, lads. Just not as terrible as we wanted. How's it possible to murder one of my tunes.'

'That's true enough now,' Billy agreed, laughing.

'Yeah, and my tunes are already murdering music,' Snot quipped.

'Right, definitely, what's all this blinkin monkey business all about?' Marty complained from the side-lines. 'No bullshit, at least try to play some fucking tune altogether.'

'*Corgi Sandwich* is next up,' Stan told them.

'*Corgi Sandwich*!' Gina said.

'What about it? Pick the hairs out.'

'What's the chords? What exactly you saying I should play?'

'Catch up.'

'Stan, bay. Give a signal to start so,' Billy suggested. 'You have to make it feckin' clear to us all now!'

'Like counting in isn't strong enough?'

'Try it at the same speed so!'

'Don't get your dirty undies in a twist, Billy,' Anna-kissed objected.

'Yes, right, just because you've played in a show band,' Herb sniggered.

'Wanna nose job, Herb bay?' Billy warned, leaning forward.

'So can you all try fucking harder this time?' Snot told them.

'Did I fuck up?' Gina wondered.

This question hung in the air, because it was so far from reality.

'I got me vocals warmed up now,' Nutcase explained. He began pacing again, like Dame Sutherland on steroids.

'Don't give us full throttle yet, Nut. Keep it to second gear, mate.'

Stan fiddled and fussed at the guitar's controls, as if he really cared.

It was still unclear why a punk band wanted to rehearse on a Sunday. I suppose it was better than watching your parents snore through *Songs of Praise* or *Sing Something Simple*.

Observing all this, Marty was twitching and wincing from a corner of Crock's Sound Studio B. For him notes were musical and leaving the bank fast.

'Hurry up, Herb. I don't wanna see your flashy Jackson Five fretwork.'

'You wouldn't know it, Stan.'

'If it kicked him up the arse,' Anna-kissed put in. She kept weighing the rhythm guitar in front of her, like Herb ought to carry it for her.

'Just keep it all simple,' Stan said.

Herb's desire to be Sly and the Family Stone was a tough call for a new punk group. Particularly as his girlfriend had only found her battered guitar in a junk shop the previous month.

In the face of this Gina decided to strum modestly. When she played discordantly, it was deliberate, not because she hit the strings like Gus the gorilla on drugs, as did most lads starting local groups. For her these approaching chord changes felt like traffic lights far ahead, while Anna-kissed and even Stan were still groping in the dark. I noticed that despite being the least musical person in the room.

'Try *Corgi Sandwich* again,' Stan prompted.

This time Gina was along with the chorus. She had a soprano that cut through Nutcase's wrenching howl. Singing well and in tune was truly subversive. There was going to be a shake-up, if Stan allowed her to stay. She injected musical talent, and it was completely taboo.

* * *

'You thought it was OK? Thanks.' Gina got tangled in her guitar strap on the way out.

'Right definitely, no bullshit Gina, from where I fucking stood it was making Pauline in Penetration sound like blinkin Barbara Dickenson. Or I must be Shirley Bassey,' the rock guru enthused.

Gina looked bashful as she rested her guitar against a speaker. 'Really? These lads play the songs so fucking fast,' she commented.

'Right definitely, you can't stop these blinkin herberts going off like a lot of bloomin trains,' he commented. 'No bullshit, like some bullet train with no blinkin handbrake pushed down the fucking hill. But fair play Gina love, this is a new little punk and I was really fucking impressed with how you was playing along,' Marty said, twisting his anxious mouth in a very encouraging shape.

'I hit a C sharp during *Sandwich*. Did you notice?'

'C sharp, Gord elp us, no need to rip all your bloomin hair out about that, is there,' Marty said, not missing an atom of the talent in front of him, smiling widely in appreciation.

'How can you be so positive? Didn't you listen properly, Mr Gorran? I made so many stupid little errors.'

'Right, definitely, a few mistakes, yeah, but what's a few blinkin bum notes among these gormless punks?' Marty jested, crinkling his eyes and exposing his imposing gaggle of ivories.

'The category of music isn't relevant,' she replied. 'Mistakes are mistakes.'

The rock mogul put a reassuring arm around her shoulders for a moment. 'Right, definitely Gina, so why don't you join Mortal and come down to the blinkin *Mad Hatter* to play their first big club gig?' he hustled.

'Truth is... don't know if I have the time, Mr Gorran. *Studying...* I've got to practice for auditions... You know, for *music* college.'

'Gord elp us, *music college*!? Straight up, don't go bloomin studying and rushing into all that blinkin classical music crap, with all those fucking fiddles and stuff. Fair play, where's all the blinkin fun and money in studying that stuff? You don't want to throw away this huge fucking opportunity to make a massive splash in the bloomin rock business,' he advised.

'Well, you gotta appreciate, Mr Gorran that...'

'No bullshit love, have you seen any of those classical music girls driving about in their own blinkin white Jaguar E Type with the fucking hood down on a bloomin country road, before their twenty first birthday?' he suggested.

'My parents don't see it that way,' she explained. 'They want me to make an honest living from classical music.'

'Straight up, *honest*, it's easier to get into that royal fucking family on that bloomin balcony, than to tinkle the blinkin ivories in the Albert Hall,' Marty argued, showing eye teeth.

'Maybe,' she agreed. 'I dunno. But I can't make any promises about playing with your band.'

'Right, definitely, you want to listen up, cos Mortal's the best bloomin little kick-arse punk group I've heard all bloomin year in the entire UK. And, no bullshit I'm taking em to the blinkin summit of this fucking pop music industry,' Marty vowed. 'Or I'm Alvin Stardust.'

'Maybe. Good luck,' she told him.

'Right, definitely, so you gonna blinkin join them? Or, straight up, you gonna get clamped up into that fucking party frock all your bloomin life?' he warned, with a doom laden nod.

The punkette considered. 'I'll have to see what dad says. My parents would be disappointed. And I don't know if I can play punk in front of all those other kids.'

'You're not recruiting her for anarchy, are you, Lord Cheese?' Stan shot to the manager.

'Right Stan mate, cos before Gina joined in you lot sounded flatter than a blinkin 'edge 'og squashed in the middle of the fucking road.'

'Yeah, right, words of fucking wisdom. What do we want with her? She plays classical piano.'

'What about it? I'm well into punk rock,' Gina objected.

Snot was looking furtively up through his thick eyebrows. 'Bollocks.'

'Don't be so juvenile,' she said.

'What do you expect?'

'Gina sounded feckin' good to me, bays,' Urine added.

'I liked her too, Stan,' said Nutcase. 'I want her. I fought she 'ad a nice voice.'

'You're the singer, Nut! You've got no equal.'

'Okay, so I don't want to spoil your little party here,' Gina remarked.

Snot was doing something to his amp again.

'I only asked Gina along as a friend,' Anna-kissed insisted.

'Straight up,' Marty addressed them, more sternly, 'are you gonna invite her or are you stupider than Ronnie Reagan's blinkin arsehole? No bullshit, she's the one difference between being up there in the bloomin charts at number one for six months, or going down to number six after one week at number blinkin fifty nine.'

Gorran grimaced at the bitter irony of failing to dent the charts for long enough.

'We can't play my crap tunes,' Stan pointed out. 'Now we've got her and she can play fucking Gershwin.'

'Right, definitely, but if you want my advice you'll get Gina into your band faster than a fucking squirrel up a pole. Otherwise, no bullshit lads, I don't have an ear for blinkin music in the first place,' Marty winced. 'Straight up, I must have cut it off and sent it off in the post again in a fucking envelope.'

'I don't mind,' Nutcase said.

'Mind fucking what?'

'I'm not able to full commit anyway. Not yet. I'll see how my studies go, right? I'll have a word with my dad.'

'Fucking 'dad', listen to it,' Snot objected. He extracted weird impatient noises from his axe.

'Right you lot, hurry up and run through your last set. Fair play, get this session done, cos I've only squared off with Crock for another hour.'

'Come on, punks,' Stan urged, plugging back in. 'I'll try you with another horror story. If I get anything out of this crap guitar. And no backing vocals, Gina. This isn't a Van Morrison record.'

'Don't be such a non-musical nob,' Billy told him.

There was going to be turmoil. I had a sense of it.

Mortal had to agree on putting together three chords. Still, I noticed that Stan was enjoying himself, playing with Gina Watson. Why would you start a band, if it wasn't fun? There was a clash of personalities. Musically they bounced off each other.

A motley collection of individuals can turn into a great band. Rivalries, tensions, egos can be forgotten as musical chemistry flows. A special group will discover their own sound; and it's brilliant to feel that happening. I knew that and was privileged to be there. For future audiences, it's something they want to hear.

Even by the end of that first session I couldn't think of Mortal without Gina. She definitely sprinkled a bit of magic dust, and it was hard to remove.

Snot tried to be difficult. You couldn't come on as Sid Vicious all the time. Not even Sid Vicious could.

8. *Ob-scene* is Born

As usual on a Saturday, I was busy in my student job at the *Co-op Superstore* all day. After turning fifteen I got a part time position in the grocery department, and built my hours up from there. The whole building was bulldozed, 'redeveloped' and replaced by something cheap and nasty, only a few years after I left. I don't know if (or how) that was significant.

Circa 'Silver Jubilee' year the *Co-op* was still the only proper department store in town. For my brother and me, accompanying our mother, it was a romantic adventure just to arrive at the entrance and push through the revolving doors. It was like *Selfridges* to us. Set over several floors the place looked massive, and stocked everything under the sun. The store even had a customers' lift.

If you ascended the carpeted central staircase instead, to the first floor, you would arrive at a very nice cafeteria. A pot of tea for three and an iced bun or a custard tart was my favourite. All those kind old people in flat caps and plastic rain capes, retired factory workers, blue or pink rinses and bad dentures (like original punks), with big smiles and kind words for the kids, between steam and smoke… What happened to them all? Where did they go?

If I remember the *Co-op* cafe was busy, the actual sales floors were comparatively empty. Other than for the presence of staff that was. You'd find at least half a dozen sales assistants, a manager and a deputy manager, for every customer. They'd generally be stood about, waiting to be mobilised. It felt like the communist block except that, either side of the January sales, you never had to queue. This army of assistants would gather together around the impressive wooden counters to enjoy sociable banter. The cash registers were not exactly over worked either. Purchases involved some type of tubular communication system, which fired metal capsules around the building. Whatever it was, it was fascinating for my brother and I to observe. If our mother bought a packet of buttons or a ball of wool for instance, this would trigger some sort of missile launch around the whole building. Eventually, following a suspenseful wait, the projectile would return to base, mission accomplished, containing – not a hydrogen bomb holocaust – but Mum's change and receipt.

Occasionally my parents went in for a bigger purchase, such as dining room furniture or beds. Finally, I remember, some be-quiffed bloke in a three-piece suit with a tape-measure, would notice and sashay over to investigate. Chuck and I were fitted here for our new school uniforms, as the summer holiday came to a close. Mum could always count on the price and the quality. Otherwise the superstore was a bit challenged in the fashion sense, even before I started dyeing my hair in bright colours.

'Look at this box-set matching tie and shirt,' Mum would point out. 'Come on Paul, try it on. That's so stylish. Put it up against yourself in the mirror. What's wrong with it? Stripes suit you. Don't you like seahorse patterns? What's wrong with you? That's smashing that is. You're not with it. Try it against the red blazer.'

Then there was our grandma, who'd rustle the sweets section like a hungry horse. She didn't worry because she didn't have a tooth in her head.

As a student worker on groceries I wore a brown overall. It was badly ill-fitting. There was enough play with hot wires and packing machines to satisfy a prog rock keyboardist. In the yard outside there was a storage shed, where Saturday staff lads would huddle between boxes of apples and cabbages. Here they'd keep out of view, chatting and smoking to kill time between tea breaks and going home.

One particular Saturday I was out labelling, sticking on prices and stacking product trays on display shelves. And who should show turn up on the floor? None other than entertainment chief Marty Gorran himself, like a night creature showing in the day.

The Co-op employed him freelance, and his assistant Steve, to create signs and displays around the store. I'd spot Marty at the centre of a shop floor gaggle, including managers and employees, animatedly in conference, offering his creative advice. Or I'd notice the outer atmosphere of his kinky blonde hair, resembling a giant dandelion, bobbing about and moving along over the top of display units; along with the soundtrack.

Although I rubbed shoulders with Marty socially, I never thought he'd take specific interest in me. Marty had little cause to shop at the *Co-op* supermarket either, because his local newsagent supplied most of his essential needs. I was startled to find him heading along the aisle towards me, where I was occupied putting fruit on display. And it could not merely be a coincidence, as his face was firing up a five-cylinder grin to burn off any doubts; as if I was his special mate, lost for years: as if the sun was shining out of my arse, and he drew my attention to that miraculous phenomenon.

I decided to neglect the apples and stuff and find out what he wanted.

'Straight up, I thought I'd catch you down here with the fucking fruit and veg,' he said.

'It's my regular date for a Saturday afternoon.'

'Yeah, fair play Paul, and I reckon you graduated from that blinkin Nulton Arts College by now, didn't you?' He winced affably, while treating me to his undivided attention.

'Yeah, I suppose.'

'Straight up, I was a blinkin student there myself once,' he reminded me. 'Gord elp us, it's been blinkin donkey's years, more than I care to bloomin think about, since I graduated. Fair play, it must have been round the time of fucking *Sticky Fingers* getting released,' he said and beamed ironically.

Why the sudden charm offensive? I felt uncomfortable to be the centre of this attention. I was a background boy.

The rock maverick noticed this and changed direction. 'Gord elp us, I know you an't going to stick down here forever, with all these bloomin fruit and veg,' Gorran predicted.

'Well, I hope not.'

'No bullshit, no matter how fucking fresh, you don't want to make a blinkin career out of it. Straight up, I expect you're gonna move on with the whole rock 'n' roll circus. Cos I knew right away you got bigger blinkin ambitions than bags of bloomin mixed salads and bunches of cut fucking flowers.' He grinned out affectionately.

Although I was part of the Co-op romance, I didn't consider this job permanent.

'Sometimes I envy Stan, cos his parents give him generous pocket money,' I admitted.

'No bullshit, Bottle, we all need a bit of blinkin loose change to rattle around in our fucking pockets,' Marty confirmed, refocusing on my dissatisfied expression. 'And Stan was offered that apprenticeship down at Drew Spiro's Design Agency in town, wasn't he?'

'Yeah, until he got expelled. Now it's all off,' I said.

'Right, definitely, what's going on there?'

'Stan's my next door neighbour,' I boasted.

'That so? Right, definitely, a good lad to have bloomin growing up in the next house along the same blinkin street,' Gorran agreed. He began to sort out his awkward teeth with the tip of his tongue.

'Yeah, the gig blew his chances of that apprenticeship. He's never going to find a job... not equal to his talents.'

'Straight up Bottle, Stan wants to be very fucking careful with that blinkin yellow goggled shark, Drew Spiro.'

'Really? So you know this Spiro bloke?'

Gorran's glad expression crumbled in uneasiness. 'Straight up, I wouldn't trust that Spiro as far as I could fucking spit, after I'd had all my blinkin teeth pulled out.'

'Oh? How would you know that?' I wanted to know.

'No bullshit Bottle, I've done a lot of blinkin jobs for Spiro's,' Marty told me. 'And I an't planning to get commissioned by Spiro for any more blinkin design work. Fair play, not even a blinkin casual doodle on me serviette at the Chinese takeaway.'

'Oh well, that's reassuring,' I considered. 'Then I should pass that on to Stan, shouldn't I.'

'No bullshit, get Snot fully blinkin clued up on that dodgy fucking company,' Marty winked and grinned.

'It was a fantastic gig Mortal Wound played at college,' I enthused. 'Almost worth getting expelled for.'

'Straight up Bottle, who needs that qualification when Snot's gonna get his first blinkin plat'num disc hanging at the end of his fucking bed,' Gorran argued.

I must have given Marty a look that said, *We agree that Mortal are brilliant, but how does it relate to me*? As a brilliant publicist and media-manipulator Gorran instantly picked up on it.

'No bullshit, I was chatting to that Julie Buckle in 'Women's' this afternoon, one of our top fashion designers, when I said it was about blinkin time I spoke to Paul Bottle about going places together in the fucking Nulton music scene.'

'You and me? Together?' I gawped.

'Right, definitely Bottle mate, we can get all my local bands up in blinkin lights, with the right type of bloomin publicity and press coverage. No bullshit, if there's somebody who knows his way around the fucking typewriter keys. Somebody who agrees with me that Mortal Wound can make a bigger bloomin splash in this country than fucking Windsor Safari Park,' he argued, reaching out.

'What's this about press coverage? How's that to do with me?' I asked. I was struggling in the backwash of this media blitz.

Other Saturday staff were staring suspiciously at us. They wondered what we were chewing about, not being able to connect Gorran to the world of rock and pop yet.

'Straight up Bottle, the band's gonna need some clever bloomin interviews and articles behind them,' he persisted.

'All right, but…'

'No bullshit Bottle, this little punk group needs some blinkin media promotion from a sharp little fucking local rock writer. Fair play, that's where I reckon you come in,' he suggested. The full-beam grin was at a full stretch. The guru's eyes twinkled over me as if I was Tom Wolfe in embryo; as if he could see the first cells dividing.

Who isn't partial to a bit of flattery?

'Okay, Marty, so you want me to help out? How do I fit in to your company?'

Gorran's beam of admiration held me in the circle, like a World War Two searchlight. The idiosyncratic map of wrinkles, dimples and crevices was put into freeze frame. He'd got an amazingly complex dial for a man in his twenties. Part of it was down to the round-midnight lifestyle, or maybe the wear and tear of big ambitions, knowing that it was never an easy road.

'Straight up Bottle, cos our Stan wants you involved and I blinkin well agree with him for once,' Gorran was delighted to inform me.

'Stan suggested me? I can't play any instrument or sing either.'

'Gord elp us, Bottle, nobody's going to ask you to fucking play any bloomin instrument. No bullshit, we've already got enough blinkin non-musicians making a fucking noise here in Nulton. Straight up, to get the rats running out of the venues with their bloomin hands over their fucking ears,' he said, half in jest.

'In punk you don't need to play well. I just don't fancy any instrument. So what else can I do?'

'Right, definitely, because Snot was telling me about all those fucking top rate blinkin articles you were writing for the college paper.'

'My stuff for *Chips and Chalk*, do you mean?'

'Straight up, whatever they fucking call that college rag, cos Stan was telling me how you've got a smart way with fucking words.'

'Not sure about that,' I replied.

Flattery had a limit. The grocery manager had an inborn suspicion of students, despite being forced to employ them. He strolled past us several times and shot long warning looks.

'No bullshit, I've never been so impressed with any article I've read in that blinkin college paper. Straight up Bottle, your writing stood out like a wart on the nose of fucking Miss Universe,' he claimed. 'No bullshit, in a positive way, and how could you fucking miss it, Bottle mate?'

Marty hung on to see if I'd agree with this idea. So the Rolling Stone mug continued to stretch out towards breaking point.

'Well, it was fun writing those pieces,' I admitted. 'I got a bit of a kick out of it.'

'Right, definitely Bottle, because *Star Materials* needs a bloomin brilliant words person like you to boost circulation. Straight up why don't you come and string together your bloomin brilliant fucking sentences for us instead? Fair play, now you're out of blinkin education.'

'What kind of stuff should I write?' I was getting uneasy as the supermarket manager watched. I didn't want to get sacked.

'Right, so Turbo Overdrive have got their debut single released next blinkin month. My Rob's had to sell his motor to pay for the first bloomin cut and so he doesn't have a pair of blinkin wheels anymore! Fair play, there's only so far the *Star Materials* artists' budget will go. Now Rob's hassling me to get some bloomin sleeve notes done for the record. Fair play Bottle, who has blinkin sleeve notes on the back of their fucking records these days?' Marty objected.

I shuffled and cast uneasy looks. 'You don't want to fall out with Rob over that.'

'Right, definitely, someone handy with a blinkin typewriter to shake up some fucking press releases for the *Nulton Chronicle*,' Marty requested. 'Straight up, what do you blinkin think about all that?'

'I can have a go,' I agreed. I couldn't help myself.

The grin of pleasure was amplified. 'Straight up, I'll let Rob know, when I see him later. He'll be chuffed to bits about those bloomin sleeve notes.'

'That shouldn't take me long,' I said.

'Right, and Stan said you ought to write the pieces for our bloomin fanzine as well. Fair play you can interview all the bands taking part in this 'Battle of the Bands competition. No bullshit, you can take down the fucking interviews with all the groups and I'll print it up in this new bloomin magazine. Fair play, then we'll sell the fanzine in the record shops and to all those punks on final night,' Gorran explained.

'Sounds a great idea,' I agreed.

Exuding positive energy, Marty observed me approvingly. I was snagged to his little finger, yo-yo fashion, like almost everybody on the scene.

'I'm doing this all by myself?' I wanted to know.

'Fair play, my mate Steve Fenton will help out. Steve can string a few blinkin words together when he's in the right fucking mood.'

It was exciting. 'Right, you're on,' I said.

'Steve's a good fucking snapper, and he can take all the photos for the mag too. I'll design the pages for you, set out the bloomin art work and layout and get some fucking advertising revenue coming in to pay for it all.'

The rock guru grinned and rubbed his dry inky hands together.

'A lot of lads are starting fanzines,' I reminded him.

'Straight up Bottle, never mind the blinkin competition, cos even all those big name fucking music papers down in London better look over their bloomin shoulders now,' Gorran confidently predicted.

'Let's see how the first edition goes.'

'Right Bottle, you got the picture, so join us at the Dragon tonight, and we'll have a longer chat about the fanzine and buy you a couple of drinks to calm your blinkin nerves.'

Marty twinkled and leered at me, the awesome 'words person'. Then he was up and out of groceries, to his next appointment in a different department of the *Co-op Superstore*.

9. Stan and the Dove of War

Gorran got into the habit of introducing me to people as 'Copy Writer in Chief'. Even before the photocopiers of his print empire had begun to overheat I was bigged up and it sent my immature imagination reeling.

That particular evening the *Dragon* was crammed with punks, Goths and bikers. It was the only venue for Alternative Nulton, between applying for a university grant or signing on.

Rival youth tribes had little to fear from rubbing leather jackets. It was because the threat came from the streets outside. The town's straights and casuals were the most hostile to any individual or group different to them. That was true of my older brother too, Chuck, who ironed *all* of his clothes, down to his socks. Of course there was danger for the punks, when TV and newspapers turned us into pantomime villains. The local fascist chapter had started up – or whatever they called themselves – and gathered on Wednesdays and Fridays in their own public house, *The Lion and Unicorn*. The publican there was an ex-sociology lecturer, thin as a broomstick and bushy bearded, by the name of Lionel Mace. He was sacked by the Tech college after writing an article for the *English bulldog* and for shagging a sixteen year old Belgian hippie during an exchange trip. I don't know what the article was about. I suppose I could guess.

Anyway, Stan arrived that evening at the *Dragon* wearing a new studded leather jacket (pocket money from mother), as well as wraparound black sun glasses. Even though he didn't approve of rock star posing he did look very cool in those shades. The true reason for putting on that garb was his fear of being recognised and getting his head kicked in. That was an added risk in the weeks and months after the Nulton Arts gig. In the words of (one of) Gorran's heroes, Gene Pitney, *he knew what a town without pity can do*. Then again, Marty knew that even better, as did every gay lad or girl growing up during those decades. Well, a sizeable minority meant him harm – or us, or them.

My only competition as a music correspondent, in our town and region at least, came from that cub reporter on the *Nulton Chronicle*. We hadn't been introduced to this mysterious lad yet. We knew he was also a would-be music journalist, already writing gig reviews for the moronic local rag. That included a review of Mortal's notorious bash at college, which had got right up Snot's nose.

'All right, you can interview us for this fanzine… if you want to,' Stan told me.

Still, we got excited about Gorran's publishing empire. Snot was tossing back the JD as well as dissecting the group's last practice. When well lubricated he admitted that Gina was a truly glam girl and a proper punk. But he was still spooked by her classical music credentials. To say it was a threat was an understatement, like saying that Cruise missiles and Soviet SS missiles were a bit of a headache to planning your weekend.

It never occurred to Snot that *he* might be talented as well. His Mum ordered 'Play Guitar in Six Weeks' from the newsagent. Snot picked it up in under five I reckon. That's how quick he was. Even during the brief period he kept those publications hidden under the bed like porn magazines. He was borrowing music books and scores from the local library. He furthered his musical education by closely watching other musicians and performers. We took in a lot of high profile punk bands that featured in the national music press. Stan would always go to the front of the stage, following finger placements and chord progressions very closely, when the gig got underway.

'Gina'll get us doing classical stuff. I don't want Mortal sounding like a bunch of prog rockers in fucking cheesecloth, trying out concept albums,' Snot objected. 'No, if we allow that, we have that big cheese Gorran entering us into fucking *Stars in their Eyes*.'

'It'll never happen,' I insisted.

'She never turns up for practice.'

There was something else on my mind too. 'What about your apprenticeship, Stan? Did the company write to you yet?'

'Not a peep out of them.'

Stan's chance of working for Drew Spiro Design was a bigger lame duck than Gerald Ford was.

'Anyway, Marty told me that Drew Spiro is a terrible employer.'

'Oh yeah? But how about you Bottle? What you planning to do now... after graduation?'

'Stuck with fruit and veg all my days?' I didn't know the store was going to get demolished a few years later. The town council was unlikely to commission any public sculptures from me. *Life* magazine hadn't asked me to pose for its next cover.

In Nulton good jobs were rarer than pink pineapple trees. We were thinking about 'what a waste' even before Ian Dury sang about it.

'Still getting shit off Pete?' Snot enquired. I reckon he noticed my despondency, even running beneath my excitement about the fanzine.

'Don't ask,' I said. 'Now they're threatening to throw me out.'

'You fucking serious or what?'

'As the state of the nation,' I insisted.

After the closing time bell and extended 'last orders', we decided to save bus fares by walking home. 'Home' was still in the road where we'd grown up, at least for a while. We pursued our usual route. In general avoiding drawing attention to ourselves (more difficult as punks), with the general psychos, black-shirts and other thugs, that were lurking about in corners and underpasses. It was a game of hard-core 'space invaders' for real. There was hardly a sign of friendly life, as if the bomb had gone off. Certainly we had always half an eye towards the sky, fearing those nukes. We discussed the topic regularly and agreed there'd be no reasonable warning. Would you want one?

'Don't go winding yourself up, Bottle. Why give a fuck about jobs and stuff? Something'll turn up.'

'How can I get by without a job… and maybe nowhere to live?'
I moaned.

'You're a punk gentleman of leisure,' Snot told me, shifting from
side to side.

'Oh yeah, like sure.'

'Why throw a wobbly over fucking career opportunities? You're
meant for a life of the fine arts.'

Loping along, head down, hands in overcoat pockets, I made a
dismissive and depressed noise.

'There's nobody who wants me sculptures.'

'C'm on, Bottle. The nation's a bunch of Philistines,' Snot
remarked, in his caustic way. 'Let's remind them about that fact.'

It sounded harsh, yet had frisson. I was hiding under the Oxfam
coat collar, as if the Philistines might recognise me.

'My dad and brother keep having a go at me!' I reported.

'Yeah, well, I've heard… all that shouting through those prison
walls,' he admitted.

'At least it's a prison with a comfy bed,' I explained. Not to
mention a roof above.

'Don't they appreciate your artistic gifts?'

'*Huh.*'

'You've got to stand up for your rights,' Snot advised me.

Bob Marley was counted as an honorary punk, along with Jimi
Hendrix, Sun era Presley and J Cash, *et al*. Snot wasn't half as
ignorant about music as he made out. He'd got the public library
behind him.

Being out of condition, weak-chested and lazy, Stan had to
concentrate his efforts and coordination on walking up hill. I had
to be careful not to stride far ahead of him, heedless of safety.
Physical disability and a weak chest didn't prevent Stan from
enjoying smoky atmospheres though.

'My folks have gone off you, Stan… after you went punk and…
got yourself expelled.'

'Tell them. I'm really fucking… offended,' he puffed.

'You're worse than a football hooligan.'

'High praise,' Snot jested.

'If it goes on like this… I'll have to pitch my tent.'

'You'd be better off.'

I shot him a look of panic. 'On the streets, d'you mean?'

* * *

Straggling back to our district, we bumped into Mick Dove. This lad spent all his evenings in the *Lion and Unicorn*. What did they have playing on the jukebox there?

Nobody was on the street, apart from us. It was so quiet you could hear some bloke snoring through a closed window. The three of us joined up on a corner, eyed each other, while chewing on raw matchsticks (this was a disgusting teen habit, most likely picked up from a movie).

Dove wouldn't say what he was up to. Not stargazing. He'd left college amongst our cohort, so we had plenty of topics of teenage frustration and resentment to discuss. Dove hadn't found any gainful employment either in that tanked economy. No shock there.

'Not a fucking sausage,' he said, with a scowl.

With that skunk's brush of red and green hair of his; adorned with shin-high bovver boots, drainpipe jeans and a swastika tee-shirt; he'd never get a ticker-tape parade of job offers anyway. On the other hand, why was he hanging about under street lamps after midnight?

Snot thought that Mick was a fascinating character. Despite derogatory talk of 'fascist regimes' the Mortal guitarist refused to condemn those violent opinions or behaviour. To Snot's way of thinking Mick's far right views and physical aggression was just very punk. I remembered how Dove had spat at and insulted Stan directly, with shocking venom, at the college gig.

'What do you expect from Dove?' Stan had argued to me. 'Bunches of flowers?'

'Don't be stupid,' I said, 'this was vitriol.'

'Better than fucking *Baby Bio*.'

During a tense street encounter, Mick explained how he'd started his own band. He had called it Steel Dildo. Despite a quiet voice and shy demeanour, Dove wasn't a likeable punk.

As I said, this extreme patter (not to mention fashion sense) impressed Snot no end. The little punk guitarist thought he'd found a fellow spirit. Steel Dildo was another punk band and Snot was excited by the competition and rivalry. For Snot this would create more gigs in town, more mayhem and more anarchy, allowing Mortal to get back into live action.

So who'd object to that?

* * *

Not many weeks after, my parents finally threw me out, as I'd anticipated. It was down to my failing to find a 'proper' job, as well as my dress sense and attitude (recently changed). To quote Rotten I was considered a 'lazy sod' and, as a failed sculptor and would-be fanzine writer, a lazy sod unlikely to join the working class any time soon, any more than I could join the aristocratic class.

Stan's showed up in my bedroom. I was surprised my older brother had let him in. Snot was still wearing the studded leather jacket, as well as a ripped bondage tee-shirt, with big strap boots and black jeans – not the fear that Chuck admired. Stan could have been menacing or dangerous, if not for his diminutive stature and those 'disabilities'.

Snot shambled closer, his big romantic eyes taking in the dramatic scene, within my bedroom or my former bedroom. He shuffled and shrugged, trying to regain his dent-chested nicotine breath.

'What the fuck's hit you, Bottle?'

Throwing my clothes in to a suitcase, shrugging, I attempted to seem hard and unfussed. No teenage lad wants to show weakness or emotion to a mate.

'Where you going?'

'Down the stairs and through the front door,' I explained.

'Then where?'

My head was still pulsating from the last blow; I felt broken, heart-racing, with 'blood in my eyes' as the expression goes. My whole past was ready for the spiritual skip.

'I reckon they've done you a favour.'

'Come off it Stan.'

I was desperately trying to hide my hands from shaking, while I stuffed jeans, shirts and other togs into the case.

'Throw away your latch key in protest.'

'You could give me a hand with this stuff!'

'So where are you going?'

'Just away from here,' I told him.

He attempted humour. '*Butlins*? Youth hostelling?'

'Fuck off Stan,' I suggested.

'We've all got to leave home one day.'

'Apart from you, that is. When do *you* leave?'

'Yeah, right, apart from me,' he agreed. 'That wasn't my decision!'

The punk musician watched my activities casually, as you'd watch those of a clever pavement artist.

'Maybe you want to thank 'em for chucking me out?'

'You're a real anarchist now,' he argued.

Then the suitcase fell unhinged to the floor, spilling my hasty efforts, and I was sorely tempted to kick it out of the window in advance.

'If you can't give me a hand.?' I pointed out.

Snot had fallen into a phlegmatic hunch at the foot of my bed. Snot's bedroom was a far better place to be.

'There's nice fucking bed and breakfast in Colditz.' He meant his place.

'Belt up.' That's what I was trying to do. Like a kamikaze pilot looking for a new pair of trousers.

'You're the young gent I'm concerned about,' Stan said, hamming it up.

'Is that right?'

'My word of fucking honour, Bottle.'

'Your word of honour?' I challenged.

'Yes, speaking as a menace to decent people.'

'This isn't a good time for it, Stan.'

His sad brown eyes watched me, within that large olive face, with its dense shadow of stubble.

'Come and stay at my house,' he offered.

'What?'

'You heard, live with us.'

'Brilliant idea!' I balled up another uncooperative tee-shirt from the Co-op. 'How's that gonna work, exactly?'

'I dunno. Just put your head on the fucking pillow... close your eyes. So our house doesn't have any stars. I mean, we're not in the RAC best hotel guide... or any shit like that.'

'You said it!'

I thought Stan was just being cynical. Obviously I'd lost my generosity along with a sense of humour. Luckily it was just temporary. We'd need a lot of humour to get that fanzine done.

'Yeah, well, we've got sleeping bags... and a fold-out sofa. The fascist regime in my house is more sympathetic,' he argued.

I turned to face him. 'What choice have I got?'

So we hauled my gear around to his place next door. (Since he was a lad Stan wasn't allowed to lift or carry anything too heavy). On the step, into the night, I pulled our front door behind me.

In fact I never set foot in that house again.

10. The Smith

Stan's parents always refused to take any rent off me. His family was incredibly generous and welcoming. They never asked me about a possible departure date. When the cooking was so great, the mattress so soft, I knew why their son was comfortable there.

Some mornings I'd hear dad revving up his Rover 75, setting off for an early shift at the vacuum factory. One or two afternoons I bumped into Mum on her return from Ray in accounts. As ever she was dressed impeccably (she worked as a telephonist), shocked to see me, speaking to me warily, quickly dashing off, clutching her handbag.

All my family, including older brother Chuck, had disowned me. They tried to ignore my mirror existence next door. They cut off the Whitmore family for harbouring me. They took no notice of me, although it must have been strange for them to realise I was behind the wall. Not wishing to take advantage of Stan's family I had to find my own place.

Snot and I had great nights out with a new crowd, despite my change of circumstances or because of it.

As a punk pub the *Pink Dragon* was our obvious regular. It was the only place in town to find interesting people of a like mind, from music to movies, books and ideas, to fashion and politics. It was definitely a university of the scrapheap. I was never an ale drinker, not even during an era when lads drowned in a bath of beer every weekend with a few salted peanuts floating on top. I wasn't exactly playing trumpet for the Salvation Army though. Anyway I was just waiting for cappuccinos to be invented.

That pub had a fantastic jukebox; filled with punk singles and EPs, as curated by Marty Gorran.

'Can't you rent a room instead?' Stan suggested. He was stood at the centre of a dense cloud of sweet smelling smoke; which Dougal usually tolerated.

'What with?' I replied.

'Sell your body?' he suggested.

'Only with the lights off.'

'I know someone looking for a flat mate. Yeah, it's a lad from college. Just graduated like us. He's sharing with one boy already. The other students went back home... after graduation. Needs a couple of lads to come in with them. Why not have a talk with him about it?'

Nervously, 'I'll think about it,' I said.

'Don't be shy, Bottle. D'you want to share my gilded cage forever?'

'*Hmm*. Sure. I can't afford much rent.' The caring and sharing of the *Co-op* had its limits.

'Reach some type of fucking agreement with him.'

Before long Stan had arranged a meeting, so that we could discuss terms.

Well it was this round shouldered, rangy lad, who bustled into the pub, in a parker, radiating energy and bonhomie. He'd got a mop of greasy, curly dark hair, with a pasty and spotty teenage complexion. He had NHS black framed spectacles, which were masking-taped together at the bridge.

'Here comes our young gent now!' Snot remarked.

Recognising the small guitarist, the lad scurried over. Hand raised up in greeting, with a friendly twinkle, he fairly bounded to our patch. Despite this vitality of purpose he got very breathless and had a forward leaning, bad posture. While cutting through the bar he had to avoid some irritable biker types. We knew that any accident with a pint pot, any jolting of a biker's drinking arm, could produce a nasty altercation with dangerous consequences.

'All right, Stan man!' he declared. 'In decent fettle, marra?'

Snot lifted his large hand to indicate this, remaining behind those shades, for safety's sake, as if copying Lou Reed or anticipating *Jesus & Mary Chain*.

'Away man, it's good to see yer again like. So this is the lad that wants to share with us mind?'

'Let me introduce Master Paul Bottle. A gentleman and a fucking officer.'

'Aw right, man,' he told me, warmly shaking my hand. 'Pleased to meet yer marra! I'm Roy. Roy Smith.'

'So you were at Nulton Arts?'

'Ai, I was on the journalism course, marra. Until that bas'tad at the newspeeper group chucked me off the course for pro-test-in', he recalled, ruefully.

'Stan here had a similar experience,' I said.

'I'm an art criminal,' Snot suggested, taking another rich drag.

'Me and my mate Paulie mind, we was both on the journalism course like. Did you ever meet Paulie? Ai, and I got expelled for bein' on a political protest, like. The college and my boss, they didn't like me takin' direct action.'

'Well, Roy, this is our homeless punk.'

Smith gave the aura of rare bath times; though that wasn't rare for lads in that era. When I was fifteen a squirt of deodorant spray was a sign of effeminacy or decadence. A blob of hair conditioner would transform you into Quentin Crisp. I should have been so lucky.

Our new radical friend, to give him his full name, was Dominic Roy Smith. He'd dropped the 'Dominic' because it sounded too middle-class as if he could even join the *Young Conservatives*. For ideological reasons he'd reverted to plain Roy Smith. Indeed the lad was a passionate member of the *Socialist Workers' Party*. My own political education was not advanced, but like me, Roy's parents had completely disowned him.

Smeary denims and an anti-Apartheid tee-shirt were signs of his politics and of left-wing street cred. I made a quick Barthesian analysis of these semiotic codes. As well as being a member of the *SWP* Roy was a big fan of *Doctor Who* and *Star Trek*; which gave him a lot in common with Snot, even before Roy said he was getting into punk.

'I come from a town called Darlow,' Roy explained.

'So where's that?'

'The *North East*, comrade. *Tyne and Wear*, mind.'

'I wanna go to the *Riverside* in Newcastle,' Snot said.

'Did Stan tell you the score mind, about the spare room? Right, so I'm gettin' thirsty again lads… Let me get another bevvy in, before I tell you all aboot it,' Roy promised. 'Can I get you lads anything in, mind?'

'Not for me,' I told him.

Stan declined as he couldn't take too much alcohol, on account of his health. Puzzled by such abstemious behaviour Roy darted away to get himself another beer. I'd already noticed that Roy was asthmatic. Either that or he'd donated his lungs to Castro. This didn't prevent him from shifting like a hare when it was required. He was only held back at the bar where long negotiations were necessary to get served.

Finally returning with a foaming pint pot, Smith offered me the spec on his hot property. 'Ai marra, we rented this house like, over term time. Now college is over there's just the two a'rus in there, comrade. Paulie and me! We need another two lads to share with us to meet the rent. So if you and another comrade want to come in… Then you'd be *morst* welcome, marra. So why don't ya come over later and take a look at the place, like?' he offered warmly.

Suddenly beginning to wheeze, his tubes rigid, in distress, Roy had to reach for his inhaler. The pub atmosphere didn't help him to breathe. Taking a few drafts from this device (whatever chemicals it contained) he felt more relaxed. A combination of asthma and nerves set off the shakes, despite fearless revolutionary politics.

'So who'd I be sharing a room with?' I asked.

Bright eyed, enthusiastic, 'Away man, you'd have your own room. Like I said, apart from you it's only *Paulie*, man. I'm sharing with this lad off the *Nulton Gazette. Paulie Wellington*,' he explained.

'Where did I hear that name before?' Snot wondered.

'Paulie's a junior reporter on the local paper, marra.'

'Oh yeah, bollocks, he's the lad wrote that review of Mortal's gig at Nulton Arts.'

Smith's ironical eyes gleamed (irony, mirth, frustration) behind the smudges of those thick rimmed and thick lensed specs. 'That's right, comrade, our Paulie covers a lot of these local gigs mind. It's what he morst enjoys writin' aboot, marra.'

'Paulie fucking Wellington. What a tosser. Did you read what he said about my band?' Stan complained.

'Not so far,' I admitted.

'Paulie doesn't mean any harm, man. Try not to take offence,' Smith said. But I noticed his hand shake as he poured down some more beer.

'That was an appalling review. I wanted to throw up.'

'Away Stan man, Paulie only tries to speak his mind, as he sees it… whatever other people might think.'

'You're sharing a loft space with that idiot?'

'Ai Stan, as I explained… I was on that journalism course with our Paulie. Unlike me, mind, he was able to graduate… with a bit of help from me like. But I can't blame him for that mind. And he does his level best to be a good comrade and a radical reporter.'

'You write for the local paper as well?' I wondered.

'*Nawh*, man, don't be daft… I was expelled, I already *toold* you.'

It was after Roy joined a Shipyard picket line on Teeside. He returned during his summer hols, and the sponsoring news group decided to spike his career as a trainee journalist. He was put into the role of an unqualified and jobless campaigning reporter. That's how he found himself stranded in Nulton. At least until he got the idea or opportunity to escape.

We left the pub together – the first of many such evenings – to go and nosey around the offered property. Smith baptised this place 'the Mansion'; situated for sure in one of Nulton's seediest districts, up behind the railway station. After we stepped off the bus, we were heckled by a line of skinny girls, lurking against a high wall. Then there was a bunch of blokes swigging from spirit bottles, leering at the girls and taunting us for being punks.

'Which side are you on, comrades?' Roy shouted back at them. 'You'd better choose, mind… before the revolution comes round!'

Smith put his head down and darted towards a socialist horizon. We tried to give close pursuit, pushing up one of the steepest hills in town. I should explain that sharp hills are a feature of Nulton topography. The gradient didn't suit my mates – not at all. Snot's physical problems were from infancy, but the aversion to any form of exercise (apart from smoking, riots and the obvious) was a cultivated habit.

At first Roy romped ahead, apparently as fit as a flea that had grown up in a circus. Watching him dash almost out of sight, we struggled to keep track of him. Except that we noticed, Roy shortly came to complete halt in the near distance. We saw him doubled over, apparently in agony, suffering pain, gripping his knees, wheezing violently. Until he managed to grope about into his parker, pull out the inhaler and to shove it back into his mouth. He knocked back a couple of doses of those vital chemicals… straightened again, allowed his lungs to ease, set his sights on the summit, and shot off again.

A short distance later we saw him ground to an anguished halt, yet again, requiring a further dosage of medicine. This routine was repeated several times along the way home. He bounded like a mountain cat for most of the way, until his lungs turned as stiff as sheet metal.

Near the summit we got our first glimpse of 'the Mansion', almost through fog. Then I was the one who needed a dose of relaxant drugs. I could imagine *The Munsters* living in there. And then I thought about the Motel in *Psycho*. I swear, that was no exaggeration.

'Almost back at our place, comrades!' Roy announced, stood waiting then, in a semi-heroic worker's posture on the approach.

The block was a big dilapidated Victorian villa, recently divided into 'flats' by some rack-rent landlord. I was supposed to be free and independent, having flown the nest or been ejected from it. Any excitement about that idea vanished in a moment.

I began to hanker after home comforts. Even of the Bottle variety.

11. Roy's Mansion

Leading us up crumbling stone entrance steps, to face an enormous flaking front door, under a blustery portico, Roy frisked his jean pockets in search of the key.

A rank shadowy hallway was home to a colony of spiders, ruled over by a single high naked bulb. Undaunted, almost cheerful, our fifth-columnist friend continued in the vanguard. Snot and I risked the dilapidated wooden staircase, which wouldn't have disgraced a *Hammer Horror* production. I gazed up nervously, expecting Christopher Lee to come down to greet us.

My spirits plunged – it was *Heartbreak Hotel*, down on lonely street. Only the vague idea of sharing with like-minded mates, spurred me on. Maybe like Charles Bukowski. Would that be enough?

Smith rummaged for a second key. 'Away lads! Make yourselves at *hoom*,' he urged.

Immediately the stench of the place – a mix tape of toilet, bad cooking, body odours, rotten socks and a blocked drain – assaulted my big hooter. On a windy night every window and fitting would rattle, like loose teeth in an old mule. Admittedly the flat was sizeable enough, because Victorian rooms were big, although damp and drafty. Even those cold drafts, hitting from us from every direction like arrows, couldn't break up the pong.

Smith noticed my first reaction; read off the slogans written up across my face. 'Don't worry about it, marra,' he assured me.

'You'll get used to it,' Snot told me.

'When I blend in?'

'Come the revolution lads, we'll pull down all these old slums mind, and have a proper house building programme, providing decent hooms for working people, mind.'

'Start with this place,' I said.

'You want the Nulton Hilton or what?' Snot said, in rebuke.

'Ai man, after the revolution we'll take over all those pricey boutiques and offices, and turn em into decent places for workin' people,' Roy pledged.

Well, I couldn't stick about in Stan's spare bedroom, with only a thin wall between me and my folks. I needed my privacy.

'Away man, even Engels had to rough it from time t'time. We have to do the same, comrades,' Smith argued.

The Trotskyist ripped off his well-travelled boots and the proletarian rabbit trimmed parker. Stan and I noticed those revolutionary holes in his capitalist socks.

'Any road marra, we're going to line all those greedy landlord bas'tads against the wall and *ma-sheen gun* the lot of 'em,' he promised – with a tremble and a determined glint in his eye.

'They'll never agree,' Stan remarked.

'They don't need to agree, comrade!' he insisted, rolling up his plaid shirt sleeves.

At last Snot felt safe enough to remove those sunglasses. 'Talk to your landlord before all that fucking shooting starts.'

'Away, what for, man?'

'Check it's in the contract. About shooting people. He might not like sudden noise.'

'Noise?'

'First you want to sort the smell. Bottle's a *sensitive* punk.'

'Away Stan, that bas'tad landlord doesn't have any fucking sense. Plenty of time for spring cleaning aboot the hoose, comrade, after we bring the struggle to an end.'

'Or get some air freshener or something,' Snot added.

'We're in the vanguard, lads. Concentrate on workers' strikes and actions before your communal living spaces, mind. Acting as the catalyst that sparks the revolution, there's plenty of time for air fresheners,' Smith reminded us. 'We know what capitalist landlords are like, so ignore maintenance problems… for the time being, comrades.'

'The first action's to plug our noses,' Stan told me.

'Away man, I've got two cans of steak and kidney pud in the kitchen cupboard,' the Trotskyist offered us. 'Won't take me five minutes to boil 'em up on the stove, man, if you're hungry.'

'Nah, it's all right. Cheers anyway, Roy mate.'

They had a decent telly and double-cassette player on offer. Paulie Wellington could afford to buy that stuff. Telly and music – fantastic – they'd got their priorities right.

'Away, lads!' The Smith told us, with a surge of optimism about the future. 'So what do you think of the place?'

'What happened to these floorboards?' Snot asked. He noticed a hole under a rug and demonstrated the soft give of wood.

'Ai, well lads, the landlord's down in my book of class enemies. That bas'tad's name's top of the list and, come the hour of the revolution mind… he's up against that fucking wall!' Smith pledged. He clenched a fist, went red, fully testing his lungs.

'He probably fucking owns the wall, and will sue you.'

'You could refuse to pay rent. 'Til this landlord agrees to repair stuff,' I suggested.

'He could be a socialist, for all you know. Maybe he's a Labour party supporter.'

'Away man, we doon't negotiate with those reformist class traitors!'

'Make him put in some new windows, new floorboards, unblock all the drains. That would be a start,' Snot said mischievously.

'No comrades, we pay our rent on time to avoid any hassle,' Roy argued.

'What's your flatmate think about it?'

'Paulie you mean? Paulie gets into a mess with his wages. He doesn't always want to pay his share on time. Only because he can't organise his budget like,' Roy explained.

'This Paulie sounds like a right fucking tosser,' Snot observed.

'Oh, Paulie's a good lad really. Always does his best, mind.'

'So how long have you lived here together?' I asked.

'I'll fill the kettle and make us all a cuppa,' Smith pledged. At this he shot off into the kitchen, which I didn't have the guts to inspect.

When Smithy returned with steaming mugs, he caught Stan gloating yet again over the Mortal gig. He was bragging about all the trouble, not about the actual music.

'Ai that was a really brilliant gig, man!' Roy agreed.

'You were there?'

'Away Stan man, 'course I was there. It was amazin'.'

'Did you get into any fights?' I wondered.

'Only *fightbacks*, comrade.'

'Delighted you had fun at our little concert,' Snot said – like he was the farmer at Glastonbury.

'Fair's fair, there was a lot of fascist violence that night,' Roy recalled, infuriated again. 'Good jab somebody gave 'em a good hidin' mind.'

'The band noticed something goin' on,' Snot said.

'Away man, the music was out of this world!'

'We don't play music,' Stan informed him.

'Right comrade, whatever you say… but are ya gonna play another gig soon?'

'Not on purpose.'

'They've got a gig at the *Mad Hatter* club, next Saturday night.'

'Bloody great, man, I'll get meself doon there to see.'

'A fiver on the door. Even to socialist revolutionaries. But as you're a *Doctor Who* fan, I'll put you on the guest list.'

'Cheers, marra!'

Stan was enjoying the couch, even when the springs got caught between his cheeks.

'We've got some new tunes. More terrible than ever,' he pledged.

'Great man, right then… so I look forward to hearing the band again.'

Smithy's eyes gleamed with enthusiastic fish-eye energy, through smudged twin-tubes of NHS specs.

'Don't take any notice a'him. Mortal's getting better, with practice.'

'The band's improving, but we can put a stop to it.'

'The SWP's in favour of punk,' Roy informed us, passionately.

'The socialists like it?'

'Anybody with bad taste's welcome,' Stan commented.

'The party's in favour of a youth movement, being *radical*ised. That's standing up to oppression and *exploit-ation*. Working class kids making their oon music man... and not being spoon-fed this capitalist pop crap!'

'Yeah true, and we're going to bankrupt the big record companies.'

'Fighting talk comrade!'

'What happens if you win? I mean, if Mortal come first in this band competition, that's coming up?' I asked.

'We take that recording contract and tear it up. Right in front of their eyes. Yeah, I'm serious. Get a million quid advance on a debut album, and then break up.'

'No way,' I said.

'Wait and see, Bottle. Don't be so cynical.'

'Yeah, right.'

'All those fat capitalists exploitin' the talent of working class kids,' Smith fumed. 'Then what happens, comrades? They sell the music back to us.'

'They've sold a few to Snot,' I agreed.

'Shed loads.'

'Ba'stads! But the whole late capitalist system is in crisis like. The whole fucking system is in decline and fallin' apart, comrades,' Roy predicted.

'Better take our million and get out,' Snot said.

'Away man, read the editorial about punk in this week's edition. Have you ever read the *Socialist Worker* newspeeper mind?'

'I don't want to crease it for you,' Stan said.

'Away man, I've got spare copies.'

'We haven't finished this week's *NME* yet,' I explained.

'Away man, all well and good, but I'll save a copy of next week's peeper for yer. I'll come to the next Mortal Wound gig too. Authentic youth protest music, Stan. I'm all in favour of it mind.'

'We want all the political extremists we can get.'

Roy took Stan's little jibe in good part. Unlike most of his party counterparts, he had a sense of humour and could take satire.

We enjoyed infusions of strong northern tea. Snot put up the collar of his leather jacket against the cold. He observed the rundown living conditions, as if a first protest song was brewing.

'Doon't forget to sup your tea, lads. Fill yer boots,' Smith encouraged us. 'Get that brew down your necks.'

Meanwhile he'd put a tape into the machine (a new one), proving he was really into the music, not just for political reasons.

'Move in when you want, Paul marra,' he told me. 'You're welcome.'

'I'll think on it.'

'Bring your suitcase ter-morra.'

'That could be a problem,' I admitted. 'Cos at present I can't think of anyone to share with me.'

'Don't fret Bottle, we'll make polite enquiries,' Snot said. 'There have to be a few more homeless punks in this town… as need a hole over their heads.'

'Ai, let us know what you've decided marra. We can talk aboot it at the next Mortal gig mind.'

'So there's just you and Paulie at the moment?'

'Ai, that's it, just Paulie and me, marra.'

'Fucking cosy.'

'So what's this lad like then?' I speculated.

'You already know. He's that wanker who wrote a shit review of our gig,' Snot reminded me.

'You don't want to pay too much attention to Paulie, mind. He always does his best now!' Smithy sounded a bit defensive. But he couldn't hide a nervous look.

'Does this Paulie share your politics?' Snot wondered.

'Away, more or less he does, Stan. He's generally on the left like. Keeps his political opinions *morstly* to himself. He's afraid of losing his jab. He's working for the local paper, so Paulie can't attend party meet-ins. But he supports the party, and takes the SWP line on morst issues. The *Nulton Chronicle* sponsors him. So he's afraid of getting the sack.'

We could sense Roy's frustration with Paulie, despite these words of support.

'Bottle here's a bit of a writer too,' Snot informed him.

Roy turned his glinting enthusiastic glance on me. 'Oh right?'

'We've started a fanzine, to cover local bands… and the contest.'

'Oh, great man! Look forward to the first edition.'

'Paulie couldn't write his way out of a paper bag,' Snot argued. 'Not if he was kidnapped and needed a fucking ransom note.'

'All right comrade, but he's just tryin' bloody hard to keep that jab on the peeper mind.'

'Where's Paulie tonight? Why isn't he here to meet and greet?'

'He must be out with one of his girlfriends, comrade.'

'*Girlfriends*?' The plural struck.

'"One" of 'em?'

'Ai, I expect he's seeing one of them or another.'

'How many fucking girlfriends does he need?' Snot said.

'Your guess is as good as mine, comrade. He's a bit of a lady killer mind.'

We stared ahead, not liking the sound of that.

'I s'pose I'd better meet him, sometime… if I'm going to share.'

'Paulie isn't really competent to organise,' Smith argued. 'Better leave arrangements to me, marra. You're welcome to meet Paulie some teem. He'd a good lad but you don't want to rely on him,' he advised. '*Nawh* man, you don't want to make that mistake.'

Stan continued to smart at Paulie's live review. It hadn't exactly been 'new journalism', more like 'old crap'. The style was definitely unmistakable:

LOCAL PUNKS MAKE A NOISE

Nulton Arts College staged a crucial live blow-out in the spacious hall tonight, when local rock band Mortal Wound appeared and blasted like a racing car on a clear day.

Punk rock has a dodgy reputation for senseless violence, up and down the nation. But this four-piece showed that good music has a positive vibe. Gut wrenching heroics burst out on the stage. The band blew us away and left a majority of punks breathless and tearful.

Lead vocalist Paul 'nutcase' Blumen, 24, married with two children, sang with despairing passion. It was an exciting night of essential music, with cool and vital local man, Jon 'Snot' Whitmore, 19, single, showing strongly, on guitar. The audience swayed with sincere compassion. There was a class for a more just world.

The idiotic antics of a few troublemakers did not spoil our enjoyment. Punk has arrived in Nulton and we need to listen, like a lion in the jungle. This incredible local band, planning more gigs, doesn't want mindless gorillas wrecking the atmosphere for peaceful punks. This was a call for compassion, from a Nulton group that doesn't invite dodgy idiots from the far right. Nothing can spoil a positive vibe for peace in this town.

This rock critic watches out for the next gig with emotion. The pleading voice of modern youth will be heard. No need to shout from the town hall, because this group speaks for a generation with feeling. They are a talented group of young musicians.

By Paulie Wellington.

12. Close Encounters with Paulie

We arranged another meeting, to meet the other flat mate or, to be accurate, for him to look me over.

We got a rapid idea about Paulie's character because he was seriously late. Checking off his battered *Timex* through impact cracks, Smith was muttering bitterly into his third pint of socialist bitter. Roy was always in the vanguard of proletarian alcohol consumption.

The Trotskyite was more infuriated, when he noticed that Paulie was standing about in another section of the bar, trying to disguise his lateness. With a superbly innocent look on his cherubic mouth, the cub reporter was trying to con us into thinking he'd been there for ages, only we'd missed stupidly him. This was a clever trick – new on Stan and me – but it wasn't fooling his sharp-eyed Trotskyite mate. Paulie even put on a look of impatience when we strolled over, as if we were messing him around. He must have tried to pull it on The Smith before.

'*Away, Paulie man!* What yer doin'? Couldn't yer see us? What are you talkin' aboot man! You wasn't early. We've been waitin' here for yer, comrade!'

'*Phoo*, Roy mate. No need to get bloody shirty about it,' Paul told him. There was a hurt, bewildered expression, as we came into a new circle.

'Right then, Paulie lad, then what the fuck kept you?' he demanded.

'*Phoo*, what's up with you now Roy, mate? Calm down, will you, mate.'

'Away man, I *toold* you we had to be here at seven thirty, to meet these lads!'

'All right, Roy mate, no need to get in my face, is there. We're all here now, aren't we, so what's the big problem?'

Paulie gave the whole pub the once over look, as if checking to see how many people had noticed Roy making an exhibition of himself.

The Trotskyist was not impressed with the excuses; he was frothing with frustration – almost literally frothing.

'Well, Roy mate, some of us have a job to do,' Paulie said. It was a pointed remark, delivered with an ironic smirk.

Wellington had joined us after the office. He was wearing his work suit and a tie, now loosened at the collar. That could have been a good excuse – stress and long hours – except that he'd visited the record shop on the way.

So what were my first impressions of Paulie? Apart from the pantomime, he came across as friendly and likeable. He was handsome in an angelic kind of way; with very blue eyes, a tall trim frame, silky blonde curls and a cherubic little nose. Like God had looked at me and said, 'Right lads, now for something completely different!'

Paulie's antics warned that his conduct was not up to the same 'A' Grade as his looks. I noticed he had an anxious skin rash, sore peeling blotches, across his hands and spreading up his arms. After finishing that journalism course at college he'd been indentured on the *Nulton Chronicle*. This first reporter's job was beginning to rock in the negative sense of the word. He wanted to fill his journalistic contact book by meeting lads like Snot on the local music scene.

After that fracas at Nulton Arts, Wellington was keen to interview Stan all right. The cub reporter was quickly in awe of the little guitarist (which went to the art provocateur's head). Paulie took an interest in me to begin with, until he learnt I wasn't in a band or ever likely to be. After that it got even worse, when he understood that I was planning to write for a new fanzine. Despite being no rival on stage or in bed, I was regarded as a threat to his status as Nulton's premier music writer.

Wellington tried to take mental notes on Stan's absurdist statements as we chatted. Snot tossed out the typical mix of cryptic comments and curious infantile sarcasm, while Paulie gawped in hero worship. But this type of counter-culture adulation didn't last long.

'Okay, Stan mate, so what impact punk's having on British youth politics?'

'I don't know, why don't you go and ask him?'

'What?' Paulie said, looking baffled and colouring.

'This supposed to be an interview? I don't talk to the press. Only *The Lady* magazine. You writing for them?'

'How do you mean?' Paulie pushed up his round little glasses and rubbed his eyes. 'That's a bit of a dodgy statement, isn't it, mate? Why would I write for a reactionary magazine like that? I'm a radical feminist and my politics are progressive, mate.'

Snot smirked and squeezed up his roach. 'Give those ladies guitars and that *would* be radical statement.'

'*Phew*, I don't see how you...'

'In those twin sets and country checks of theirs. A couple of Pointer dogs chasing after them on stage.'

The cub reporter gave his face a rub. '*Phoo, dodgy*, how can that be radical?' he objected.

'Talentless punk morons like us aren't proper ladies.'

Severely confused look. 'What I mean to ask, Stan mate, is what's the politics of punk? Are you really on the left, or you got reactionary sympathies?'

'Politics is a bigger cliché than rock,' Snot sneered.

'Away man!'

'D'you want to change the political system mate, or not?'

Stan peered around the public bar with disinterest. 'Only if you'll buy me another pint.'

'What kind of socialism do you want?'

'It's a kebab.'

'Yes, right, Stan mate, I'll get you a kebab after... if you want... but what about the bloody late capitalist system? Can you give me a quote on the class struggle?'

'A quote?' Snot's attention had definitely wandered. 'Well, I don't know, maybe if you put some punks in the cabinet... with a few Mods and some bikers in the civil service... just for political imbalance of mind.'

'What's your attitude to mindless moronic violence at gigs?'

Snot pulled on his cascade of black ringlets. 'I try to encourage it.'

'*Phew*, Roy mate, did you hear what he just said? Really dodgy opinions,' he noted, ironically.

In this way Stan's outlaw punk charm was wearing thin for the cub reporter. But he attempted a few more lines of questioning, to get some printable quotes.

'What's your message to those hard right gorillas?'

'I dunno. Get a haircut? Pull your fingernails out?'

'That would be *torture*, wouldn't it, mate?'

Straight faced, 'You heard my band playing, didn't you?'

Wellington's neck burn cranked up. 'All right, so what you going to say to the Met about their harassment of black youth, with the SUS law, down in south London?'

'Come on, get your hand off my dick,' Snot suggested.

At this I couldn't suppress a raucous laugh. In some ways I was a bit of a hanger-on and sidekick. If you wanted to be any kind of journalist, isn't that what you had to do?

Fortunately Roy intervened. 'Away lads! Interview time's over. Ai, so let's all get in another round of bevies, shall we, before closing time?' Fraternal feelings overcame his annoyance with Paulie and Stan. The radical socialist had a positive and optimistic view of human nature. 'Come on Paulie man, get another bevvy down yer neck!'

'It's just a shandy, Roy mate. I have to get back early into the 'paper tomorrow.'

'Away man, don't worry yer-self over work now. This is Paul Bottle, the lad I was telling you about, marra, who wants to rent the other room in the house like.'

Paulie gave me another split second once-over, without apparent interest.

'You heard that Bottle's a rock writer,' Stan told him. 'You two'll have much to talk about, won't you?'

'Ai, we can discuss politics, punk, culture, lots of subjects, comrades!'

Roy memorised our orders and bounded over to the bar to get them. We watched as he tried to flag down a barmaid or barman.

It must have been the radical tee-shirt in need of a change that put them off.

'So where are you from Paulie?' I asked – making conversation.

'You asking *me*? You want to know where *I* come from?'

'Yeah, yeah, I was asking about your home town,' I said.

'That isn't good for a reporter, being fucking hard of hearing,' Snot commented.

'If you want to know, I happen to be an East Ender, and my native borough is Stepney,' he told us, turning solemn.

'What happened to your cockney accent, me old sparrow?'

The cub reporter shrugged off this punk sarcasm. 'That's where I was born and raised.'

Paulie's story about his origins didn't sound credible, not even to generous Roy. All the same, a few years later, a nostalgic article about Stepney *did* appear in the London *Evening Standard*, with Paulie Wellington as a by-line. Somehow Paulie was able to bluff a features editor on the subject. Then again, he wasn't the only lad to put on a 'mockney accent'. He wasn't the only character to entirely invent and reinvent himself. It was just a standard rock 'n' roll swindle of the time. It was the stuff that pop music and culture was made on, especially in Nulton.

'Do you fancy yourself as John Lennon?' Stan said.

'Why do you say that? Not anymore I don't, no.'

'I mean those little round granny glasses of yours.'

'Well, all right, I'm going to change them soon.'

'You having a 'bed-in', are you?'

'Are you some kind of hippie then, Paulie?' I asked, out of curiosity.

The cub reporter blew air and chuckled scornfully.

Roy had returned with an armful of beer. '*Nawh*, he got his hair cut last week, marra. It came all the way down 'is back, didn't it Paulie man? Ai, amazing long blonde hair he had. Woulda been beautiful even on a girl, comrades.'

'Come on Roy, mate. It wasn't down my back!'

'Ai, he's been dead keen on punk music lately. Since I introduced it to him, mind. Paulie went out and sold all his old jazz records on the spot.'

'I'm good mates with Joe Strummer and the boys.'

'Oh, you are? You're mates with the Clash?' Stan tried not to sound envious.

'Along with the rest of the audience,' I commented.

The news reporter ignored my remark. 'Yeah, that's right Stan, they're real Londoners as well. Great lads, The Clash. Really have a good peaceful vibe going on with their sound.'

'We're talking about the same Clash,' Stan checked.

'Is there another band, mate, capable of *Tommy Gun* and *White Riot*?'

'How long have you known Strummer then?'

'Bloody ages, mate. I was down Kilburn, after one of their gigs… and Joe just invited me back to his squat… '

'What did you fucking do there?'

'What did we *do*, Stan mate? We talked music… chatted about politics and radical stuff… smoked a bit of dope together,' the reporter explained, with a gurgle of pleasure.

'Right, so what was their squat like?'

'Really cool. A fantastic place off Camden, mate,' Paulie told him. He puckered his lips. 'Really creative. A really positive vibe.'

13. Paulie as a Punk-Reggae Star

'Did you hear? I'm getting my own group,' Paulie said.

This was a bombshell on the Nulton music scene. It stunned the population – or at least us.

'You can't be a punk,' Snot told him.

A wounded, baffled look. 'Why can't I be a punk, mate?'

'So what kind of music do you play?'

'I've got my own original ideas. Anyway I want my group to be blacker.'

'Away Paulie, don't be so daft man,' Roy objected.

'You're maybe the roadie for Marley,' Stan mocked.

Paulie brushed it off. He considered himself an expert in music. He'd been the owner a substantial record collection – mainly jazz and classic rock – which he'd sold for a tenner (a common blunder).

'What's this band of yours called?' I asked.

'Got to decide on a name.'

'So what's your sound gonna be like?' Stan persisted.

'Reggae, rock, soul, punk…'

'Ah, come on Paulie. Away, man! He doesn't even have this group a' his put together mind.'

The cub reporter looked put out. 'Come on Roy, mate, what do you mean by that?'

Smith avoided drowning in bitter. 'There's only him in this group so far, comrades!' he spluttered.

'No name. No other members. I'm starting to like the sound of this,' Snot admitted.

'Come on, Paulie, don't start messing around with music, when you doon't have a clue aboot it, comrade. Ai, just stick to talkin' about your newspaper… and what you're doin' at work, man. Things you *noo* aboot.'

The band leader was looking pink and stung. 'All right, Roy. I'm putting out feelers for a guitarist, a bass player and female backing singers,' he explained.

We struggled to imagine what his group could be like.

'Away Paulie, that's impossible, you daft bas'tad!' Roy objected finally, with a violent shake.

Snot looked on with big sardonic eyes. 'Sounds like it's only you so far, Paulie.'

'Can you help find me some local musicians Stan, mate?'

'You forgot your drummer. You want a drummer in this group… right?' the guitarist considered.

Wellington's mental cogs span and failed to cohere. 'Yeah, we want some good rhythms, mate. Sure. But it doesn't have to be exactly a drummer.'

'How does that work?' Snot wondered, genuinely baffled.

Smith fumed. 'Away man, what you on about… you need a drummer in this group!' he said, trembling and shaking his locks.

'Keep calm, will you Roy mate. Wait until I explain. You don't need to have a drummer in your group. The way I see it, we're gonna try something different than rock music. I'm going to find an all-round percussionist.'

'*Awh now*, a fucking percussionist mind!'

'Come on, Roy, what's your big problem. You won't even give it a bloody chance,' Paulie objected.

'Be a bit clearer on this, Paulie. What type of sound you trying to achieve? I mean, is this a punk group or what?'

'We're definitely punk, Stan mate. But we're trying to bring in the Jamaican sound as well.'

'Reggae?'

'Jammin!' Paulie declared, picking up on the enthusiasm.

'Away Paulie, this is complete shite!' Smith complained. The Trotskyite agitator nearly choked on his ale, and threw a puddle of it away in protest.

Snot's mug had a knowing look. Wellington's plan seemed like a fantasy, yet the challenge appealed. His fusion concept was in tune with the shifting musical culture. The Clash were experimenting with Jamaican sounds, from dub to 'lovers' rock'. Paulie claimed to know Joe and the lads. He'd been hanging around with them at their squat. Punk had come across until then as very white and male: The Clash began to challenge and subvert that narrow image. In fact Stan had a stack of Trojan Records, and Jamaican sounds which had featured regularly on John Peel's show.

'If you want the Jamaican sound, it's all in the rhythm,' Stan advised.

The junior reporter was bewitched. 'I want to get a bit of toasting in my vocal style,' he cooed.

'You're the fuckin' *vor-calist* marra?'

'Sure mate, I'm going to be skanking on stage. Maybe we'll get some Ska into the mix as well,' he promised.

'Get it focussed. You're going to need a drummer and a bass player who can play in those styles,' Snot argued.

'Yeah, right Stan. Now you're talking, mate!'

'*What* are you talkin' aboot, Paulie man? When you don't even have a group together yet?' Smith simmered.

'Come on, Roy mate, give us a chance will you?'

'You can't even play an instrument mind!'

'That's the whole point of punk,' I remarked. 'You don't have to know one end of a guitar from…'

'I've got charisma. That's what you need in a bloody front man. You need somebody with stage presence,' Wellington told us.

'Yeah, you can get any stupid tosser up there,' Snot agreed.

'Right mate, right… but… That's what I've got, Roy mate,' the cub reporter insisted. He offered an amiable and tolerant chuckle. 'I've got musical charisma and stage presence, in bags, mate. Go ask Joe, Mick and the boys.'

* * *

Our town was never going to rival the big punk scenes developing in the cities, like Birmingham or Manchester – where Shelley and Devoto were more than scratching about – but we weren't aimed at the AOR charts either.

'Where you looking for your band members?'

'I've put an ad in *Melody Maker*. I put something in the musicians wanted pages,' Paulie explained.

We looked at each other in amazement.

'Isn't that a bit ambitious, Paulie?'

'Do they have a *non*-musicians section?'

'Away Paulie! What you talking about man? Yer must be jerkin, yer daft bas'tad!' Roy complained. He was choking with rage again. 'What're yer doin advertising in the *Melody Meeker* mind?'

'Come on, Roy mate, why shouldn't I?'

'Charismatic front man in search of a band,' I offered.

'You're in danger of getting too big for your desert boots,' Snot advised.

'C'mon Paulie, it's too soon to advertise in *Melody Meeker*. Be sensible, marra, you've never played in a band before now. You can't even sing mind.'

Wellington was bemused and hurt. ''Cors I can bloody sing, mate. Why would I bother otherwise? What's wrong with putting an ad in a national music paper? That's the only way to find good musicians,' he argued. 'What would *you* suggest, Roy?' He made a frustrated scoffing sound.

'Away, you daft bugger!' Smith was determined to shock him back to reality. 'I doon't want to hear any more about this band nonsense mind.'

'That's how the best new bands get together.' Injured vanity was written all over Paulie's face.

'Maybe you'll have Rick Wakeman,' Snot said.

This provoked a bit of a sarcastic teenage chortle among us, which even cheered up the Trotskyite.

'Listen comrades, he definitely can't sing, mind! Not from what I've heard, any roads.'

'Leave off, Roy mate! When did you ever hear me sing?'

'Away man, where do you think? I've heard you singing in the bath, comrade.'

'That sounds really dodgy.'

'Fuck off, we share the same flat!'

'Come on, Roy, don't be a reactionary, cos I've got a bloody good voice.'

'You don't have to be a trained Milan opera singer to be punk.' Snot argued, turned magnanimous.

'Better if you're tone deaf,' I said – picking up the punk ethic.

'If you want to start this band up, master Paulie, take my fucking advice. Don't advertise in the national music press. Find your musicians locally around Nulton. More chance of success that way.'

'Ai, spot on marra, because late capitalism just exploits the talent of these young working class kids mind. Then the bosses sell everything back to us for profit, comrades. The party supports punk cos it resists this abs'lutely vile exploit-ative system and builds a proper socialist alternative, mind.'

'That's what I'm bloody trying to do,' Wellington told him.

Snot sank back to his typical phlegmatic hunch.

Could socialism or punk survive Paulie? I didn't rate either of their chances.

'The whole point's that Paulie gets up and makes a prick of himself on stage,' I clarified. 'Like everybody else.'

'Yeah, that's the spirit. And I might be able to find him a drummer,' Snot offered.

The reporter's visage brightened. 'That would be bloody excellent, mate.'

'My mate Dennis knows all the Jamaican styles of drumming. Inside out, no problem to him. He should, cos he's Jamaican. Punk's a piece of piss to him too, if that's what you want. Standard four four, if necessary. I'll have a word with him.

'Cheers, mate!'

'Yeah, I'll explain you're looking for a reggae thing. If we come into the pub often enough, we'll bump into him.'

'*Crucial*,' Paulie came back, 'but are you sure this Dennis is really black?'

'Away Paulie! Are you *jorkin*'? What rubbish you're talking now man!' The Smith protested.

'You can ask Dennis if he's really black if you like,' Snot suggested.

The little guitarist and I had another snigger at Wellington's expense.

'I want to get talented female musicians,' Paulie added. 'I don't want to be bloody sexist with my group.'

Already I had an uncomfortable feeling that Wellington should stay away from our 'talented' Gina Watson.

'Paulie, don't be such a *buffoon* man!' Smith exploded, losing patience.

'All right, Roy mate, don't get bloody wound up. At the present time we're only discussing the line-up. There's nothing definite yet. You heard, Stan knows a drummer and he may know some female singers as well.'

Indignant Smith took a step back, beside himself and unable to articulate anything coherent for several seconds.

'We got Anna-kissed in our band, cos she's my mate,' Snot explained. Well, she used to be!'

'Sure, crucial. I heard you playing at Nulton Arts. Incredible performance that night. Really strong emotions,' Paulie remembered.

'Yeah, we read about it,' I commented.

'We got another gig… at the *Hatter*. Come if you want,' Snot suggested. 'So long as you promise not to fucking write anything about it.'

'Why not, mate? That's my bloody day job, isn't it…? I'm the paper's new reporter… the youngest one on the staff, who has an interest in punk… and it's my task to cover the local music scene.'

'Anyway, come and destroy our reputation.'

This was a confusing suggestion. 'Right, I'll come to your gig.'

Thickening his skin against unflattering quips, Paulie further loosened his tie and shirt collar and relaxed.

All the same, I noticed bitten fingernails and that spreading rash. No doubt that job at the *Chronicle* wasn't as enviable as I thought. Something was eating him up. Something was eating us all. Why couldn't this society let us be?

'D'you hear about this Battle of the Bands competition? One of the judges is an A and R man from EMI Records in London. They're offering a record contract and a major tour.'

'*Phew*, Bottle mate, I already got the all the facts on that story… I'm ahead on it. I'm going to write my big piece next week,' he told me.

Set to assemble his own band, Paulie's interest in the competition was more than journalistic.

'Mortal isn't signing for any fucking dinosaur record company,' Snot reminded us.

'After the revolution, comrades, working class musicians'll be releasing their own records,' Smith added. Humanitarian and calm again, he was finally back with a twinkle.

'There are already a lot of independent labels,' I pointed out.

'Away Paulie, cos after the revolution we'll put those record company execs. up against the wall and mow em down with fucking machine guns. That's if they don't redistribute profits,' he said (with a shiver of anticipation).

Wellington stared at his housemate in bemusement. 'All right, Roy mate, calm down, will you?' he laughed, a bit shocked.

'I'm happy to report that Mortal don't stand a chance,' Stan insisted. 'We're crap and repellent… and we stay that way. We're not going to fucking win, it's only a laugh. If we take part we can finish second at best. That way we might get some new gear.'

'Right,' Paulie said. 'So that leaves the contest open to me.' It was a Eureka moment.

'After you've found some girl backing singers?'

'Crucial, Stan mate.'

'That shouldn't take him very long, mind. Not on past form.'

'*Phoo*, what's that supposed to mean, Roy?'

'So what type of girly reggae band you putting together? Pans People or something like that?' Snot sneered.

Word got around the local circuit that Paulie – reporter on the paper – was looking for girl singers and musicians. As he'd written that cack-handed gig review for the local rag, he'd got a bit of cred from lads who couldn't read straight.

Apparently a new punk group was born every minute.

14. The 'Curry Run'

Stan introduced the new band leader to Dennis McDonald. At first mention the Jamaican-styles drummer and percussionist was interested. His previous and long-time group, The Kingston Klingons, had to break up when their vocalist became a pastry chef (Sam the cook).

Wellington stared, naively open-mouthed, during the negotiation. If he could recruit a musician of this quality, the record contract with EMI was more or less his. So his gig reviews for the *Chronicle* were merely a hobby, or run-up to global pop stardom. He was impressed by Dennis' hairstyle, mesmerised by his Caribbean patter (Dennis' parents had arrived in 1955: his Mum was a florist and his dad a driver).

The fact that Wellington was a complete novice was lost in the mix. It didn't seem to matter much during that punk period. After a break from playing live, Dennis was eager for a new project. He couldn't wait to reassemble that complicated drum kit of his; a sort of percussive 'Spaghetti Junction'. Recovering his cheery matiness, Paulie was soon full of ideas about this embryonic punk reggae fusion band. The reporter definitely made all the right noises and musical references. He probably fitted the bill as a front man, though it would have killed us to admit it. A shame he'd cut his hair off, because he might have teased it into dreads. Dennis didn't notice the disgusted faces we were pulling in the background, as negotiations and plans proceeded.

'Cheers, Dennis mate! Really *sound*. I 'n' I says *crucial*!'

'Okay, Paulie man, it all sound cool to me.'

'Meantime I'll get my group rehearsal time booked. How long do you think it'll take? Maybe a couple of hours or so, mate?'

The drummed believed this was a droll comment. He threw back his head and laughed richly at the reporter's witty repartee.

'This feels good, Paulie man. We likes the relax' character!'

If only he'd noticed the reporter's bafflement. But as leader (song writer and vocal genius) Paulie had to deal with these eccentric musician types, (so he reasoned with himself). 'All right then, Dennis mate, so I'll take down your home telephone number. Roy and me don't have a home telephone yet. So here's my office number, mate. Top secret. If you get through to another journalist don't mention anything about me moonlighting in a band.'

'Your secret's safe with me, man.'

'My bloody sub-editor will get on my back. Maybe it's best to wait 'til you hear my voice, before you say anything.'

'All right, Paulie, I got it clear,' the drummer assured him.

Wellington pouted thoughtfully. 'Then I'm looking for some girl backing singers. Any ideas about that? Maybe two or three... or even four, if they're really good.'

The drummer's eyes widened. '*Four* girls, man?'

'*Phoo*, yes, why not, mate? Why not, if this is a feminist band? Yeah, if they are really clued up, with great stage presence, mate.'

The sticks genius pondered. 'Okay, Paulie man, let me have a think... I took down yer number. Get on the blower, when you got it all worked out.'

'Great, cheers Den! *I 'n' I* says get playing. So what kind of reggae sound do you make, mate?'

Paulie has orgasms as Dennis checked off Bob Marley, Gregory Isaacs, Bunny Wailer, the Twinkle Brothers and other classics; or closer to home, Steel Pulse and Aswad.

'Dennis is mates with Eddie Grant,' Snot put in. 'Well, Dennis played bass on some early recordings a'his.'

'Crucial.' Wellington stared with numbed awe at the global recording star in front of him.

'No need ta mention that, Jon man. I just puts down a few lickle lines on Eddie's demo tracks.'

Not long after Paulie noticed a girl in the pub and left with her. Their eyes had met across the bar room, he made over there, almost before we could notice. After a quick conversation between the pair of them, a snog and a hug, she was putting her coat back on to leave. This scene put my young ego (and zero experience) into traumatic meltdown. Smithy witnessed the same horrifying scene. Our panicked glances met:

- *Did you see that?*
- *Unfortunately I did, marra!*
- *But he doesn't know the girl*
- *That's the score, comrade*
- *She's never seen him before*
- *Nothing new, comrade*
- *Didn't even speak to her*
- *Ai, he doesn't need to say anything mind!*
- *So how often does this happen?*
- *All the time, marra!*
- *Terrible! Shocking!*
- *Nothing we can do about it, marra*

My brother Chuck always goaded me about never finding a girlfriend. I didn't have my older sibling's little red book, only a catalogue of humiliation. How long did I intend to be stuck on zero?

This was a nightmare for The Smith and me. We'd watch Paulie scoring and scoring again, night after night, like Pele in a testimonial match.

* * *

Short of Paulie's company we all decided to go for a curry. That evening, it was Stan, Roy, Dennis, Fiona (the drummer's girlfriend) and me. Roy had his final DHHS Giro through and he wanted to treat us all to a meal. That was typical of the revolutionary. There was never a more generous and self-less lad – he lived up to the left wing propaganda. Around this time he'd applied successfully for a job at the Inland Revenue Office. Even if you disagreed with Trotsky's take on socialism (and everything else) you had to admit Roy was true to his word. He didn't talk politics with the Inland Revenue. The topic hadn't come up at interview. After the revolution he'd probably be Chancellor of the Exchequer anyway.

We took our window table at *The Star of the Taj Mahal* restaurant in town. We ordered *Tiger* beers and began to leaf through the menus, ceremoniously handed to us by Bangladeshi waiters.

'Away, comrades! Choose whatever you want tonight. Come on, have a proper read. Fill yer boots, lads. *Enjay* yourselves. Here's to the revolution!' Smith declared, a bit inebriated.

A crackly tape of Raga music was playing, so it was a good place to talk about punk and revolution.

I'd warmed to Roy – with his political principles and obsession with *Doctor Who* and *Star Trek*. As a fellow flatmate I could easily tolerate Paulie. I was determined to take the spare room, assuming I could find another lad to move in with me.

'Yeah, Fi-ona, so this boy comes up to me, an' he begins tellin me how he's got dis lickle band startin up. How he wants me to come back and play some drums for him.' Dennis is explaining the situation to Fiona.

'That's wonderful. You can start playing with a band again. A long time since the Kingston Klingons broke up,' Fiona said.

In truth she was a dead straight kind of girl; the type that danced around her handbag at the *Flamingo*. Course she must have liked the reggae and Ska sounds too.

'Yeah, Fi, like he wants another boy to come in an play riddum, so I thought like I was 'vailable… and it'd be nice and relaxed to mek some music agen with this boy's group like,' he said. 'So I tells this cat to tek down me 'oome number an keep in contac'. The plan is that we start rehearsin soon as possible and put down some wicked tunes.'

Nobody wanted to disillusion the lad. We'd have to leave that to Paulie.

'Bottle, mate. Did you know Les Phoenix got a big support slot for Betsy Dandie?' Stan told me. 'She and the Screamers are gonna open for Pat Benatar.'

'No? They pulled that off?'

'They're the first act on the UK leg of the fucking European leg of the World tour,' Snot explained.

'Straight up?'

'That's what the big cheese told me. Just be grateful they're not giving out free tickets.'

'Right, definitely,' I said, with a laugh.

Stan's punk sneer cut through the restaurant's subdued lighting and chintzy red atmosphere.

'Make sure you're not a hundred miles of the concert hall. You'll be able to hear her play Birmingham from fucking Coventry,' he predicted.

'You'd expect a good PA at that venue,' I said.

Anyway, main courses were served. We lost further track of those real life boring issues, such as work, money and somewhere to live. Discussing new bands, the local punk scene, the *SWP* and watching Smith's glasses steam up, we forgot about our problems. Dennis insisted that, with his thunderous, metronomic style, he could back any singer, even Paulie (who allegedly only sung badly in the bath).

Unfortunately this lively varied conversation was cut short. We had to recoil, to cover our faces, because the glass of restaurant's front window *shatter*ed over us. There was hardly time to gasp or to scream or comment. The big pane broke over us in dangerous pieces like an enormous jigsaw puzzle. There was a variety of lethal bits around us; fragments in our hair, in our meals and sticking out of fingerbowls and wine glasses.

After a delay of disbelief and confusion, Fiona – a secretary at BHS – screamed out hysterically and shook glass from her hair. Dennis, raised gingerly to his feet again, gaped in shock through the empty space where the window should have been (used to be).

Smithy was stunned breathless: he trembled violently from head to foot, juggling with his specs and temper. Our Trotskyite benefactor started to gasp and battled to locate that vital inhaler. Stan and I were glued to our seats, horrified at the scene, with our meals still before us; but we were not enjoying our mouthfuls of biryani.

In a flash the waiters swept in to clear up, brandishing brushes and pans, as if they were used to bricks coming through the windows. We struggled to make sense of this, while freezing air struck a nasty surprise and flapped the ends of tablecloths.

'What the fuck?' Stan began.

'I'll tell you, Stan man, it was dem National Front boys,' Dennis said.

'I don't know, I had my back to them.'

'Yeah, I see'd em as clear as I see you man. They must be out on their curry run.'

'Fascist bast'ads!'

We heard another window getting smashed, with commotion around the 'Asian' district of town. The manager of the *The Star of the Taj Mahal* was calling up the local cop shop, with a confident middle finger. But we knew the NF boys would be tucked up in bed before the law arrived.

Roy pulled a reformist twenty quid note from his jeans' back pocket; and he tossed it down on the wrecked table arrangement. Then he inflated his chest manfully and urged us to join him on the street.

'Away, comrades! Let's go and fight them fascist bast'ads!'

He pumped himself up and punched out an SWP salute, before jumping back outside through the now vacant window bay.

'You not having any dessert?' Snot asked.

'Away, comrade! No time for pudding now. The struggle's on. We've got to tackle em on the streets!'

'I'm full up,' I announced.

As we negotiated the back streets – emptier and darker than Alexandria Palace after it was burnt down – we began to hear echoing chants and steel-capped boots ahead. Either Nulton Athletic Football Club had been playing a mid-week fixture, the territorial army was out practicing for World War Three (which was a risk) or those NF boot boys were out 'Paki bashing'. None of these activities had any appeal to me.

'Watch out boys, here come dem NF t'ugs now!' Dennis warned. At which we stared down the gloomy street, to distinguish the acned shock troops of those neo SS dickheads.

'Away comrades, stand your ground and fight!' the Smith called.

'Not on your life, Roy. We're going home,' Fiona objected.

'Away man, fightin's the only language these fascist bas'tads understand mind!'

'We came out for a quiet meal.'

Roy had assumed the middle of the road (as opposed to his musical tastes) shouting and clenching revolutionary fists. The Trotskyite awaited a gang of shaven-headed, big-booted thugs, as they marched in our direction. Even if the Tyne and Wear-sider was brave enough – which we couldn't doubt – would he have the breath to follow through?

'He's dangerous,' Snot told me.

'Political apathy can be attractive.'

'Yeah, especially when you wake up tomorrow.'

'Away comrades, we can't let these Nazi bas'tads gerraway with violence an' intimidation. It's about time the working classes got organised for the fight back!'

'You can fight for yourself,' Fiona argued.

'Not fer much longer Fi. This lad's got a wheezin' chest an they go break his neck.'

'Come on, Dennis lad, remember Cable Street when the working class united… and they kicked Mosley's Black Shirts off the streets man!'

'These are the Nulton streets,' Snot objected.

'Brave talk, Roy man. But there's too many of dem boys.'

'You've got to listen, Roy. He's bloody right,' I insisted.

'Fancy the long scenic route home?' Stan confided.

Without a guitar in his hands he was lost.

'No Stan, they'll get you.'

'Away comrades, no retreat in the face of Nazi thugs! No surrender to threats and intimidation!' The Smith foamed. Already he was fighting for breath. The inhaler was pumping like John Wayne's shotgun.

'Spe'k for yourself, Roy man!'

'Come on Dennis, we got to make the streets safe. Overthrow capitalism and fight for the socialist alternative, man!'

'I think I'm going to throw up,' Fiona said.

'*Look wh'appen she!*'

Roy strutted off towards the drain-piped thugs, stomping down the narrow street, assuming that we were following closely behind. Drawn up to a size and strength beyond the usual, he was a socialist man of steel. Roy was up on his toes, shouting slogans, as if on the terraces of Roker Park. In seconds he was way ahead, like a revolutionary majorette.

Stan put his chest through a marathon of stress. A cat shrieked and dustbin lids crashed, and shutters came down and buildings fell into dark. Apart from an express train, rattling through the ghostly station, there wasn't another sound or movement.

Before long we got a view of the fascist gang. They may have thought we were a group of Pakistani lads. Until they began to hear surprising left-wing slogans and – in amazement - spotted a strident lad stomping towards them, pumping a clenched fist and with the hood of a parka coat pulled up, with a pair of thick NHS specs poking out between the rabbit fur trim.

'The workers united'll never be defeated. Kick the fascists off the street, let Asian workers speak!' Roy yelled angrily. I recognised these lyrics from his newspaper.

Meanwhile the rest of us followed in a timid huddle, not in any hurry to join the fray. If Roy had looked back over his shoulder, he would have realised we were many paces behind. It looked like the Smith and the revolution had lost its vanguard.

Stan was no coward – as Nulton Arts College knew – but he wasn't a street fighting man. I'd never seen him in a violent situation, off stage. Obviously we didn't want Snot to come to any harm. Of course his hands were not insured. To my mind his fingers were worth a million each. We didn't want him throwing punches.

So Roy was unaware of being a single-comrade Marxist army. Punches were soon flying as Roy plunged into the suede head group. Dennis had no choice but to get involved. Fiona shrieked as he lunged forward to help out the Darlow radical. The sight of an NF boy being launched into orbit possibly calmed her nerves. When this lad landed again he seemed to believe that reality was an extended dub re-mix by Lee 'Scratch' Perry.

A chunky thug in a cap-sleeve tee-shirt took hold of Stan. This meaty extremist began to swing the Mortal guitarist around, holding him by the collar of his leather jacket. The sight angered me so that an almost communist red mist rose before my eyes. In blind rage I landed a punch on the beefy boy's jaw, before he put any more extreme views into Stan. I just leant back, closed my eyes and launched. Dad's home boxing lessons came in handy. A split second later the young fascist's wiring started to short, and he was crumpled up on the seat of his drain-pipes. I felt a spring had snapped in my wrist. That took weeks to repair itself. Luckily I was not a musician. It wasn't too much trouble at the typewriter.

A lot of mayhem resulted. Stan was on the floor, so was Roy before long, and many of the fascists dropped on the battlefield with only dreams of the Fuhrer. Our friend Fiona tried to smother her tears in Dennis' silky shirt, while he was wiping away smears of blood. The drummer was a quiet lad who only enjoyed action behind his kit.

As we tried to recover from this painful mayhem, I recognised Mick Dove among the retreating mob. He recognised me too. His pinched ghostly face took it all in. After that he was out of there at a quick march.

I understood what Dove and his Steel Dildo group was all about. You couldn't say 'stood for', could you.

15. Stan's Move

Limping back to the Mansion, we made as many horrible groaning noises as the building's plumbing.

Roy continued to be puffed up with revolutionary fervour and whatever was in his inhaler. 'Away comrades, no need to be down-hearted at the setback. Ai, we put up a good fight mind! We stood up to that fascist scum, comrades!' he declared. Wound up, surging with adrenaline, The Smith was springing up and down the living room, menacing the dodgy floorboards.

'Tek it easy, will ya man,' Dennis advised.

'He's making my head spin, just watching him,' Fiona complained.

'Yeah, Roy man, in *foo-tcha* fight your own *p'lit'cal* battles. Gettin me street fightin with dem Nazi boys,' he objected. 'Las' time I voted Liberal, man.'

That came as a shocking revelation to the Darlow communist. 'Ai, c'mon Dennis, you don't vote for those reformist parties, man! Away, those Nazi bas'tads only respond to a united front on the streets! There's no two wees aboot it man... cos only an organised mass protest from workers and students can stop these bas'tads!' He fulminated, eyes bulging brightly. He had to pump down another two shots, as he turned around at the top of the room and began another length of paces in front of us.

'Ya don't wanna go looking for punch ups, Roy man.'

'Don't go and spoil Roy's evening,' Fiona said. 'This was one of the best nights of his political career.'

'Away Fiona, it might not be pretty, but you'll never defeat those scum from the comfort of an armchair mind. *Nawh*, we don't want to hear that type of defeatist talk here at the Mansion, marra,' he said, chopping the air.

'I bruised my bottom,' she objected.

'If that's what it takes, comrade.'

'Give the Trot manifesto a rest,' Stan suggested. Scuffs on his jacket were the biggest worry. 'I'm not going to eat out with you again either.'

I was sitting next to him rubbing my swollen hand.

'You'll never destroy the Nazis with that attitude, comrade,' Roy warned, still on the move.

'I'd let them fuck me, if it didn't hurt so much,' the punk argued.

The Trotskyite was shocked. 'Oh, no man, you can't talk like that about the class struggle. Away man, you don't want anything to do with these fascists. We've got to speak out for a real socialist alternative.'

'Si' down man, you're mekin me neck stiff. We don't want any more *polit-cal agi-tation*!' Dennis spelt out, blood rising.

'Does anyone know what's happened to Paulie?' I wondered.

'Away Bottle, you noo where that daft fucker's gonna be.'

'He got picked up in the Dragon, didn't he,' Stan reminded me.

'Yeah, but shouldn't he be home by now?'

'This might be a stupid question,' Snot said, turning to me. 'But didn't your old man ever give you a bit of a talk?'

'What do you mean 'a talk'? You mean about the facts of life and stuff?'

'Away man, he's off shaggin' some lass, as you sit there.'

Fat chance of Wellington sleeping in his own bed that night. He was busy auditioning another punkette. It gave the idea of backing vocals a whole different twist. He wouldn't return home until after work the next evening. These night-moves affected his work and added to his problems at the newspaper office.

This gave me a chance to peep into Casanova's room. His new punk record collection was stacking up – many recent purchases, with stickers and cellophane attached. The decor had changed too, with CND, Johnny Rotten and Talking Heads posters attached. Apparently he was still living out of a suitcase, as if he expected the sack before long. It was the same trunk that came down with him, from his parents' house, in a village near Norwich. His dad (a Head Teacher) must have been very proud of his son graduating from the journalism course and finding a staff job very quickly. I began to feel sorry for him. For Paulie, that is.

Extremist politics have more success in troubled times. It was hard right and hard left, wherever you looked. The 'centre' was about as appealing as a mouldy orange chocolate cream, picked off the floor. Our tango with the NF boys demonstrated the state of local politics. It wasn't difficult to get into a bitter arguments with your dad or anyone. Thinking back on that punk era, many us were displaced persons. We had to create our own culture and art. We improvised our marginal lives, our uncertain identities and the 'no future'.

Later, after we had calmed from that fight, Roy was at my shoulder, while I stared curiously into a spare bedroom. 'So why don't you move in with us, Paul, marra?' he suggested. The Smith was soothing class-war jitters by swigging on a fat bottle of 'Dog': *Newcastle Brown* beer.

'Don't you want me to bring in another flat mate?'

'*Nawh*, Bottle, forget about any conditions. I'm inviting you to take the room, man. Don't worry about it.'

Roy's mirthful, friendly eyes, much calmer, settled on me fraternally, magnified within double TV tubes.

'That's really generous. Sure about that?'

'Away man!'

'What's Paulie going to think about it?' I wondered.

'What does he ever think, marra?'

'Right, but you'd better *tell* him.'

'C'mon Bottle comrade, I'm responsible for that, move in will yer? It's nothing to do with Paulie. Anyway he won't mind, marra. There'd be trouble if I invite a couple of girls to take those rooms, cos he'll only go and seduce em, mind.'

Roy adopted a comradely, manly posture as he knocked back his 'dog'.

I was still preoccupied with Paulie's prolific number of conquests.

'You spreading legends about me again?' Stan appeared.

'Only when your back's turned,' I jested.

'What you two planning?'

'Roy's going to let me take one of the rooms. He's relaxed about me coming in by myself.'

'Oh, yeah, that's sound,' Snot came back.

'No trouble comrades, I can put another ad into the *Nulton Chronicle*,' Roy considered. 'Paulie can put ads in for nowt like. It's one of the perks of his jab. Anyway lads, after the revolution, everybody'll have a decent place to live. We won't need to *ad-ver-ise* in the cap'list media. We'll redevelop all those fancy boutiques and offices for affordable rental, comrades.'

'But that other spare bedroom's still available, right? Technically?' Stan added.

'Away, there's a room there for you, if you want it, marra!'

I turned to the punk guitarist in amazement. 'What you saying? You're thinking of coming in too?'

'I know about all your bad habits, Bottle.'

'Get off, cos I always keep a wall between us,' I laughed.

'I can get on with my song writing.'

'What's wrong with living at home? *Your* home, that is.'

'Living with the enemy?'

'Your family made me really welcome. You got no reason to complain.'

'Yeah, but I don't want to retire there, do I. I don't want Mum to bring me breakfast in bed every morning. Where would Keith Richards be, if his Mum had been there every morning?'

'Away Stan, you're welcome to move in. Whenever you want, marra.'

'You're an officer and a gentleman of the red army.'

'Like Trotsky,' I said.

'Away lads, you have to read the article about rock and racism. It's in this week's copy of the peeper mind,' he encouraged. Adding, 'Ten pence cheaper for the unwaged, comrades!'

'I work in the Co-op,' I reminded him. 'Don't forget.'

'Caring and sharing,' Stan said.

'Ai, it's a start man.'

As for finding a place to live, you couldn't say we were settled. But at least we had a leaky roof over our punk hairstyles.

16. Uncle Luigi's Guitar

Stan moved in to the room next to mine. This change was a seminal moment for the music scene, like Strummer leaving the 101ers to form The Clash with Jones and Simenon.

Snot's folks were distraught at news of his departure. His Mum, Apostolia, spoilt and pampered him more than usual.

Stan and I attended the last supper. The meal consisted of a delicious linguine, with tiramisu for dessert – all homemade. There was no sign of life from the house next door; the place I had grown up. There was not a twitch from those double lined curtains. After the meal we had to gather Stan's stuff and move it across town. The punk axe hero didn't tell his parents where the Mansion was located – for obvious reasons. Instead of getting a lift off his dad, we made excuses and called a taxi. If they knew where their son lived, they wouldn't keep away from him.

'Jonny, darlin', *call me*! Call me, soon as you arrive! *Promise?!*' Apostolia was tearful, gripping his hands, hugging him, gazing long into his eyes; and then she was caressing his bristly cheeks and pushing money into his hands. The scene was different to when I was leaving home.

Snot's parents gave him a magnificent leaving present. I'm not talking about the dinner and a wad of notes either. The gift was a vintage guitar, which dated from 1952, once belonging to his Uncle Luigi. This maternal relative of his, much loved by all, had been a musician in numerous bands. Stan was dismissive of rock culture and heritage, yet had a taste and respect for Chuck Berry, Elvis Presley, Lee-Lewis and Little Richard. Thanks to the library he'd got to hear vintage rock 'n' roll and learnt a lot from the recordings.

When Snot received his venerable instrument, it was in decent condition, apart from needing new strings. Just a bit of restoration and tuning up required. As I remember it had three knobs and a lever that changed octave or bent notes. Snot was interested in devices that changed a guitar's factory sound. With Luigi's guitar he relied less on technological effects than before. When he'd first started playing it he'd simply hit the strings randomly of course. This classic instrument from Uncle Luigi had a beautiful smooth sound, requiring firmer and more precise fingering. Curiously Snot was the only one who ever knew how to play it. The instrument was almost fated to him.

'This guitar feels amazing,' he admitted. 'The love of my life can't be better.'

He couldn't find a manufacturer's mark. He took the instrument to music shops asking them to identify it. Nobody could say where it came from or explain much about origination. Mysteriously the instrument had different characteristics, which couldn't be traced precisely to any particular manufacturer. Stan wondered if the guitar had been made by a back street craftsman in Naples. By strict definition the guitar was just a replica, a hybrid or even a forgery, no matter how fantastic it sounded. And that wasn't its only strange characteristic.

His uncle stopped playing due to arthritis in the finger joints. This trouble came from years working in a brick kiln, rather than from musicianship. Despite his love for rock 'n' roll, Luigi was forced to hang up his blue suede shoes. We went to visit him in sheltered accommodation, and he played his old record collection and reminisced. Certainly his fingers were thickened and gnarled, serviceable only for card games. The elderly Italian's suits looked a bit thin, but he was as rich as Nero with musical memories.

The best story Luigi's told concerned how, during the summer of 1962, Elvis Presley flew over to England from Germany (where he was stationed) to play a one-off secret gig. It was the only gig the King ever played in Britain – so secret that the press and public never learnt about it. Elvis took an American Airforce plane over, to land at an airfield near Lincoln, accompanied by a group of good scratch musicians. This was necessary to avoid the attentions of the Colonel – Presley's notorious manager

– who'd forbidden any concerts in England, due to his own shady past.

Presley and the boys had turned up at the venue, ready for a sound check. Of course the King was in disguise, allowing his short army haircut to go back to its natural blonde. Luigi said that the King had a great sense of humour and took delight in wearing heavy fake specs. At the sound check his guitarist found that his own regular instrument was damaged and no longer playable. The whole secret gig was put at risk by that, with just a few hours remaining until the venue opened.

Uncle Luigi was employed as a ground crew worker at the airfield. After finding out about Presley's plans he was immediately outside the stage door. An employee at the hall mentioned the guitarist's predicament and, in a flash, Luigi dashed home and returned with his own guitar as a replacement. So that night James Burton – it was none other than him – took Luigi's special guitar into his special hands. Burton was brilliant enough to adjust, shaking out those classic riffs to early Presley hits, in that superbly crisp and understated style.

After the gig Luigi was invited backstage and introduced to Elvis. Luigi was very proud when Burton came over to speak to him, full of praise for that borrowed guitar. Burton said how impressed he'd been by its full sound and easy handling. Only reluctantly did Burton give it back. He told the modest Luigi that he'd 'got himself a mighty fine guitar. Pure as a bell. Where did you find this beaut'. man?' Yet even Luigi was unsure.

Before it was passed to young Jon, the guitar had been locked in its case, gathering dust; catches rusted, on top of a wardrobe. His uncle heard a lot about the terrible punks. He was scandalised by the expletives filled performances. On the other hand, he knew there were other scandals in popular music history. The punks were not the first or last in this music. Otherwise you were not worthy of the title of a rock 'n' roll rebel.

* * *

Outside of Snot's family nostalgia, Mortal's rehearsals showed signs of improvement. Musical riffs went along with personality tiffs.

We noticed that Herb was keeping away and working longer hours at the hair salon. Turned out, Anna-kissed had got herself hooked up with Paulie. Their eyes had met at the Looking Glass disco. It had been undying lust for an entire night. Only she couldn't stop thinking and talking about him for weeks afterwards, even if Wellington struggled to place her.

'I'm playing guitar in his new band,' Anna-kissed admitted.

Herb was outraged. 'You doing what? Let's get this straight, shall we Henrietta? You're suggesting that you're playing for that plonker and for his band now?' he screamed.

'Don't judge,' she suggested.

'You shouldn't have agreed,' Snot said, 'without saying anything to us first.'

'I'm just doing Paulie a favour, until he gets this group together.'

'Oh yes, Henrietta, we understand about favours to Paulie,' objected Herb.

'I'm a free girl,' she retorted.

'Fine, but I'm not sharing.'

Anna-kissed had a green Doc Marten boot on two different stages. She'd have to choose between punk trash and punk dub. While Herb and she were arguing and fighting, more seriously, they disrupted band practice.

Meanwhile, to cover for Anna-kissed, Gina Watson – or 'Sour Cat' as she now preferred to be called – alternated instruments to fill in, depending who was absent. Gina could tickle anything with a key or a string. Snot regretted that Paulie had ever met Anna-kissed. Wellington couldn't take one of his musicians scot-free. It came to a head in the Dragon one night.

'Find your own fucking musicians,' he snarled.

'*Phew*, calm down, Stan, will you?' Wellington's features were a picture of innocence besmirched. 'Who twanged your strings, mate?'

'D'you fancy anybody else in our band? Lucky fucking dip, is it?'

'That's really dodgy. Why should I fancy anybody,' he laughed.

'I hope you don't shag the way you write.'

'*Phew*, no need to be so bloody offensive, is there mate? That comment sounds a bit sexist, to be honest. What's the matter, you jealous of my job at the paper?' Paulie ticked him off.

'Just keep out of their knickers,' Snot warned.

Wellington offered that innocent and maligned look, as if revolutionary socialism wouldn't melt in his mouth. There was a razor-blade atmosphere between them, even though Paulie couldn't see the problem.

Whatever the truth of his brush with Anna-kissed, he'd created erotic mayhem among the punks. He'd a true gift as a natural born lady killer and a wrecker of musical careers.

Around this period Stan seemed to be getting closer to Gina. Despite their constant bickering he relied on her talent, to shape the band sound. Sour Cat was the only one who could tackle his new material, which was getting more complicated. Snot would get her to harmonise the material and to advise on the most natural chord changes. She taught him how to change key smoothly and to introduce a middle eight. To complicate matters even more, I realised that I was jealous.

Not that Sour Cat got to all the rehearsals or was fully dedicated. She was fickle with her presence as the name suggested. 'Dad said I couldn't come today. I've got some of those exams and, well, I just wouldn't feel confident.' Or: 'Mum doesn't like me being in a rock group. She doesn't want me staying out late. I had to tell them I was going shopping. Otherwise they make me stay in and practice.'

Other times she'd got a hangover from clubbing. We assumed she'd been staying in Sheffield over the weekend, as we'd been told. She had relatives in that city and they gave her more freedom, which she took full advantage of.

When Stan saw a band down in London he'd get a good lie-in next day. If you couldn't rely on him to be on time, then who was left to rescue Marty's bank balance?

While this punk soap-opera ran, Nutcase was the only trustworthy band character. This was despite him being fully employed and a responsible parent. His wife was pregnant again and he had domestic bills hanging over his Mohican cut like a hatchet.

Snot was settling into his new rock star condo, which was directly next to mine. During the evenings we'd listen to music tapes, including all Bowie's Berlin recordings and other so-called 'Kraut Rock' recordings (Roy's tastes were eclectic. There was more to him than just leftist politics). Paulie was usually out late, or distracted, with his pretty conquests. He didn't share our company that often. The reporter certainly had a racy social life. Paulie slept with so many girls he didn't even recognise their faces, not to mention their names. It was awkward to be in the pub with him, when a forgotten past conquest approached him, and demanded an answer. Despite that appealing 'little boy lost' look he had and – apparently – a sexual magnetism – he had the same effect on the female population as The Incredible Hulk on interior design.

It was a laugh when Paulie tried to join in with SWP political discussions at the flat. Roy sometimes held branch meetings in the living room and, if we were there too, we'd be drawn in to the debates. These could last long into the night, and be interesting, with a varied bunch of political characters taking part. Roy was the about the sanest one among them, in my view. Stan was bored and liked to wind them all up with controversial and contrary views. He sounded a bit like Paul Weller, when the 'Modfather' once claimed to be supporting the Tories.

Meanwhile I signed up for a journalism night course. The idea was to develop writing skills in advance of Marty's new fanzine. When I began to interview local bands I realised how hard it was to get anything quotable from them. It could be painfully monosyllabic. When I had an interesting question, they'd just stare back at me in bewilderment, as if I said something like 'how much do you enjoy mineral water?'

On top of these efforts I began reading the weekly music papers regularly. At the *Hope and Anchor* in Islington we saw Stiff acts, such as Wreckless Eric, Nick Lowe and Elvis Costello. This took us up a notch or two.

17. Fly-posting

Mortal's first gig under *Star Materials* management was, so to speak, just around the corner. The levers of Gorran's slick PR and promotion machine were thrust into over-drive. The boss regularly sent Roy and I out fly-posting around the town centre, usually during the early morning hours. Marty designed and produced these posters, of several designs, using a flatbed three colour method. Day-Glo shades were much in favour during the punk period. Apart from essential gig information the posters, and flyers, showed a punk-pirate figure; a Captain Morgan in bondage pants and safety pins.

The council and the police already regarded these garish artefacts as a public menace, litter and vandalism. There were dire warnings in the *Chronicle*, though thankfully Paulie didn't shop us. I don't know why they got so worked up about the issue, since Nulton was a ghost town in that period. Even the pigeons used to drop dead out of the railway bridges. The council was doing their best to catch the perpetrators and to eliminate the posters – with gangs of YOPs in bibs going around stripping them off afterwards. The cops were eager to get us, and to close down the printing shop as well.

Roy and I were off on midnight sprees, as soon as the ink had dried on Marty's fresh factory batch. We'd head out of the workshop with a fat roll of these bills under our arms, along with a bucket of wallpaper paste and brush. Empty or boarded-up shops presented the best surfaces. There was no shortage of vacant retail units during those times. Bus shelters, a boarded-up cinema, a network of concrete walkways, tunnels and low-level hoardings – the best pasting spaces.

All our efforts went towards making Mortal's first club gig a huge success. If that went down a storm the band could play a date at *The Limit* club in Sheffield; thanks to a recommendation from Gina to the owner. Gina went to see bands there at the weekend; she went clubbing and her cousin worked in the cloakroom for a student type job.

Our fly posting technique was like this: Roy had to stretch up on the tips of his springy toes, to hold the poster high against a wall or surface, while I reached up and plastered the bill over with gluey paste. By next morning the paper would have dried, shrunk and stuck fast, so that it was hard to remove, even for those YOP degenerates with chemical aerosols, as well as buckets of soapy water and scrapers. It was their punishment for getting caught.

It was in the small hours, while we were busy posting around the Sting Hotel, that Roy noticed a patrol vehicle creeping closer. Silently to avoid detection, the cop car was edging up the side street, suddenly intrigued by a sign of life in that urban desert. Bafflingly the car turned off and disappeared again. Ten minutes later it had come back, having done a circuit of one-way streets, picking up speed as it bore down on us. Then it arrested our senses with a blast of the siren, pulled up sharply into the curb, catching us in full headlight beams.

Frozen into guilty postures, holding our materials, we had a 'you will be prosecuted' look. There was a roll of garish bills still under my arm, like a forger of Panamanian dollars. And if this wasn't a roll of posters, it was the biggest spliff you'd seen in your life.

Like a US highway patrolman, this solitary cop got out lazily from his Ford Cortina. Basking in the swishes of a revolving blue lamp, he straightened his cap, pulled up his trousers, strolled around the side of his car, making cautiously towards us; the unpredictable juvenile delinquents.

'*Orl roight*! What are you lads up to? Why you 'angin round these streets at this time'a *noight*?'

'Away man, what do you think we're doing? We're just puttin' up a few of these *porsters* here, mind. We're only wanting to support our mates – playing in a band – who've gorra gig soon,' Roy explained.

The copper was unimpressed. 'You can't stick those up! What you doin?'

'As my mate told you… it's just for a gig,' I added.

'Gig? I'll gi' you a gig, lad. Where's your permit? Where is it? You're gonna need permission to do it?' the cop challenged.

'We don't have one,' I admitted.

'What you're doing is ille-*gal*. You got to hand all that stuff over to me. You're in serious trouble, you lads.'

'*Awh now*, away with you, man! What harm we doin? Trying to put on some music in the town like? Trying to get local youth to do something positive and go to a concert, man!'

'Look, you can read for yourself,' I said. 'Go on, take one and have a read… if you want. They're a great little band.'

'I don't wan' one!' the cop replied, irritably. 'I don't want to read your blasted *post*-ers. You're coming with me. Back to the station.'

'C'mon, man, gi' us a break now. Don't support this reactionary society. What side of the law you on, comrade? Just because they pay you a wage, the police don't need to support this capitalist oppression. *Doon't* be a wage slave officer. Come and join our revolutionary struggle in the party, man.'

The policeman drew himself up. 'You cheeky li'le Trot toe rag!'

'Away officer, no need to be a slave to the Tory establishment!'

'You're one of these commies!' declared the cop. 'If you don't like it 'ere, get back to Russia.'

Radical politics aside, The Smith wasn't so daft as to confront the state security-apparatus by himself. Best to avoid arrest (and sack from the Inland Revenue) and to continue the struggle (with reinforcements) on a more progressive-feeling day.

The police officer produced a notebook and pencil. And he began to take notes about the incident; as if he wanted to be a rock journalist too.

The thing was, he took his eye off us. The cop assumed we were too scared to move, while he wandered back to his patrol car to report back to the station.

Oscar Delta Bravo. Over. Can you send another car to me in Manchester Street? Over. I got a couple of herberts sticking up bill-

posters here. Over. Yeah, you know, those disgusting pink things that are turning up all over the shop? With the blinkin Pirate? Yeah. Over. Well I've got the lads here. Got them with a bucket of paste and a roll on em. Over. Yeah, enough to decorate your bathroom with. Over. Yeah, if you can find a free car. Over. I'm across the street from the Sting Hotel. Over.

By the time he looked up Roy and I – after swapping an informative look – had scarpered. We dropped our tools and the gunged glue and were out of there. Somehow I kept hold of the rolls of posters and flyers, as they'd taken Gorran so long to prepare. Roy scrambled away at full tilt, dodgy lungs or not. I wasn't too far behind. We heard a siren start up in pursuit and, soon, a second one. I was afraid that we had incriminated *Star Materials*. What would Marty think if Roy and I had to stand up in the dock? Any copper with half a brain would follow the trail back to the pop guru's workshop.

Luckily for Gorran any prosecution would get stymied, as soon as Dave Crock got second-wind. Dave would be on his hot line to the Chief Inspector, who had a twenty percent stake in his pubs and shared a round of golf twice a week. That would end the ridiculous matter.

Roy was in a bad condition and worse mood when we finally got back home. It wasn't as if we were paid, or that it furthered the revolution. The good-hearted Trot needed a couple of bottles of 'dog' before bedtime, or was it breakfast, just to calm down.

What would those cops have charged us with anyway? Disturbing the dead? Breaking the depression, or The Depression?

18. Dancing Barefoot

Mortal Wound's long-anticipated first club date finally came around. There was a big excited queue of punks stretching around the block of the *Mad Hatter* club.

The Smith and I were really smug and pleased, as we crossed out our names on the guest list.

Dave Crock teetered at the summit of the entrance, delighted by the huge turnout (in and out of focus) before his eyes. The retired central defender was stuffed into a crushed velvet suit and a ruffled shirt. Estimating overall takings and brandishing the rock-size coal of his cigar, he was well chuffed. The only fire regulations he respected were on the back of a box of *Swan Vestas*.

'Great turnart. Very fuckin satisfyin'. More the merrier, I always said. If they got a fiver let em in. Let em enjoy em'selves. I ain't never been no fuckin kill joy,' Crock told his snooker men. At this point of the evening he held his thugs back in readiness for trouble. The snooker men could sweat out a long break before they got back to the table. There was plenty of time to clear up stray balls.

Roy and I shouldered through to the saloon bar. We were already looking for Marty. Stan and the band should have been occupied with a sound-check. Hopefully they were practicing arrangements, not just trying out some arguments.

Gina – or Sour Cat – should have been taking part. Unfortunately we got a jolt as we saw her hanging around the bar. She was in the right outfit and heavily made up, ready for a killing on stage, yet she was alone and broody at the counter. She was drinking as well, *seriously* drinking, chasing down cider with vodka. This behaviour wasn't completely surprising for a punk maybe. We were shocked because she wasn't meant to be there – she was supposed to be with the others, or even striding about doing those weird vocal exercises she went in for. What was she doing sticking to the counter like a hardened bar fly? Where had happened to her musical composure? We had to find out and do something, before this came to Marty's attention.

'What you lads bugging me for? Can't I have nerves?' she admitted. 'What about it? Leave me alone. You have any problem with that? I had the same thing with Chopin.' She was shouting at us, only because the saloon was so packed, being extra full with punks and miscreant youths of all types. The mood was very loud and enthusiastic, in readiness for Mortal's big headline gig. There was a great sense of anticipation, now that the JWG debacle was behind them. Except that many local punks didn't yet know Gina, and they didn't associate her with us herberts.

'Away man, you'll be fine,' Smith insisted.

'You can't be nervous now,' I said.

'What do you know about it?'

'Well, it's too late for nerves! You're gonna be on stage soon.'

'I don't give a shit about that.'

'And you've got too much talent.'

'Huh, "talent",' she scoffed, polishing off the cider in a single slide.

I boggled at her throat, wondering what I'd said wrong. 'So you're *not* talented?'

'Bottle! Don't be so cheeky.'

'This is a massive gig,' I argued.

'And you're a massive pain in the bum. That's why I joined this punk group in the first place. I don't want to be a rock goddess, any more'n a classical diva.'

'Even though you've got the potential.' I pulled up my spiky hair.

'No, Bottle. Don't just gawp at me. You should listen.'

'Away Gina man, are you getting the pre-gig jitters?' Roy asked.

'Well, I've haven't played rock music to this many people,' she admitted.

Roy's eyes widened behind his specs. 'You haven't? *Oh, hell.*'

'No, don't worry about it Gina. You'll be fine, once you start playing.'

'First I need to get smashed,' she advised. 'Can you stand me a couple?'

'No, no, you don't! You're very talent... you're very *good*.'

'Not until I'm out of my head, I'm not. Otherwise I'm a failure. You don't want to see a failure, do you?'

'Away man, you're going to be absolutely fantastic tonight, mind. Just don't keep knocking back those bevies and spirits back, Gina man. It's not goin to do yer nerves any good.'

'Don't call me a man, Roy. I'm a girl,' she said curtly.

'It's just an expression of his,' I offered.

'Ai, we're all equal in the class struggle, comrades.'

She widened her eyes at us. 'All right, *ladies!*'

It was definitely the vodka. She'd got herself into a right state. Any more vodka encores and she'd be finished. Her beautiful blue-gray eyes resembled smashed pebbles, within those rings of kohl thick as crude oil. Despite this, even under lurid punk cosmetics, she seemed pinched and pale. Could it be Mortal's unpredictable sound that made her anxious? Not to mention the group's large raucous following.

The Smith and I finally spotted Marty Gorran in the room. Naturally he was fully occupied in schlepping the room, for business and recreational reasons. Eventually he moved in our direction, because the bar area was crammed with local rock cognoscenti figures. The filaments of his candyfloss hair were infused with colourful light, which also splashed across his bumpy pasty features. Gorran was almost made for the disco arena like some type of counter culture cyborg. Following his expressions and gesticulations, his versatile grins and winning ways, I knew he'd eventually see Gina and have pop puppies.

What was up with her nerves anyway? At band practice she was cool as refrigerated cucumber.

'This is a different set up. I don't think I can handle it. This helps though,' she said, tossing back a fresh tumbler.

'Hold on,' I told her. 'If you play half as good, it's going to be a sensation.'

'Won't happen!'

137

'This is just a punk gig,' I argued. 'It's not *The Rite of Spring*.'

She was not impressed with the first classical music record I had borrowed from the local library that week.

'Away Gina, listen to us, you'll be fine man!'

'Be quiet, will you, Roy woman? What does Stan want from me? I don't know which instrument I'm supposed to play?'

'How's that? Which instrument?'

The Smith was bemused. 'What do you mean, comrade, that you don't know which instrument?'

'Anna-kissed and Herb had a big row. Right? You didn't know about it? She wants to play for another group. Not only Mortal.'

'We heard something,' I told her.

'If she joins them, Herb says he won't play. I was on rhythm guitar, then I was playing bass in Herb's place. How am I going to fit in?'

'Away man, now I'm totally confused,' Roy admitted. You'd think he'd grasp the ins and outs, if he could get *Das Kapital*.

'This must be Paulie and his new group,' I said.

'Oh god he's causin' absolute mayhem with 'em, comrade.'

'Who's in this group, *Viscous Kittens*? Why does Anna-kissed want to play with them for?' Gina complained. She tilted back a pint pot and drained it.

'Steady on, marra!' Roy warned, touching her elbow.

'Is Paulie even in the building yet? What's the point of being support act tonight, if he can't even *get* here?'

'Ai, this def'nitley has Paulie written all over it,' Smith agreed. It wasn't one of Paulie's trivial everyday absurdities at home or work to savour.

Gina narrowed her sparkling, too sparkling eyes.

'This lad, Paulie Wellington, is their singer,' I told her.

'Did I meet him yet?' she wondered.

'Soon enough,' I remarked, gloomily.

'*Fit*, is he?'

I hoped and prayed that Gina would be one girl to resist his disarmingly magnetic angelic sex appeal. The thought of Paulie showing her his record collection was nauseating.

'Still no sign,' Roy confirmed, checking off his battered timepiece. 'He's got to turn up. He can't let his group down!'

Dennis had arrived early to set up his drum kit. Steve, the bass player was down there too, after completing a mundane job. Even a couple of the 'sassy feminist' girl singers were getting changed.

'Ai, these lasses came and said they were friends of Paulie like… here to provide backing *vorcals*. But def'nitely noo sign of that buffoon Wellington in the building, comrade,' Roy grumbled. He shook his mop pessimistically.

'Why isn't Anna-kissed talking to me?' Gina said.

'So you reckon Paulie has blown it?' I speculated.

The subversive was shaking his head gloomily. 'I doon't know what's going on with that idiot, comrade. Your guess is as good as mine like.'

'They'll have to cancel.'

'Well, the rest of the band say they can play without him. They'll go on and do their instrumen'als like, if Paulie doesn't shoo.'

'Terrible. Instrumentals? How's that going to work?'

'Away man, you haven't heard Paulie sing yet,' Roy warned.

'No, I haven't yet,' I admitted.

'Ai, he might be a pain in the arse, sometimes, marra. But Paulie always means well. He doesn't want to cause people hassle, mind. I reckon he's just tryin to be a decent *soo*-cialist like the rest of us, comrade.'

I was more optimistic that there would be a workers' revolution soon. 'He'll let his mates down! He's gonna ruin the first gig for them.'

'Ai, they're none too happy at the moo-ment, marra,' Roy admitted, with a full body tremble of dread and astonishment.

Roy knew his way around the racks. He was into Siouxsie and the Banshees from the beginning, as well as Talking Heads, Television, and later The Gang of Four, the Comsat Angels, the Tom Robinson Band – that period of febrile musical energy, seeing the rebirth of rock, all starting from the punk movement.

'Paulie's been rehearsin' all week, mind! Didn't you notice? How he hasn't been out sleepin' with so many girls?'

'No, yeah… I didn't meet any girls at breakfast this week.'

'It's like a tell you marra. Paulie's been cuttin' doon on his sex life mind. After work he was busy practicin' with his group.'

'Then what's keeping him tonight?'

19. Ego Clash

Marty Gorran was heading for us through the crush. A high voltage smile sent numbing electricity through us. 'Hel-lo! *Hel-lo*, you lot! How're you all doing?' It didn't clock immediately that Gina was slouched next to us.

'In fine fettle, cheers Marty man,' Roy replied, enjoying his own bevy.

Marty and Roy should have been total opposites; one being a Marxist and the other a media capitalist. However, they somehow they clicked: popular and unpopular music was the uniting factor. Marty even hired him to look after *Star Materials* finances. In fact the music mogul had hundreds of quid stashed away in numerous nooks and crannies. The cash was in boxes and containers around his flat or at the workshop. All the money was income from gigs and first record sales.

Roy was pleased to get involved with the local music scene. He'd got the extra cred of being employed by the Inland Revenue office. If only our Tory dad knew that his tax returns were being processed by a Socialist Workers Party member. In Smith's mind, under the stage of late capitalism, there was no contradiction between the revenue and the revolution.

'Paulie hasn't turned up,' I explained.

'Gord 'elp us, you mean that lad off the blinkin local rag? Right, definitely, so where do I get another fucking support act from? What I heard about him he's off with another gel. Straight up, somewhere with his bloomin trousers around his ankles,' Marty said, wincing at his woes.

'Away man, your guess is as good as ours like. The rest of his group are all here and weetin downstairs for 'im like.'

'Straight up, I've never heard this bloomin Viscous Kittens lot.

141

No bullshit, I booked 'em on trust.'

'He's not going to show,' I lamented.

At this point Marty suffered a rude awakening. His troubles quadrupled as he noticed that 'Sour Cat' was next to me. 'Gord 'elp us, *Gina*, no bullshit, what the blue monkeys with a fucking hard-on are you doin up here?' he wanted to know.

'Leave me alone, you slave driver.'

Filled with angst Marty's amiable grimace crumbled. He saw how drunk she was. A pickled musical rat was chewing at the cables of rock superstardom.

'No bullshit gel, what's the big blinkin idea? No bullshit, loitering with all these blinkin headbangers and knocking back crates of fucking orangeades at this time?' he complained. The Pop maverick looked her over anxiously, checking off his spattered watch.

'Leave me alone, okay?' Gina let off a cackle, tilted her head back and tried to get a last drop of vodka out of the glass.

Marty observed this behaviour in horror, as if watching a multi-million pounds record deal trickling down the drain.

'Straight up you lads, why didn't you bloomin stop her drinking herself under the fucking table like this?'

'She got here before we did,' I objected.

'Gord 'elp us Bottle, how many of them fucking cherry pops has she been tossing against her bloomin tonsils?' A pained grin stretched those features in reprimand and angst.

'You don't own me, cheesy. You can't tell me what to do,' she slurred.

'Away man, we can't pump oot her stomach,' Roy argued.

'Viscous Kittens are due on stage in ten minutes,' I commented.

'Right, definitely, so you entertain the fucking crowd, Bottle.'

'Yeah, I'm a free woman.'

The plaster was falling out of Marty's rococo features.

Les Phoenix swept into the venue (on his night off) and immediately came to join the throng. As he noticed the scene of discord, a smile of condescension played up and down his crafty smirk, like Jools Holland's fingers over a pianoforte.

'Gee Marty, havin a piece of trouble with your artists. Or what's the jive with these guys?' he observed with a drawl.

'Right, definitely Les mate, nothing I can't blinkin handle.'

'Don't cut em any slack, Marty.'

'Fair play, Les, but I look after my own blinkin big-name bands in my own fucking way, don't I?' The teeth were clamped together in defensive formation.

He lit a charoot and killed the match. 'Remember the old Colonel Parker, baby.'

Phoenix, in the role of exiled American rock mastermind, kept to the shadows. He gloated under a gas-guzzling hat, and began to sup an original American malt. A rock manager/promoter's fur coat insulated against the cold and damp of the English climate. He dismissed any of the rumours that he originally came from Stoke-on-Trent. Les didn't hold with such petty small town gossip and rumours. He kept the wide-angle of the big country in his mind.

'Hey boys! How ya all doin?' Betsy Dandie greeted us. She'd a bouncy enthusiasm, a radiant smile, though her dental dazzle rivalled Marty's. They were as large as quarterbacks – only more polished and regular. She was in black, a type of a spider's web blouse, with leather trousers and thigh boots. She resembled Dolly Parton out on Halloween.

She swished the mane. 'How's the big gig prep goin, Marty?' she called to him, bubbling and sparkling before us.

Gina's punk costume helped her to blend in. She observed Betsy shyly, as a younger girl sometimes looks at a confident older woman. Even if the glamorous Baltimore rocker had a derivative sound, her rock 'n' roll cred were authentic. Betsy was never a common or garden character around our neck of the woods.

'The Screamers gig with Benatar was awesome, guys,' Les reported. 'Did you read that freakin rave review she got in *Sounds* last week?'

'Straight up, Les mate, I might have noticed something. And I definitely picked out a few bloomin earth tremors.'

'Geez, man, it was *sweet*. You should have freakin been there. This reporter from the *Birmin'ham Post* buzzed me for an interview. This guy agreed Betsy blew Benatar out of the goddamn arena,' Les bragged.

'Quite a night,' Betsy cut in. Leaving further hype and promotion to Phoenix, she began to socialise with her lead guitarist.

'So this guy tells me how Benatar's roadies were gonna pull the freakin plug on my Betsy,' Les recalled. His shrewd sharp eyes aimed their rays just over our heads. 'Benatar was one relieved chick when the Screamers packed up their gear and took the freeway home.' He tapped the side of his impressive conk.

'Right, definitely...'

'I've gotta level with you, Marty baby... cos one of the Screamers' roadies overheard some little guy from *Kerrang!* sayin how Dandie has the most huge female rock voice of the century,' Phoenix reported.

'No bullshit, Les mate, but how can you bloomin measure something like that?'

'This guy said like, we blew out a window in the cathedral,' Betsy said, putting in her piece.

'No bull here, Marty baby, cos I've already got the goddamn track list sorted for Betsy's epony-mouse debut album,' Phoenix informed us. He touched the crown of his Stetson. With a dry catch in his voice, Les told us, 'Sure thing, man, I already know what the first freakin US hit single's gonna be.'

'Fair play, Les mate, I heard the gig went blinkin well.'

'The way Betsy and the boys is rockin, Marty baby, she's a freakin shoe in for this Battle of the Bands... here in little ole Nulton town,' he told us. Les chuckled and raised his glass in ironic salute to the place.

'Right, definitely, Les mate, but I wou'n't be too over blinkin confident about your chances of winning,' Marty warned. He seemed to get a sudden tooth ache which cracked his grin.

'We always get a fuckin full ouse when our little Betsy's on,' Dave Crock bellowed at us, with a wink. The ex-centre-half returned to a strong position at the bar beside us.

'Me, Betsy and the boys are goin back to the States this Fall. We're ready to sign on the freakin line with Bonnie Tyler. After that we're back on the godamn road, man. The band bus's swingin

South to join up with the Kiss show. We're on the *sk-edule* for joinin those Kiss boys during their stadium dates. Gee Marty, it's gonna be a sweet tour, man.'

'Cheers everybody!' Crock interjected. He sank another pint, looking flushed and glassy, while keeping a free hand flat on the counter.

'Right, definitely, but you don't want to be out of blinkin touch with the British music scene. Straight up, there's a lot of bloomin exciting new bands springing up here in blinkin England. And no bullshit, Les mate, you don't want to miss the next wave of bloomin exciting music. Like someone eyed blinkin Californian surfer missing the next fucking big one, Les mate.' Gorran grinned about the circle of punks and hangers on in anguish, being stung by his rival's US-centric view of rock.

'Gee Marty, you're too impressed by these bunches of English friggin punks. There ain't nothin you British guys can teach us about rock 'n' roll. Man, you shoulda taken up my invite for Birmin'ham. One day you're gonna ask yourself where you was that night. No shit, it was the Stones at the Rosebowl. And our Betsy's gonna be a big star in the US of A one day, man. These little punk guys of yours gonna be cryin into their freakin mugs of warm beer, Marty baby. Or *milky tea*,' he added.

'Fair play, Les mate, but you can't avoid punk rock happening big here in the bloomin UK,' Gorran winced, dragging deeply on his latest ciggie, to order his thoughts. 'All those blinkin yanks are looking our fucking way right now.'

'Sure baby, I'm listenin but, shoot, man... take some advice about this business. Like gee, I'd been in this industry for three freakin decades. Yeah man, for real. Find a beautiful chick with a big voice, writing her own freakin toons. Get yourself a great gel with a goddamned big voice that hits the back row of the shittin bleakers, man... a gel singer who gets the freakin hairs on the back of your neck freakin twanging.' Cheeks colouring a little, Phoenix moistened his lizard lips with Jack D.

'Fair play, she definitely gets the hairs in my blinkin *ears* twanging,' Marty remarked.

'Our little Betsy's welcome at the 'Atter,' Crock boomed. The club owner raised a full pint towards the American rock magnate, before he downed it in tribute to takings.

'It's a goddamn done deal, Marty baby. Don't waste your energy promotin' that bunch of freakin British hooligans,' Phoenix advised.

'Little Betsy's always welcome ere at the 'Atter!' Crock shouted. 'She pulls the punters. Tight fuckers open up 'eir wallets. No, no, no… No trouble to Dave Crock. I ain't got no complaints bart er. Beautiful little gel, Betsy!' Crock brayed. He managed to lock his knees to secure his grip. 'Nah, nah, an if any fuckin dirty tosser gets is filfy ands on er,' he promised.

The Beverley Hills rock mogul came to the rescue. 'You're welcome, sir. We salute your freakin good taste. Betsy's a goddamn east coast classic. *Period.*'

'You can say that agen, Joe!' Crock roared.

'Right, definitely, all well and bloomin good Les mate, but you don't want to ignore a fucking talented little punk rock band like mine,' Gorran argued, going through contortions of protest.

'Gee Marty, what's with you and these scruffy bad teeth losers man? My Betsy and the Screamers is gonna blow every goddamn little Brit punk group of yours out of the freakin pond.'

'Fair play Les mate, you want to hear Mortal blinkin Wound play live tonight,' Marty argued. He continued to grimace with confidence, waving his ciggie about in the air.

'Let me be freakin straight with you Marty, they don't stand no chance against Betsy, in this god damned Battle of the Bands,' Les crowed.

'You can take a fuckin compliment, can't you love?'

'Straight up, you're in for a blinkin shock. Mortal's the best new group I've heard this side of the Dolls knocking 'em dead at the bloomin Garden last year,' Gorran insisted. He grinned in wonder at the great rock memory. 'Or I'm Farah Fosset Majors.'

'No chance of beatin *us*, matey,' Betsy added, overhearing.

Phoenix clicked the back of his cowboy boots and stared ironically at the heavens. 'You're never gonna get to second base with those freakin British thugs,' Phoenix insisted.

19. Ego Clash

The corporate rock chieftain narrowed his wind-stung, icy blue prairie eyes at a wider distant horizon, to concentrate on those big American Billboard dreams of rock stardom, coming along on the side of the freeway.

20. New HQ

'Enjoy yerselves, lads! Get some more pints down yer froats!' Crock urged our party. Old-fashioned gentlemen's manners were lost on these little uptight American rock stars.

Roy observed the club owner out of nervous fascination. He wasn't sure how to take the man or where to place him on the political scale. I wasn't any more socially at ease.

'Right, definitely Dave mate, I appreciate all your blinkin support,' Gorran said. 'Only, fair play, I'd like to call in your promise to get me office space here at the *Hatter*.'

The publican's eyes sharpened. 'Office space? Ere? What yer talkin bart?' he asked, leaning over in a menacing whisper.

'Right, definitely Dave mate, you offered me a room down in the blinkin basement, payment in bloomin kind for Alice in fucking wonderland,' Gorran recalled. Marty gave a wavering smile to help him remember and keep a promise. There was always a first.

'What ya need a fuckin office foo-er, Marty boy? You can't play fuckin moosic darn there!'

'Right, Dave mate, what do you think? Fair play, it's about bloomin admin and organisation. Straight up, we've been scratching around for a blinkin HQ. Definitely, I'm starting up this new bloomin publishing venture of mine,' Gorran explained.

'Publishin?' he spluttered. 'Printin'?'

'Right Dave, soon as possible I'm going to blinkin bed with this new music fanzine project.'

'Goin' to fuckin bed? How does this in-foo-ence my mags?'

'Right, definitely Dave, this don't affect your bloomin erotic mag range. Fair play, cos the idea's to promote all our *Star Materials* artists taking part in this Battle of the bloomin Bands contest coming up soon Dave, that those local council crooks is blinkin promoting.'

'Don't worry bart them fuckin nosy wankers, Marty boy.'

Gorran made a face. 'Right, straight up, we've all had enough of them meddling tossers, Dave mate.'

'So what's this all abart *offices*? What you twistin my fuckin arm for now, Marty boy?'

Gorran offered up his friendly smiling mug through a cloud of amiable ciggie smoke. 'Straight up Dave, *Star Materials* has got to have its own bloomin office some place. No bullshit, the editorial staff's got to blinkin spread out and have its own bloomin base somewhere, doesn't it,' Gorran explained.

'A base? *Staff*?' Losing contact with gravity, staggering a few steps, Crock just about rescued himself. 'What is it?'

'Right, definitely Dave mate, steady on, cos you already mentioned something about our office,' Marty said, jogging his memory.

'That's your business, Marty boy,' Crock insisted, firmly planted, only wavering. '*Moosic!*'

'No bullshit Dave, let's turn a huge bloomin profit on my first edition, quicker'n James Hunt can get his fucking Lotus out of the garage,' Marty argued. He flinched at the prospect. 'Fair play let's get my blinkin new editorial staff settled in there.'

'What fuckin staff you tawkin bart?' Crock demanded.

'Right, definitely Dave mate, this lad.'

'This lad? This geeky shitface ere?'

'Right, definitely, it's Paul Bottle's our new Copywriter and Editor in chief, Dave mate.' The punk genius grinned certainty and assurance.

'An oos this scruffy fuck next to im?'

Attention focussed on Roy, who blinked in surprise through the taped-up NHS frames, beginning to roast in his parker.

'This is our new blinkin Treasurer in Chief for Star Materials music corporation,' Gorran informed him. He took a swivel and opened an arm. 'Roy Smith, *Dave Crock*. Dave Crock, *Roy Smith*.'

'Fuckin delighted, Mr Smith...is it? What yer drinkin? C'mon, c'mon, I got me own fuckin tab ere. I own the fuckin place. Dream come true. Ain't bought a fuckin drink for twenty years! Perks'a the trade son, after more'n a decade defendin in the fuckin first team.'

'No bullshit Dave, that Alice in Wonderful cost me a blinkin arm an' a leg, what with that truck load of fucking emulsion. Straight up, it took me best part of six months to get the fucking rick out of my bloomin neck,' Marty recalled.

Crock began to tunnel back in time. 'What you planning next, Marty boy?' he pressed.

Gorran exercised his features to meet the challenge. 'Fair play, we've already got more than five hundred blinkin quid saved up in our kitty. Straight up, I've got to keep all that bloomin loot safe together some place, with Roy here helping out. No bullshit, cos the idea's to enter all my blinkin Star Materials bands in this Battle of the Bands competition. Definitely cos that five hundred quid's got to cover the entrances fees for them all,' Marty explained.

Crock rocked back with another beer and drained it. He was overcome with sentimental respect for his DJ's genius. 'You've always played fair an fuckin square wi me, Marty boy. You can ave yer office. Ave it. We talkin *good money*, Marty? So what we talkin? More n a few monkeys?'

'Right, definitely, Dave mate, more than monkeys, that's the bloomin big idea, Dave mate.' Marty was twinkling and grinning optimistically at full power.

'Well then, I'll get a fuckin strong box put in. Ave a word wiv my boy, Troy,' Crock offered, woozily. 'You never done a sneaky one rarnd the fuckin side. You always put on a fuckin nice show. Wi them fuckin dreadful fuckin bands a yours. I'm lookin forward to that gig t'night. I've eard a lot abart this new fuckin rock group a yours.'

'No bullshit, Mortal Wound.'

'It's a good ouse. I'm appy, Marty boy. I'm very pleased, son. You're on the fuckin ball. No fancy tricks. You ain't never fuckin megged me.'

21. The Thin White Legs

With the support slot late, nobody could say where Paulie might be.

The *Music Box* lager lake was rising and soaking into my boot leather. It felt as if every punk rocker in the town and beyond had come to see Mortal Wound's comeback gig. Marty continued to get all the hype in edgewise for the big occasion. Roy was equally busy trying to recruit disaffected youth for the SWP, showing no fear of even the most fearsome clans, undaunted by threats or apathy.

Les Phoenix had opted to come downstairs to see what all the hype was about. Like an eagle on a distant rock ledge, or the best-selling AOR section at the *Record Shack*, Les kept a tasteful and imperial distance.

More sinisterly Mick Dove and mates loitered stage front. They intended to cause mayhem and wanted to single Stan out, as being the ideal target for their hate.

Dove's transformation into a thuggish proto-skinhead was a puzzle. He had been brought up by his Grandparents, after losing both his parents early. As a Junior School boy he would invite me back to his house for tea and tarts. His grandparents seemed all right – just typical grandparents. You couldn't blame them for his extreme views (as far as I knew). Mick left the Sixth Form with good A Levels. He'd been a hard working student at Nulton Arts. What was his big problem? Mick came over as a shy studious lad, a bit of a painful introvert. Except he'd share nasty psychotic fantasies with me on the way, sexual as much as political, told in a sinister whisper.

There was a girl in the fashion department that Mick began to fancy. She turned him down politely, only he wouldn't take no for an answer. One afternoon, as I wandered back into the studio, I noticed a row going on between them. Dove suddenly shoved the girl and sent her flying. While she screamed on the floor he coldly wandered away, hardly looking back. After that I took a different route home and we became suspicious enemies. I knew he was involved in a suede head gang and they launched revenge attacks on students they disliked.

Meanwhile, back at the *Hatter*'s basement live venue, a swirling, packed crowd, was in a restless and rowdy mood. Not only were all these drunk and doped-up lads packed like proverbial oily fish in a can, but a long delay stretched their patience like whale gut.

Viscous Kittens name had featured on posters and all promotional material as official support. Most of the Kittens, of both genders, were ready to appear. Unfortunately, sharing ironical looks, Roy and I didn't have high hopes that Paulie would turn up.

DJ for the night was Steve Fenton. This gave everyone the chance to hear Marty's new record selection (plucked from the indie network that week), including a lot of stuff from The Ramones. Marty visited had gone into *Stiff*, *Rough Trade* and *Honest Jon's* for the latest imported 45s, EPs and LPs. Gorran wasn't insular in musical view, despite his passionate support for British acts. The underground American punk scene and, soon to be, the 'new wave' movement, began to fill boxes and to cover his decks too.

Nulton's Stray Cat wasn't even in the building then, or ever likely to be. Probably he was hanging about at home, or prevaricating, or fornicating, or developing a new interest in something. Or maybe he was just sweating about an overdue news report.

'No Kittens tonight,' I predicted.

Roy was broiling in his parker next to me. 'Away man, there's time for the comrade yet.'

'How can they play, on a few hours practice?'

'Paulie can't drop out now, marra. He's been rehearsin' hard, like.'

'More chance of sticky ribs than Viscous Kittens,' I complained.

'Away Bottle, you've got to keep optimistic about the future.'

'That lad'll be late for his own funeral.'

'So long as he's not late for the revolution, mind,' Roy said, in earnest faith.

'Don't set your bloody alarm clock.'

'I told Paulie every decent socialist has got to be ready, to man the barricades, marra…when the big moo-ment of the revolution finally arrives.' The Darlow radical grew misty eyed.

'He'll spoil everyone's big day,' I joked.

'Away man!' Roy covered his mouth to disguise hilarity. However furious with Paulie, he could savour the absurdity of his antics: at least until the revolution came. 'I hope you're wrong about that, marra. I don't wanna put our Paulie up against the wall. Paulie's always done his best to be a good socialist, mind.'

However, I didn't share Roy's confidence about Paulie's Scarlet Pimpernel proclivities.

Something positive, because next minute we gave a jump, as the club's PA came live. House lights dipped and flickered, and Fenton faded out his final Damned record. Roy and I exchanged uneasy looks of suspense: was Viscous Kittens finally ready? Had Wellington found the motivation for his big moment of pop destiny? Or was Mortal Wound planning to come on early? Butterflies entered my stomach; bloody huge ones like those that hatch out and flutter all around the Amazon.

'Can it really be him?' I peered towards the stage and wondered.

'More likely Marty found a diff'rent support act, marra.'

The atmosphere spiked with frustration and violence, Dennis MacDonald dared to stick his neck out. The percussionist seemed fully relaxed, with his swinging stride, and settled comfortably behind the kit. Giving a quick warm-up on those skins, getting a feel for the acoustics; giving some testing kicks on the bass drum, with a bit of tinkling around of snares and symbols; Dennis finally got the show underway. The place was hopping immediately. Dennis had the groove and a blissful look.

Steve Fenton had played for heavy rock and even HM groups, such as Hammer Blow or Sturm Troop. So at first these Caribbean poly-rhythms had been a challenge to him.

Kittens started with an instrumental percussion track – an anxious extended-play B side. Fiona offered support to Dennis by smashing a tambourine. But she couldn't avoid a beer shampoo from some of Dove's fascists.

Anna-kissed came on next and plugged in her rhythm guitar. One by one, three backing singers wandered on stage. These were Paulie's erotic conquests from the previous fortnight. I knew them by sight – and a few polite words over toast and cornflakes. Did Anna-kissed realise how her 'band mates' had been recruited? Judging by her willingness to appear that night, she didn't yet. When she finally *did* Viscous Kittens wouldn't last any longer than their original one-night stand. That was even before Herb got wind of the episode, so that he would, literally, search the whole town in search of Paulie, intending to get his balls in a pair of hot curling tongs.

But had Paulie turned up, after all?

Anna-kissed played with her back rounded and turned against the mob. You couldn't doubt her pluck, even if musically she was breaking her nails and was lost in dub space.

The Viscous Kittens were dunked in spit and beer, and in danger of drowning. Except that punk bands were not easily defeated. Getting canned off, abused and spat at, was an accolade. Maybe that was less obvious for a reggae fusion band. Anyhow, after the first number, Anna-kissed unplugged her instrument and stalked off in fury. Obviously she didn't think Paulie was going to show up. The group's sound held without her in-put, because she was hardly competent. Dennis was longing for the glory days of The Kingston Klingons, even in the roughest dance hall. The drummer was a pro and he'd finish their set and collect his pay, even if it nearly killed him.

The thing was, just as we gave up, completely against the odds, Wellington showed. Suddenly, like an apparition of a flaxen haired Apollo in the wings, or even a Peter Frampton in a spot, he jumped up on that stage and was cavorting with his group and groupies.

'Fuck me, comrade, if it isn't our Paulie!' Roy declared – suddenly animated. Instead of a communist clenched fist, he was pointing in disbelief.

'Can it really be true?' I wondered.

'Ai, I reckon so, marra. It's hard to believe m'eyes, but it's him aw-right!'

'It's a miracle!'

'Ai, it's hard to credit. Just don't go believing in all that religious mumbo-jumbo, comrade.'

'He must've warmed up his feet.'

'What's the daft ba'stad doing, mind?' Roy said.

Our eyes boggled at the prancing, bespectacled figure of our Paulie. He was doing a weird dance in a blouse-like costume – and no trousers. It was his idea of getting punk and being original, only with a hippie hangover. His vocals were a 'heavy breathing down the phone' style. The distorted sensual noise was produced by puckering those cherubic lips too close to the microphone. The lyrics had a peace love and understanding slant to them. It was like Donovan had turned into a punk. Afterwards lads argued that Paulie had a lot of guts to get up there. But Paulie compared himself to Marley, Dylan or Lennon (depending on his audience).

The other Kittens were just relieved to have a vocalist and finally to play a proper gig. Wellington was their front man, pluses and minuses, and he took a blizzard of spit and some plastic pint pots on the chin.

Not even the fascists knew how to categorise him. Some took him as an iconoclastic Hindi mystic.

'What's the daft bast'ad *wearing* mind?' The Smith marvelled.

'I don't know. I couldn't say,' I replied. Probably my mouth was hanging open like a shark knocked on the head.

Apart from that hippie blouse, the reporter wasn't wearing much. He'd got a brand new pair of red *Doc Marten's* boots – I'd enviously noticed the box at home- and he had his skinny white legs poking out of those. His silky hair was streaked with red dye and pushed up. The colour had to be washable type, because he was afraid of upsetting Beer Belly and Back Slapper at the office. For them CND, punk rock (and all things deviant or lefty) was worse than the Masons or the Klan.

'What's he trying to do? Prancing around, looking like that?'

'Don't ask me, marra,' Roy told me, shaking his tangled mop in amazement.

'This is bloody terrible,' I remarked.

'Ai man, he doesn't seem to have much of a clue. Not a clue, marra.'

Roy's breathing became worse. This time it wasn't just a smoky atmosphere.

Responding to the audience, Dennis recovered his percussive touch. He had amazing talent on those skins and rims. Steve got the swing of the sound and put down some vital bass lines. Anna returned on stage and there was space to make a few creative mistakes. Only the presence of those cooing and crooning backing singers was risible. *The Supremes* they were not.

Paulie was far too passionate with the mic. And his songs caused distress and confusion to many people. The words were disguised by extreme volume and bottom-end vibration.

> *Rasta, rude boy, the rebel*
> *Out on the streets at night*
> *Gettin in to the fights*
> *For love and justice mighty*
> *Just trying to make the peace!*
>
> *Oh, Rasta, rude boy, rebel*
> *Looking for love and light*
> *The racists full of spite*
> *Kicks you in the balls*
> *Home to bed you crawl!*
>
> *Oh, Rasta, rude boy, rebel*
> *Get to reach your heaven*
> *Make the socialist decision*
> *Give the world a hug*
> *Kiss your girl on the rug!*

If he was terrible, could it have been in a sublime way? Like Deborah Harry's blonde streak or Joey Ramone's trousers? The local punks had to work out where they stood. It was too early for me to write a review. If Wellington got the band on the John Peel show, it could be a clincher.

At the end of 'Rude boy Rebel' Viscous Kittens segued into a more experimental number, incorporating dub effects.

Decibel! Decibel!
Feel the vibration
Punk and reggae nation!

Decibel! Massive decibel!
Shake me to ma foundations
White and black dub stations

Decibel, oh big decibel!
Get my people high
Sexy revolution style!

A final 'decibel' resounded and ricocheted, as the Kittens ran out of any more tunes to play. Paulie would need to sit down at the kitchen table and sweat out a few more tracks for them.

Viscous Kittens didn't get too much rough treatment by punk rock standards. Maybe it was a case of confused musical identity for them, or just – in Paulie Wellington's case – confused identity.

22. Mortal Rocked

Meanwhile (stage rear) Mortal Wound was in the middle of yet another bust up. Even while he was on stage (where you'd think he'd be harmless) Wellington was having a wrecking influence on Nulton's punk rock community.

Herb refused to play music (or anything) with Anna-kissed. They'd been an item from their first year at college. To other students and teenagers they seemed like an inseparable couple, always together. That was until Wellington's and her eyes met across a sprung dance floor. Moments later they were making back to her place. Her parents were away on a golfing weekend. Herb was occupied at a Hairdressers' convention in Hartlepool.

In the ramshackle dressing room, Herb was smarting, 'Why are you sleeping with that blonde sensation? He puts highlights into his hair, by the way. You didn't think it had *natural* lights, did you? I never want to play with you again!'

She gave an outraged and confused laugh. 'Stick your bass right up your bum!'

'Why do you have to shag that idiot? What's wrong with a bit of loyalty?' the bassist objected. 'We've been together so long. I trusted you. Couldn't you resist?'

'We're not The Carpenters,' Anna-kissed told him.

'They were siblings!'

'C'mon lads, cut out all the feckin *arg*-ments. We've still got a gig to play or did you forget!' Billy objected. Grabbing his towels and rubbing his hands in talcum powder, the band's mighty drummer was ready to roll.

The musical couple didn't give a middle-eight for such advice. Herb didn't yet grasp the truth that Paulie never stayed long with any of his girlfriends. One night stands were his usual score. By the next morning these girls were already as much toast as what they were eating. Roy and I knew it, because obviously, we'd often join them at the table. It was almost a 'fact of life' that our cherubic superstar had the erotic memory of a swatted mosquito. So if Herb could just forgive and forget that incident Mortal didn't need to suffer. The scandal would blow over quicker than a Ramones song –only less memorably!

The rest of the group was caught up in their row for a while. The entire Mortal come-back gig was put at risk.

'What we gunna do?' Nutcase agonised. 'We an't got a band no more.'

'No sweat Nut. We'll go out and abuse the audience. Maybe we'll have another riot,' Stan argued, smirking and strumming.

'Any more broight ideas from you now, Stan bay?'

He could have devised a new line-up, exploiting Gina's multi-musical talents. Sadly, while the punk pair was in crisis, Sour Cat was busy getting wrecked upstairs. Nulton's answer to Joni Mitchell was busy pouring more petrol on to the fire. The Smith and I should have kept a closer eye on her.

At some point Gina remembered that she was in a band, and that they were due to play. Or maybe one of the *Hatter*'s drunken sexist oafs got a bit too personal. Anyway she staggered in to them, bleary eyed and confused. She got a full blast of teen frustration.

Snot looked up, 'Fuck me, if it ain't Tina Turner.'

It was a poor taste joke, even for Stan.

'Where you been, Gina? Are you going to explain yourself?' Herb challenged. He was still riled from his romantic duel.

'Clearing my head,' she proposed. Vodka was written all across her face in original Russian.

'Until you're out of your skull,' Anna-kissed complained, in disgust.

'What about it?'

'That's really professional of you, isn't it,' Herb told her.

'Professional musicians are killing music,' Snot said.

'I don't need to be sober,' she claimed. 'To play in *this* band.'

'Obviously not,' said Herb.

'My tunes are moronic enough,' Snot said. 'So she's pissed. What's the problem?'

'Thanks Snot, you're a gentleman.'

'C'mon, lads. Feckin hurry up, will ya'all, now? We're got to get out there and play so!'

'Not with me,' Anna-kissed insisted.

'Without a trained bass player, you're sunk.'

'You're a feckin nob you are bay!'

'You *need* me,' Herb insisted.

'If you play with Kittens, you're out,' Snot told her.

The band was under severe stress, as the mob awaited. Mortal Wound wasn't yet so famous as to read about their disasters (as triumphs) in music paper gossip columns.

'I can play the guitar parts. All of them. A piece of cake,' Gina said to them, gagging and wobbling.

'Just because you can play *Flight of the Bumblebee*!'

'You're thinking of taking my place? Didn't you call me a friend once?' Anna-kissed said.

'Why don't you all snog and make up?' Snot suggested.

'Ai, Gina plays guitar better'n you lads now.'

'Go and lay some more bricks!'

'Feck off.'

'The show goes on,' Snot said.

'I can't stand any more a this fuckin arguin,' Nutcase complained. He covered his ears and slumped on the bench.

'This group isn't credible without me,' Herb said.

'What yer talkin' about, yer feckin nob!'

'Gina can play bass,' Stan insisted.

'The fuck will she!'

'She can play a nose-flute,' Anna-kissed complained.

'You couldn't even play *that*,' Gina cut back.

'Herb and Anna are out of my band.'

'Oh right Stan, maybe we're going to do that!' Herb snapped.

'I can cover all the guitar parts,' Gina explained.

'If you're playing my guitar bits, then I'm out.'

'She's out,' Billy commented.

'Not just out of tune,' Gina remarked. She giggled.

'Go hang… in your bloody guitar strap.'

'I quit,' Herb shouted. 'Did you notice?'

At the moment of grave crisis and potential eye-gouging, Marty Gorran arrived into the dressing room to sort them out.

'Hello, hello, what the fuck in a tank is this? Straight up you lads, what exactly in the name of blinkin Johnny Cash might be going on in this changing room?'

The charismatic DJ and hustler projected amiable bafflement. In this situation he came over as the big brother you'd never wish to disappoint.

'We're breaking up,' Anna-kissed said, looking away.

'Gord 'elp us, are you gonna explain this to me, cos how do you expect me to arrange a big tour on the blinkin London pub circuit, if you're busy cutting your own bloomin throats?'

Marty threw the great rock 'n' roll swindle at them. Suddenly the Mortal members were looking about in shame, fiddling nervously, avoiding his gaze and each other's.

'Right, definitely, then why don't you lot get your blinkin instruments and get on bloomin stage? No bullshit, before those psychotic punks wreck the place and Dave Crock's got my bloomin guts for his bedroom curtains,' he said, with a warning grin.

In fact Crock was standing out in the *Music Box* at that moment. He'd find himself out of pocket and in a vengeful mood if his DJ cancelled. The consequences were more unpredictable than the punk rock movement itself.

Neither Herb nor Anna had any sympathy for Gorran's troubles, as they promptly left the dressing room, going in separate directions (for a while).

* * *

Snot remained in confident and smug mood, while trying a new opening riff. He knew that Gina could pick up any stray bass line from Herb. He was eager to try Uncle Luigi's guitar on a live audience. Although Nutcase was upset by this rumpus, he would soon start to relax. Billy Urine knew how to relieve tension by smacking the lights out of his skins. They all wanted to keep Mortal alive and possibly Marty too. It was all about taking the cue, striking an opening chord and jumping in to scissor kicks.

After a stressful set with Viscous Kittens, Steve Fenton offered to lend his bass to Gina. In readiness Billy flexed his rippling arms and exposed the iron filings of his bare chest. Gina was wearing ripped fishnets, a *Lurex* 'space girl' blouse and a pink tutu that failed to cover her arse. Quickly and clumsily she touched up her cosmetics and hairstyle. She had no time to sober up, so she was well and truly smashed. I wondered if this was representative of classical music: even if they knew how to sit still.

Some hardened musicians could play well drunk. So to speak, they took it all in their stride. Stan and I frequently caught punk acts doing it badly. It could be entertaining to watch a shambolic band, new or established. I wasn't sure how Sour Cat was going to cope. We'd never seen her playing rock music live. But after all this was a punk group.

It happens that, when performers leave the *Hatter*'s artists' dressing room (rudimentary as it was) to make for the *Music Box* stage, they needed to negotiate a long, ill-lit and cluttered corridor. Gina was following behind the others in that direction, very dizzy with booze and (worse) turning rigid with stage fright.

Snot noticed her lagging behind. 'Hurry up Gina,' he called. 'You'll be late for the encores.' Snot being nerveless on stage, he was taking the lead; his hunched gait in shadow and that guitar slung over his shoulder like a rifle.

What happened was, at this point, Gina's stiletto heel got caught at the top of a set of steps. As she was straggling, none of the other lads could rush to break her fall. Tumbling down in a clatter of limbs, the back of her head struck the last concrete step.

There was a sickening *thwack*. Startled, the rest of the band turned to see her, in a heap. Gina was crumpled and the borrowed bass was snapped in two. To begin with they feared she'd broken her neck or something. It looked as bad as that. Their panicked voices echoed into the dingy corridor.

'*Tawk* to us, Gina,' Nutcase urged. The giant shouter was down on his knees, cradling her, squeezing her miniature hands (compared to his).

'Oh jeysus! Speak to us, Gina, will yer!' Billy despaired.

'Right, definitely you lot, no bullshit, what you doing fucking loitering back here? Fair play, there's a gig to play tonight,' Gorran called, as he rushed to investigate.

'It's Gina, Marty, she's taken a nasty bump to 'er 'ead,' Nutcase explained.

'Gord elp us, and it's no bloomin wonder is it, when she's been knocking back that blinkin orange juice. No bullshit, like all the fruit farms got fucking frostbite,' he pointed out. 'Why didn't one of you punks keep a weather bloomin eye on her up there?' he complained, kneeling down to the side of his stricken musical genius.

The band was too occupied in trying to revive her.

'No bullshit, somebody go and call a blinkin ambulance,' Marty concluded.

* * *

Unnecessary to report, there was no Mortal Wound revival that night. Marty had to call on Turbo Overdrive as last-minute replacement. Lucky that Turbo's vocalist, Rob Shaw, was in the venue. Along with the group's guitar hero, Spike Murray, he agreed to play a set. The heavy rock duo teamed up with Billy and Steve. Together they formed a decent scratch group.

The sudden change didn't impress punks, suede heads, casuals, Goths or even fascists for that matter. They'd all turned out to see the return of Wound. The regular *Hatter* drunks and psychos didn't care who was on, so long as they got some entertainment. Dave Crock couldn't distinguish one wall of white noise from another. It didn't matter so long as he collected enough door money. His snooker men threw a group of Casuals out through the back fire escape (hauling them up to the second floor first), when they dared to ask for a refund.

A rumour spread about how Snot had taken a heroin overdose and collapsed before the gig. To my knowledge he never tried that drug or scotched the rumour. The local music cognoscenti related how he'd been rushed to hospital for a clean-up.

A make-shift Turbo Overdrive wasn't as slick as usual. The gig was too loud for audience complaints. Like a jumbo jet warming up in a tiled bathroom, technical problems were masked. Spike and Rob always put on a hilarious show. They didn't leave their macho moves and camp routines at home. I wasn't in the venue to watch them at that point.

Turbo was another *Star Materials* act entered into the Battle of the Bands. They had a decent chance of winning. They intended to blow the local opposition away. They took their Led Zep, Hawkwind, Sabbath and Purple influences at high velocity.

No, you couldn't dismiss their chances. We feared that Mortal Wound was finished after Gina's bad accident. They would be forced to go back to their day jobs or get a grant for university or, more likely, sign back on to the dole queue.

23. Cat Hospital

If not for youth culture in Nulton the emergency services would have been out of work. Paramedics swooped on the club and didn't even pay a fiver to get in. The snooker men stood back for a while.

We managed to bring the punk princess back around. After checking on her senses, the ambulance crew lifted and moved her, with a baby blanket over her lurid outfit. Gina's face seemed to be a narrow mask of pain. My heart fell into my boots at the sight.

Turbo Overdrive were already on stage as replacement headliners. Their heavy rock pounded the entire building, in a soundtrack to our panic. Gina was taken out on a stretcher and slid into the waiting ambulance. The medic team climbed back with her and whisked her away to the punk repair shop. As a siren bounced and faded around the downtown district, all the voyeurs slowly returned inside the *Hatter*. In the end there was only me standing out there, staring down the street after her, at the receding siren and lights.

The following day Gorran organised a hospital visit. I arranged to meet him beforehand at his workshop. As usual his workplace was crammed with signs in progress, paints and inks, paper and card, tools and materials. I always associated our friendship with those materials and the pungent smell of Cow's Gum glue. Locking up shop early we set off to pick up the others.

Marty, Snot, Nutcase and me turned up at the *Prince of Wales' Nulton and Duncehead General Hospital*, right on cue for evening visiting time. Out of the Mortal posse only Billy Urine was absent. Billy had got well-paid work on a new housing site. In those days Irishmen still worked on building sites, rather than web sites. Of course Herb and Anna-kissed were off in a huff, bothering the manager with late calls. Nutcase didn't soften his style for the visit; he turned up in bondage trousers, chunky dog collar and that green Mohican, which made him look about seven feet tall. His dog's collar was another luxury accessory from *Boots* the chemist: *Boot's did* have a pets department in those days. Nut would pop in to make his purchase, even in normal work clothes, after knocking off early. He went up to Pets' (they didn't stock actual live animals) and picked a nice chunky canine collar. The assistant asked, 'Can I put that into a bag for you, young man?' 'Ah, no fanks, it's all right,' Nut explained. 'I'm gonna wear it now.'

The Mortal crew created a stir at hospital reception. Obviously doctors and nurses hadn't got much direct experience of punks. Only what had been filtered through the tabloid press, *Nationwide* or the Bill Grundy dust up, like everybody else. Or what was beginning to file through *A&E* at weekends. Luckily they remembered how Gina had been dressed on arrival.

Marty had his eccentricities, which always made people sit up a bit or startle. On the other hand he did have a proper day job – he worked and made something for a living. He applied those winning grins to reassure the hospital staff. He knew how to turn the schmooze to full volume. Not even the NHS could resist Marty's rock 'n' roll charisma. He gave them the idea that he could run the health service better than anyone. He'd got all the self-confidence, the know-how and the contacts. So they let him pass, and us lot with him.

We set off down a big mixed ward, which had that whispering tea-trolley atmosphere. Our assorted appearance turned heads and froze conversations. People were gawping at us, digging elbows into each other. The reaction was either fear or laughter, as we picked off the aisle and passed by.

We found Gina in one of those iron framed beds of the period, with bedclothes like stationary. Her head was turbaned up like a Sikh. She was even paler than usual, very tired, black-eyed – not from cosmetics. Her greyish blue eyes opened as our arrival stirred her attention.

'Hello, *hello*, Gina love. Straight up, we all popped down to the hospital together to find out how you're fucking doing,' Marty said in greeting.

And he posted himself at the foot of her military bed. He radiated more caring authority than Consultants on their rounds.

'Glad you could come,' she told us, meekly.

'How yer doing?' Stan asked, hunched and sniffling. They'd amputated the guitar from his hands for a few hours.

'Break a leg!' Cat told him.

'Ow yer doin?' Nutcase wondered, shuffling closer, blocking the view.

'Not too bad, Nut. Kind of you to ask. But I'm getting a bit of a headache.'

'Right, definitely Gina, never mind that, you gave us all a blinkin heart attack last night. No bullshit, why'd you want to throw yourself off the top of the fucking stairs like that?'

'I'm feeling a lot better,' she said pointedly.

'Do you remember anything about it?' I asked.

Gina's lovely gaze burnt a hole through me. 'Not much, Bottle. I only came around this morning. I just remembered… picking up Steve's bass… leaving the dressing room and walking into the corridor… at the *Hatter*… nothing else! Except now I have a big lump on the back of my head. You can't see it under this. I felt sick when I opened my eyes…'

'Right definitely, Gina, so did that paranoid little doctor back there give you any idea when you can start blinkin gigging again?'

'Are you serious or what?' She jolted up in protest.

'No bullshit, am I blinkin serious? Straight up, when we got this big London pub tour with Doctor Feelgood and the Rods on the bloomin horizon? When we need to get this blinkin little punk band on the road again, quicker than Frank Sinatra can change his suit.'

'I'm much better, Marty, thanks for asking,' she said. She bounced on the mattress a bit. And hospital mattresses didn't have much bounce then.

'She just needs to change her bandages,' Snot suggested. 'Or sprinkle a bit of blood on them.'

Gorran conducted her from the bottom of the metal bed. 'Right, definitely, I'd already got all these big name fucking promoters lined up. No bullshit, Gina love, we're all excited to see where you'll go next. Straight up, we all want to see you 'op back out of that hard bed quick as bloomin possible.'

'Well, okay. Let's see how it goes.'

'I 'eard you walkin' be'ind me. Next minute… I looked back. Your 'igh eels in the fuckin air,' Nutcase recalled, shaking his intimidating crest.

Nut hadn't slept all night. He was sensitive, he felt everything keenly; except when he was performing under a hail of missiles and spit.

'When I woke up again, it was like the Screamers had been playing in my head all night,' Gina told us.

'Right, definitely, that would explain almost everything,' Gorran agreed, with a laugh.

'I could hardly put my head on the pillow,' she said.

'Not surprising. We thought you'd gone and croaked on us,' Snot remarked.

'You was out cold. We was worried,' Nut pursued.

'She still looks very pale and tired, doesn't she,' I added.

My friends all gave me a certain look.

'Right, definitely Bottle, but our Gina always looking blinkin pale,' Marty reminded me. 'Straight up, that's her bloomin style.'

'Lucky I only fell on the *back* of my head,' Gina joked.

'Right, definitely.'

'Anyway, you're looking brilliant now,' I said.

Immediately I regretted having made that comment.

Nevertheless she managed, 'Thanks, Bottle. I've definitely got my head screwed on,' she added.

We all attempted to find some levity in the remark.

'When are they going to discharge you?' I asked.

She was looking brighter, while enjoying hiding under covers. 'The doctor told me I'm under observation. I should stay in a bit longer.'

It wasn't music to the pop guru's ears. 'Straight up, I don't care about that, cos you gotta watch these blinkin handsome young doctors, waltzing around these wards just wanting somebody to fucking practice on,' Marty warned.

'Sorry Marty, no band practice tonight,' she told him.

'Right, definitely, so what's the point of me booking Mortal in for a week at the Marque Club with X Ray Specs? No bullshit, what's blinkin Eddie and the Hot Rods going to say?'

'For fuck's sake, Marty. Do me a favour,' she objected. She threw another chocolate into the black circle of her mouth.

Nutcase blushed and looked around in embarrassment.

'She lost consciousness,' I reminded him.

'Yeah, not her fucking voice,' Snot said.

'No bullshit Snot, without Gina your group got as much hope as a three legged donkey at a fucking greyhound track,' Gorran argued, suffering a facial tremor.

'Any roads, Gina's lookin' better, int she,' Nutcase insisted.

Gina had pulled the crisp sheet up to her pointy chin. 'I told you, I'm still under close observation. I'm not coming out yet.'

'Gord elp us, so how long does this go on for? Fair play, drugged up to the fucking eye balls and confined to your bloomin bed. Cos, no bullshit love, you're led there like Marianne Fateful waiting for the fucking Stones to come back home,' he warned.

'Leave off, Marty. I'm not drugged up. Just a few pain killers.'

'Right, definitely, and that's what she said as well.'

'You gonna drag her out of bed?' Stan said. 'What you going to do?'

'Give her more time to recover,' I suggested.

Marty had a big inky hand on each nob of the bed end. 'Right, definitely, and what's going on with Herb and Anna-kissed? Fair play, when I got Herb blinkin bitching about how she's gone orf with another bloke. Straight up, and Gina and Stan are pushing him about?' Marty asked.

'They resigned and I accepted,' Stan said.

'No bullshit, what's all this blinkin baloney about Anna-kissed sleeping with that bloomin reporter lad in another group? Straight up, Herby claims she picked him up in the Looking Glass the other night.'

'Herb's definitely out of the group,' Snot stated.

'That would be Paulie, wouldn't it?' I considered.

'No bullshit, get all these names sorted out. Gord elp us, I'll have to get on the phone to Abba next,' he objected, revealing the gnashers. 'Right, definitely, so who's playing blinkin bass in future?' Gorran asked, snapping some facial muscles under the tension.

'We don't know the line up yet,' Stan replied. 'Gina was meant to be on bass... for last night's gig. Before she threw herself off the stairs.'

'She couldn't help that,' I argued.

'No? She could have taken fucking precautions,' my friend argued.

'Right, so if Gina's gonna play bloomin bass for you, then who you got playing on blinkin rhythm guitar?' Marty challenged.

'Cat is,' Nutcase put in, anxiously. 'Cat's on rhythm... Int she?'

'Yeah, I can play rhythm as well,' Gina told him.

'Right, no bullshit lads, at the same fucking time?' Marty remarked, holding the grin of amazement. 'No bullshit, you telling me she's got five fucking arms?'

'Singing and playing together isn't any problem.'

'Just no keyboards or lead vocals,' Snot cut in.

'She can do backin' vocals,' Nutcase suggested.

'Gord elp us, backing vocals an' all? I can't blinkin keep up wi' you lot. Fair play should I get on the blower and have a chat to those Fleetwood dirty Mac people? See if they want a bloomin new manager. Unless old Les has flown em back from LA already and signed em up to his Red Rooster roster,' Marty protested.

'Dunt worry, Mr Gorran,' Nutcase assured him.

'Cat isn't doing the singing. That's final.'

'I'm still up for it,' Gina told their manager.

'Straight up, I might as well open my blinkin wallet all the fucking way and get Leo Sayer. Fair play, he'd got some blinkin hit albums left in him.'

'Anna wunt 'appy,' Nutcase explained. 'So she left.' His massive shoulders shrugged inside the studded leather jacket.

'She couldn't hold a note anyway,' Gina argued. She observed her toes as she wiggled them through the tight sheets.

'Right, definitely. Straight up, do you have any more fucking toys to throw out of your blinkin pram?' the rock guru wondered.

'I fink so, Mr Gorran.'

'Straight up, Nut, no bloomin good just thinking about it.'

Stan was making a show of ignoring him.

'Don't worry, I'm fully committed,' Gina told them.

'Good girl,' Nut told her.

'Right, definitely, tell me I don't have to rummage about for your original fucking contract,' Gorran suggested, pained.

'No way,' I said. 'Don't do that. Don't cancel the contract. They're still viable,' I argued.

'We're up for it,' Nutcase added.

'If we agree who's playing what instrument, then I want to stay,' she said. Obviously she was in denial about her stage fright.

'If you don't throw yourself off a roof,' Snot told her.

Gina narrowed her slate eyes. Luckily she thought better of it. 'Look, you want to share some of these chocolates? I got a truck load.'

'You already scoffed a box,' Stan pointed out.

'Help me out,' she told us. Really she was looking shocked, drained, but much better.

'Good to see colour back in your cheeks,' Nut was saying.

'You lot always put colour into my cheeks.'

'Usually green and purple.'

Then who should turn up in the ward, but her parents. While we were tucking into the confectionary like Christmas, we saw a middle-aged couple approaching. They had every right, however badly timed. I became even more conscious of the red streaks in my hair. I was naturally an alien with nervous tics too many.

'Regina? What's going on here?' the mother remarked.

What did she think?

24. First Heat of Battle

Marty couldn't get his hands completely on Gina's career. In such a way Mortal was cut down to a three-piece. That doesn't have to imply any loss of creative energy – think of the Jam or, later, the Manics – only Stan's band wasn't made that way. It was hard to lose lads such as Herb, Anna-kissed and Gina; a mix of personalities that gave the band their vital ingredients, however volatile. Somehow the group didn't fire without Cat. Everyone was dispirited during this period.

At its lowest ebb Mortal was reduced to a duo, because Nutcase didn't play any instrument, unless you counted his throat. You couldn't describe him as being a 'singer' exactly, more of a 'gate mouth shouter', like Solomon Burke or Clarence Brown, to stretch it a bit.

Even if Snot was against musicianship, he understood that Cat improved the sound and that he was always learning from her.

Over the following weeks Marty returned to the musical drawing board. Not only did he have other artists' careers to promote, such as Turbo Overdrive, but he had to pay for them. The punk impresario described the condition of Mortal as 'awful'. But he refused to push the reject button straight away. He decided to wait and see how events developed.

What was happening with Gina, following the accident at the *Hatter*? Her parents kept her away from the local music scene and us. They locked her up in her chamber music to practice for exams and auditions. She found it easy to turn back into a recluse, obsessed with scores and exercises, to avoid her problem with stage fright.

She suffered dizzy spells and headaches for weeks. She suffered Neil Young style bouts of feedback. The doctor called every day to see how she was. As I've said, this gave plenty of excuses to remain at the pianoforte. The doctor, she told me later, said how fortunate she'd been, not to suffer more serious consequences.

Our first sighting of Gina around town came much later. It was like spotting John Lennon walking about Manhattan or Joni Mitchell at her easel. One tea time Roy Smith rushed back from the Inland Revenue office, saying how he'd recognised her, carrying that electric keyboard. Most likely she was on her way to Nulton Arts, to use one of the rehearsal rooms (you could hire a room, if you had some money or hadn't been expelled). At that time she wouldn't recognise The Smith, as they hadn't been properly introduced. Gina didn't move in the same revolutionary circles as we did.

Then Nutcase bumped into her at the *Record Shack* one Saturday afternoon. She was pleased to see him, though tight-lipped while flipping through Morten Treble's new punk singles racks. These reports gave me hope that she'd recapture the original punk spirit, like a gaudy moth around the flame of a disposable lighter.

What else was going on? Marty got his office at the *Mad Hatter*. I'd regularly rendezvous with him. I began to bash out a first draft of our new *Ob-scene* fanzine. It was a hard-boiled type of writing environment. The office was a windowless, dingy concrete basement space. It was reached by going along the same hazardous corridor that had upended Gina. Not that we were bothered about the surroundings – it was cool to be underground. We were pleased to have a base, somewhere to work and scheme.

Marty thought I'd want some help to write copy for *Ob-scene*. He couldn't find another wanna be rock hack. No one was prepared to write for nothing and sometimes through the night. In that category Paul Bottle was the town's one-off celebrity music writer. Steve Fenton could hardly knock two sentences together, by his own admission. Marty pressurised him, or verbalised him, to make a contribution. Fenton would agonise for hours over putting together a piece. I'd show some mercy and offer to re-write his interview or review, often returning to his raw interview tape or notebook. That took extra work, which submerged me in my own Alphabet City, letters spinning like the New York Dolls on acid.

Nevertheless I had some brilliant times writing that fanzine. For me it was fun working through the night to meet deadlines. The memory of my brother's 'lazy sod' type insults goaded me on. After dawn had cracked the night I'd meet Marty, enjoying an early breakfast at his favourite café. This was a place called *Bet's Baps*, situated down an impossibly narrow (and wonderfully hidden) passageway in Nulton town centre. Over the bacon and eggs we'd continue to discuss how things (musical and literary) were going. Fantastic times these were. I was high from writing and the music, from the caffeine and ideas. Gorran was great company of course, full of the new music, creating a buzz of ambition. I wouldn't worry about lack of sleep, or tiredness, until a steel door of fatigue finally shut me down, as other people were going to work.

So Marty installed me as Nulton's version of the New *Musical Express* – and I had to write like one too. It was hard to keep up with Marty. He could have put Warhol into bed.

* * *

Like any legendary rock hustler, Marty understood the power and reach of the media. He knew how to play it, to call on it, to spin and manipulate and control it: even if just local media. Yet occasionally, as the fanzine came together, he leant on me to favour Robb and Turbo. It was a rare example of disagreement between us.

'Bottle mate, why don't we put my Rob on the first blinkin cover of this 'zine? Fair play, he really enjoyed those bloomin sleeve notes you wrote up for his debut single. Straight up Bottle, I promised him you'd give this record a proper boost in the first issue, so why not give him a bit of a fucking splash on the front cover? Fair play, so what would you say to that?'

'We can't do it. Sounds like favouritism.'

Stubbornly I insisted on writing my own copy, expressing my genuine opinions, without any special favour to his *Star Materials* artists. Even if they won that EMI record contract, I wouldn't turn into Truman Capote by hype.

'Otherwise the fanzine won't be taken seriously,' I argued.

Marty would work quietly and with great concentration, alongside me, designing posters, record sleeves, all types of publicity and promotional materials. Really the office contained everything he couldn't get into his workshop. Most significantly this included a filing cabinet and even a new security box, provided by Crock's son.

* * *

Journalism night classes were improving my technique. With my crush on Gina I needed a class on flirting and dating, but of course they didn't run them in those days.

Unfortunately, not long after moving our 'zine into the basement office, we suffered a potential bombshell:

'Here's an exclusive for you, Bottle. Mortal's going to split,' Stan revealed.

'No!'

'That's the way it is.'

'Don't go and do that,' I said, pleading with him.

'It's definite. Do you wanna quote?'

'Give it time. Sort it out. Call a meeting. Talk to each other.'

'What's the odds, Bottle? One band splits up and you start another one.'

'It wouldn't be the same!'

'Better!'

'No, that wouldn't work.'

'We've got to try, unless we just stop playing.'

'Have you given up on Gina?'

'Don't need her.'

'You jealous of her?'

'She can play second piano for the Royal Philharmonic, far as I'm concerned,' he grumbled.

'What about the band competition?'

'Not such a big deal.'

'Only a bloody record deal.'

'Who needs that? One of 'em's only gonna drown in our swimming pool.'

'Marty already entered you,' I objected. 'He's paid your entrance fee. You're not going to let him down?'

'Steady on, Bottle. Why are you so loyal to the Big Cheese? He owes me more than fifty quid.'

'You owe him, more like.'

'You already sound like a fucking journalist.'

'No, no, that isn't true. He's always throwing money at you... and the band! Anyway, don't you want Mortal signed up to a record label?'

'I'd rather sign on the fucking dole.'

'Try something new,' I suggested.

'I like the people down there,' he replied.

'With an A and R man coming to town, this is Mortal's big chance. You can make something of the band. Get known. Get a deal,' I argued. 'Get reviewed!'

'You're spending too much time with that motor mouth. The big cheese. You don't get it. Neither of you. This... being in a band and stuff... is only a good laugh,' Snot insisted. 'Or it used to be.'

I certainly got hot under the dog collar.

* * *

Not such a 'good laugh' if the Royal College of Music had kidnapped Gina Watson. Herb and Anna-kissed were no longer the Sid and Nancy of Nulton's punk scene. A tense atmosphere reigned at the Mansion – Stan might have cut Paulie with a knife. Especially as the cub reporter was extra cheerful as he got into rehearsals with the Kittens.

The Battle of the Bands progressed in local pubs and other venues, while Mortal was in peril. There wasn't enough time for Stan to get a new band together, not even during those punk years. Anyway Marty had already entered them as 'Mortal Wound' on the council form. The rules were strict about changes of name and personnel, once you'd played in a heat. Luckily Snot was more sensitive about losing face and credibility with his mates and associates. That Nulton music scene was very cliquey, or pathetically small, depending on your point of view.

The venue for Mortal's first heat was the *Pink Dragon*. That would be an advantage for our favourite band, because obviously it was their regular haunt. Publican Dougal was himself a punk rock fan who was keen to promote regular gigs. He'd turned the place into a haven for punks and punk bands. Dougal wasn't intimidated by punks, greasers, Mods or any other youth clan. He'd worked as a lifeguard back in his home town of Perth: he had once rescued a Japanese au-pair from a white shark by punching its nose. For Mortal a gig at the *Dragon* would be like playing our own living room – just with more reliable floor boards and a higher ambient temperature.

Stan was hostile to big music corporations (after EMI staff had refused to pack *Anarchy in the UK* and the label eventually dropped Sex Pistols like a hot Halloween pumpkin) but wanted to keep playing 'music'. We didn't know what was coming next on the punk scene (as Gina reminded us) and Snot wanted to hang in.

At this point Mortal Wound was reduced to Fenton, Nutcase, Billy and Snot. Arguably you couldn't spot much 'star materials' there. They didn't have a single girl in the band anymore. The sound wasn't enough to whet Marty's musical appetite, assuming it didn't kill off his taste buds. He asked Steve Fenton to cancel a big job at a skittle hall in Duncehead to play bass for them. At least they wouldn't embarrass the big-haired pop promoter – or would they?

The Dragon was a medium sized pub. It always had a great atmosphere and (allegedly) acoustics; and the room was packed out with amps, speakers, woofers, sub-woofers, mix desks and greaser-style roadies. When we looked at the running-order we noticed that Snot's combo was up against Turbo Overdrive, Steel Dildo, Plastic Underpants and Gob.

To my recollection, the competition's rules allowed each band to play four 'songs' in total. Many of them barely had four songs in the repertoire! There was a panel of judges who compared notes and scores. In total there would be ten first heats in the Battle, played over the summer weeks, with the top two groups in each going through. Then there was a discretionary best third place, at the judges' mercy. At the initial stage there wasn't any big record company type on duty. The presence of an A&R man (it was always a man then) would be reserved for the grand finale.

The *Dragon* was crammed with a startling variety of youth cult haircuts and outfits. After just a handful of gigs Mortal Wound had built up their following. There was anticipation, expectation as usual, for any rare gig they played – and that included me.

Despite losing that original line up – re-jigged and reduced – Mortal plugged in and 'tuned up', amid an electric mood of anticipation. Stan didn't flinch from crashing into the typical material, including *Social Worker*, *Punk Spunk* and *Storm the Garden Party*. With this band – just to cover deficiencies – Snot had an aggressive, high-volume, almost thrash-metal sound. Stan came across more macho, posturing with that guitar (admittedly a potent weapon in his hands), than I was used to. It was amplified by the bruising figures of Urine, Fenton and Nutcase alongside him, who nearly dwarfed him (apart from the sound).

Even if the crowd did go mad that night; even if musical shortcomings were masked by hormones and rebellion, alcohol and amplification; Mortal were not interesting to Marty and me. The swaggering display did not make up for the loss of their former wit and verve. The reasons for those shortcomings were obvious. They were away in a bedroom somewhere, busy with something else.

All the same, Snot carried it; he was amazing and even put in backing vocals. Billy's drumming was a demolition ball on a metronome. Fenton was putting down bass lines like slab pathing. We were grateful that a band personality came through. The uninspired chaos of Gob and Plastic Underpants didn't offer much competition. Admittedly Gob's usual singer had been taken into detention that week.

So the gig wasn't low on entertainment. It was splendid punk pandemonium. Dougal was clicking his fingers behind the bar. Unfortunately the anarchistic party was cut short. Musical disaster struck, as Nutcase's vocal cords snapped. At some point in the third chorus of *Garden Party* his voice went mid-shriek. His iron throat died in action, like a foghorn thrown into the sea. Suddenly Nut was gulping like a beached whale. Later he admitted to having had a sore throat the previous week, except that – no pun intended – he decided to keep quiet about it. 'Dint wanna let the band down,' he croaked, almost in tears. He'd tried some gargling and gentle exercises on his throat. Even so, those vocal cords were shredded as if slashed by a hedge-strimmer.

Nut stared out in despair – over the variegated cuts of the moshing punks before him. The band kept playing for a while. The whole Mortal sound ground to a halt, like a Salvation Army Band marched over the end of a pier. Snot shuffled over to Nut to find out what the problem was. It was pretty obvious to us in the pub. Despair etched into the shouter's big bumpy face, he had to abandon stage. As we know, Nutcase was a sensitive type of lad.

The gigantean screamer was at breaking point. Gorran was waiting to console him with open arms and a cold drink. The maverick was flapping a paint-spattered wallet at Dougal's bar staff, without a moment's hesitation, like any true manager. A pint of lager didn't bring the voice back though: the iron throat had been breached, like a torpedoed battleship.

Billy, Steve and Stan muscled through the last number. Talk about 'no more heroes'. Snot wasn't looking for sympathy votes, yet the judges gave them to Nutcase regardless. The band tumbled off stage in pools of sweat, too frazzled to acknowledge cheers from diehards. They got through that heat by the skin of a guitar string.

Well, Turbo Overdrive was next up and won the heat. Marty was delighted and it almost made amends for the tragedy. Turbo's charismatic, polished heavy rock was a hit with those judges. Turbo knew how to put on a great show for those guys out of the British blues revival. The group had a sardonic swagger, which adapted to the punk times and was not far removed from punk. Many almost veteran groups adjusted their sound to their times. They even tweaked their image to fit in with fashions; just as in the future rock bands transformed into electro dance outfits.

To our amazement, Steel Dildo (playing their usual jagged and furious set) came through in third position. You couldn't account for politics or taste. They should have been eliminated. Snot didn't agree with me.

* * *

Encouraged by weekly journalism classes, I began to write in to the 'readers' page' of the *Music Mail*. The title was a national weekly music paper, in an age of ink before the glossies. To my surprise they eventually published one of these letters and others followed. The subjects I chose related to music controversies of the punk period. The sub-editor came up with titles for them:

Why the Stranglers are Punk
Get Tough with Fascism in Rock
Punk Style in the North
The Caribbean Sound in Camden

These rock polemics were deadly serious to us during the period. I'd take hours writing them up, usually sat late at the kitchen table, avoiding Paulie's sorties to find out what I was doing. The very curious cub-reporter would pretend to be making another cup of tea while trying to look over my shoulder.

'So what you writing, mate?'

Anyway I got to see my name in print for the first time. That was a great thrill in that – I wouldn't claim otherwise. Every 'winning letter' would earn me a five-quid record token, to spend down at *Our Price* (not valid at the Record Shack). That was the equivalent of working a whole evening with string beans at the *Co-op* supermarket. And it impressed my mates.

I was really excited to go into the newsagent's on a Wednesday morning, picking up *Music Mail* and thumbing through to see if they'd published my letter that week. Possibly – just possibly – I'd filed my first paragraph as a music journalist.

When he found out, Marty Gorran was hyping and praising the discovery of a new celebrity rock writer in town. 'Right, definitely Bottle, so was that was your blinkin piece in the fucking *Music*

Mail I spotted this week?' he declared, beaming.

'More like a letter,' I argued.

'Fair play Bottle, *congratulations*! No bullshit, how do you get all those blinkin long words down on the fucking paper like that? Yeah, definitely, I've got plenty of ideas in my blinkin head an' all, but I can't express them on bloomin paper the way you can.'

I shrugged, then lost for words.

'Right, definitely Bottle mate, you got a fucking talent to make the blinkin music come to life for us,' he said, as if in wonder. 'So, no bullshit, why didn't you mention something about your bloomin *gift*? How you got writing copy for the bloomin *Music Mail*?' Marty took in the miracle and grinned gratitude at the god's gift.

Of course it was a bit overwhelming and embarrassing. 'Well...' I floundered.

From that point Gorran spread my rock writer celebrity status around town. Everyone assumed I that I had to know what I was talking about. Marty was convinced that my journalistic fame would raise his own profile even higher. It brought music-biz world domination a few stages closer. It propelled his whole *Star Materials* publicity bandwagon.

So when we were in the pub: 'Right definitely everybody, have you been properly introduced to my new Editor-in-Chief at Star Materials' publishing? Straight up lads, you didn't know how our mate Bottle's been writing fucking feature articles... for, no bullshit, fucking *Music Mail* down there in blinkin London.' For him it was true because it had to be. We lived this collective half-fantasy. Arguably it was no more real or fake than any other scene.

What's more scary is that I soon got used to this role. Every local band wanted me to review or interview them. They were convinced I could get something into *Music Mail*. My nose only had to show around the *Dragon*, before lads in bands came and approached me for publicity. They'd try to bribe me with free drinks or, sometimes, even press bags of dope and tabs of acid on me. Gorran boasted how Paul Bottle was now, not only one of his closest sidekicks, but also a *staff writer* for *Music Mail*. Thanks to him this was a well-known fact, and added to the frenzy.

'Right, definitely Bottle mate, so what's your blinkin opinion about this new group?' Marty would say. He'd say this in front of our punk crowd in the pub or club; clearing a space for my wise words. 'Straight up, fucking listen up everybody, and get the opinion of our own blinkin *Music Mail* reporter,' he warned. After a while I got used to these plaudits and stopped giving a jump of alarm when all eyes turned in my direction. The background boy was put in the spotlight.

Well, I was famous for almost fourteen minutes.

25. Nutcase Spends More Time With His Family

In contrast to my growing reputation as music mag sage, Snot didn't have any reasons to be cheerful.

The reduced band didn't improve or develop from playing several more gigs. Unlike the (sometimes) shambolic groups that Snot and Gorran championed, such as the NY Dolls, Flamin' Groovies, The Stooges and even Velvet Underground, they didn't have glamour or develop a buzz. Mortal Wound had certainly lost their dynamism and edge since that riot at Nulton Arts. You could say they were riding their luck, or taking a ghost train to obscurity.

In the evenings Stan would lock himself up in the bedroom to practice; brooding, hiding his doubts. He continued to rehearse every weekend at Crock Sound with the survivors, without any sign of excitement.

Another hammer blow fell when Nutcase decided to retire on health grounds. Like some cabinet minister bonking his secretary or the nanny, Nut announced that he was going to spend more time with his family in future. Anyhow, Nutcase put in an emotional early-hours phone call to Billy. Stan and I went to the Nut's place, intending to persuade him to change his mind – along with his future singing style.

We sat around a very bare looking front room, listening to another version of his resignation speech. He worked as a plasterer, with some painting and decorating. The family had recently moved into this house, to be fair to them. Removal crates were taking the roles of armchairs.

'The missus is 'avin 'er baby in a coupla months,' he explained. 'There's a lot of work to do. I still ain't painted the kids' room.'

'You had time for the band before,' Snot complained.

'So when you've finished decorating, you can come back,' I hinted. I could hear my voice echoing like a Scott Walker record – *Scott 3*.

Despite being crestfallen, Nut's green Mohican still touched the ceiling. He hadn't shaved it off in protest or anything, which we took as a hopeful sign.

'Sandra dunt want me playin' no more gigs. She dunt like me bein' late nights,' he said. There was a wobble to his damaged voice.

'You fucking love the music,' Snot objected.

'Fanks Stan, mate. I gotta fink of the wife and kids.'

'Mortal fucking needs you. How are we gonna replace you?'

'Cheers, Stan, it scared me when I lost me voice,' he admitted, shrugging his huge shoulders like subsiding cliffs.

'We were screwed before, but now we're double screwed.' The charismatic axe man leant forward, so that his thick leather jacket – like it was made from Rhino hide – creaked in protest.

'Your voice'll come back,' I argued.

'It's been playin' on me mind.'

'Give it a few more weeks.'

'The doctor told me I 'ad to rest up. Sandra told me to listen. The doc said I need to fuckin' shut up. Or I'll lose it permanent.'

'What do the doctors know about fucking vocals?' Snot remarked.

'He said I got fuckin colics.'

'Don't you mean fucking *polyps*?' Snot corrected.

Nut scratched that huge boxy chin, staring out miserably to space.

'I don't suppose you got many vocal cords left.'

'I dunt know, mate.'

'You're part of the Mortal sound.'

'What would the Pistols be like without Rotten? Or the Buzzcocks without Pete Shelley,' I burst out.

'Cheers, Bottle.'

'What are the Pistols like without Matlock?' Snot said.

'I dunt want to stretch it. Me voice.'

'No, no… course not, Nut… but give it a try.'

'You've got to train your voice,' I suggested. 'That's what Gina warned you about, wasn't it. You'd damage your cords if you abused them. She said you'd got to warm them up.'

'Fucking Gina.' Snot gave me a look.

'I'm too busy on the estate.' Nutcase shrugged and parked his enormous boot on a box opposite.

'Get your polyps snipped off and see how you feel,' Stan argued.

Nutcase was pessimistic. 'We'll see ow me and Sandra get on wiv the noo baby.'

'Oh, yeah, the new baby...' Snot had a gloomy look as if he going to change nappies himself.

'Mortal's a great little band. I'm gonna miss it.'

'You're a fucking original blues belter,' Stan praised.

'It ain't been easy.'

We sat with mugs of tea. There was a pink tricycle in the hallway, belonging to Nutcase's first kid. The kid's tricycle seemed to be the only domestic object on view. The former tenants had taken everything with them, down to light fixtures and kitchen pipes – *de-decorated*.

'Gina can sing for yer,' Nutcase suggested.

'Don't mention that girl to me.'

'Why not?'

'We haven't seen much of her... apart from a big bump on the back of her head,' Stan recalled.

'She really went with a bang,' I remembered. Mortal as a whole was going with a bang.

'She 'ad a great voice, Stan.'

'Not our type.'

'No?'

'No. She hasn't even called me up or nothing,' Snot informed him.

'Nah?'

'Not a peep.'

'What the 'ell's 'appened to 'er?'

'It's her stuck-up fucking parents, isn't it,' Stan said, 'keeping her bloody prisoner.'

185

'They won't let 'er out the 'ouse?'

'Chained her to the fucking piano.'

'Until she's note perfect,' I said.

'She sings like a fuckin angel,' Nut recalled, generously.

'That's the fucking trouble, isn't it,' Stan retorted. 'Who wants an angel in this band? It's like putting fucking Judy Collins in fucking Motorhead.'

'It's got to mellow one day,' I said – selfishly.

'She's a caged canary.'

'You wanna let 'er out,' Nutcase advised, eating another Garibaldi biscuit and rubbing crumbs off his great mitts.

'How are we going to do that? Who do you think she is, Patty Hearst?'

'I dunno, Snot mate.' He began to pull on his rubbery ears. As if the multiple piercings were itching.

'She's got other priorities,' I objected.

'The band doesn't compare to the Royal Philharmonic, or whatever that bunch of arseholes call 'emselves these days.'

'Give her a chance to sort out her problems at home,' I argued.

'You mean like *you* did?' Stan told me.

'That's different,' I replied.

'Anyway, maybe you'd like her to move in with you?' Snot jibed.

I shrugged and blushed, like a kettle turned on with no water. Oddly the image of Paulie came into my head.

'If only she 'adn't got pissed or wore them 'igh eels.'

'She's far from being punk.'

'You're too rough on 'er. An' she plays keyboards great,' Nut said.

'Fucking bollocks.'

Each of us attended to our own thoughts. With just a bit of percussion from the direction of the kitchen.

'I can't do any vocals. I can't fucking sing,' Snot declared finally.

'No?'

'I can't even scare anybody, Nut, the way you can.'

'I'm fucking sorry about it, Stan mate. Honest.'

26. Marty has his Loot Stolen

Days after Mortal lost their vocalist, musical heaven collapsed on *Star Materials* as well.

Somebody or bodies had broken into our new 'office' at the *Hatter*. Marty and I turned up for another night shift as usual. We discovered a scene of carnage as I switched on the single naked light bulb. My typewriter was twisted up into positions it was never designed for. Marty's art work in progress had been torn and scattered. All the desk drawers and filing cabinets had been emptied and vandalised. This depressing scene provoked Marty into riffs of agony and despair.

But, as we stared at the ruins, there was even worse. Marty realised that his new safe deposit box had been prised open. Rushing over and giving it a futile shake, he realised that the entire *Star Materials'* deposit (for band entry fees and fanzine printing) had been stolen. That theft had been the main intention of the break-in. All the destruction was gratuitous and meant to be a type of decoy.

'They've torn up my writing… all my articles,' I told him.

'Straight up Bottle, forget about your bloomin articles. How are we gonna enter all our blinkin bands, when we got bloomin tom diddly squit to enter em all with?' he bewailed.

'Maybe I've got some rough drafts at home,' I replied, sorting through scraps of paper.

Marty's nocturnally porous features – voluntarily deprived of light, sleep or boredom – were contorted into despair and strangely flushed. Of course his hair stood on end naturally – but now it had good reason. He began to sift and assess the damage. He got caught in a physical battle with his best draughtsboard, while attempting to reassemble it, which he eventually had to throw away in a heap.

'*Gord 'elp us, who's responsible?*'

I pressed unhelpfully, 'Why keep your money down here?'

'Right, definitely, *where did you think I'd keep it?*' he grimaced, keeping tolerant.

'How much did you have?' I wondered. 'Altogether?' Like Jean Genet's lost first draft on prison toilet paper, I was still clutching at shreds.

'Straight up, there was more than five hundred bloomin quid, when you added it all together,' Gorran admitted.

Such a massive sum forced an involuntary whistle. 'So was that a good idea?'

'Right Bottle, you think we'd put it with the blinkin high street bank or something? In the fucking *building society?*' Gorran said. He winced with incredulity at my financial naivety.

'Why not the building society? That's where I put five pounds of my Co-op wages, every week,' I explained

Marty gave me an old-fashioned look. 'Right, definitely Bottle, go and line their blinkin pockets. No bullshit, while they lend it back to you from their fucking sun beds,' he argued, forcing a sardonic laugh.

'Oh, right, I see.' I didn't really.

'Straight up, I had the blinkin sense to go out and buy us a strong box to keep all that bloomin money in.'

And how effective had that been?

'Straight up Bottle, I'm not Madame fucking Curie looking into the blinkin future, am I,' he objected.

'Who got in here, to smash the place up and steal our money?' I objected.

'Fair play, there was only me, you, Steve Fenton and that Smithy who knew about our bloomin loot,' Gorran elaborated.

'Roy's as honest as his political convictions,' I pointed out.

'Right, definitely, and those commies aren't interested in fucking money anyway, are they?' he agreed.

'Not Roy. Apart from throwing his salary at us.'

'Fair play, it couldn't have been Steve Fenton, because he hasn't taken a postage stamp off me, all the time I've known him, even though he used to do some bloomin breaking and entering in his time,' Gorran said.

'Really?'

'Straight up, in the past, fucking years ago, in his blinkin spare time, he did.'

'Dave Crock could use your five hundred quid.'

'No bullshit, I've seen Dave Crock put five hundred fucking quid into a blinkin fruit machine, before now,' Marty informed me. 'Straight up, just to check they're blinkin working.'

'Well, maybe he owned those fruit machines.'

'Right, definitely, *of course he fucking owned them*, Bottle. But, fair play, you need to be bloomin careful what you say about Dave Crock and his family. Otherwise you could end up like that blinkin Graham Gross.'

'Point taken,' I said, while beginning to tidy the office.

'Straight up, I reckon this must have been an inside job somewhere down the blinkin line,' Gorran argued. 'There's no sign of a break-in here far as I can see.'

'It wasn't us. We proved that.'

'Right, so we've got our bloomin suspicions. Only we still want to be careful about making any big fucking accusations against Dave Crock and family.'

'So he had a key to your safe box? Is that what you're saying?'

'No bullshit, our lives have got to be more bloomin valuable than you think. Straight up, your life's more precious than five hundred blinkin quid, if you understand me,' Marty warned, grimacing. 'Less you want to wake up in the middle of the night with some blinkin ugly mug putting double barrels up your fucking nostrils.'

'You don't have to be Kojak to work that one out,' I said.

'Right, definitely, not even Starsky and blinkin Hutch,' Marty admitted.

'Your bands depend on that money. That's their entrance fees for the contest, isn't it? We've got to pay printing costs for our fanzine,' I thought out loud. 'I don't want to waste my words.'

* * *

After tidying up, as best we could, Marty and I returned to the saloon bar. I needed a vodka and coke to calm my nerves and Marty more addictive substances.

Dave Crock had taken up his central position for extra time; spraying saliva at the faces of his cronies. It was just as if Graham Gross, a legend out on the wing for Athletic, had never even pulled on the shirt.

Marty and I got within inches of the purple cauliflower nose, silvery grey ringlets and bleary eyes. Gorran told him what had happened in our office. Talk of robbery close to home almost sobered him.

'If I find art oo did it, Marty boy, I'll kick the shit art of im,' the publican promised.

'Right, definitely Dave mate, glad you're in the picture, cos we'd blinkin appreciate a clue about who pulled this off,' Marty informed him.

The ex-footballer shuffled closer, to dampen the DJ's ear. 'Wot you sayin, Marty boy?'

'Straight up, the only people that knew anything about our blinkin money was us,' he explained, leering amiably, holding his hands up. 'Right, definitely, leaving out your good self, Dave mate, and anybody you might bloomin know about.'

'Ain't got no *sus-picts*?' Crock leaned in further, red eyes narrowed, struggling to keep steady. 'Fair's fair, Marty boy, you're the fuckin moosic man… I ain't got nuffin to do wiv any fuckin stolen money.'

'Right, definitely, Dave mate, it's just about five hundred bloomin quid altogether down there.'

'No, no, I dunt go abart rippin' off me own fuckin gaff, do I?'

'Why don't we just call in the cops?' I suggested, eagerly.

The former central defender leant back uproariously. He noticed me again and took in the ridiculous sight. '*Ha, ha*, son! Call in the fuckin cops! Ha, ha. Get yer lugs over this lad.'

I didn't get it. 'Why not?'

'*Ha, ha*, young fella. *Call in the fuckin cops!*' He banged my shoulders appreciatively. 'What a fuckin laugh, you is. Where you get this funny little fuck, Marty boy? *Kinter-garden*?'

I was puzzled by his merriment.

Gorran began to look alarmed at this interchange. 'Right definitely, well spotted Dave mate. No bullshit, Bottle's got a dry sense of fucking humour. Fair play, and he's just been appointed as a new fucking staff writer for *Music Maker* magazine no less, down there in the bloomin smoke, Dave mate. No bullshit, you need a good sense of fucking humour, along with a blinkin sharp ear for new music, to write for a top fucking rock organ like that.'

Crock tried to focus and get a second look. '*Congratulations*, son. You knows yer moosic.'

Dave gave a bit of a shimmy, a surprisingly nimble move, to sink another pint. He achieved a result with a single dilation of his throat muscles. Quicker than an elephant seal sucking down a tossed fish. A barmaid banged down another pint of ale, the moment the defender's empty pot hit the counter.

'*Cheers everybody!*'

'Right, definitely, and we want some expert inside blinkin knowledge of the fucking criminal world, Dave mate… to find out who got into the office and cracked open my bloomin deposit box.'

'Dunt go an' stress yerself art, Marty boy. I'll get to the bottom of this fuckin nasty little bus'ness,' the landlord predicted.

'Right, definitely Dave, we appreciate any blinkin help,' Gorran said, unusually stressed.

'Did these fucks nick anyfin else?' The ex-footballer had a corrective hand on Marty's shoulder.

'Right, definitely, now you mention it, there was a set of my best blinkin artist's pens and brushes taken,' Gorran explained.

'It'd set a dangerous president, to let these fuckin little feeves in me club.'

'No bullshit Dave, that's what I blinkin thought and…'

'Marty knows is moosic. *You done good, boy!* You ain't no fuckin trouble. No fuckin fancy stuff neither. No fuckin megs.'

'Fair play Dave, if we lose that money we might as well jump down the bloomin crap chute and pull the blinkin cord behind us,' Marty agonised. His facial muscles snapped like a Bootsy Collins bass line.

Crock was impressed by the suffering. 'Don't lose art, Marty boy. Leave it wi me,' he suggested. The club owner gestured at the barmaid again, pulling on an imaginary tap, sticking out his tongue and tilting backwards.

'No bullshit, my lads in Turbo just put out their first blinkin single and we an't paid off all the fucking promotion costs,' Marty admitted.

'No fucker breaks inta me gaff. We'll find 'oo steals dosh from the Atter. We'll see ow the fucker likes is legs broke.' Crock drained and downed the next one.

'Cos, straight up, I didn't spot any signs of a blinkin break-in down there,' Marty said, dragging deeply and squinting through the cloud.

'No signs of a fuckin break in?'

'Right, definitely, that's what I noticed when I blinkin looked. Fair play, I reckon this must have been an inside job, Dave mate.'

'*Inside* job? Never!' Crock barked. He was scandalised.

'Straight up, that's what it bloomin well looks like to me,' Gorran argued, giving an apprehensive wince.

'*Nah, nah,* 'inside job', *impossible*, Marty boy. Fair's fair, don't give yerself a fuckin 'eart attack over this box. I'll find the fucker and break is legs,' Crock repeated, drinking up.

'Right, definitely Dave mate, but…'

'No buts, Marty boy. The only lads wot knew abart your box was… me, your lot an… my boy Troy.'

'Right, straight up, so you went and told your bloomin Troy about this blinkin strong box?'

'Yeah, e's the one what fuckin bought it! He's gotta know bout sec-urity matters in me club, Marty boy,' the publican grinned, licking foam from his moustaches.

'Gord 'elp us, Dave mate, why did you want to go and tell blinkin Troy for?' Marty wanted to know. He was grinning with cautious outrage.

For a threatening moment, the landlord sobered. '*Nah, nah.* If you got some notes stashed, Troy as to know abart it. E's me Security Man'ger. You got a problem wiv it, Marty boy?'

'Right, definitely, that's a big bloomin weight off my blinkin mind,' Gorran said ironically.

'Troy's a fuckin profesh'nal. He'll smash their fuckin faces in for yer,' Crock reassured us.

'Right, definitely, Dave mate, if we can get our money back I'd be interested to hear his blinkin side of the story,' Marty replied, unable to resist a sardonic scoff.

'My boy Troy'll sort it art. Everyfin nice, clean and p'fesh'nal.'

27. Paulie Turns Out to Have a Heart of Glass

Stan was disgusted by the Pistols when they mimed on *Top of the Pops* ('Holidays in the Sun'). This sell out or self-destruct (take your pick) was even pointing the way for other punk groups, and that might include Mortal Wound. Snot spent hours, days and nights, shut up in his room doodling on that strange guitar. Band rehearsals were 'crap' and put him into a foul mood. So he'd come back and lock himself away with a new riff: Just waiting for John Peel to come on between ten and midnight.

Something completely out of the Blues happened. By habit the three of us would stay up late (teenagers suddenly without parents or guardians) drinking and smoking, talking and watching late movies. I had got back from my journalism night school. Roy had been redistributing wealth at the tax office. He came back to the Mansion with 'bevies' for us all, from the 'Offy'. That was the real 'trickle-down effect'. During this period – while his band was unhealthy – Stan smoked away like an express train, as if trying to buckle his chest completely. Hectares of marijuana and tobacco went up in flames.

It was roundabout midnight, and Paulie was still out. Either he was on the pull, or very late back from the office. Wellington didn't keep us up to date with the swings or the roundabouts. We got the idea that his indenture as a newspaper reporter wasn't going well. Beer Belly and Back Slapper were on his case. The editors would shout, reprimand and order him to search Nulton for 'exclusive stories'. That was a thankless and futile task. Not surprisingly Paulie would gravitate towards the record shop instead. I'd bumped into him a few times in the *Record Shack*. Rather than getting any

194

story for the *Chronicle*, Paulie was hunting down the latest punk releases (hoping to take Stan by surprise), as well as the classic Al Green and James Brown funk-soul recordings that were his true taste. He'd take his new records home (he had bought himself an impressive turntable) and, inspired, practiced his bongos along to them, as well as trying to write new songs.

'We don't pay you to sit around on your arse all day,' Beer Belly told him. 'Get out and prove yourself as a reporter. Find some stories!'

In response Paulie's skin condition deteriorated, with rashes spreading up his forearms.

Despite that, his love life roared away like Aryton Senna taking a wrong turn and going down a ski jump. His conquests were as spectacularly varied as ever. He even picked somebody up during a stuffy *Nulton Chronicle* staff social evening. It was the most unpromising erotic situation you'd ever think up. At first Paulie was stood in a group of male hacks, draining the beer, trying to firm up relationships. The cub reporter soon forgot to network with them, as his attention was captivated by a Mod girl stood feeding ten pences into the jukebox. First contact achieved the two of them were leaving together. That huddle of newspaper staff, laughing too loudly, telling jokes and anecdotes, hardly noticed Paulie move. The *Chronicle* might have run the incident as a mysterious disappearance story. If only Wellington had such an eye for a story.

Roy hadn't been present for that *Chronicle* killing. Generally he turned communist red at Paulie's antics – despite egalitarian principles. He'd be fuming on the sofa and working those asthmatic lungs like ripped airbeds. Stan (who wasn't exactly Alan Bennett material either) ran cynical advance bets on the likely colour of the girl's hair, in the event that Wellington brought her back to the Mansion. 'Who's brave enough to risk a crisp fiver on a blonde?' he taunted. After a while I couldn't resist the challenge. These 'wagers' would be exchanged before the BBC played the national anthem of the 'fascist regime'.

Roy and I were obvious virgins: we could have formed a secret society of the chaste. We were both lonely and inexperienced lads, even if we barely referred to the fact. We were so revved up with hormones and frustration, with no direction to take them. Some nights we might have looked twice at a dirty mop.

Paulie Wellington was on a different planet. Obviously Planet Sex. He had no idea about our situation vis-a-vis the *opposite* sex. If he was a James Brown type sex machine it was generally on the quiet. His appeal was an unconscious gift and he had no need to brag. Well, fine, but Paulie would usually forget her name, or even the girl's face (yeah, really) by the very next day. You could describe him as a sexual amnesiac. All of this, don't forget, while he claimed to be a 'radical feminist'. If/when a girl confronted him about this, Paulie – with the forgotten experience of their amorous night – would stare back, completely mystified, chaste as a besmirched choir boy.

'*Phoo*, dodgy. She was a bit hostile. Bloody hell, what got into her?'

Smithy and I would recognise the girl without any problem. Unfortunately that didn't give us any satisfaction.

The ultimate nightmare came true one evening. It was when Paulie returned home with Gina Watson. Really. You might imagine my shock and horror when she stumbled into the flat after him. Roy choked in mid-gulp of his *Newcastle Brown* and his specs practically *shatter*ed on first sight.

'Away, Paulie, what's goin' on?' he startled.

As usual Wellington attempted to sneak around the side of the living room (it was a large space) with the girl, expecting us to either to not notice or not to be bothered.

Gina was shocked to find us there, arranged about that tawdry living room, almost as if waiting. The punk rock circle of Nulton was paddling pool sized, yet Wellington hadn't mentioned these living arrangements. Amazingly he failed to recall that Gina had been involved with Stan's band, or more. Even worse he failed to identify her, apart from her mysterious attractions. That was all too ridiculous and typical of his amorous routine. For Wellington this was just another girl who mistook him for her long-lost soul mate.

Nobody knew what to say or how to react in this situation. Only Paulie, with a theatrical type of bemusement, didn't see the problem. He was pretending to be offended, as if we were a bunch of Mary Whitehouses who had a moral gripe with Gina's natural desires.

'*This* is your place Paulie?' Gina stuttered.

'What's the problem?' he told her.

'With Stan and Paul here?'

'*Gina!*' I mouthed.

'Away Paulie, what's the big *i*-dea, man? What the fuckin' hell are you doin', bringin' her back hoom here, mind!' Indignant, Roy was up on his feet to challenge the hapless roving reporter.

Stan hadn't moved a muscle meanwhile. He just focussed on the film and said coolly, 'Welcome to our rock star pad.'

'Paulie asked me back for a… a *night cap*… Only one more, that's all,' she insisted, colouring through the pancake. 'You know, one more for the road. Why didn't you tell me about them, Paulie?'

For once she was just merry, not pissed; as if the prospect of sex didn't make her nervous at all.

'So what's keeping you? Get on up and get down,' said Snot.

'What you doing back here, Gina?' I wondered.

'We were chatting about music and stuff… and so Paulie suggested we, you know… go back to his place and, you know… listen to his Cat Stevens albums.'

'Cat Stevens? Are you sick?' Snot demanded.

'Come on, Stan. You're so narrow-minded,' she told him.

'I've got a delicate fucking stomach,' he agreed.

'This comes as a surprise. Even a *shock*,' I insisted.

Gina offered me a quick look. 'I didn't expect to find you punks.'

Afraid that he was becoming marginal to the gathering, Paulie put in: 'Okay, so you lads know each other, right? Or am I getting the wrong signals here?' He laughed dryly and nodded ironically around at us.

'*Paulie man!*' Smithy began to rage, hands on hips.

'Where d'you drag up this daffy wanker?' Snot wondered.

'*Phew*, Stan, that's really dodgy! No need to play the macho man, is there mate,' he said, starting to huff and puff.

'Did you bump into each other? This evening, did you?' I asked.

'I was at the *Looking Glass*,' Gina explained. 'You have a problem with that? I have a life away from your band. There's more to me than punk music!'

'Come on, you lads, lighten up, will you? We met each other at the disco tonight,' the reporter insisted. 'Got anything against having a good bloody dance?'

'You can't censor my social life,' Gina objected, 'or tell me who to dance with!'

She was dressed in an outrageous style; lots of bare flesh, great for the disco, showing she was a musical maverick. If I'd false teeth I would have swallowed them.

'He picked you up?' Snot remarked.

'Maybe I picked *him* up. We didn't want to end the night there.'

'Okay, are you boys gonna explain what's going on here?' Wellington demanded. He decided to keep a high moral tone with us.

'Away Paulie, when are ya ever gonna learn, comrade?' Roy demanded, boggle eyed behind the specs, and shaking his mop in bafflement.

A numb look spread over the pop idol's face and froze his angelic mug. '*Phew, Roy*, what you getting so wound up about? What's the big pickle, mate? *Who* I bring home?' he wondered.

The Trotskyite began to shake and tremble. 'What's the 'big pickle'? Ai, you really want to nooo, comrade? This lass is a friend of theirs, man. Gina's a member of their *band*,' Roy informed him. 'Of course you knew about it, comrade. *Mortal Wooond*, man! What yer tryin' to pull here, Paulie? What yer doin bringin' her back hoom here mind, yer daft bas'tad? Ai, at this time of night, man.'

'She's guitarist, keyboardist and vocalist for Mortal Wound,' I pointed out.

'Not any more, I'm not,' Gina she told me.

It was bloody hurtful. My heart was in my Doc. Marten's.

'Right Paulie, anybody else in this fucking band, past or present, you fancy?' Snot wondered.

'Why should I fancy them? You're bloody out of line, Stan mate.'

'Maybe you want to shag *me* as well? First you pull Anna-kissed behind Herb's back. You know what I'm talking about. Now you chatted up Gina and brought her back here...to hear Cat Stevens, wink fucking wink. That's good going, Paulie, isn't it?'

'Really dodgy Stan, cos it wasn't anything like that,' he insisted.

'Away, Paulie man, why don't you have more fucking sense, marra?'

'Nobody picked me up!' Gina yelled.

'Ain't it *Just Like a Woman*,' Stan sneered.

Paulie stared in open mouthed horror at his slanderers; as if the terrible truth about our characters was occurring to him. Why was he sharing a flat with these dodgy anti-feminists?

'Away Paulie, why don't you stick to one girlfriend mind... for a time?'

There was a stunned hurt look. 'What you trying to suggest, Roy mate?'

'Why are you having a go at him for? Paulie's a lovely bloke. He lifted himself out of poverty to be a newspaper reporter. Can't you admire a story like that?' Gina challenged us.

'Cheers, Gemma. I really appreciate it,' Wellington said. 'If she doesn't have a problem with this, then why do you lads?'

Snot was the only one not fazed. It proved that he didn't have his own thing about Gina! 'So your parents let you out, did they?'

Gina was standing very awkwardly before us. 'I let myself out,' she said. 'It's Gina! Or Sour Cat now.'

'Sour Cat Stevens?'

'I knew that. That's what I said, isn't it?'

'A rebellious teenager. I reckon that's the way it was,' Stan needled.

Bewildered, lips apart, Paulie tried to understand the dispute unfolding. This hadn't been part of his plan for the early hours.

'So I got strict parents. They don't like me mixing with you, do they? Who can blame them? So I have to get out of the house... After dark... after they've gone to bed.'

'They don't mind you sleeping over with this wanker?' Stan pressed.

'Fuck off, I'll deal with that,' she snapped back at him.

The Smith was pacing the creaky boards. 'Away Paulie, didn't you think whether Stan and the lads would be here, comrade? Ai, don't you see how embarrassin' it is like?' Roy fumed – his glasses steamed up. He was a risk of imploding with helpless fury.

Gina objected. Her elbows and high heels stuck out at angles. 'Hold on, Lenin. What's Paulie done wrong? Don't you allow females into this cheap hotel of yours?'

The Trotskyite tried to calm himself. 'Away, Gina man, I know Paulie can't always help it, like. Maybe he sleeps with a different girl every night, but I noo he supports the party. Paulie tries to be a good socialist mind, even if he's a complete buffoon.'

'How's your head now, Gina?' I asked. 'Clearer?'

'What?' Cat struggled to adjust to my comment. 'Oh, you know, I get dizzy spells sometimes.'

'Still looking at the world through a bottle,' said Snot. 'The bottom of a fucking vodka bottle.'

'Fuck off, will you Snot. You can't talk, with all that smoking.'

The lead-guitarist crossed his arms and concentrated back on the western movie, as if nothing had occurred.

The Smith still hadn't spoken his full piece, trying to redeem his comrade. 'Paulie man, why didn't you think aboot how our Gina's in the grooop? This isn't comradely behaviour, man.'

'All right, Roy mate, calm down, will you?' he said, observing his friend's frantic progress around the room (as if measuring how many capitalists it might fit).

'Away Paulie, I don't want to calm down!'

'You're upset.'

'I knoo I'm fookin upset!'

'She only came back to look through my bloody record collection. What's your big problem with that, Roy mate?'

'I wouldn't sleep on this sofa, Gina. Not unless you want a fucking spring up your arse,' Stan warned.

'Heard of a taxi service?' Gina shot back at him.

'Fast work, even for Paulie,' the guitarist remarked – as Victor Mature took a slug and grovelled in the dust.

Paulie affected a shocked expression. 'That's a really dodgy sexist comment,' he pointed out.

'He just asked me back…for a bit… to read the lyrics to *Just Like a Woman*,' she insisted.

They all laughed at that. It was too hilarious.

'His theme song!' Snot argued. 'I warned you, didn't I?'

'What are you talking about? Dylan's not hip any longer?'

'He gives you Dylan after his life story. After he tells how he was raised a n'orphan from Stepney,' he sneered. 'Then after that he whips off your knickers, old sparrow.'

'*Phew, dodgy*! What's your point here, Stan?'

'Away Paulie, I doon't believe my eyes, man!' Roy groped for his inhaler finally. Throwing back his head, and trying to apply vital doses of calming chemicals, he was boggling in amazement.

'He's better looking than you lot,' Gina said.

There were noises of male disgruntlement.

'Come and join us,' Snot suggested – setting off a mushroom cloud of dust.

'Don't take any notice of that dodgy bloke,' Paulie advised.

'Make yourself cosy,' Stan invited.

Gina wavered. 'What the fuck does this have to do with you?'

'Go and screw James Taylor if you want to.'

There was still a lot of shooting happening on television.

Paulie kept aloof like a slandered angel. He was convinced of superior sexual politics.

'You've got a problem about rival musicians?' Gina implied.

'Away Gina, Paulie can only play bongos, comrade,' Roy informed her.

'Don't try to be funny. Paulie's a singer and he knows a lot of instruments.'

Roy halted and shook his lank locks. '*Nooh*, he only sings and plays bongos like.'

'Why should I believe that?'

'You want him to bring them out and try them for you?' Snot suggested. He snuggled down further into the sofa, as the final reel approached.

'That's rubbish. I don't believe you.'

'No, honestly, it's just the bongos,' I confirmed.

'Fuck knows, he keeps us all awake with slapping 'em and everything.'

'What's your problem? I'm lead singer and percussionist in my own band.'

She stared into his innocent eyes. 'Bongos? Really?'

'Phew, didn't I tell you about my bongos? I've got my own band together now. Viscous Kittens,' he reminded her. 'I'm the lead singer. I play all percussion. I'm adding my female backing singers.'

'Come on, Paulie, don't be a buffoon!'

'Paulie's groupies,' Snot said, helpfully. He kept his interest on the shoot-out.

'Come to the next Kittens' gig. It's going to be fantastic,' said the bongo player.

'Yeah, maybe.' Gina allowed herself to flop into the sofa between Snot and me.

'Been up to much recently, Gina?' I enquired politely.

'This and that,' she said, without looking at us.

'Away, Gina man, do you fancy a brew?' Roy offered. 'To settle your nerves, mind?'

'Put a couple of sugars in it.'

'Hey, Bottle, you owe me a fiver,' Snot told me.

'What? How do you mean, a fiver?'

'*Blonde*! She's blonde,' he pointed out.

Sour Cat turned to give him a look.

'Ah, leave off her Stan, marra. I'll just go to the kitchen, mind. Ai, I reckon we could all use a brew now, comrade.'

'*Phoo*, I'm going to bed,' Paulie told us.

* * *

Paulie did Mortal a big favour by getting them together socially. The situation left a bad taste in the mouth – even for punk.

'I went to the *RCM*,' she told us. 'No, I didn't get in. Bastards turned me down. Smug arseholes. Never mind. It was a tight squeeze. Fell down at the audition.'

'Sorry to hear that,' I replied.

'So what's your plan, marra?' Roy asked, encouragingly.

'I applied to Leeds School of Music now. They invited me to go up and meet them. It looks a really top place,' she enthused. 'I've got some new pieces to learn for the audition. I was thinking of some Chopin, and a bit of Ellington. *Single Petal of a Rose*, maybe,' she thought. 'Oh god, I really love that piece.'

All of us lads looked at each other in bafflement.

She was upset to hear about the delicate health of Mortal. I could tell she was burning with passion for the band. She was longing for the thrill of making obnoxious noise. Whatever obstacles she faced, Gina still had the punk spirit.

As the final credits rolled for Gary Cooper, she was starting to enjoy our company again. Paulie had slunk back into his room, and the patter of bongos started up for a while. Then again, despite his success with the opposite sex, I never once heard him boasting about it. You could never accuse him of doing that. The evening was a total embarrassment for everybody, but not for him. Next morning, as he whistled over his cornflakes, the entire fiasco (and Gina) was a distant memory.

Gina eventually got a taxi back home. She had a hidden stepladder, tucked away in the back garden behind her dad's shed, to get back indoors by, without waking up either parent.

28. 'Hercules' Poirot Confronts Junior Crock

At this point we should return to the theft at *Star Materials*. Deadlines approaching, Gorran was desperate. As we know, the rock guru had debts and promises to keep. Turbo had blown their PA while playing second support to Hawkwind at Aylesbury *Friars*': a roadie had his hair singed off and tried to sue the group for compensation.

Gorran Kept up the day job and earnt fees as an in-demand DJ, but he still had to cover living expenses. He was a music impresario, not a charity. Marty didn't want to mix up *Star Materials* finances with his own. Roy advised him strongly against that dangerous idea. It was a tricky case and Marty had to solve it. He couldn't let *Star Materials* go bankrupt before getting his first number one. And Turbo wanted a new *Bedford* tour van.

One of Troy Crock's duties, as CEO of *Crock Security Group*, had been to expertly install our strong box. Troy definitely had strength to tease open a mid-price security device. In the past Troy had been a local celebrity himself, as a multiple 'Iron Man' champion. He'd dragged a fire engine down Nulton high street, live on regional TV, by a wire between his teeth. He was an ex-boxer and power lifter, even if his dad was gutted that he never made the squad at Nulton Athletic. Despite taking out five ambitious strikers in a youth trial, it still hadn't impressed the scout. Troy Boy had been too slow to drop his team mates. As a teenager he'd been a Judo brown belt; kick-boxed, cage fought, bare-knuckled, armed robbed, everything. For half a season he was captain of *Nulton Falcons* American Football Team, until he took a life-time ban.

After giving up an active role in sports Troy took on a few of his dad's pubs. He was offered a managerial position shortly after Graham Gross got woken up by a shotgun, albeit briefly. Troy developed a portfolio that included entertainment, sports and gambling enterprises; a sports centre, a sports shop and some porn shops.

'No bullshit, you don't have to be Hercules Poirot to work out who's behind this blinkin crime,' Gorran argued.

There was some circumstantial evidence. Steve Fenton had noticed Crock hanging about in the corridor outside the office. The Screamers' drummer, Brad Donut, had seen Troy with his hand on the door knob.

'So this guy must have been round six feet tall. Chubby, right? Shaved scalp? Pouty little mouth? Flat head? Cross eyes?' Brad recounted.

'Sounds just like him,' I said.

'Fair play, what would Troy Boy want with our measly bloomin five hundred quid? Straight up, he puts more'n that on his dad's fucking nag. He was blinkin bragging how he put a grand each-way on that Flying Boot at Towcester last week. The horse came in third out of a field of bloomin four and he didn't even bother to cash the fucking ticket.'

'Was it our money he was betting?'

'Gord elp us,' Gorran said, reacting with a wince.

We didn't have any other suspects in our ID parade. So what were we going to do about it? We went to have a few private words with Troy at his studios: Steve, Marty and me went along that day.

Squeezed into a new red tracksuit Crock Junior was wedged behind an enormous office desk – probably half a tree from the Amazon. He had a problem with his nose tubes that complicated his breathing, like a bull that had got its dick stuck in a gate.

'Really fuckin sorry to ear abart yer feft,' he told us, already bored.

Troy made a big show of doing his accounts books. Proud of his writing prowess, he ran down his daily bookings with a gold fountain pen, inscribed with his name on the cap. He'd an annoying habit of licking a finger and thumb before turning pages in a big ledger, checking the month's bookings at Crock Sound Studios.

'Right, definitely Troy mate, we appreciate you're bloomin busy at the moment, but we need some of your blinkin 'elp. Fair play, help us get to the bottom of all this bloomin funny stuff down in the basement,' Marty urged, with a squint and wince.

'You musta been gutted, Marty. I woo'n't criticise, if you went art and wasted those feevin fuckers,' he argued. The eyes darted up to us for a moment, before returning to the figures. 'Nah, nah, that's a lotta juice to you lads.'

'That's why we want it back,' Fenton informed him. As ever he operated straight as a telegraph pole. 'All of it.'

Troy turned up the piggy eyes with a glint of menace. 'You lads wunt me to get art my own fuckin wallet and give you a fuckin loan? Or what's this abart?'

'Right, definitely Troy mate, we appreciate your blinkin brain power, because our Steve spotted you lurking about outside our fucking office on the very day of the bloomin break-in.' The punk guru grinned helpfully.

'So how're you going to explain that?' Fenton challenged, taking a step closer.

'It was about the same time as the robbery,' I clarified.

In a surprising movement, Troy began stabbing the nib of his pen through the air towards us. '*Nah, nah*, you lads! You wanna be fuckin careful… chuckin arand fuckin accoosations,' he warned. Colouring, enraged, he brushed the surface of his buzz cut. 'You wanna show some respec' boys. No justice without fuckin proofs.'

Marty continued to grin reassuringly if painfully. 'No bullshit, we just want to know if you saw anything blinkin suspicious outside our *Star Materials* office, while you were down there at the time, Troy mate, lurking about and checking the bloomin door.'

Jolting a crick out of his neck vertebrae, shifting his bulk in the soft spring chair, Troy's brain blanked. 'Nah, not a fuckin mouse, Marty. Can't be of any assis'ance to yer. Now if you don't fuckin mind,' he suggested, shaking his wrist to move along his bracelet.

'No bullshit Troy, how can you be so fucking sure about that?' Marty burst out. Money could make him emotional sometimes.

'I could take fuckin offence at yer attitood.'

'What do you know?' Steve demanded. 'Give us the info.' The versatile bass player came straight out with this, as if ordering a plain omelette from our favourite cafe.

'Inside, artside, wotever… it ain't my fuckin problem, dick ed. Fink! What'd I wunt with five hundred poxy notes yours?' he asked rhetorically. 'That's never bin my game lads.'

Tossing down the expensive pen, Troy leant back heavily on his cushiony leather seat. A couple of deep creases formed at the centre of his minimal forehead.

'You look arter your business, Marty, an I'll look arter me own.'

'Right, definitely Troy, we hear what you're blinkin saying, but we can't afford to lose our dosh to just anyone who walks by and has a blinkin look,' Gorran said, agonising, as if picking the words from between his teeth.

The thug smoothed the front of his shiny red jacket. 'What ya tryin to say, Marty boy?'

Marty's tortured grimace set off premature wrinkles. 'Straight up Troy, if we don't recover our money my company'll be finished quicker than James Hunt splashing through a dirty puddle. So fair play, Troy mate, we're going to need a bit of your blinkin help, to get to the bloomin bottom of this.'

'Why leave yer money darn there? You stupid or wot?'

'That's your advice?' Fenton challenged. 'That's your expert opinion?'

Troy was instantly pumped with aggression. 'That's right, dick ed, listen up and wash yer fuckin mouth art.' He could have shoved another bus down the road at this point. 'My advice, take it or fuckin leave it, dick ed.'

'Fair play, Troy mate, but you're supposed to be chief blinkin security officer.'

'I dunt poke abart in fings which ain't my fuckin bus'ness. What would I want with five poxy undred? What I wunt with a lotta artist's pens? That's why.'

'Right, definitely Troy, so you know those bloomin artist's pens went missing?'

'But it dunt belong to me!'

'No bullshit, Troy mate, but I already blinkin know they don't fucking belong to you,' Marty told him, laughing dryly.

'Ain't nuffin to do wi me, Marty boy, none of it. Now, if you lads dunt mind,' he suggested. He shook out his arms, tried to get the fountain pen comfortable in his grip and dabbed the nib on his short fat furry tongue. I noticed that he already had a blue blot on the tip.

'You've some questions to answer,' Fenton argued.

'Takin the piss, dick ed? I dunt answer any moo-er yer stoopid fuckin questions.'

'Straight up, Troy, so we've had your side of the blinkin story b'now, so if you hear any suspicious fucking talk from any other bloomin local criminals, no bullshit, we'd be grateful if you told us about it,' Gorran suggested.

'I ain't makin no promises.'

'Right, definitely, cos if we don't get our money back I might have to pack up my blinkin turntables at the *Hatter* for good,' Gorran warned.

Suddenly Junior Crock looked concerned. 'Stop yer DJ-ing? Stop pullin in the punters? *Nah, nah*, Marty. You dunt wanna think abart it. What ud me dad say?'

'No bullshit Troy, you'd better go and blinkin ask him, cos I've got this bloomin Battle of the Bands jamboree coming up. Fair play and my Turbo have a 'Black Forest Chateau' tour of Germany on the fucking horizon. So, straight up, Troy mate, how am I going to finance all this blinkin business now? Fair play, we've got Jack Squit chance of covering it all,' Marty bemoaned.

'I'll let you know,' Troy replied.

'Not if you hear from us first,' Steve said.

'I ain't dishonest, Marty boy. Dad brought me up honest. I got fuckin efics. Never do nufink under the ref's nose. Keep in wi' the law,' Troy advised, taking a solemn tone. 'Me dad's prouda me. All right, so I wunt cut art to play fuckin football. So what about it? I'm a man's man.'

Soon after the meeting he offered Marty some free rehearsal time for the bands. So we drove back to Crock Sound Studios – room 2 – where Snot and Billy were smoking rather than practicing, as if all their (creative) capital had grown legs, jumped out of the box and escaped by itself, as well.

29. A Misguided Tour of Troy's Gaff

Marty was desperate to rescue his cash flow. He brooded over that testy altercation with Troy. In the end Fenton came up with a plan: we would go and explore Crock's house without any invitation. Steve was at risk of going back to old back ways, if not more cramped living arrangements. It would be his first house break in years. Maybe he was rusty. Failing to come up with any better ideas, despite many pub conferences, the rest of us had to go along with the idea.

Fenton carried out all necessary groundwork. The old skills hadn't deserted him: He seemed to get a lot of pleasure out of it. He even followed Troy home, before he left for Spain, to that suburb of a suburb. As soon as we had confirmation of the Crock family's departure to Marbella, we went off on our Sunday afternoon trip to the thug's dream home.

Coolly Fenton threw his tool bag into the back seat of Gorran's Austin *Sunbeam*. This was proof for me that Fenton, for all his other talents, had many ways to earn a good living. I knew the lad was straight by then, but not inflexible.

They took Roy Smith and me along with them – as look-outs. It seemed a bit shocking for a socialist (as well as a tax officer) to get mixed up in common crime.

'Ai man, the bas'tad's a class traitor, nothing more. He's been stealing from the working class for years, comrades! Appealing to their worst instincts, mind, and takin' their wages. Let's storm the place and put him up against the wall, comrades. Away, his name's already written down here in my little book of traitors and class enemies,' Roy insisted. He really did have that book – a diary or notepad – stuffed into an inside pocket of his parka.

'Keep a grip on yourself Roy. No bullshit, I'll be blinkin happy just to get my loot back and keep my bloomin nose in the same shape,' Marty argued. While driving he was trying to work out a Rubik's Cube of a new roundabout in town. Instead of finding Crock's patch we might head off to Scotland by mistake.

Troy had a big detached house on a new *Parrots*' Estate, stuck out on the outskirts. Steve's info about family hols in Marbella proved accurate, because the place had a shut-down look: there were no vehicles on the driveway. Hopefully the oldest boy, Seth Crock, had gone with his parents too. Even at fourteen and on the short side, the lad was already a junior power lifter and kickboxer on a short fuse.

'That's his gaff,' Fenton confirmed.

'He's doing well for himself,' I remarked.

'Yeah, a drug dealers' neighbourhood.'

'Away lads, under-occupied mansions for the bourgeoisie! After the revolution we'll turn em all into flats for young homeless people, comrades.'

'Great idea. Put me down on the waiting list,' I suggested.

'Right, definitely Roy, leave your bloomin reds' revolution to another day, will you? Straight up, we're blinkin busy right now and a bit fucking stressed out. So, fair play, let's hop out of the car and take a closer blinkin look,' Marty instructed us, cracking the driver's side.

We had to move carefully, into the full glare of the suburban afternoon. There were plenty of their neighbours about; playing kids, lawn mowers, barbecuers, sprinklers, gardeners, loungers. We definitely stood out as a bunch of punks on an away-day crime jaunt.

'Plenty of class traitors around here, comrades,' Roy observed.

'Fair play Smith, keep your blinkin specs clean, and your bloomin hood down. No bullshit, get yourself over on the corner for me,' Marty told him.

The rock maverick was hopping about, in case any of those suburbanites grew suspicious. No, they weren't used to seeing punks on their streets, just reading about us.

'Straight up Bottle, hang around on the bloomin corner along with him. No bullshit, and keep a sharp eye for any more blinkin nosey fucking parkers,' Marty instructed, wincing away.

'No problem, comrade,' Roy said, tugging his hood forward, despite the warm temperature. 'We're in the vanguard of the movement comrade. No need to worry, cos I've plenty of practice in class action mind.'

'Fair play Roy, no more blinkin punch-ups with crew-cuts or anybody,' the pop impresario advised.

So Gorran and Fenton set off, trying to look casual, towards the Crock property. Smithy and I positioned ourselves, using privet hedges as partial cover. I was inconspicuous as a hedgehog dipped into paint pots.

Body language jerky, globe of frizzy hair backlit by the sunset, Gorran dashed off and fixed a powerful smile for any potential passers-by.

Fenton cut a ramrod and unfussed figure alongside. Though he was dressed in black, carrying a carpetbag toolkit – right out of criminal central casting – the bass player was looking as calm and casual as Rod Stewart trying to pull at his own birthday party.

Marty – with a gas ball of dandelion hair, narrow shoulders, springy steps, knock-knees and new fluffy orange jumper – vanished from our view, around the hedge corner. The rest of this account follows from what they lived to tell me:

Gorran kept jangling nerves in check as, after scrambling over the wall, he set off up the Crock driveway. Steve evaluated doors and windows, based on years of experience. Fenton had many anonymous mentions in the *Chronicle*, apart from gig reviews. The Mortal bassist decided against cracking the front door, because Troy's domestic security system was tighter than the Pentagon's.

The *Star Materials* team went around the side of the house; Fenton scored out a double section of glass on suction pads. After neatly completing this work – casual as if working at his own home – Marty was urged to squeeze in through the resulting hole, making full use of Steve's hands as stirrups.

The pop Svengali reluctantly did as he was told, for once. Despite whinges, complaints, curses and bad omens, Marty managed to wriggle through – he was skinny and wiry enough – until he tumbled into a corner settee arrangement within. Despite years of backstage ligging through the night and juggernaut loads of *B&H*s, Gorran sprang back up on to his black-suede pixie boots.

'Gord elp us, I hope you're sure he's off on these fucking holidays.'

Untroubled, Fenton told him to release the window catch – cos he wasn't so skinny.

'Fair play, Steve mate, mind where you're putting your bloomin winkle pickers,' Marty complained.

In fact they were *DM*s.

Fenton expertly surveyed the room. The place was rigged up with laser-triggers, fanning around the spaces; one just inches above the (shaggy white) carpet.

'Get under the beam, Marty. Crawl along to the control box. I'll tell you what to do.'

'Right definitely, good idea Steve mate,' he objected. 'Straight up, I'm starting to blinkin regret this plan of yours. Fair play, remind me whose blinkin bright idea this was?'

'Just shape up, Marty. No time for complaints. We want our money back.'

So Marty dropped to his knock-knees, pressed down his crinkly hair low as possible (maybe it was too nebulous to set off alarms) and began groping along Crock's shag pile. Inch by inch he went, threaded nimbly in and out and between that pattern of blue pin-prick light beams (like an ELO lightshow at Wembley in miniature) – each one connected to a control board, which was rigged to the local cop shop. One false move and the Nulton fuzz would descend on Troy's house, perks and promotion depending on in. With these risks torturing his mind Gorran moved forward like a go-go girl caught in slow mo. At last, Fenton calmly calling last minute instructions, the pop guru managed get through, slip into the hallway, so as to disarm vital switches.

'Thank Gord for that. I was wearing out the knees on these bloomin new jeans. Fair play, I thought was about to die of a blinkin heart attack in there,' Gorran gasped.

'Nice big house,' Fenton observed, without pleasure or admiration.

'Right, definitely Steve, but let's make it fucking lively. Fair play, I don't want to be hanging about in this blinkin playpen,' Marty warned, grinning grimly.

'Troy don't keep money down here,' Fenton decided. 'He'd keep everything close. Most of all during the night time. That's when he risks closing his eyes,' Fenton suggested.

'Right, definitely, don't go giving me the blinkin creeps. No bullshit, if you reckon our loot's stashed upstairs then lead the bloomin way.'

'Upstairs, Marty,' Fenton decided.

The thing was, at this point, something dreadful began to develop. There was a feeling of something sinister. A feeling, or an *atmosphere*, almost a *smell*. Marty hardly got his knobbly painted fingers on the banister, before he was shocked by the low registers of a hideous sound. This noise was approaching, gaining volume, from the end of the hallway. When the charismatic promoter looked back, he realised that the devil was rushing towards him. That's right, as far as *he* was concerned, it *had* to be the devil, bearing down on him.

Marty was too terrified to even twitch a muscle, never mind to run or to shout out, in warning or horror. He couldn't get enough air in his chest to reach scream level. The devil – red-eyed, drooling, ruthless and enraged, knotted with raw power and solid muscle – closed in a fury on our media-manipulator. The Mortal manager was locked into a posture of complete terror and surprise: even though he didn't normally believe all that occult mumbo-jumbo. 'Worst nightmare' didn't do this justice.

The devil was pounding towards him over new parquet flooring. This diabolical creature then launched itself, reared up on powerful back haunches. It *flew* through the air, leapt, exposing awful pointed fangs, making a truly blood-curdling howl (a roar of despairing fury) directed at the pop promoter, and closing.

If Marty hadn't turned his back and slumped to the floor, at that very moment, the devil would have ripped his throat out, like Troy tucking into a burger. All the same, the creature's rippling limbs clenched around Gorran's wiry human frame, in a hug of horror, you might say; its fangs sinking viciously, into the back of the punk maverick's trendy King's Road fleecy orange jumper.

Cringing, Marty felt warm gob soaking through to his neck (surely this was a punk from hell), a desperate gnawing at the tender flesh. Horrified, reluctant, Marty twisted to make eye contact. He found two mad little, reddened black eyes, rolling back into sockets, in the middle of a sleek black face. As this the dark lord began to moan (in an almost sexual way) until Marty was not too optimistic about rock destiny. What had the Mortal manager ever done to deserve this?

As we might guess, this beast wasn't really the devil incarnate. No, this dreadful creature was just 'Archie', the Crock family's pet Rottweiler. He was a big beefy dog, bred for work in Germany, but not evil by nature, only nurture. Sadly Archie hadn't been invited for a fortnight in Marbella with the rest of his family. Miffed, Archie had been lounging in the back garden, trying to fill his Sunday, feeling a bit bored, chewing over his latest basketball. This was his test – he couldn't believe it. His master had taken him to special classes on how to maul humans who didn't smell precisely like a Crock. Archie didn't need to take a second sniff. His master would give him another biscuit as his reward.

Unfortunately the second bad-smelling (to him) human smell got away, and returned to whack him over the skull with a steak tenderiser. There wasn't much Archie could do about that – even as a schooled Rottweiler. Feeling the impact he was gradually forced to loosen his grip. Howling, disorientated (brains mincemeat), woozy, Archie decided to tuck his stump between his haunches, and creep back out into the garden to regain his instincts. Really he wasn't a devil, he was just a bit of a baby.

* * *

'Brush yourself down, Marty.'

'Gord elp us Fenton, all right for you to fucking talk! No bullshit mate, you got that mutt just in the nick of blinkin time. Straight up, I need a bloomin sponge to mop up all this fucking doggie spittle,' he objected.

'Did he break the skin?'

'And a fucking tetanus jab up my blinkin arse!'

Still, he managed to calm down and refocus. Marty wasn't ready to forget about his stolen money and the Battle of the Bands. Fenton's feeling of hidden treasure was more powerful than the dog's sense of smell. So our pair of music personalities continued to venture up Troy's mock-Tudor Staircase: it was right out of *Dallas*; Grecian statuettes, Persian rugs, porcelain displays, the lot. There was a full-scale *Airfix* reproduction of a superbike proudly displayed on the landing. That plastic model of a racing motor cycle must have taken Troy months, if not years, of painstaking careful work, piece by piece to glue and to paint. Fenton destroyed it within a matter of seconds, by putting his boot through it.

'Crock must have a safe box in the main bedroom. Trophy bride and family treasure close together at night.'

'Right definitely, Steve mate, but let's find this master bedroom, take back our loot and get our blinkin arses out of his bloomin dream home,' Gorran suggested.

'Get a grip, Marty.'

'No bullshit, Steve, you didn't have that blinkin hound in a bear hug, chewing your bloomin neck to the bone, did you.'

'Second door to your right.'

The duo shuffled into the Crock couple's frilly front bedroom. Steve only needed a few seconds to work the space out. He located a safe deposit box hidden at the head of their curtained four-poster. It was further concealed behind a reproduction painting of wild horses running through a raging river, resembling that Seeger LP cover, apparently designed by *Woolworth's*. Fenton tossed down his kit bag on the shag and got to work. He picked out the appropriate tools and set about cracking the box. It made him feel nostalgic, except that no explosive charges were involved this time. With a gentle tap on a needle the safe door swung open.

The punk maestro leaned in to get a view of its interior. He saw that set of artists' pens, which had once belonged to him.

'Right, definitely, these are mine, but I don't see our blinkin loot in here,' Marty said, peering over the bassist's shoulder.

'Only a pile of videos,' Steve reported.

'Right, definitely, so Troy left us with a set of lot of blinkin movies.'

'Let's take em anyway. We don't know what's on those vids. At least we won't go empty handed. And Troy's got our calling card,' he remarked.

Back in the *Sunbeam* – out of sorts and half savaged – Marty grated through gears, to complete a U turn in violent jolts, and set off back into town.

'Ai man, fascist propaganda films, most like,' Roy predicted.

'Right, definitely Smith, what do I care what's on them. No bullshit, I'll take em all home and record over the top of the blinkin lot of them,' Marty complained.

'Don't be too hasty,' Fenton advised.

The rock guru stared grimly down the dual-carriageway, brooding over his steering wheel, big hair squashed under the interior lining.

Maybe he didn't get the stolen loot back, but those videos definitely proved to interesting viewing and no more left-leaning than Roy said.

30. Home Movies

Our next gig was at the maternity ward, when Nut's missus gave birth. We were getting around the different departments of that hospital. Once again our appearance caused a rumpus, even before Sandra's screams had ricocheted around the delivery room and surrounding corridors, as if in tribute to her partner's vocal style.

Nutcase was a proud and humble new dad, grateful for our visit. 'Fanks for comin lads,' he told us. The baby resembled him, not only because it had a Mohican haircut at birth – though not a green one. 'We're really chuffed,' he explained tearfully. There were sore rings of happiness around his puffy eyes. 'I can't believe my Sandra brought another rock fan in the world. It's a fuckin miracle,' he choked up.

'Ai lads, look at him will ya, the little fella's the spit a him like!'

Billy had taken an extra tea-break to join us.

Nut's broad pasty features screwed up, 'You're right, the kids ave def'nitely changed me. *Def'nitely*. I look at life different. I aint the same bloke.'

He'd been present for the birth; *very present*, in studded dog collar and bondage trousers. Sadly he didn't change his mind about leaving Mortal.

'Doctor said I still got nodules on me froat. Sorry lads. Scares the shit out of me… losin' me voice.'

'Come back when you want,' Snot said.

'I was up on stage singin' and nuffin came out. I felt like a cockerel with grease up its arse,' Nut recalled.

'What happens to a cockerel… when it's got grease up its arse?' I wondered.

'Same fing as 'appened to me,' Nutcase cut back.

'What did you think he means, Bottle?' Stan said.

Anyway we were all thrilled at Little Nut's first gig.

The semi-finals of the Battle of the Bands were fast approaching. Snot was trying to find new 'musicians'. Reluctantly Snot was wrestling with lead vocals himself. As a self-taught musician he struggled to combine singing with playing. Recently he'd received a formal letter from *Spiro's* confirming that he'd lost his apprenticeship (as a technical designer). Obviously that was weighing on his mind. Even if he didn't discuss the matter, dark thoughts about 'failure' were playing over and over in his mind like a crackly old LP on repeat; like Nick Drake, Tim Buckley or even Van Gogh or somebody.

Gorran wasn't in an up-beat mood either. The traumatic memory of Archie's jaws still gave him waking nightmares. Marty didn't abandon his plans for global domination, understanding that the music business was defined by hits and misses (like Phil Spector) although this was a setback.

Furthermore (in the guise of Hercules Poirot) our criminal investigation was on-going - even into the dark. It soon took an unexpected turn and I was called as an expert witness.

'Right, definitely Bottle, come back to my place afterwards, will you, cos I've got something blinkin important to show you. Don't worry, you blinkin herbert, you can keep your bloomin trousers on this time,' he objected. 'Straight up, who'd fancy you anyway?' he joked affectionately.

'Nothing planned,' I admitted.

So we took another ride out in his *Sunbeam*. We drove past the entrance to *Electromax UK*, where my dad and brother worked, probably on night shift – giving everything they'd got.

We arrived at the council estate, even driving by Les's rusty *Cadillac*. Marty had a nice flat above a laundrette (it was quiet at night time). The pop maverick reversed up into a space at the parade, with numerous mechanical jerks and rethinks. Going backwards wasn't his strong point. Jolting into a position he hopped out and led the way, in his knobbly, gawky way, up outside concrete steps that lead to a blustery open corridor, towards a line of front doors.

Marty had his flat looking stylish, moodily lit, with a flair for colour and design. Every shelf and niche was packed with his record collection; and items of rock 'n' roll memorabilia. It was the first time I'd been invited to Marty's place to see this. The effect was instant fascination, which added to Marty's glamour and wisdom.

Punk enthusiasts like Marty were obsessed with 1950s rock singers and artists. Snot also considered the early rock 'n' rollers as authentic and rough edged. The punks went back to the essential ingredients of rock, as if bands could start again, ditching bullshit, pretension and multi-tracking. They wanted something raw and immediate, simple and direct, capturing the new generations.

What did I notice in particular around Marty's pop pad? As well as screen prints of Iggy, Bowie, Lou Reed, the Velvets and the Dolls, Marty also had big prints of young Presley, Gene Vincent, Little Richard, all along walls and shelves. Marty could talk about these artists with passion, and mixed their classic tracks into his punk nights.

'Right, definitely, make yourself at home, Bottle. I'll fix us both a cup of bloomin tea, before I explain what this meeting is all about. Fair play, I know you don't drink much and we'll both need blinkin clear heads for all this,' he argued, in a sardonic tone.

'This is a proper mystery,' I told him, settling.

The pop genius was posed in the arch before his kitchen. 'Straight up, it's all about as clear as bloomin alphabet soup in a puddle of vomit,' he admitted, pulling his wiry mop into better shape.

On returning with our brews – his mug was Sweet, mine was Slade – he kneeled to mess around with his video machine. He pushed a tape into the new player – VHS state of the art.

'Straight up, it's been giving me blinkin nightmares,' he warned. 'Gord elp us, what with that ferocious mutt and these videos, my blinkin nerves are bloomin all shredded,' he admitted, contorting his spongy night-club features.

'You've got more info on the break-in?' I wondered.

Gorran went and switched on an oil lamp (straight from the *Co-op* home department). The soft pink light turned his big hair into a coral reef. Twitchily, he reached over to a new pack of ciggies and tore away the cellophane wrap. He seemed full of a dread of anticipation, while putting a death-stick into his Mae West moosh. He lit up using a chunky US lighter which had been a gift from Les. He dragged exotically, and waved it around like Liz Taylor gossiping to Lizza Minelli at a top New York nightspot.

At last the strip of video tape ran through spacings and symbols. With hisses and crackles, boiling dots and streaking lines, the 'movie' began to settle into a definite picture.

'A pirate version of *Rocky*?' I quipped.

'Straight up you couldn't watch anything more fucking rocky than this,' he warned.

Elvis Presley gazed petulantly from the wall, Gene Vincent had a similar sullen look. Little Richard was scandalised, even as he enjoyed the joke.

I shuffled on the rock maverick's white leather armchair. 'So when's the action going to start?'

'Gord elp us, Bottle, why don't you have a bit of blinkin patience?'

Then it all came up, between smoke, pink lighting and the steam of our tea. Honest, I was glad I didn't have anything else to choke on.

A hand-held camera zoomed in and out of shot. In crude racks of focus the image changed perspective. It required a few seconds for me to determine what was in the scene. Obviously it was one of those blue movies. I'd heard about them.

'What are they up to?' I called out.

Our pop guru squinted through his smoke. 'Fair play, give it a few more bloomin minutes to settle,' he chastised.

Recently I'd been disturbed by erotic dreams about Gina. I didn't know what to do about them. On the following days I'd be tortured by them. Why didn't some of Paulie's confidence rub off on me?

I sensed that Marty's interest in Rob Shaw wasn't just musical – I wasn't *that* naive. In fact the punk promoter didn't even *like* heavy metal as a genre. I didn't want to pry into their relationship.

What they did in the privacy of their homes, in a locked dressing room, or on a last minute holiday was their affair. They were mates of mine.

'I can't make it out,' I admitted. 'The picture's a bit fuzzy.'

Erratic camera work refocused towards male forms that were writhing and cavorting on a bed.

'Straight up, Bottle, next up you'll be asking me for blinkin popcorn,' Gorran said. 'Why don't you try to blinkin concentrate? Don't you have any fucking smart rock writer's ideas?'

'Who do you think I am? *Roland Barthes*?' I enjoyed making this obscure reference.

Scratchy frames of the amateur flick lit on my pupils. The lens sharpened gradually to expose the centre of action, which included a huge flabby form that resembled a boiled walrus.

'Fuck me, isn't that Troy Crock!'

'Right, definitely, mind your French, while you're in my blinkin house,' Gorran remarked.

'Is this shot in Troy's house? That's the bedroom we broke in to, isn't it? What's Troy up to? Oh, *horrible!*' I said. I'd picked up a cushion and half covered my eyes with it. This was much worse than *Doctor Who*.

'Straight up Bottle, a penny for your blinkin thoughts,' Marty ticked me off. 'Fair play, behave yourself, cos a regular writer for blinkin *Music Mail* ought to have a decent opinion about any type of movie.'

'I only write reviews on music,' I pointed out.

'No bullshit, maybe I would have invited Barry fucking Norman back here to give his bloomin review instead,' he commented.

'How am I supposed to understand all this? Disgusting.'

'Fair play, as a music writer, do you have any blinkin idea what this porn flick has to do with our blinkin stolen loot?' he agonised.

'This is disgusting.'

'Straight up, which fucking monastery did you come out of?'

'What's on all the other tapes?' I wondered.

'Just blinkin sequels to this one! What did you bloomin think?'

'Is Troy Boy in all of them?'

'Straight up, Nulton's male version of fucking *Emmanuelle*,' he grimaced.

A few scenes later I got another shock, when I also recognised the form of Mick Dove. His smooth skinny torso was captured there on 8mm (the film was transferred to video). They had no more bodily secrets than top brass Nazis sharing a bunker together.

'As I bloomin suspected, Bottle, and I reckon I've seen his horrible blinkin mug around the *Hatter* before now.'

'He's the singer in that Steel Dildo. You know, the suede-head band that got third position in their heat.'

'Straight up, those bloomin boot boys? Thanks to one of those fucking bent judges anyway.'

'The same,' I confirmed.

'Fair play, I wouldn't want to wake up with that fucking creepy crop-head lying next to me under the bloomin covers.' The punk maverick gave a shudder, which concluded with a shivering drag on his ciggie.

'Me neither, Marty. Dove moves in far right circles. He hates Stan, you know. He's a troublemaker when Mortal plays. Provokes fights whenever they have a gig. And I recognise some of his mates there.'

'Straight up, that's all blinkin useful information. Only, no bullshit Bottle, I'm still scratching my blinkin head, trying to figure out the link between this and our stolen band money.'

'I can't work it out either,' I admitted.

'Straight up, what's this bloomin fascist orgy got to do with the break-in at *Star Materials* headquarters?'

'Better get the *Washington Post* on this one,' I said.

'Right, definitely Bottle, you get all the blinkin expert guidance you need. Fair play, make some notes and talk to people, cos we need all the fucking assistance we can blinkin muster to solve this crime.'

'I want to go home now,' I said. 'Can you turn this off?'

'Right, so I don't want to upset you with fucking Troy 'deep throat' Crock on his four poster.'

'What's the next move?'

'Straight up, Fenton and me had better go and have another bloomin talk with Troy. No bullshit, I'll let him know I've been watching these vids.'

'Is it a clever idea?' I said, pulling on my Oxfam coat.

'Straight up, I reckon it's our only hope to confront him and hear what he's got to say. No bullshit, use these blue movies as a bargaining chip. Otherwise *Star Materials* goes down the blinkin toilet without a bloomin rudder,' he warned, indelicately.

'Thanks for asking me over,' I said.

It wasn't the best late night screening I'd attended.

* * *

While nosing around the Record Shack one Saturday – during my lunch 'hour' – I stumbled into Mick Dove. On other days Snot and I would be in there searching for vinyl together. After buying an LP or a few singles – as much as we could afford – we'd go off to a favourite Asian delicatessen. We'd sit at the front window, discussing our purchases, taking tea and fruity Asian confectionary, which resembled slabs of coloured ice.

The *Record Shack* was the town's only outlet for independent punk releases, as we know. The chain stores wouldn't yet touch punk records; either they didn't get the scene or have contacts with independent companies. Not until punk began to move into the mainstream and develop more commercial offshoots. Morton Treble stocked every label or release he could get hold of (from the independent distributors) and those obscurities, to which local punks referred him. In addition the shop displayed promotional material for local gigs. And Milton sold advance tickets from the counter. The shop was a massively useful resource for the local music scene, if you were starting a band or just interested in going along.

Morton was an unlikely punk fan, slight and gnomic, with the expression of a frightened mouse. He must have been considerably older than us (or so we thought) wearing a pointed beard and being partial to baggy sweaters. We could never work

224

out if his enigmatic young assistant, Siobhan, was his daughter, niece, girlfriend or even his wife (we were too naive to look at her fingers). She also had a helpful knowledge of music, although she had a very neutral type of personality. In fact she served without a flicker of apparent enthusiasm or interest. Roy insisted that she must be a creature from *Doctor Who*.

Dove and I gave a jump as we noticed each other that Saturday. We moved about the store eyeing each other over the racks. Suddenly I didn't only think of him as the vocalist in a band. I was getting flashbacks of him performing in blue movies, as well as crushing skulls. For a while we pretended to ignore each other. Unfortunately, flipping through the same section, we were forced to rub shoulders.

'Ah, for fuck's sake, it's that Bottle. How's the communist movement?'

I tried to avoid eye contact and focus on sleeves. 'S'long as you keep out of my way.'

'They're mates of yours. All of them Trotskyites,' he sneered, down his nose. 'You was out socialising with em.' Dove had a quiet, insinuating tone of voice, as if someone had taken the whistle out of his neck.

'I like to socialise with socialists. Do you want me to discriminate?'

'You couldn't be tighter. Fighting on their side.'

'We were defending ourselves,' I said.

'Why you attacking white boys? Where's your loyalty?'

I couldn't help finding that ironic. His pale eyes puzzled over me. I noticed that his hands were fisted up.

'See? Don't listen to all that red propaganda. Join the patriots. Don't sell England down the river.'

'Not much of a river in Nulton,' I pointed out.

'Don't betray your people.'

He was trying to recruit me – to sway my mind. All of them were selling you their party, like Club Ibiza for political extremists.

'I'm a floating voter,' I remarked.

'You believe in this system?'

'I've yet to make my mind up… politically.' This was a dangerous admission.

'The indigenous people got to stick together,' he argued.

How did he get so twisted up? Consensus was a dirty word in Britain – compromise was rotting in the streets – and people were ready to try extreme solutions for a change. It was that type of disillusioned boredom that produced punk as well.

'How'd you get involved with Troy Crock?' I retorted. Never mind the economy or politics, that issue was uppermost.

The Golem-like fascist was taken aback. 'I'm not discussing another party member with you or anyone,' he snarled.

'Really? Since when were you *Made in Britain*?' I wondered.

Morton and Siobhan picked up on the menacing conversation. The timid look on Morton's visage was a deceptive one. They began to sense the risk of violence in their beloved shop. Morton didn't look like a hard man, but he was ready to intervene to save his records and everything. Despite a peaceable nature, he'd look after his singles, double packs and picture discs, with his life.

'Troy's a true patriot. Well respected in party ranks. Don't disrespect him. You won't always have those commies to protect you.'

'Right, Mick, so I could almost be intimidated,' I retorted.

'Troy's a generous lad. He supports the party… to build a strong Britain, improving the lives of working class British people,' Dove told me.

I processed the information. Essentially it was 'national socialism'.

'He's definitely got a soft spot for the Hitler youth,' I said. Really I was taunting him, to find out more.

'You aren't fit to eat cornflakes out of his fucking hand.'

'So long as it's just his hand,' I replied.

Dove's face puckered with fury. 'You wanna feel *my* hand?'

Morton noticed the disagreement. After giving Siobhan a reassuring look, the record shop owner turned a warning glance at us, without blinking. So I stepped aside and began to explore another box of records. Anyway Morton knew I was a polite regular customer. I wasn't the aggressive type – I'd blush when Siobhan looked at me.

'What do you know about punk? Why you buying those records?' Dove confronted me.

'Why shouldn't I?'

'This is white working class music,' he argued, sneering.

'You reckon?'

'Not for commie traitors and mates.'

'Give me elbow room, Dovey.'

'Why do you rate Snot's band? Tell him Steel Dildo's getting stronger. We've got a new rehearsal space. We're really fucking tight. And we're taking the message to the people,' he said. 'Any dream Stan's got of a recording contract is over,' he goaded.

'May the best band win,' I replied, 'but what were you doing in Troy's porno flicks?' I just came out and asked him.

Dove wrinkled up his mask with cold hate. Then he jabbed a clammy forefinger at my chest. 'Me and the English patriots are gonna win this Battle of the Bands contest.'

'What got into you, to take part in those dirty movies?' I persisted.

'We're gonna bring back the death penalty, Bottle, for all queers, not just the commies and traitors,' he warned. 'That's the people's justice.'

Firing squads, nooses, take your pick!

I watched his superior race making an exit.

31. One Man's Band

Not many RPMs later I collided with the Dove of War yet again. This was during his other job fronting up a punk band called Steel Dildo.

After the combo came a poor third in their previous heat, they should have been thrown out. Only an intimidating challenge to the judges table, which reached a far-right councillor on the panel, put them through as 'best runner-ups'.

Snot and I stood at the back of the *Dragon*, getting a head of Dildo's violent thrash and hate. I was finding them hard to take, although Stan was more laidback. He argued that the band was entertaining; claimed to enjoy their edgy set. Snot thought extremism and aggression was an exciting and risky part of punk. I went along with him to a fashion, except that I wanted irony or humour in the music too. The best groups had a bit of thought and cuteness to the sound and to the lyrics. There should be some art involved, with the performance element, to put alongside the music, beyond anger and gobbing.

Politics aside – as Snot would tell me – Steel Dildo was playing better; and they had stage presence. Their 'songs' consisted of angry three minute blasts and harangues. Assuming you liked them, which I didn't, they could whip up a mob frenzy. My spiky coloured hair seemed to stand up on end, even as I felt something cold and slimy down my neck (not gob this time). A Steel Dildo gig was high camp, low farce and a snake pit, all mixed together. Surely they couldn't win the Battle of the Bands, or could they?

Mick Dove's vocal style was weird; it obscured his furious lyrics. Maybe a lot of lads pogo-ing about didn't listen or get his lyrics. Even on stage he sounded as if he was whispering, although it was a sinister whisper, like fingerprints over your brain. Just numbskull stuff like *People of the World Disunite*, or rabble rousing choruses of *Asians Against Caucasians*. It would be years before a left-wing skinhead group, such as The Redskins, came along to challenge the ideology. Meanwhile Dildo came over as a right wing version of Dead Kennedys – that brilliantly sardonic (later) American punk band – of *Holidays In Cambodia* fame or notoriety (they didn't suspect that holidays in Cambodia *would* become fashionable). But as I said before, Dildo completely lacked irony and humour.

'How you gonna win the argument? By silencing them?' Snot challenged.

'They would silence *you*,' I reminded my friend.

'You wanna have their songs banned or what? You want to censor free speech? You want to stop free expression?'

There was no need to answer that one. I just looked back sceptically.

'Don't get worked up about it, Bottle. These are just wind ups. Symbols. Situations and hoaxes,' he claimed. In that sense he was a typical art student, looking for attention and provocation.

During and after Dildo's short set the crowd was in a riotous frenzy. Snot was getting great pleasure from the spectacle, as from his own band. Marty Gorran was DJ and he was forced to make an urgent appeal for calm over the PA, as if he was Big Brother. In some ways he was our 'big brother' – since mine wouldn't speak to me or recognise me in the street.

'Straight up, Gord elp us all, if all you blinkin herberts don't stop throwing things and smacking each other. Straight up I'm gonna pull the fucking plug on this whole bloomin gig before long,' Marty warned. He came over as an anxious booming voice through the PA.

'Fair play, cut out the gobbing, all right? No bullshit, how do you expect me to play any fucking records if the stylus is slipping all across the blinkin grooves!' he objected. 'Fair play, I'll send you the blinkin cleaning bills and all. If you don't cut it out, I'm out of this place. Fair play, faster than a squirrel picking up its nuts and running back up its fucking tree!' he threatened.

You could distinguish his sinewy lines, the electric halo of hair, behind a bank of coloured stage lighting, stood over his console.

'Right, definitely, otherwise the blinkin management are going to get these fucking bouncers to sort you all out. Straight up lads, it's your last bloomin warning now, because the blokes can empty this place quicker than fucking Olive Newton John,' he warned. Marty wasn't so up on popular country sounds.

Finally the bouncers had to go into action against Dildo's mob. They took to the floor in numbers and, putting in some tasty screw shots on those neo-Nazis, cleared the table in style. Despite the views of his eldest boy, Troy, nobody could accuse Dave Crock of being a racist. He would hack down the opposition, regardless of race, creed or political views. It was a sport for men and everybody was fair game.

After Dildo it was surreal to have Viscous Kittens playing next. This time Paulie had miraculously turned up early. He jumped on stage first, and was bashing his bongos, pouting and prancing about, to please and entertain the crowd. The unlikely pair of Dennis on drums and Herb on bass formed a great rhythm section. Anna-kissed was chopping away at guitar, jagged and abstract to suit the sound. The whole venue shook with lower end vibrations and wicked bass lines; everybody in the room *dancing, dancing, dancing*.

Herb had been recruited back into the group, when he realised that Paulie had forgotten about Anna-kissed (in bedroom lighting). The cub reporter was no longer any threat to their relationship. Typically the pop idol had lost sexual interest in her by dawn - as soon as the first ray of sunlight had cut through his bedroom curtains. The only interest in her by then was as a member of the group. That was positive – it was almost a step towards true feminism.

Viscous Kittens had been rehearsing, with and without their leader. Their sound was rejuvenated like an old Rastafarian with a fresh sack of ganja. After a while I stopped staring at Paulie's stage antics because the music was so great. A lot of the girls in the crowd that night came to the front to watch his performance closely. Wellington had a trio of female backing singers on stage too and he was lapping up the attention. One of these girls was a dressmaker and she made the band some new stage costumes. Unfortunately these were to Wellington's instructions. Their outfits were baggy smocks with large orange sun images at the centre. It had to be a wind up for the punks. I've no idea how Paulie got the other musicians to wear them.

Arguably the ridiculous stage image was just a minor distraction. Even Paulie himself was just a distraction. The reason was, Viscous Kittens had put together a brilliant sound. The fusion of influences, somewhere between Trench Town and Notting Hill, had worked triumphantly.

Miraculously Paulie's groupies were entirely in tune, even if Paulie had no idea about harmonising. Before the gig started Wellington had argued that his singers were a radical feminist statement. This claim was underlined by knowing that he'd slept with them all. That was really Paulie's only talent. But you couldn't overlook it: I would have traded it sometimes.

The judges that evening were ageing rockists to a man. The panel ranged down the table, like Robert Plant, Van Halen and Phil Lynott together on a stag night.

Thank the lord that Gina wasn't around. And she had resisted the pop god's charms that notorious evening. That calamity was only avoided because we'd stayed up late to watch a classic film. Just imagine if we'd taken an early night or stayed in our rooms. If it hadn't been for us Sour Cat might have turned into a Viscous Kitten. By next morning Paulie would have disowned all knowledge of her as a sexual partner. It would have been too late for her by breakfast time. Such a calamity would have damaged her music career, not to mention her sex life. It was a big might-have-been of rock music history. And it was too horrible to think about – although I did.

What would happen if Paulie really succeeded and won the Battle of the Bands? We shared a recurring nightmare of Paulie as a famous global pop star. Terrible images of Paulie as a rock idol, adored by every girl, spread over the centre pages of *Smash Hits* with a staple through his belly. Oh god, it was too dreadful to think about.

You only had to look at the record charts every week. The music business was a crazy mix of the ridiculous and the sublime. Particularly the singles chart. Paulie on *Top of the Pops*, breaking young girls' hearts, stuck at number one for umpteenth weeks. Paulie being interviewed by Richard Skinner on Radio One, grinning on the cover of *Rolling Stone*, Paulie cracking America and Europe. It wouldn't have been any surprise to Paulie himself.

There was only one other local band able to stop him, in my view. Unfortunately Mortal wasn't in any shape. If Snot's band had been a person it would have been in hospital too.

* * *

To recap the story to this point (for those readers who may be tracing Mortal's rock family tree): Nutcase was retired with his polyps: Herb Slasher and Ann-kissed had fallen under Wellington's influence: Sour Cat had dropped her punk name and given up rock (according to rumours *Gina Watson* was a complete neurotic and a prisoner in her own music room). Steve Fenton was entertaining 'corporate clients' on Marty's behalf at Duncehead's *Bernie Inn*. Only the drummer Billy Urine was prepared to play.

After the robbery Marty was desperate for income. He wanted to enter all his bands for the contest, and to subsidise *S&M* music enterprises. To finance these ambitions he had to take on more work as a sign writer/designer and was DJ-ing around the clock.

Not having any musicians or a band, Snot faced elimination from the Battle. Mortal's name was up on the poster, and a lot of his old college mates had turned up. He decided to go solo to avoid dropping out altogether. Later we understood that solo performances were not allowed, according to the small print of the rules. The competition had been advertised as a band competition. Fortunately for Snot nobody made a fuss at the heats stage.

'I got to level with you, Bottle,' Snot admitted. 'I hate doing this on my own. It's against the whole idea of punk. But I haven't got any choice… do I? Yeah, well, so it has to be me, the guitar and a few of my crap songs.'

'I'd like to help out,' I told him. I was happy with my chisel and a typewriter.

We glued ourselves to the bar, letting Snot imbibe more courage and to inhale extra sweet inspiration.

Gorran was busy hustling, working his plastic features, with big talk about pop's future. Obviously he hadn't noticed how few musicians remained in Mortal. Archie the Rottweiler was still gnawing at his nerves. I reckoned we'd have to persuade Sour Cat back, to stand any chance. For all his persuasive power and PR genius, Gorran wasn't always a wizard. Not away from his turntables.

When Mortal Wound's turn came, Snot clambered up. To begin with the audience didn't realise he would be alone. After fussing, tuning and throat clearing, Stan began to strum and sing. That evening he had an acoustic guitar. He could have passed as a folk singer, even direct from the Village. He was solitary at the mic, blinking under a hot spot. If it hadn't been for the spiky coloured hair, sundry piercings, ripped 'Sex' tee-shirt, bondage pants with a chain through the loops, he could have been related to Dylan or even Pete Seeger.

'Yeah, right, I've always been me own punk.' Stan continued to fiddle with the neck of Luigi's axe, still tuning up twitchily into a crackly PA. 'The band took one look at you ugly punks and ran away,' he joked. 'Well, anyway, don't mind me, finish your fucking conversations. I'll just stand here and play a few of my terrible songs. Maybe I'll entertain you... before you all fall over dead drunk.

'Do you lot appreciate the Velvet Underground? So I'll kick off with my version of *All Tomorrow's Parties.*

'Fuck me, Bottle mate, glad you didn't want to sing this one!

'After that I'll croon a couple of me own fuck-up songs... just to let these judges know I have my own derivative material. Not that you're gonna rate it. No apologies. If there's any music lovers out there... best to leave now.'

Snot cut an opening chord. Under the spot he's the same small, hunched, vulnerable looking lad. Same big ego, charisma and obvious (if denied) talent. He didn't have a 'good' voice, but he restricted himself to his range. Obviously, choosing a Velvets' song, there was something extra to mere tunefulness. Or tunelessness.

'I'm never gonna croon again,' he admitted afterwards.

After a full programme of shouty bands, so desperate to impress, Snot sounded fresh. Apart from a few hesitations, and that awkward style, Stan got through it. He'd got such a gift with the guitar. The only risk was in the vocals. He had to keep under control, to avoid severe limitations. Holding down volume, avoiding theatrics, building tension, he managed to catch the ear.

The guitar was held up in a high position, hiding his poor narrow chest. He'd look up for the next verse, keeping time by tapping his foot on the boards. There'd be a shrug of the shoulder as he changed chords or went into the bridge. Most of all you noticed his hands, large yet delicate – a strangler's hands, as they say.

'I don't want to upset you, Stan mate,' I joked afterwards. 'I wouldn't like to mention Joan Baez.'

'I fucking wouldn't do that,' he agreed.

Stan was one of those natural talents, hard to explain, like Errol Garner or Jimi Hendrix. He'd just discovered this talent by chance and accident – as we saw – entirely self-taught. You didn't want to tell him this. Often I'd sit at the end of the bed, listening to him, completely dazzled. In fact I was open mouthed.

The judges put him third, so he went through. Somehow he'd pulled it off. Once again he'd hypnotised us all. But it would be years before we had any appreciation Joan Baez.

32. Work Out at Troy's Gym

A rematch with Troy Crock wasn't such a smart move. But we had to present him with the latest circumstantial evidence.

This time we rang the front door bell of Troy's pseudo-Grecian pile. After some deduction – not yet needing to hire *Columbo*, *Ironside* or *Kojak* – Marty realised that the Crock clan really wasn't at home. This time they were out shopping or eating, because they had flown back in from Marbella the previous week.

Steve gripped the edge of the back fence and peered over, just in case. There was only Archie spread on the lawn, chewing erotically on another new basketball. We had no wish to provoke the evil side of Archie's nature again. So Marty told us we should leave the area; we clambered back aboard the Austin and he gunned back into town (if you count the exhaust as a gun). Unfortunately we didn't find Troy in the *Crock Sound Studios* complex either, or down in the office of the *Flamingo* club either. We were shooting about Nulton all that afternoon, as in an indie (or idle) reconstruction of *The Italian Job*.

Acting on a tip off, Marty understood that Troy must be on duty at the Duncehead branch of *Troy Crock Health & Fitness Centre*. To get an address Marty consulted a rain warped copy of the *Yellow Pages* book, from a vandalised telephone box. In those days it was the closest thing to a sat-nav. Even now I smell piss and rain every time I look up an address.

Nobody on the local music scene had much dice with health and fitness. Most of my mates were heavy smokers, drinkers, often mixing other additions (or addictions): most of them only had with an inch of spare lung capacity. Any breath left was reserved for knobbing or more alcohol. This made sense to them; because it was hard to imagine Jimi Hendrix sipping apple juice in a sauna.

Again Steve Fenton was fearless in confronting Nulton's pre-eminent thug. When it came to (understanding) his emotions Steve was Steve Austen of *The Bionic Man*. Either that or he didn't have a nerve in his body to start with. Overall Steve had a nervous system like a fretless bass.

The *S&M* party (so to speak) arrived at the Crock's leisure centre and hustled past reception without a prior booking. Hoping to be missed, we ignored a huddle of employees in tight shorts, sneakers and carrot tans. Unfortunately these highly-tuned health workers noticed our rush. They were desperate to check-up on our membership status. Gorran's lack of sporting condition was glaringly obvious, as it was startling. That didn't stop the music exec shifting like a chased hare when required (not only with a dog after him). The rock maverick's unique appearance, with that spindly gait and natural puff of hair (enhanced by punk fashions), created an immediate panic in a leisure and sports centre.

Compared to Gorran I was in reasonable shape, despite a Richard Hell type haircut and ripped fetish trousers (which impeded my progress). I was already wearing big Oxfam overcoats (most likely from dead men), as if anticipating my passion for groups such as Joy Division, The Cure or The Sound.

Leisure centre staff was kitted out to join Brotherhood of Man, Bucks Fizz or even S Club Seven. Abba had won Eurovision the previous year and the Swedish ensemble encouraged a certain look of glowing health, like Tantric sex in the sauna. Anyway it was the first time I'd been chased by such a bunch of bronzed and determined blondes. There's a first and last time for everything. We managed to give that LA beach party crowd the slip – we'd already had plenty of practice. I felt like Winston Smith out of *Nineteen Eighty Four*, roaming long empty corridors, with a terror of toned studs instead of rats. The Centre Director's office, when we eventually found it, was as empty as the post holder's moral conscience.

'*Gord elp us*, I'm all at bloomin sixes and sevens.' Marty was gasping for breath and this pain set off the fissures and drill holes of his craggy features.

'That goon's here somewhere,' Fenton insisted.

'Right, definitely Steve, be blinkin careful how you deal with the Crock family. Straight up, in case they wake you up in the blinkin small hours of the morning. Fair play, with a couple of steel barrels pointing up your bloomin nostrils. No bullshit, you want to keep a hand on the switch of your fucking bedside lamp,' Marty advised. He winced with disorientation.

'Don't let Troy Boy bother you. We'll find that ape and put him back in his cage,' Steve said.

'Right, definitely, mind how you handle him.'

We hung about on a gallery overlooking squash courts, following all the thwacking and grunting. It wasn't the best place to do our thinking. Despite his anxieties (which resembled free jazz at this point) Marty refused to give up the treasure hunt, certainly not without a fair shot at making it big in the record business.

That posse of honed trainers crashed through double-doors in pursuit. Fortunately, as these body fascists slowed and smirked at us ready for the kill, Steve located Troy Boy. The local fear figure was to be found relaxing and spreading out in his bar area. Why didn't we think of that? We shot off down the gallery to join him.

The flabby bulk of the 'Leisure Centre Director' was squeezed into a plastic sofa. This was a bloke who once pulled a steam engine up a hill, by a strap between his teeth. That was an awesome feat and you had to respect it. Even if he'd gone completely to hay seed by then, he used to be a magnificent animal. By this time he was simply an animal. You just wanted to stick a rosette on his neck – if you could find his neck. He'd done it all live on TV and even been interviewed by Sue Lawley on *Nationwide* afterwards.

Junior Crock wasn't thrilled to be reunited with us punk herberts. For him we were as appetising as a stale hamburger tarted up with spicy pickle. Even so he couldn't avoid the rock glitterati of Nulton for long. He couldn't overlook a music industry giant like Marty Gorran. The punk genius brought a glittering cloud of charisma and pizzazz with him. You couldn't turn away Marty, any more than tax payers (or local businesses or construction workers) could afford to ignore Dave Crock.

Troy was immersed in his own private sauna of cigarette smoke. 'Jesus wept, its Marty boy. What you fuckers doin ere, in my sports centre? You ain't workin out, are you?' The portly blubber was zipped into a XXL silk tracksuit. He threw some more hard liquor on to the hot coals. His Costa del Sol burn hadn't yet started to calm into a tan.

Marty had the big grin ready to work magic. As if bumping into that zippered gorilla was the biggest pleasure and surprise of his week. '*Hello, hello* there, if it an't our good mate Troy. How're you been blinkin keeping? What a fucking pleasant surprise. Straight up, we just popped by on the fucking off chance, to see how well you're doing. No bullshit Troy, I was just telling these lads here, how we ought to keep you updated about all our investigations into that blinkin theft in our HQ,' Gorran explained, offering his challenging dental work.

'Yer chicken shit robbery agen?' Making an impatient noise Troy peered off into the distance, through the billows of a drag.

'What you hiding?' Fenton challenged.

'Ah, if it ain't you again dick ed? You obnoxious fuck. Marty got you on a bit of fuckin string or what? When I finish with you, son, your own muvver wont want yer,' Troy fumed. He pulled down the neck of his tracksuit. The top of his head was flat as a Kent cliff, or a melon sliced clean by a cutlass. 'If you ain't fuckin careful dick ed...' he muttered.

'Right, definitely, your theories are always blinkin welcome in these quarters. Fair play, I've got a blinkin international music company to run, Troy mate. Straight up, that and all these bloomin promising new bands of mine, wanting to win the contest, keen as fucking *Flying Boot*.'

'Fuckin get on wi' it!'

'No bullshit Troy, and they all wanna make it blinkin huge in the fucking charts this year and make all of Nulton bloomin proud of 'em. So fair play, they want me as their manager, promoter and adviser, Troy. So now our mate Steve here is just fucking very anxious about our stolen bloomin money and all the blinkin good fortunes of all our talented young Nulton artists. Straight up, same as you are, Troy mate.'

'And who's this dopey goop? *This* one 'ere.'

It seemed that Troy was referring to me. It gave me a jump to be recognised at the wrong moment.

'Right, definitely Troy, glad you noticed our blinkin star reporter and fucking editor-in-chief at *Ob-scene* fanzine,' Marty said.

'Fanzine? What's that? Fuckin' Bay City Rollers? *E's writin' somepink*? What with?'

'Yeah, straight up Troy, didn't you hear something how our Paul Bottle's got himself a big fucking name in the world of rock journalism? So, no bullshit, he's got himself a regular weekly column for fucking *Music Mail* down there in blinkin London, Troy, on the national bloomin music press in Holborn,' Gorran gloated. He was nodding at the thug knowingly, with an arm around my shoulder.

Crock gave his peeling pug nose a vigorous rub. He was no more a music fan than he was a pacifist. For a split second his squinty eyes got me into focus and back out again. 'What do I care about yer fuckin music papers? D'you fink I read that fuckin shite in the press?'

'Right, definitely Troy, but even if you don't take a close fucking interest in the punk rock scene, blinkin *Music Mail* is one of the biggest selling weekly papers both sides of the fucking pond. Straight up, with a couple of sentences Bottle can make or break any blinkin new group,' Gorran argued. Much to my discomfort.

The thug sucked back snot. 'I ain't int'rested, Marty boy. You wanna speak to me dad.'

'Straight up Troy, cos as a leading blinkin journalist and editor in chief Bottle can fill you in about our crime investigations,' Gorran said, with a flinch.

Suddenly my Adam's apple shot up and down, as if Troy had struck my button with a hammer. 'Crime investigations? *Me*?'

'I dunt give a flyin fart in a jam jar about your fuckin money.'

'Well mister Crock, you know, it's like this… it's a lot of money for Marty and his artists to lose, given that…' I began to stammer a response.

'Wot the fuck you on abart, gimp face?'

Troy gestured to the bar. Even if he couldn't play football like dad, he could drink like him.

Somehow I had to spit out the story, in true punk fashion.

'Never mind the fuckin sob story, gimp. Do you lot fink its right to break into somebody's 'ouse?' Crock said, in retaliation.

'Yeah but on the other hand, mister Crock, it's worth considering that…'

Gorran frowned deeply and signalled with the glowing end of his ciggie that I should end my contribution. Now it was his turn to add some gloss, a bit of pathos, and even a hidden threat.

* * *

Although Troy had turned to flab, he still knew how to throw it around. What's more, he employed a full squad of hard men who had twenty-four hours access to weight machines and a subsidised bar.

'Bottle didn't mention a break in at your house,' Fenton pointed out.

'Watch your marf.'

'But we did get those videos.'

'You left your fuckin boot marks over my wife's fuckin shag pile, dick ed.'

'What about it?'

Crock tipped forward in his sofa, taking it with him. 'What abart it, dick ed? I'll tell yer *What abart it*? You broke in and went rarnd my fuckin arse. You went up into the fuckin master bedroom and broke into me safe,' Troy accused, stabbing his meaty forefinger at the bassist.

'Straight up, *Gord elp us* Troy mate, try to be blinkin calmer, before all your bloomin hair grows out. No bullshit, like Elton John under a blinking Hoover,' Gorran said, grinning with sympathy.

'An' what you do to my fuckin dog? E wouldn come back into the fuckin arse agen. E sleeps in the fuckin garden. What you do to my kids' pet? Was it you, you fuckin dick ed?' the villain accused, fuming red.

'Right, definitely, *fair play* Troy mate, but what in all the blinkin monkeys in a cage were you doing cavorting around with all those little fascists on your own bloomin bed?' the punk maestro wanted to know.

The former Iron Man flushed and went rigid. His purse mouth spluttered, as he said, 'Mind your own businesses, Marty boy.'

'Straight up, Troy, your own blinkin private life an't no interest of mine, only what the fart in *Marks* were you doing prancing around on that bloomin mattress? No bullshit, giving those fuckin little extremists some pocket money?' Gorran asked, with a marvelling expression of incredulity. He drew a shape with a fresh cigarette, much as a gymnast might twirl a ribbon.

'Keep to yer moosic, Marty boy. Nobody tells me what to do wiv money.'

'No bullshit Troy, I'm more concerned what you did with *our* fucking money. Straight up, not who you're pokin' up the blimmin bum in the comfort of your own bloomin home,' the pop mogul argued. He gave a wince at the distinction.

'It's payback time,' Steve flatly explained.

'*Pay back*? What's that mean, Dick ed?'

I began to wonder if Fenton had watched the *Death Wish* series: personally I'd walked out while I still had the chance.

'Right, definitely, pay back our blinkin money, Troy mate.'

There was a lot of snuffling, menacing, breathing. '*Your* money, dick ed?'

'Right, definitely, Troy mate, it would be *our* money,' Marty confirmed, exposing his large teeth encouragingly. 'Last time I blinkin checked it was.'

'What'd I want with a poxy five hundred quid?'

'We've got a full set of your video nasties,' Fenton said, staring coldly.

'Leave it out wanker, or I'll flatten your fuckin ed, 'til your fuckin ears stick together,' Troy warned. 'I'll twist your ugly face 'til you're looking at your own fuckin arsehole.' He revealed his sharp little fangs, giving a demonstration of the action with his hands.

'Any time after closing,' Fenton insisted.

PUNK STORY

'Any more shite from you, dick ed, and you'll be blowing bubbles in a block of fuckin concrete,' Junior Crock warned.

'Right definitely, Troy mate, we don't want to get under your bloomin feet or anything. Only, straight up, but did you tell your missus about these other blinkin hobbies of yours?' Gorran asked. He grinned amiably as he enjoyed his smoke.

'Leave my missus art of this, Marty boy.'

'Straight up, what's she gonna say, if she blinkin discovers you've been making all these fucking blue movies on her own bloomin Slumperland? Fair play, Troy mate, while her blinkin back's turned and she's orf down the fucking shopping centre, sipping those blinkin cold spritzers, with all those bloomin pricey girlfriends of hers?' Marty suggested. He hunched up his narrow shoulders in the fluffy orange jumper.

'She ain't interested in the movie business,' Crock insisted.

'She's interested in your credits,' Fenton suggested.

I gave an uneasy shuffle. 'How long have you been involved with local fascists?' I asked.

'What's that? Fuck off, gimp face,' Troy told me. He threw some more spirit on to the flames.

'Right, definitely Troy, we just popped by to say hello and get some fucking advice. Fair play, then we'll be out of your leisure centre faster than your best greyhound with a fucking bazooka up its blinkin arse,' Marty promised. The wide smile betrayed some insecurity.

'Just sign us a cheque. For the full amount,' Fenton told him. 'Make sure it don't bounce neither.'

'*You'll* bounce dick ed. I'll shove your ed through one of my fuckin fruit machines. Then I'll pull art your fuckin tongue and pick the change out of your fuckin marth.' Troy Boy jerked a forefinger towards Fenton.

'How do you know Mick Dove?' I asked, shuffling.

'Where'd you get this streak a piss, Marty? Outa fuckin Bernardo's?' He leered with malice. 'Or was it Battersea?'

'You want to take this outside?' Steve suggested, straightening up.

'I'll put you in a fuckin skip, dick ed.'

242

'Right, definitely, let's leave out the blinkin handbags, how did you get bloomin mixed up with that dodgy fucking suede head in the first place, Troy?' Marty asked. He tried to arrange his mouth into a more comfortable shape.

But overall Gorran relaxed into a friendlier body language. The clink of glasses, sociable chatter and aroma of tobacco always softened the edges.

'They does well all over Europe, my sexy vids.' Any revenue stream cheered him up.

'Right, definitely, but what's the blinkin world coming to, Troy mate. No bullshit, and you film everything on blinkin super eight and put the dirty movies into the safe above your other half's blinkin head?' the pop mogul said.

'What you doin messin wiv my private life, Marty boy?' He desperately tried to loosen his tracksuit top.

'Straight up Troy mate, why d'you get blinkin involved with this horrible Mick Dove character. No bullshit, and let him fucking blackmail you into the bargain?' Gorran said.

He wasn't called Hercules Poirot for nothing.

'Like I said, Marty boy, we all make mistakes,' Troy regretted. 'Ask me dad.'

'Right, definitely Troy mate, but what the pig in a fucking tutu were you up to nosing about in our bloomin office and nicking the money from your own strong box?'

The thug seemed regretful. 'Dove boy got your five hundred quid now. It's moved on, Marty boy.'

'Dove got new equipment for his band,' I pointed out.

Marty's diplomatic grin was under severe pressure.

Troy Boy removed a pressing crick from his neck. 'I told yer. Nuffin to do wiv me. Dove's got yer loot.'

At this point Fenton went to make a move on the leisure centre boss.

'I wouldn't advise that dick ed. My lads'll tread over your face 'til it's just a bit of fuckin coc'nut mattin. Dunt even think abart it. Unless you want a buncha little girls in fuckin leotards treadin all over your ugly fuckin mug.'

'Right, definitely Troy mate, but you've gone and left me out of blinkin pocket now,' Gorran objected. 'Straight up, what are we going to do about these bloomin bands of mine that need to enter the Battle of the Bands competition?'

'Now, if you lads dunt mind,' Crock suggested. Hands flat on the table before him, Troy eased his buttocks from the sofa. With sweat breaking out, he hauled himself back to a vertical, cushioned by pricey sneakers. 'Yeah lads, I've got me treadmills to shift. Some of us as got businesses to run,' he implied. He slunk off, arms and legs stuck out at big angles. There was just a contemptuous backward glance.

We faced a difficult situation – not only from the fitness fascists. Blackmailing Troy could have been an option, except that such dirty tactics was not Marty's style. His taste in music was more likely to get middle of the road.

We never did get to the bottom of it, so to speak.

33. Preparations for Battle

*O*fficial 'Battle' posters and leaflets began to appear around town, produced by order of a sub-sub-committee of the council's Leisure team. Like jelly hurled at a kids' party, the council was chucking rate payers' money at the youth vote.

Marty Gorran's printing machines were punching away like the Royal Mint. Using flat bed and screen printing methods Marty experimented with typesets, hand lettering, combinations of colours, patterns and production techniques. There was no doubting his craft.

I always loved the atmosphere of Gorran's bare bricked workshop; the thick, sharp smells of paints, inks, glues, paper and spirits; the packed-full higgledy piggledy cupboards and shelves.

'*Gord elp us* Bottle, just keep your blinkin fingers still while I pour out this bloomin paint, will you?' he scalded.

I was assisting him at the wonderful, yet simple mechanics of a wooden screen-print machine. Of the *S&M* crowd I was the most interested and, usually, had enough patience with the process.

That particular evening, I recall, an unrelated controversy developed between us. This was a result of Nulton & Duncehead FM inviting Marty on to Barry Dazzle's popular evening *Traffic Jam Show*. They wanted him to chat to about the forthcoming Battle of the Bands competition and the chances of his *S&M* groups. Gorran had accepted the invitation, even though he hated the show and derided the choice of music, which was MOR as *cats' eyes*.

'Aren't you worried about selling out?' I wondered.

'Right, definitely Bottle, before you get on your blinkin music critic's high horse again. Fair play, just you concentrate on getting some interesting quotes from these bloomin local bands of ours,' he advised. 'Most of em can't remember their own blinkin address.'

Dismissing my quibbles, Marty concentrated on the mechanics of printing. He'd got patches of colour into the squiggles of his puffy hair.

'Yeah, right, Marty, but Barry Dazzle? What interest does he have in punk or Mortal Wound?'

'Straight up, *Motown* wasn't built in a day and *Sun Studio* didn't get a blinkin reputation inside a week. Sam and Johnny had to iron out a few bloomin molehills before they could walk the blinkin line.'

'It's all publicity,' I agreed.

'Hold that bloomin paper still while I'm pouring. All blinkin smudged like Gina's makeup,' he complained drolly.

I improved my concentration, steadied my grip. 'All the same, Marty, I don't see where the money's coming from, after the five hundred was stolen. How can you get around that?' I argued.

'Right, definitely Bottle, and who put all those fucking ants in your blinkin trousers tonight?' he objected.

'What's the point doing all this work… if we don't have money to enter the bands?'

'Fair play, even Harvey blinkin Goldsmith had a few money troubles along the way to mega success,' Gorran argued.

'I still don't get you,' I admitted.

'Because, fair play, I already went and solved the problem with our stolen five hundred quid,' Gorran said. He gave a celebratory smile as he let this slip.

There must have been a look of astonishment over my gawky features in response. 'How'd you sort that one out?'

Gorran took his time, walking across the studio, to fetch over a fresh canister of pink paint. He was producing a three-colour image for Turbo Overdrive – a labour of love. 'Fair play, I found another blinkin way to raise the fucking loot,' he said.

'You're not winding me up?'

'No bullshit, you don't need any winding-up, Bottle mate,' he told me.

Not to be distracted, Marty's paint grimed hands operated the swinging arm of the wooden printing machine. While he concentrated there, with a grin of pleasure at the task, he also had a knowing look.

With studied force he pulled the arm over, fully across the bed of the machine, to make an impression of colour shapes on the thick paper.

'Les Phoenix and I might be bloomin rivals in the music industry, but even old Les knows there's no Battle of the Bands without *Star Materials*. Fair play, what fun would that be, so in the end he advanced me five hundred blinkin quid, up against my new Austin *Sunbeam*.'

'You bet your new car on that?' I said. 'You didn't! But you might lose your wheels, Marty. How can you get us all around town if that happens?' I objected.

'Fair play, I an't finished these posters yet,' he ordered me. 'So I bet my little motor against Les that one of my *Star Materials* acts is gonna win this competition.'

'Mortal Wound isn't even talking to each other at the moment.'

'Fair play Bottle, leave all those blinkin teenage egos to me. That's my fucking headache as their bloomin agent, tour manager and mentor. Les is offering us five hundred blinkin quid up front, so I can't refuse his bloomin offer. No bullshit, you don't get your blinkin New York fucking loft if you can't put your mortgage on it.'

'What if you lose?' I challenged.

'Straight up, when you drop your blinkin toast on the floor, does it always land up on the wrong fucking side?' Marty argued.

'I don't know. I don't generally drop my toast. At this moment in time Mortal is just Snot. There's nobody else in the Wound,' I pointed out. 'You might as well drive that little Sunbeam of yours into the scrapyard and get it cubed.'

'Right, definitely Bottle, you won't be so blinkin pessimistic after you get your first fat cheque as a music industry copywriter,' Marty predicted. His eyes popped at me, with a stubbornly optimistic grimace.

'Well, I don't know, I can't imagine myself. We'll have to see about all that.'

'Right, definitely, you'll see. So maybe we can finish off these blinkin Turbo Overdrive posters now. Otherwise, straight up, I'll have to get back to Les Phoenix and try to bloomin sub-let my fucking council flat as well.'

* * *

It'd take more than a lick of fresh paint to knock Mortal back to life.

While their competitors rehearsed like Springsteen without a wristwatch, they were occupied bickering with each other. Our chance of winning the contest was more of a non-starter than Dave Crock's canner.

We didn't get news updates about Gina's health or musical development. Would she get any free time from 'A' levels to re-join? As for the racy wet dreams about her, I didn't know where or how far to go.

Except, one afternoon, I decided to take the bus out to Gina's district. In every sense her mother was shocked by my appearance. She wasn't touched by my concern for her daughter. Just the usual stuff about how Sour Cat had to work to get into the Conservatoire. If Gina was upstairs at the time of my call, she didn't catch on or let on. As I walked back down the hill towards town, her mother was spying on me. Either that or she was searching for other punks in the shrubbery. After that I was even more worried about Mortal's multi-instrumentalist.

On top of that, Nutcase was suffering sleepless nights with Little Nut. Otherwise the baby was doing all right – growing and extending his vocal range. The original Mortal belter wasn't in any hurry to make a comeback. He was too busy rocking his baby to sleep by (only) humming Clash and Pistols tracks.

Potentially the road ahead was as rocky for them as for Marty's Austin *Sunbeam*. I was afraid that handy little car might be parked out alongside Les's *Caddy* - a colt tied to a mustang.

Then there was *Ob-scene* to put to bed. The fanzine had a subtle bias towards *S&M* acts. The cover price would help to raise extra funds. After the break-in all my articles and interviews had been trashed. I jigsawed the scraps of my work in emulation William Boroughs's cut up technique. There were fresh interviews to add, and I could rewrite some pieces, thanks to a battered replacement typewriter with arthritic keys, taken from Co-op stores. Writing away amidst the blue fog of Marty keeping me company, I'd be tapping away into the small hours, with that fantasy of being a cross between Dashiell Hammet and Tony Parsons.

Marty had a double lock fitted to our office to prevent any second break-in. It was definitely like locking the stable door after *Flying Boot* had bolted: or even after *Flying Boot* had been shot, butchered into portions, deep frozen and fed to Archie.

Like any notorious media magnate Gorran could sometimes behave punkishly towards his own staff. He couldn't help it. I knew he had financial worries, along with that dodgy bet with Phoenix. On the other hand, nobody was paying Marty for his services; for his time and trouble, even if he enjoyed it. So I was prepared to hammer keys under the midnight oil, for no obvious recompense.

Steve Fenton wasn't just a cool head with nerves of steel. He was a talented calligrapher, as well as being a semi-retired house breaker and a versatile bass player. Marty got him to do all the headings and sub-headings for our mag by hand. It was superior to the typical photo-copied fanzines that came out. Each example was unique as a fingerprint and the overall result was beautiful. Marty would do a typical punk era 'cut up and paste' job on copy, graphics and pictures. After I'd typed up my columns he'd literally stick them on a 'master page' using cow gum. Writing and publishing was more tactile in those days.

Steve did his best to help me with writing duties. He'd torture himself, chewing down a pencil, reaching for an opening sentence. He'd finish in a pool of sweat as if he'd played a gig with The Grateful Dead.

Every punk with an amp was waiting for this EMI A&R man. I reckon they had round-the-clock spotters. This stranger was the *Top Cat* in the alley, and we waited for him and that fat cheque. Indeed, weeks in advance, lads claimed to have seen him disembarking, either at the train or at the bus station. This mythical rock scout was more elusive than George Harrison: more important than the American President. To a lot of us the real President of the USA was Iggy Pop of course. *Mr Pop, sir.*

Bullshit circulated about lavish prizes and kickbacks on offer. People told about suitcases of payola, boxes of drugs, recording sessions in New York with David Bowie at the controls; and even a *Granada* TV series with Tony Wilson producing. Marty didn't offer any counterpoints to dampen these wild rumours, or to contradict the hype that one of his *S&M* bands was a boot-in. Particularly after a track off the second Turbo Overdrive EP, *Bumper Bronco Gel*, got a spin on the Kid Jensen evening show on Radio One. This relative success helped to refill the company coffers. Jensen didn't mention my sleeve notes.

The first edition of *Ob-scene* finally hit the streets. Marty had good trade links to local printers, so arranged a reasonable price. Bundles of the mag were distributed to local newsagents and other outlets around Nulton and Duncehead, including those owned by the Crock family. That was good going: Morton Treble had it 'sale or return' at the *Record Shack*.

Marty had a master plan for his publishing move. He aimed to be a rival to *Sniffin' Glue*, before he went and put *IPC* out of business. His greatest coup was to get permission to have *Ob-scene* accepted as the official programme for the Battle of the Bands. This meant that we could sell our mag during semi-finals and at the final itself. The only condition attached was that we must cover all bands involved.

That was reasonable (even for a one-man staff) except that I eventually had to write something about Steel Dildo. I didn't need to have the mind of Umberto Eco to work out their opinions. Dove was furious when he saw we didn't want to publish anything positive about him. Stan argued that our decision was just censorship. Fortunately Stan didn't get any say about the mag's editorial policy. If he or Dove was keen to publicise Dildo, let them publish their own 'zine. You don't hand a weapon to somebody intending to kill you or harm you. Do you offer full freedom to people who don't respect that freedom? Who want to take your freedom away from you and others they disapprove of? Dove sold his party's newspaper in town, usually on Saturdays. He did eventually bring out a fanzine, called *Hard As Nails*, which never featured British reggae groups such as Aswad or Steel Pulse, or any alternative viewpoints.

To begin with Snot was fascinated with *Hard As Nails*. He would read bits out loud, just to annoy me. The smirk soon dropped after he read a vitriolic article about Mortal in issue two. There was a 'battle of the mags' before the music final got underway. This created more enmity between Mortal and Dildo. Fortunately for us there were 'class traitor reformists' in the town hall, rather than those true to their principles of killing everyone else.

Don't forget, local music fans were convinced I was a star writer at *Music Mail*, thanks to Marty's constant plugging. They believed that a few positive words from me could launch their careers. This put a lot of pressure on me, not to mention social aggravation. I didn't like to disillusion them. Marty and I had a type of understanding, without needing to puncture our balloon.

Many bands accused me of being biased. If you smooth the ego of one rock star, you will rough up the ego of their rival. They'd complain about alleged misquotes or unflattering angles. A few times a musician or band would even physically threaten me. All the same, all of those would-be superstars wanted to read about him or herself. This type of rivalry or vanity definitely sold more copies of our magazine. In fact *Ob-scene* began to go like hot cakes after a strike at the bakery. You'd think a lucrative record contract was printed up on the back cover, just needing a signature.

Marty's fly posters were up on every surface in town – empty shop windows, rough walls and lamp posts, like layers of acne. Roy and I didn't have to avoid the cops any more. Everything was sanctioned by the council. The cops were instructed (by local politicians and organised criminals) to turn a blind eye to punk antics.

Even Paulie Wellington was writing bits for the *Nulton Chronicle*, fully testing the idea that any publicity was good publicity.

Despite his rock star ego Paulie didn't write anything about himself. He justifiably feared that Beer Belly and Backslapper would accuse him of moonlighting and sack him on the spotlight.

Even the stray cats up trees realised that Paulie didn't have his wits about him.

* * *

Keeping good time Marty and I called into *Nulton & Duncehead FM* to be interviewed for once.

Barry's playlist was as MOR as a three wheeled invalid car. The function of music on Dazzle's show was to punctuate his toe-curling gabble. We doubted that any punks would be tuned in to Baz's *Traffic Jam Show*. It was the producer who had invited us. Baz never scanned the pages of *NME* or *Sounds*, not to mention *Sniffin' Glue* or *Ob-scene*. His favourite group of all time was REO Speedwagon or Chicago.

Dazzle's original claim to rock fame was to have bought Bonnie Tyler a drink at the Wembley Holiday Inn once. Dazzle was a recognisable local figure, hired to open fetes and (one year) to turn on the Christmas lights. The self-obsessed DJ drove about in his distinctive purple 4x4 Jeep with his name sprayed along the side. Naturally he was a fan of Betsy Dandie and had played her indie EP. That was something.

Dazzle's producer kept us fidgeting in reception. Marty shuffled his bony buttocks on the edge of the seat, chain smoking. We were stranded in the waiting area outside Studio A, listening to weather reports and prattle. Marty and I feared our promo slot would be squeezed out.

Finally, the producer returned and led us towards the studio. There was only five minutes left before Friday evening gardening tips.

Goofing behind his console, as Barbara Dickson faded out, Dazzle hailed us forward to the console. He told us to move in closer towards big fluffy green mics and to put on headphones. Barry sported bushy sideburns and his new Eagles tour tee-shirt. He was spray-tanned, fifty something, with crinkly blue eyes, a big nose and bottle blonde permed hair. He was also prone to a shit-eating music biz grin. His dental work made Barry Gibb resemble Shane McGowan.

Marty knew how to address a radio mic, his reputation behind the decks was legendary and he was no media amateur.

It quickly became obvious to us that Dazzle was paranoidly suspicious of the punk maestro. The producer had made this booking, and Dazzle had zero interest in punk rock, national, local or galactic. Like other normal subjects Dazzle's awareness of punk came from the *Today* programme fiasco and tabloid fright and spite. Otherwise he had no curiosity about the music or the street fashion scene.

Dazzle came back live, as a Cliff Richard tuned out. Baz got the fake chit chat with Marty underway and immediately looked alarmed. Dazzle wanted to avoid revealing his own ignorance and indifference, particularly after he understood that Gorran in the studio.

Dazzle's orange wrinkles took on a panicky expression; and Marty chewed the fat like an Inuit on acid.

'*Super*, Marty, me old mate,' Dazzle interrupted. 'So what'd you say's the name of this little band of yours? Turgid Overdrive, *ha, ha*. Well, hey *Fernando*, that one'll stick in the ole lug oles. So you folks at home, or driving home from work, pin back your flaps and get a load of this Turgid Overdrive group, *ha ha*. Get your glad rags out of the wardrobe, girls! Treat yourself to a Nulton night out. Just listen to your *Pilot of the Airwaves*, Baz Dazzle, my friends. Have yourselves a jolly night out. Marty's band's down there at the Civic Hall for this *Battle of the Bands* contest. And he's hoping it's not his Waterloo, *ha ha*,' he chuckled, in that smoky baritone.

'*Ha, ha*, it's been ever so *super*, Marty. The best of British to you, son. It's been an absolute pleasure. So have a good one, will you? May the best band win on the night!'

'Right, definitely Baz, but…'

'Are you gonna make them a star, Marty?' Baz concluded our package, cutting out his rival's microphone, and talking over. '*Ha, ha*, well that'll be the day!'

After this the studio technician faded in Doctor Hook's *When You're In Love with a Beautiful Woman*. And that was the signal for us to take off our headphones.

'Right, that's it boys. Thanks for coming in,' Dazzle told us. The grin and bonhomie was dropped.

'Gord elp us,' Marty protested afterwards, as we exited. 'I reckon that blinkin wanker's on the same space ship as bloomin Earth Wind and Fire.'

'With none of their talent or melodies!' I agreed.

'Straight up, you got the picture, cos that Dazzle's never had to get a crowd up dancing on the blinkin floor. No bullshit, I hope they don't make that blinkin show poodle one of the fucking judges.'

During the interview I wasn't allowed a single word in edgewise. That was rough on a celebrity rock writer. However dire our appearance on the radio, it acted as another big plug for the competition.

34. Attacked from Both Sides

Nulton Civic Hall was the largest and most prestigious venue in town. It typically offered a programme of classical concerts, touring theatre, as well as the Christmas panto and even Uri Geller the Israeli spoon bender. Geller's psychic energy had caused a sensation by stopping the town hall clock dead and even melting off the big hand. There was a team of engineers dangling and swinging off ropes for weeks, trying to fix the mechanism and then to solder on a new long arm.

Both members of Parliament were invited to the final of the Battle, together with town councillors, the staff of the DHSS, the Nulton Athletic football squad and numerous business and media figures. The politicians came on a jolly, only to get the biggest shock of their lives.

The Civic Hall offered every 'act' its own dressing room. Each band had its name pinned to the door like true rock stars. For one night Turbo could strut about like Van Halen. Considering this was the punk period – and many groups had only been together for a few months – that was incredible enough. Mortal Wound was now only Stan Snot, yet he had a changing room to himself. The little guitarist crossed his fingers for a last ditch group reunion.

Solo performers were banned under the contest rules. Stan wanted to get away with that breach, but somebody had shopped him. I knew that it had to be Dove, or one of his legions.

Some old bloke with a greasy comb-over, heavy black glasses, a brown corduroy suit barged in. He was waving around a clipboard, to inform our diminutive axe hero of his dire fate.

'No solo artistes, son. We've already had a complaint about you. I uphold the complaint,' the man confirmed. 'No, no, this won't do.'

'That lad complaining's a fascist,' I objected.

'Well, this lad's not going out solo!'

'Don't listen to petty complaints!' Snot whined.

'You're not allowed. You know the rules, son. We posted a copy out to the lot of you. That's that.'

'So it's final for the final,' Snot quipped.

'*Solo not allowed*. Read for yourself. This is a competition for new local *groups*,' he emphasised, breaking sweat, waving the clipboard.

'I've got a weak chest,' Stan remarked – satirically.

'Yes, have a heart, will you?' I added.

'He's not playing anything by himself.'

'That's bollocks that is.'

'No, no, it's certainly not. Unless you produce your group, in a couple of minutes,' he explained, checking his wristwatch, 'you're out.'

'You're a fascist as well?'

'Don't be cheeky to me, son.'

'My group's off playing on a cruise ship,' Stan claimed.

'What do you want me to do? Throw 'em a life boat? Good luck. You can't play this concert on your own. You're out, son.'

Snot's career as a punk rock icon was at risk. Fortunately, as this critical moment of pop history, Gorran made another timely entrance. With an inborn sense of a looming crisis, the guru came to check on preparations. The reality was not encouraging.

'Right, definitely Snot mate, what the jack up the beanstalk's going on in here?' he wondered. '*Gord elp us* mate, what are you doing waving a bloomin clip board in front of their noses? Straight up, this is a contest for blinkin rock bands not for fucking prize potatoes.'

'Who are *you*, *when* you're at 'ome?' He was startled by Marty's charismatic style. 'What gives you the *or-thority* to speak to me in that blunt manner?' Offended, he blinked and snuffled.

Marty's smile pulled rank. 'Straight up, get into the picture, because I'm the blinkin manager of this fucking top little rock band,' Marty explained. 'No bullshit, and who the fuck are you, when you an't out on your blinkin milk round?' he wondered.

'You want washing out with soap and water.'

'The establishment's kicking me out,' Stan remarked.

'No more complaints from you, sonny Jim,' the official pronounced, perspiring freshly. He took another quick look at the printed sheet on his clipboard.

'Straight up, listen to this fucking Mister Ten blinkin Bob's Worth,' Marty objected. 'Straight up, how are you gonna explain what you're doing, hanging about in my artists' changing room?'

'What you insinuating?' The steward adjusted himself against the barbs. 'This competition's only for groups. Do you get me? Solo is against the rules. No solo! *Point six, paragraph three,*' he pointed out, rapping the document.

'Gord elp us, no bullshit, you're letting power go to your blinkin head, mate. No bullshit, we came out to the Civic Hall tonight to cop a few cracking fucking local rock bands. Not to argue with some bloke in a brown coat reading out an act of bloomin Parliament,' Gorran objected, grinning in amazement.

'That lad can pack away that guitar and go home,' the gentleman insisted.

The punk maestro's temperature was raised. 'Right, definitely, we didn't come out to listen to some bloomin concert by the North Korean fucking male voice choir,' Marty objected, wincing.

'Technically they'd be a group,' I pointed out.

'Not without instruments,' Stan insisted.

An official finger was aimed at our local pop impresario. 'Talk to the chairman of judges. He'll tell you the same. No solo artistes tonight!'

'Fair play, we didn't put on our glad rags for some jumped up usherette to start reading out the fucking riot act,' Marty replied. Agonised frustration crushed his features.

'Watch your mouth, son! I can't stand about 'ere all night, arguing with you,' said the official. 'You can't be doing anything about it. *The rules is the rules.* Judges' word is final,' he told us.

The official left in high dudgeon.

'That's the end of my solo career,' Snot commented.

'Straight up Snot, what a blinkin shambles this is,' Marty rebuked. 'No bullshit, not for the first time.'

'Well, I didn't want you as our manager,' Stan replied.

'Come off it, Stan,' I said.

'Let the big cheese find another punk band.'

'Right, definitely Snot, now you blinkin mention it,' Marty said. 'Fair play, maybe I'd better go off and see if the blinkin Damned want a new fucking manager. Or I've always fancied going orf to New York some time to offer my services to blinkin Suicide.'

Billy Urine arrived. '*All roight lads!*? What's the scandal? What do I hear about some bas'tad putting in a complaint about our Stan so?' he wondered.

'That's right,' I informed. 'Stan can't play the gig solo. Officially it's not allowed.'

'Straight up Billy, what does this bloomin contest matter to you, with Snot throwing his fucking rattle out of the pram?' Gorran complained, rinsing his hair.

'I'm ready to play,' Snot assured the drummer.

'Who made this feckin complaint now? Fair play lads, who'd be so sneaky as to object? When everybody's turned up and ready to play the gig?' Urine speculated.

'It has to be Mick Dove,' I said.

The drummer snatched a quick breath. 'Ai now, the Dildo vocalist, mind?'

'He's the only lad who hates Stan enough. Our band's a threat to Dildo's chances. Take us out, it's easier to win. Dove wants the recording contract.'

'Right, definitely, Bottle's got his finger on the blinkin pulse about that bloomin little boot boy. Or I must be Tom Jones,' Marty agreed, in a hunch.

The truth flashed in our eyes, like warning lights on Turbo Overdrive's sound desk.

'Why don't we tell the judges?'

'Right, definitely Bottle, what a good bloomin idea, when Dove's got Troy Boy in his back pocket and a couple of politicians to keep 'em company,' Gorran warned. 'Straight up, just try going down to that fucking town hall to complain about your blinkin rent,' he suggested, battling with some fresh tics.

'Look on the *broight* side now, lads,' Billy cut in. 'I'm avail'ble and you got Steve on bass. No need to go feckin solo and t'ink about gettin *disqualifoyed*. Fair play lads, don't get down hearted. We're *satis-foyin* the rules so. Let's get ready and play this feckin gig.'

Billy inspired us. He had arrived with some of his drum cases. To emphasise the change he picked up his sticks and began to beat a tattoo on the table.

'You've been *rehearsing* as a three piece,' I reminded Snot. 'Why not go for it?'

'Play as a three piece Stan, so you can. We've been playin all the songs. Don't be a stubborn *ee-diot*.'

'Right, definitely Billy, but when I heard you lot rehearsing as a three piece I've heard more fucking sparks from a box of wet blinkin fireworks.'

'We're total crap in that format,' Stan agreed. 'Complete bollocks and no Sex Pistols.'

'So we're just going home?' I said. 'Is that your plan?'

'Right, definitely Snot, he's got a blinkin point, because if you can't get your original fucking band together, you'd better play the final with Steve and Billy. Otherwise, no bullshit, the organisers are going to send me to the fucking cleaners, quicker than one of Dean Martin's blinkin suits,' Gorran warned, shrinking down into his shoulders.

* * *

While we harangued with Stan, our dispute was rudely interrupted. Mick Dove burst in with his thugs and began to give us all a good kicking. That's the only way to put it. There was no advance warning and we were caught by total surprise.

Apparently Dove had seen Billy turning up at the venue. The fascist frontman knew that Urine had spoken to Fenton about forming a scratch band. After making an official complaint to the judges, Dove was afraid that his Civic Hall putsch would fail.

He didn't know that Stan refused to perform as a three-piece, or admit how he missed Sour Cat.

These right-wing lads were harder and meaner than hammers and crowbars. This time my dad's boxing lessons – enthusiastic but amateurish – didn't come in very handy. I could only put my hands up in futile defence.

Before I could catch second wind one of the thugs had punched me off my feet. In a baffling moment I found myself across the floor. As if Sugar Ray Robinson had danced in, I'd no idea what had hit me. Suddenly I was gazing at the world from two inches off the ground. It was just me and the fluff down there.

In actual fact Mick and the NF boys knocked three chords out of us. Dove's intention was to cause Stan more lasting damage. Marty was beaten into a corner, curled into a ball, yelping. In the words of the song, he was a talker not a fighter.

'Get yer feckin hands off me!' Billy screamed. Despite a pugnacious reputation he could hardly flex a muscle. With no chance to retaliate, the Mortal Wound stickman was skittled like a bar game.

Like the epilogue of *Mein Kampf*, they'd been saving the worst for us. I felt the end of their boots between my ribs. Dove's small face was screwed up into a small fist of hatred; resembling a furious worm. We were vanquished. The NF boys stood sneering over us, fists and jaws clenched up, hearts and minds closed. From this extremist angle, I was forced to look up one of Dove's drainpipes. I nervously counted the eyelets on his boots, while praying for my life. There was no opportunity for a socialist fightback, as Roy would have urged, if he'd been there.

A groaning and moaning heap, we'd nothing to add to the political debate.

'Don't fuck with patriots,' Dove hissed. Attempting to raise his voice, it came out in a weird, hushed pitch. Even when he was enraged, you had to strain your ears. Vocally he was a type of Tom Thumb in jackboots.

'Nothing else to say, Bottle? You ain't playing this gig, Snot. You heard the patriotic councillor. People want the truth. We're not tolerating your leftist agenda.'

'Right, definitely, felthead, but I reckon you still owe me five hundred quid,' Marty complained. 'Straight up, I'll send you all my fucking medical and laundry bills after this.'

The thugs left the scene. The Mortal crowd was scattered as if a bomb had gone off.

'Oh bays, it's brutal, I can't even raise me feckin arms,' Billy complained.

'Right, definitely Billy, I definitely don't want to bump into those blinkin ugly zombies again, down a fucking dark alley,' Marty agreed, brushing off his music manager's jacket.

'I reckon we already did,' I pointed out. Lucky I didn't play any instruments.

Marty soon proved that rock dreams are indestructible. Our music mogul clambered back on to his pixie boots, pulling up his Ramones' jeans and was knocking the dust out of his puffy hair.

I stayed on the ground for a while longer, tasting blood and cobwebs, in a bitter satire of poetic bliss.

I almost regretted that we took music so seriously. I knew that Abba never got this type of treatment.

35. Another Girl, Another Planet

Our National Front Disco experience provoked Marty Gorran to urgent action. While other bands were going through sound checks, out in the auditorium, we decided to go and persuade Gina to make a punk comeback.

Everybody on the Nulton rock scene knew that Sour Cat – regardless of her talent – had problems. She was agoraphobic, claustrophobic, Paulie-phobic, everything phobic. Sightings were rarer than the sound of a cuckoo in winter.

'She's twitchier than Joe Cocker,' Stan said.

'Cocker's into the music,' I said. 'He's got stage presence!' Sometimes my friend's music taste posturing – on the thermometer of cool – could irritate me.

Not only did Cat stop attending gigs, including local pub gigs, she didn't even go out dancing or socialise anymore. What was getting in to her? She was beginning to make Greta Garbo's social life look like Liz Taylor's.

The Watsons' house was so gloomy the Brönte sisters would have refused to go in there; not even on a *Forte* hotels weekend-break special offer. Marty told me to do all the talking on the doorstep, reasoning that her Mum had already met me. I tried to explain that her mother generally regarded me like Charles Bukowski. But she was *even more* alarmed by Gorran and by his turns of phrase.

Anyway they didn't answer the bell. There was not a movement from inside or a light, in response; only an exterior coach light that showed up all our garish anxious faces. If her mother *had* been home again, most likely the cops would have joined us.

However, as we huddled together under the porch, we began to pick out sounds of brittle notes. We decided it must be Gina going through keyboard exercises. Presumably she was practising for her appointment at Leeds School of Music. Maybe she decided to continue and ignore the knocks and chimes. Or subconsciously, at an infantile pre-mirror stage, she wanted us to go and rescue her, like some punk princess in a MOR tower. Sometimes our dreams can trap us, no matter how pretty they look.

'Right, definitely, don't hang about looking at each other like a bunch of blinkin electrocuted street cats. Straight up, take those blinkin chains off your trousers too. This an't fucking Halloween,' Gorran told the band members. 'Or no bullshit the whole blinkin neighbourhood will hear the clanking and start running orf in bloomin horror.'

'Why can't she make it simple like? And just answer the feckin door?' Urine objected.

'Cat's got unconscious internal conflicts to resolve,' I analysed.

'*Gord elp us* Bottle, is that the bullshit you want to write for fucking *Music Mail* every week?'

'Let's go home and forget all about it,' Snot suggested.

Gorran was in no mood for punk cynicism while going to all this trouble.

'Bang the knocker one more time,' I suggested.

'She must be feckin deaf now!'

'She's getting her Beethoven complex,' Stan argued.

'No bullshit, it'd be easier to rouse that blinkin Maria Callous to come out and sing at the fucking Albert Hall.'

Ironically it was probably a Beethoven piece she was playing; some dreamy run of Romantic notes that went fluttering away into the street. But you could pick up her nerves too, as the piece was regularly halted and restarted. Whatever the explanation, we were in no mood to stand about listening.

'Gina's lost herself in the classical world.'

'Feck off Snot, and get your t'inking cap on,' Billy rebuked.

'Right, definitely,' Marty agreed, 'we have to break into fucking Colditz here and put some blinkin sense into that dented head of hers. No bullshit, not only some taste in bloomin music,' he argued, grimacing. Gorran didn't like any musician in a periwig, especially after Adam Ant sold out.

'What yer t'inkin, Marty? Looks like they got this big house under lock and key,' Billy said. He cast a wary look over the daunting facade of the Watson villa.

'Right, definitely, just blinkin spread yourselves out and look for open windows,' Marty instructed, shooing us.

'Not another break in,' I commented.

'Right, definitely, stop whinging.'

'I don't like it,' Snot said, as if he was being handed a concept album.

After getting assaulted by Dove and his cronies, we were a bit sore. Music business aside, life in general was less rosy. We pushed through shrubberies and trampled flowerbeds to get into the back garden. Eventually we regathered on the Watson's undulating lawn, like porcupines from hell. Immediately we noticed there was a light on upstairs. We distinguished some movement behind curtains. Gina had a bedroom on the second storey. It was definitely quite a pad.

'Either that's her bedroom, or they got a phantom of the opera,' Snot said.

'Fair play, if you can't be any more help, Stan bay.'

Gina didn't respond to subtle whistles or calls. We had to rely on Gorran's media-manipulator mind to come up with a brilliant idea. The punk maverick organised us into a human ladder, to scale the exterior wall and reach her bedroom window. What a crazy idea. It was a type of circus version of the balcony scene in *Romeo and Juliet*. As the strongest Billy Urine was anchor man. Rather than a hod of bricks he held *me* up on his shoulders; and Snot was stood on mine. Unfortunately he was the Romeo, but he *was* the smallest.

Gorran was hanging about as ring master. Snot's ample thighs squeezed my cheeks, as if I was stuck between Miss Piggy's arse cheeks. Billy must have tripped, because he folded and the three of us went sprawling over the lawn. Luckily it was only grass to land on. As top man Snot went with a thump and a howl on impact, adding a bit of relish to his bruises. He might have sued Gorran for breach of contract.

With our second attempt – staggering like a pissed giraffe – we had more success. Billy made a desperate rush and collapsed our noses against bricks. After clawing and scrambling against the wall of the house, Snot was high enough to reach Juliet's window ledge. Tense and awkward, as if he could plunge at any moment, Stan nervously raised a knuckle to tap on the glass. No rock guitar-hero should have gone through this ordeal. Fortunately there was a rapid reaction as the sash was thrown up. Somebody had come to the window to look down.

'What's this? You put on a growth spurt Stan?' It was Cat's voice.

'Not funny,' he said.

She'd no problem recognising Snot's melancholy eyes and piratical face, peering up at her from under the ledge. Gina stared down, a hand over her mouth, as she recognised us all in turn. It was shocking that Gorran had forced a disabled person to perform this. But like everyone, she didn't mention the fact. Nobody thought of Stan in regard to his 'disabilities'.

'What an amazing trick, boys. I'm impressed!'

'Course it was the Big Cheese.'

'All right, Gina?' I called.

Billy Urine's voice came up shakily. 'Fer feck's sake Gina, come down and let us in!'

'What else can you boys do?!'

'It's finals night,' Snot told her, ironically.

'The Battle of the Bands? That came around quick.'

'Didn't it! Time flies!' I called.

Even Billy's rope-like neck muscles were at risk.

'So what are you doing here?' she asked.

'As a three piece we're shit,' Stan explained.

'The rules stop him playing solo,' I added.

'Give me a song, I'll give my opinion,' Cat teased.

'Right, definitely Gina love, so why don't you blinkin hop down quick? Straight up, before this bunch of monkeys do 'emselves more mischief?' Marty called up. His wiry bony frame was silhouetted in moonlight below her – with just a fuzzy halo about his hair.

'Try this in your stage show,' Gina teased.

Snot kept his artistic fingers hooked over the ledge.

'Fair play Gina, just do as we bloomin ask and let us in. Or, no bullshit, we gonna lose that blinkin record contract faster than Ravi Shanker tunes up a one string fucking lute,' Marty warned.

'What're you doing here, mop head?'

Apart from that distinctive puff of hair and star dust, Marty was in obscurity. Only he was still larger than ordinary life.

Finally we were able to collapse our human ladder. We could only hope that Cat had listened to Mortal's legendary manager.

* * *

The house radiated affluence and cultural taste, from the hallway through. I was able to read off tell-tale signs like Roland Barthes. Or like Jacques Derrida, I had a shrewd eye for contradictions. Her father could afford these things, because he ran those paper mills and a paper products company. Joseph Watson had a good reputation as an employer and was respected. More than this he was a big music fan and he sponsored concerts, even though, as yet, not punk concerts.

Gina wasn't dressed to shock that evening. I'd never seen her without theatrical makeup and shocking fashions. She was just in a plain blouse and a pleated skirt, like a character from a dystopian science fiction novel. Somehow she looked really good. Or maybe it was just me. Snot thought she'd given up Rotten and all that punk.

Without heavy punk cosmetics her features were cooler. She was looking tired though and there were dark smudges under her eyes. Generally I was mad about her. Past experience with girls taught me not to show my feelings too obviously. She might have been a pussy cat, but I was still a platypus.

Gina was shocked by our latest appearance – and it had nothing to do with punk. This was after our pre-gig warm up, when Dove and his mates had slapped us about. Snot had a cut on his cheek and a display of psychedelic colours developing. At this stage she was more concerned about Snot's injuries than mine. That grieved me. I guess he was the key member of Mortal, whereas I just typed up interviews. He got her sympathy and concern, while I dished out a naive compliments.

'What happened to you? Oh my god!'

Snot gave her a summary, 'Some lads did us over in the changing room,' he explained.

'Them right wing t'ugs gave us a roight good kickin' so!' Billy admitted. 'It was shockin'!'

'They got us by surprise. I was pushed on the floor, before I knew anything,' I said. 'One of them was kicking me in the ribs… while I was on the ground.'

'Not a sight for sore eyes,' she told us. 'Come into the front room, will you. Just for a while… to recover… take the weight off your boots.'

We followed but we must have looked anxious. With a band sound check overdue, we were up against the town hall clock, fortunately repaired.

'Don't worry, my parents are out… late shopping. Anyway they rarely come into the front room. The house is too big for them to use.'

'No bullshit Gina, I reckon you've got a few blinkin ghosts wandering about this creepy fucking castle,' Gorran agreed.

'Mozart,' Snot suggested.

Besides the skirt and blouse, Gina was modelling fluffy slippers. We could almost be shocked. She definitely wasn't in Sour Cat costume.

If Mortal didn't make their sound check, in some shape and number, they would be disqualified. But how could you even sound check, if you didn't have a band?

We sunk into a couple of Chesterfield sofas, but couldn't afford to hang around. A bit of talking and negotiation was necessary to persuade Sour Cat. Gorran sensed a weak spot towards us – a chink of sympathy – and he was the PR negotiator to work on it.

To begin with his heartfelt riffs, about human adversity and rock destiny, didn't make any impact. 'Why should I come back to the band now… just to help you lot out of a fix?' she said.

Good question. Freud or the beat poets couldn't help me. She sat looking sceptical, opposite to us, wringing her hands, as if to get the stiffness out of her fingers. It looked as if she was sitting in a cold draft. She was pleased to see us again, but she was far from her old punk self.

'Right, definitely Gina,' Marty set off again, leaning forward between his bony knees, clasping those dyed hands, turning up a tragi-comic mask. 'No bullshit love, if you don't come back into Mortal Wound tonight, then those bloomin arrogant wankers on the council are gonna disqualify them. Straight up, quicker than David Bailey gets the blinkin angles on all those fucking models of his.'

'I'd like to help,' she commented.

'Straight up Gina, what harm can it do to play rhythm guitar and contribute your bloomin musical talents and backing vocals? No bullshit, so Mortal Wound can pick up that winners' cheque tonight and get that blinkin lucrative recording contract into their fucking back pockets.' The rock supremo attempted to twinkle confident reassurance.

It was a hard pitch, even if a chipped tooth and a half-closed eye added pathos and anti-hero appeal.

'Can't you take no as an answer? You want me to put it in a tattoo... on my ass?' she cut back. Gina remained on her feet, ready to show us out and return to her studies.

'Fair play now Gina, where's the harm in it, so?' Billy wanted to know. 'Just play the gig *tonoight* will yer... an' help us win the contest, because, jeysus, we gotta play our best now.' There seemed to be a lump in Urine's throat.

She folded her arms and tapped a tempo with her slipper. 'Why'd I want to do that? To get gobbed at and abused? When I got good music upstairs to think about?'

'Right, definitely, so you're gonna hide away in that blinkin bedroom of yours? Straight up, pull the fucking curtains on the blinkin world and tap away on that fucking little keyboard?' he said.

She turned away, anxious.

'Straight up, you're gonna have that on your guilty blinkin conscience for the rest of your life,' the pop maverick argued.

'How did you work that out?'

'No bullshit, having big regrets that you condemned a fucking great little punk band to bloomin obscurity for future generations. Straight up, that you help to launch 'em back down the fucking plug hole of rock 'n' roll destiny,' Marty objected, diplomatically. On the edge of his seat, he winced at such a terrible event.

'I'm not a regular member,' Gina argued.

'They need you,' I said. 'Without you, they're just… also rans.'

'Never rans,' Stan put in.

Sour cat merely shrugged and stared fixedly ahead.

'Right, definitely, you want to listen to Bottle here, the top fucking rock writer on that blinkin *Music Mail* paper down in London. No bullshit Gina, if you an't playing the gig tonight I might as well take Snot here and drop 'im back down at the bus station. Straight up, so he can get out his instrument and start fucking busking,' Marty argued.

'What cheek you want the tattoo?' Cat commented.

'Fuck off, will I.'

'Right, definitely Snot, so Mortal's going over those Niagara Falls blindfolded on a fucking handcart,' the pop maverick told him. He was struggling to sort out his facial muscles in this crisis.

Gina stayed put and wasn't moved.

'Honest, you're the heart and soul of this band,' I declared.

'Until I pass my exams and get into music school, I can't commit to anything. I read about the final in the *Chronicle*. I support you… hope you do really well… but it's difficult for me to re-join.'

'You can still read that paper?' I wondered.

'We're lost our mojo, Gina, without yer. Fair play, so we have. Won't you reconsider coming back to us like?' Billy urged.

She flinched under pressure. 'You've got to understand… it's important for my future… last time I made a hash of the Bach piece. It was so bloody embarrassing. All those teachers observing me… twitching their beards and stuff. I wanted the floor to open up.'

269

'Right, definitely, Gina, never mind those blinkin fiddle slashing dinosaurs, get your bloomin guitar back over your shoulder and out of the fucking house. Otherwise, straight up, Mortal have got no chance of triumphing in the competition and putting a bloomin three album deal into their jacket pockets. No bullshit, Gina, you're losing your sense of fucking reality,' Gorran warned.

The star vocalist and multi-instrumentalist stared ahead blankly; chewing her lips.

'You're absolutely brilliant,' I said.

Sour Cat gave me a curious look. And the others turned to check me out too.

'You're vital to the band now.'

'Since you first walked into practice at Crock Studios,' Billy admitted. 'Honest to God, I don't care what you moight say now, Stan bay. That's the *troot*. We lost our feckin sound, way back so. It changed when she joined us, so it did.'

'If I can do the vocals,' Gina said. 'I'd consider it.'

'Lead vocals? No way.'

'Listen to you now, Stan bay, you was desperate for her a moment ago.'

'Just desperate,' Snot remarked.

'Go and spin on it,' Gina suggested.

'She has to stick to rhythm guitar. I'm doing the vocals and lead guitar,' the head punk insisted.

'Right, definitely Snot, go and bloomin listen to yourself will you? No bullshit Snot, squawking up on that stage like Bob blinkin Dylan with a fucking nose peg on. Straight up, you lot, if Gina wants to do bloomin vocals and add a few licks on guitar, I'm telling you as your blinkin manager to take her on board. No bullshit, Snot, your vocals give me the bloomin shakes, like a lot of blinkin neutron bombs,' Marty grimaced.

'Get a chunk of the big cheese.'

'I'll definitely try some lead vocals, if you're really asking me,' she said. 'What happened to Nutcase, anyway?' she wondered.

'Vocal nodules,' I explained.

'Oh, poor Nut! Is he on the mend or what?'

'Straight up, we got a bloomin sound check coming up. No bullshit, Mortal's gonna piss away that record deal like Ollie Reed against a blinkin lamp post,' Marty warned, fighting with a pained look.

'Live concerts don't agree with me. Remember?'

'Don't get fussed, Gina, cos we'll look after you,' I promised.

'Maybe I'll think about it. Buy me a drink before it starts.'

'Gord elp us, just stay away from the blinkin orange juice, will you?'

'You've got to include my songs on the album,' she stated.

'Bollocks will we,' Snot bristled.

'Right, definitely Gina, don't listen any more cos he's not in a position to blinkin negotiate. Fair play, glad you're being more bloomin positive and getting into the right mood. Straight up, go and grab your bloomin coat, will you?' Marty told her.

'What's my dad going to say?' she wondered.

36. The Rock Aristocracy Gathers

Gina insisted that we get Nutcase back, as a pre-condition for her. Cat agreed to play rhythm guitar, adding only backing vocals and splashes of keyboard. She was definitely in a strong negotiating position.

Marty faced the challenge of appealing to Nutcase's best instincts and returning him for a sound check. The big name DJ had to throw the little Austin around town as if entered into the cross-Sahara rally race – if not in a purple haze, definitely in a blue haze of exhaust smoke.

We found Mrs Nut and Little Nut fast asleep, but not Big Nut. Sandra wasn't delighted to see us gathered on her doorstep again. Luckily she already knew us, because we didn't look wholesome, not even to a heavy metal fan married to a Mohican punk.

'My Paul's not at 'ome, lads,' she explained. 'He's workin' on those 'ouses Parrots are throwin' up.'

The *S&M* gang had to scramble back into the *Sunbeam* in a good impression of the *Keystone Cops*. Grinding gears and burning North Sea oil (just then beginning to pump into giros) the pop impresario grimaced forward over the wheel with grim determination.

I thumbed through a copy of the *Nulton A – D*, to try to determine the location of this half-built 'Paradise' Estate. It was right off Purgatory. At last we caught up with Nutcase, after Gorran had negotiated security staff: he managed to baffle them with enough hype. The pop magnate had two verbal talents; either he'd charm the pants off them or make them desperate to get rid of him. After jogging along muddy streets-in-embryo, trying to avoid trucks and machinery, we found our vocalist at his alternative labours. He was painting ceilings, tilting his head back like Michelangelo filling in clouds. Apparently he'd given up the idea of being a rock god, or even a punk rock hate figure.

Gina whined that the doctor's advice about resting and medicating was just bullshit. She argued that you didn't get rid of nodules by pampering them, you blasted them with screams instead (his own, that is). Either that or you shrank them with vodka. Nutcase listened to her wide eyed, taking in the expert advice. Meanwhile he was dabbing white-spirit into a cloth and wiping his thick fingers. He never wanted to disappoint Gina or hurt her feelings. He highly respected her playing and singing and she took advantage. So he listened to her dubious advice, even though a ship load of Vikings wouldn't have budged him otherwise.

'Right, Gina. I 'eard yer out. What you 'ad to say. If you lads want me back… Well, right… To be honest, I've missed it. A gig 'ud do me good,' he decided. His bison chest expanded as the crazy thrill returned.

So we scrambled back to the car (now sprayed with mud from a passing tipper truck). Complaining bitterly Gorran geared back to Nulton's bright light. There was no time for Nut to take off paint spattered work overalls. Marty thought they'd be an effective costume for the gig. 'Straight up Nut, it's all about making a blinkin impact,' the pop genius argued. As ever we genuflected. 'No bullshit Nut, listen to me, cos they'll be hanging those blinkin paint spattered overalls of yours in a window down the fucking King's Road this time next year.'

'You reckon, Marty?'

'It's not so far-fetched,' I said. I was his most gullible mouthpiece at this time.

The Mortal screamer crammed his glued-up green bristles under the roof. Luckily he'd kept that hair style, which resembled a green flying saucer stuck through the centre of his head.

'I've been missin' the buzz,' he admitted.

We flew back into town, with no more hold-ups, for our date with rock 'n' roll destiny. So we hoped. And when we got there (after Marty had parked at a zigzag) we noticed a Les's old Caddy

(*Buick, Pontiac, Cadillac – Empire Coach/Attleboro MA*) slunk into the kerb of the high street, in defiance of regulations. This enormous flattened looking automobile was a vintage landmark for the town. Phoenix had resprayed its rusty arches especially for the Battle of the Bands final.

The more cynical of Nulton's youth – and older generations too – doubted Les's Texan origins. From time to time, the topic came up. They detected more than a hint of Stoke-on-Trent in that Lone Star twang of his. Most people on the Nulton music scene preferred to go along with him. We were happy to hitchhike along his freeway, particularly with a genuine US girl like Betsy hitched for the ride. Nobody could doubt that Betsy came from Baltimore. Phoenix definitely had a half-sister in Pittsburgh, who'd married an American sailor (his job was to pull back the elastic on aircraft carriers). A few lads had been introduced to her in the *Dragon*, when she came over to visit family. She definitely had an American accent. It was enough to keep Phoenix's American credibility alive.

'Straight up lads, be blinkin sensitive with Les tonight, after the bloomin King went and fucking pegged it,' Marty advised.

'Don't worry,' I told him. 'We're all sad about it.'

'Fair play, Les was his biggest fan and it takes a lot of blinkin courage to drag himself out of *Gracelands* tonight,' the rock guru briefed us.

As our bunch headed towards the Hall, a Cadillac door opened before us, with an almighty creak at the joints. At first we thought it must be Springsteen about to jump out on to the Nulton sidewalk. Unfortunately it wasn't the New Jersey legend, it was Betsy Dandie and a couple of her Screamers. A tight ball of energy, smiling dazzlingly, kitted out in black leather, with her pointy boots and a blaze of blonde hair, she definitely looked like a million dollar record contract. Betsy had certain traits in common with Bruce.

Gina looked at the woman admiringly, 'She looks like the winner,' she said.

'*Gord elp us*, Gina love, don't be taken in by all that *Red Rooster* hype. Straight up, put your blinkin chin up and have a bit more bloomin self-confidence,' Marty suggested. 'No bullshit, you got more talent in one of your blinkin tonsils than she'd got in her whole bloomin body.'

There wasn't exactly a red carpet for Betsy, or any explosion of flash bulbs, only the typical crowd of spotty youths. Even so they were star struck, even allowing for hormones. The glitzy rock starlet was making her rapid show biz entrance.

We were heading towards the stage door. 'Right, definitely, we'll let Les have his moment in the blinkin spotlight,' Marty told us. 'Fair play, if Betsy and the Screamers win this competition, then I'll cut off my own fucking ears and pop em into an envelope for 'em.'

'Remember what he just told us,' Stan said.

We looked back down the alley to where the *Red Rooster* entourage had assembled. Phoenix sniffed the evening air (just as polluted as LA) smelling rock 'n' roll destiny, like Jasmine in Austin (Texas). The CEO of Red Rooster was dignified, sombre, all in black (in respect to Presley) a trademark fur draped over his shoulders and the Stetson cocked forward. For the big night he'd asked his friend (Al from next door) to drive him and the artists to the venue. The diminutive pensioner was kitted out awkwardly in a hired chauffeur's uniform and cap.

No back entrances for Red Rooster.

'No bullshit, that's the only way old Les can get his blinkin head through,' Marty jested. 'Straight up, even if he took his blinkin hat *orf.*'

Gina was no better in the Diva stakes. She was stood looking at her guitar case and keyboard. All of a sudden it was too much for her. 'Thank you. Will you boys carry my gear for me? Or what should I do?'

'We'll figure out the set list,' Snot was saying.

'You only got three songs to play, max,' I reminded them.

'We'll get through the sound check first. I've got a few new songs. A couple of obnoxious rackets. We can include them for the gig.'

'Maybe *Faber*'ll publish your collected song lyrics one day,' Gina teased.

'My songs are so crap nobody would ever want to sing em.'

'Good. At least you're honest about your talents.'

'Out of self-respect and love for music,' he said.

'Why bother to write and play them in the first place?' Gina challenged.

'They're not for your ears,' Snot said, snappishly.

'Thank god for that.'

'Right, definitely, cut out all this blinkin bickering you two, will you? No bullshit, you've only got a few bloomin minutes to sort it all out,' their manager warned.

'Keep your hair on, Marty,' Cat told him.

Yet the rock mogul was patting her shoulders reassuringly. He didn't want his biggest asset losing her nerve and running off.

'Listen up to the big Cheese,' Snot quipped.

'It makes sense,' I insisted.

So we agreed to carry Sour Cat's equipment. Nutcase was afraid she'd fall off her stilettos again, on the way in.

'Don't worry, I know my limits, mop head,' Cat teased.

'Gord elp us, Gina love, we all know about your fucking limits!'

Gorran was trying to spot the rival big hair from EMI. He calculated that the music exec. should be in the building. The fast train had arrived and this EMI big wig had to be hanging about some place. The high-rolling A&R man could be intercepted and schmoozed in advance. He'd surely never met an impresario with such dazzle as Marty Gorran. Even if this EMI A&R bloke was a big power player, he'd be boggle eyed and twitching at Marty's spiel, like that bunny in the headlights down a country lane.

Backstage, excitement was building. The cream of Nulton punk – and other youth cults – was in attendance. Most of the Viscous Kittens litter was gathered, just not their tom cat feminist. His absence was more predictable than the three-day week. Under pressure the Kitten crowd was forced to sound check without him. In terms of personnel and gigging, The Who was a more settled outfit: the Kinks was more harmonious: Led Zep was more abstemious. As a result the other Kittens hung about, alternating between the changing room and the corridor outside, looking lost and miserable; including the new backing singers, known as The Fem Felines, at least for five minutes.

The grumpy bloke with a clipboard was still loitering, and desperate to catch people out. Luckily Marty was able to pester and bamboozle him for a sound check slot. By the time Gorran had finished, this official didn't want to stay in earshot, and he wouldn't be able to tell Dolly Parton from Pavarotti.

'Right, definitely everybody, hop along with those blinkin instruments,' Gorran urged, having secured the deal. He shooed Mortal out of its changing room.

Moreover he rushed off to hustle in advance. A severe dose of pre-gig hype could prove vital. And even if it didn't he still enjoyed it.

* * *

It happened that Gorran found the A&R man. The rock biz visitor was corked on a high stool at the foyer bar. The guy was nursing a whisky and soda by himself, keeping out of the way, doing some outstanding office admin. Despite a fulsome welcome at the leaky train station, where a council leisure committee was stood about as if for a Royal party, Jez Starry seemed a bit lost. He'd been to Nashville and Tokyo that year, only Starry didn't know what to make of Nulton. Gorran thought it was a case of severe culture shock and urban alienation. Our local rock guru wanted to make the A&R power broker welcome, as well as to twist his arm and refine his taste in music.

Therefore Nulton's rock supremo chose the best approach; turning the flexible grin to the correct angle; the friendly hunch to an ideal ingratiating posture. Humbly approaching, feigning surprise, subtly finding the stool next door, Marty's conversation turned to the local music scene; and to his roster of *S&M* groups in particular.

Starry cut a trim, trendy figure, no more than thirty five: in a red silk shirt and black jeans tight as ink stains. He definitely brought the atmosphere of the international music business with him; a rare atmosphere of glamour, money and excess. Marty could almost taste it on his limber and furry tongue, as he closed in, preparing a killer pitch. If Gorran had just a single string of inferiority in his skinny frame, then Starry was the guy to play on it. Marty had never met such a crafty and unreadable character – a rock biz exotic. He half expected Starry to perish in our world, crumble to star dust, quicker than a dog shot up into space.

Marty hid this uncomfortable feeling as he broke the thin ice. Starry lost patience with this pre-gig blurb, because rightly, as head judge, he couldn't be influenced.

Starry's suntan – acquired from a session in Montserrat – tightened like a dry banana. He refused to listen to any more of Marty's verbal payola.

'Yeah, sure Marty, see you later,' Jez said. 'You going to the après gig party, man?'

* * *

While this encounter was taking place – in the main foyer bar – Mortal had a nasty surprise waiting. Yes, another one.

After the NF Disco mauling, racing off to find Gina and Nutcase, the band had had to leave most of their gear behind in the changing room. On their return, anticipating a sound check (which Gorran had extracted with difficulty) they discovered that much of their stuff had been vandalised. There was also graffiti; insults and obscenities; scrawled across walls and over the mirror. Mick Dove had left his calling card.

'I don't want to look inside that boy's head,' Gina said, reading it off.

'Fuck that, look at our gear,' Snot complained.

'This is where the fascists jumped us,' I explained to Gina.

'They've put a dent in your cymbals, Billy.'

'Feckin Nazi nobs,' declared the group's drummer.

'It's awful. I'm gutted,' Nutcase said, devastated. It was far worse than any kitchen wall he'd ever plastered. 'I feel for yer. Honest.' It was one advantage of having your instrument in your throat.

'We've got to get through a sound check… somehow,' Gina reminded them.

'What with? How? As a fucking skiffle group, or what?' Stan objected.

'Fair play, Stan bay, why the feck not? I'm goin up there and playing somet'ing. No matter what you lads say, so!'

'If it was good enough for The Beatles,' Gina argued.

'We aren't the fucking Beatles. When are you going to cut out that shit?'

'Fair play, we gotta get on stage so,' Billy considered.

'Or we're disqualified. Not long before it all starts. They'll let the audience in soon,' Gina said.

'We'll have another riot on our hands, so we will, lads!'

As we began to sort through the mess, Stan suddenly became very distressed. He was gripped by panic, which wasn't like him. He let out a kind of wail, even worse than his singing. Our little Mortal axe man was plunged into despair, practically in tears.

'What's up with you?' Cat wanted to know.

'Me guitar.'

'Your guitar?'

'Yeah, I can't find it. My uncle's guitar has gone. Those fuckers must have stolen it.'

Most of the gear had simply been tossed about – it was retrievable. We sifted and searched thoroughly, but we couldn't find Stan's instrument. Finally we had to admit that his magic guitar was missing, presumed stolen.

Snot was frantic (how'd he explain this to his family). Somehow Gina and the rest coaxed him to participate in a sound check. Anna-kissed leant him her guitar (despite frosty inter-band relations). Paulie was still nowhere to be found, so her band loyalties were under severe strain.

The arm twisting with Starry abandoned, Gorran came to the wings, stage right, pulling his big flossy hair out. Stan was really miserable, looking smaller, more hunched, pigeon-chested and awkward than ever. At the same time he didn't want to get disqualified. Not with all the punks rooting for him.

The group hadn't practiced in this line-up for weeks. They had to get the feel for each other again in rapid time. The sound engineers were patient and helped out. There was a lot of stressful fumbling. The group began to get its exciting edge back. The lads began to enjoy their musical company. Obviously the same wasn't true about off stage relationships. The technicians were beginning to smile. Admittedly, not as broadly as Gorran was.

Snot had to adjust to a borrowed guitar, very different to Luigi's mysterious model. Cat meanwhile had to get a feel for his new songs (two of them). He shouted the changes out to her. The shimmer of keyboards was great, even if the sound wasn't entirely together.

Snot was unsettled by the theft. I wondered if his heart would be in the contest, after such a disaster. Somehow he had to find the guitar and recover his punk spirit.

37. Paulie Drowns His Kittens (And Gets a Shock)

Meanwhile, there was still no sign of Paulie. Not a hair or a sexed-up *meow*. Already he'd missed a sound-check and the Kittens were frantic. Admittedly the cub reporter was famous for erratic behaviour and late appearances. Nobody had been able to get in touch with him during the day, either at home or work. Obviously he was out of touch during the night. They didn't want to guess his intentions because his mind was like the Bermuda Triangle.

Then, the clock ticking, just when his group was beginning to mutiny, Wellington amazed everybody by showing. They were huddled in an emergency conference, deciding how to continue, slagging him off, when he put his head around the door. He breezed in as if he was doing them and the whole music business a massive favour. Oddly, at this moment, he had his work suit jacket hooked over his shoulder, as if merely calling by. In a charming and matey mood, those blue eyes gleaming with cheer, he greeted his hired musicians, as if wristwatches and promises had never been invented.

Dennis noticed him first. 'Hey everybody, it's dat Paulie boy. Wha'ppen wi you Paulie? We didn' expect you so late? Where you been hangin' out, man?'

'Paulie's here!' Herb declared.

'What the fuck time do you call this?' Anna-kissed shouted at him.

'Knock me down with feather,' Dennis remarked, on his feet.

'We've had the sound check. We've gone through your songs, trying to make sense of them. I wasn't going to sing that rubbish… unless *you* did, mate!' Anna confronted him.

'Phew, calm down lads, what's up with you lot? What's the big deal, eh? I'm here now, aren't I? Where do you think I was?' Wellington wondered, with an ironic chuckle.

'Fucking Shetland Islands,' Herb objected.

'Yeah, maybe, so just give us a bit of notice, Paulie man,' Dennis suggested.

'You already got permission to leave work early. To get our gear…to change… to go through the sound check,' Anna-kissed reminded him. 'Don't give us any more fucking stories.'

'Okay Anna, but *some of us* have got a *real* job to do,' Paulie commented.

'You got this band final scheduled, weeks ago,' Herb said.

'Paulie man, we already been and done a sound check. You wasn't anywhere, man! You're just wastin' dis band's time!' The sticks magician had changed into a string vest and sweat bands.

As if inspired by this observation, Wellington protested. 'Come on Dennis mate, keep your bloody shirt on. I've been slaving away in the bloody newspaper office all day, if you must know.'

'Seen, Paulie man, bu' you knew we had the big gig tonight!' Dennis said, glaring. 'Y'want to get here on time, boy! Why yer messin us about for?'

'Okay, *phoo*, don't get into a heavy atmosphere, Dennis mate. Here I am now. I'm still bloody vocalist and songwriter, aren't I? So I got here as soon as I *humanly* could,' Paulie argued. He was stunned by their unreasonable insensitivity.

'You didn't rehearse or practice this week,' said the Kittens guitarist.

'Come on, Anna, you don't need me for last minute practice. You got the tunes by now. They're all my bloody songs, aren't they? I took ages over those tracks. Anyway, I know how to sing… and I know my own songs, don't I. So help me out on this.' He had a hurt expression.

'Incredible you ever jumped into bed with this idiot,' Herb remarked.

'Right, *phew*, so you want to be a sexist now as well, do you Herb?' Paulie challenged.

'Right so where's your gear Paulie?' Anna-kissed asked. She noticed him standing about, pink faced, yet empty handed.

'I got here from the bloody office,' he told her numbly.

'So what are you telling us?' Herb told him, furiously.

'Get you, Paulie. Do you think we're all fucking dimwits?' she yelled.

'What yer up to, Paulie man?'

'*Phoo, relax.* I only popped by to see how you were doing. Thanks a lot for the support. Now I've got to nip back home to change… to find my instrument and stuff.'

'Not those ludicrous bongos,' Herb despaired.

'Oh my god!'

'And don't think I'm wearing that stupid blouse you came up with.'

'What do you mean? Those are our stage costumes,' Paulie reminded him. 'What's bloody wrong with the costumes, all of a sudden?'

'Wipe your arse with them,' Herb suggested.

'*Phew*, that's a really dodgy comment!'

'I'm this town's Brian Ferry. Tell him, Anna. I'm not wearing those smocks. I love fashion.'

'Those are Egyptian suns, like bloody Sun Ra mate,' Wellington rebuked him.

'Suns? Or giant egg stains? You want to come over like Joni Mitchell or what's the idea?'

'Okay, I hear you. So keep your cool, Herb mate… you should mind that bloody ego of yours, mate,' Paulie suggested, with an ironic laugh. 'It's getting out of control.'

'There's no time for return 'ome trip now, Paulie man,' Dennis warned.

'What if we're first on? How can you get home and back again… in time to play our slot?'

'All right, Anna, I'll get back as soon as I humanly can, all right. I just dropped in to say hello to you lads. Why did I bloody bother?' Wellington said, huffing in disappointment, loosening his tie a jot.

'That's great isn't it? You expect us to hang around, in the remote hope that you may join us on time.'

'Come on Herb, don't get your knickers in a twist, mate. You're not on that stage yet,' Paulie protested, with a sarcastic noise.

'Are you committed to this group or not?' Anna challenged.

'*Phoo*, it's *my* group, isn't it? I invited you to join, didn't I?'

'He's a waste of space.'

'*Phew*, a really dodgy attitude. There's no need to be aggressive. Who pulled *your* nose?' Wellington wanted to know.

'Okay, Paulie, don't yer hang around man. If ya late, I'm t'rowin down me sticks an callin' the whole gig off. D'ya get me, Paulie man?' McDonald warned. 'I didn' join ya band to be mucked about like this.'

'Come on Dennis, bloody hell, who's mucking who around?' Paulie told him, blowing air. The lead Kitten looked hurt and surprised by unjustified criticisms. He was a genius surrounded by these unfeeling dullards.

Apart from the sex, you had to say, his life was a complete shambles.

* * *

Roy Smith came along later. He wasn't in any group, so he wasn't under any pressure, not even to recruit new *SWP* members. In his case he really was doing us a favour. Finishing his hours at the tax office, he'd changed into his after-work proletarian-wear.

Roy and I intended to sell copies of *Ob-scene* fanzine. In addition he wanted to flog a whole alternative bookshop of radical publications. All that stuff had to go under the counter. In Roy's opinion, if the punks kicked up an insurrection, it might be the trigger for a worldwide revolution.

'Away, Bottle, you're not lookin' in such fine fettle tonight, man. So what the bloody hell happened to yer, marra?' Roy wondered. He noticed all the cuts and bruises.

'Another close shave with those NF boys,' I explained.

'Oh nawh! *Norragen*, comrade! When did this happen mind?'

'In the changing room. Before the band sound-checked. What's worse, we reckon they nicked Stan's guitar.'

He wrung his lank fringe in anguish. The eyes glittered with indignation. 'Away man, what's he going to do now?'

'Well, he borrowed Anna-kissed's guitar. No, it doesn't sound too bad. Better than nothing… Snot isn't happy though.'

'M'be we'll find them fascist bast'ads and gerrit back off 'em, mind!'

'I'm not sure if that magic guitar's in one piece… even if we got time to negotiate,' I remarked.

Then, afraid that Paulie would let down his Kittens, we went to have a warning word with him. Maybe he was already losing enthusiasm for punk music. That was likely because he was easily distracted from one cultural style to another. Paulie's hairstyle had changed even more regularly than youth fashions. He'd sold his record collection several times in recent memory. That was a first warning sign. How to stop him selling-out his punk rock collection too?

We caught up with him.

'Come on Roy mate. You can't expect me to perform those songs on an empty stomach.'

'What are you tawkin' aboot, marra? Away Paulie, there's a good Chinese takeaway just down the road,' Smith suggested. 'Just go there and buy something quick and ge' back here, comrade.'

'No, I can't survive on take-aways, Roy.'

This was an ironic reference to the Trotskyite's notoriously unhealthy diet. Boiled-in-the-can steak and kidney pies definitely had revolutionary effects on the lower orders.

'Ai Paulie, get some fish 'n' chips in, man!' he suggested. He was working his way through the entire *SWP* cookbook. Certainly fish 'n' chips always tasted best during an *SWP* camp at Skeggy – wrapped in back copies of the paper no doubt.

'Come on, Roy mate, I've just got to pop home, to pick up my bongos and change clothes,' the reporter said. 'I'll get a bite to eat at the Mansion, won't I?'

The big hearted Trotskyite was struggling with his breath. 'Away Paulie, so mek sure you're back here at the Hall… in good time for the band contest, comrade.'

'All right, Roy mate, what're you getting excited about? I know all that. There's no need to remind me.' He watched his friend's agitation with amusement.

'Ai, just so long as you do, comrade. There's no pint qualifying for the final, marra, if you don't… if you doon't take it seriously mind. You've already missed the sound check!' Smith reminded him, starting to fume.

'Okay, Roy, what are you upset about? I can join them later on, mate, when it all gets going. They can't do without me, Roy.'

'Away, Paulie, is that the case, mind? Just mek sure you get yourself back on time, or them Kittens is gonna kick yar arse. Don't say I haven't warned you, comrade!'

'*Phew*, that's *really* dodgy, Roy mate,' he puffed. 'That came over as a bit bloody aggressive… if I'm being honest with you.'

Roy was trying to knock some sense that wasn't there, like trying to put in a brick after the house has been built.

'Come on, Roy mate, get off my bloody back, will you?'

'Off your back, man? This is the final Paulie, so no second chances, comrade.'

'Don't hassle me, Roy. You think I'd let my own band down?'

'Ai, I do. That's exactly what I'm thinking, man.'

'All right, so I'm just going home to get a quick bite to eat… pick up my bongos… and I'll be back here in a bloody flash, Roy mate,' he pledged.

'Away Paulie, make sure you don't have any dis'ractions.'

Rarely, if only to avoid Roy's criticisms, the reporter turned his attention to me. 'So you think I can win tonight, Bottle?'

I backed up Roy. 'They have no chance if you don't turn up.'

'That's what I thought. This group of mine's roots and radical,' Paulie play-acted. 'Crucial! We've got this peace and love vibe going on.'

'Paulie, don't be such a *buff-oon* man! Just get hoom an' pick up those bongos!'

* * *

Mick Dove was in the foyer with Dildo band-mates and supporters. These lads gave us a look of hatred as instant as powdered potato. Hatred was the drug *they* were thinking of. But, with my background, I wasn't afraid of Dove's fists, or any other part of him. Typically his type relied on dark nights, the element of surprise and greater numbers.

He hissed at me. 'What the fuck you doing here, Bottle? Didn't you get our writing on the wall?'

You had to strain your ears to get his sinister voice.

'Completely lost on me, that was,' I told him.

'You can't read?'

'Away, you fascist bast'ads, Bottle's here to review all the groops tonight. Ai, he's a regular cont-rib-utor to *Music Mail* mind… one of the biggest sellin weekly music peepers.'

Even Roy had swallowed Gorran's tide of hype about my rock writing.

'No sweat Roy, I'll settle this one,' I said. As if they hadn't spoiled my funny looks.

Anyway Dove wasn't impressed. As yet there were only a few people around the foyer; waiters stocking up the bars, students unstacking chairs, a few roadies taking early refreshments, council officials and probably the EMI A&R man. I couldn't pick out Starry – I didn't have the Mortal manager's instincts.

'Mortal needs to retire,' Dove scoffed.

'They're not leaving this building without a record contract,' I said.

'Fuck off home, commie wankers.'

'*Phew*, did you hear what he just said to us, Roy. Phew, that was *really dodgy*,' the cub reporter observed.

'Ai, well said comrade. These Nazi lads have no place upsettin' the working class in these late capitalist times,' Roy reposted.

'Get back to Mexico, Trotsky,' Dove told him.

'This isn't one of your Hitler youth rallies,' I said.

'Watch your mouth, you geeky faced wanker.'

Paulie stared in open-mouthed astonishment at this abuse from real-life fascists.

'I'm almost scared,' I bragged.

'You don't understand youth music,' Dove argued – adenoidal, through his teeth. 'You don't get Steel Dildo.'

'I get you.' They wouldn't be featuring in *Smash Hits* this side of the beer hall putsch.

Dove further narrowed his eyes at me. 'You don't understand the music of the native people,' he argued.

'You don't intimidate us,' I insisted – though his mates were having a very good try.

'Away man, cos the working class's gonna start the fight back… the fight back against the fascist scum,' Roy began to rage. 'We're gonna take back the streets, until our communities are safe mind. *Seef* for all races and creeds in a post capitalist *sorci-ety*!' At the end of his breath, Roy was beginning to spit - like a police water cannon threatening to turn on.

'Fuck off Trot.'

'Away, cos all yas fascists do is exploit the demoralisation of the working class… faced with mass unemployment… the lack of a real socialist alternative in this *cun-ree* mind,' he spluttered. Roy was pumping himself up towards an SWP clenched fist.

'Who's this little Trot, Mick?' wondered the Dildo drummer. This sidekick was a lad off the Tech college metalwork course; a beefy skin with huge red ears, in a 'patriotic' tee and regulation steam-pressed drainpipes. Smithy was changed into his Marxist slogan tee and heroically ripped and scuffed jeans. He'd shrugged out of the Inland Revenue gear.

'Don't you get our youth policy?' Dove hissed.

'Your policy isn't working on us,' I said.

'Native youth's waking up. They don't want the agenda of socialist punks.'

Frozen with shock, expelling air, Paulie said, '*Phew*, that's really dodgy!'

'Ai, Paulie marra, *doon't* worry man. It's dis-gustin' propa-ganda. I heard *exac-ly* what he said. Fascist scum, take your fucking Nazi shite back down the sewer… where it belongs, will yer!'

'Native youth doesn't want commie crap,' Dove informed us.

'Ai, the only way's to fight 'em on the streets!'

There were at least a dozen of this scum fronting up. In my view you had to choose your battles. Otherwise our bruises would get bruises.

'We ain't going to tolerate lefty bands,' Dove smirked.

'Did you hear what he just said, Roy? It's really dodgy stuff, isn't it.'

Dove finally turned his attention to the distraught cub reporter. 'Who asked your view? You're that idiot… with all those girls hanging off you,' he mocked. Another of the 'Jealous Minds'.

'*Phew*, I reckon this lad's really sexist as well… really dodgy in his political views, Roy mate.' Pinking, Paulie made a disapproving noise and flipped his eyes up in horror.

'An' that fucking awful reggae noise! Grass skirts and coc'anuts.'

There was startlingly loose and unrestrained laughter. 'Where's your dress tonight, Paulie?' wondered the Dildo drummer.

'*Phew*, that's really out of order, mate. You can't say that kind of stuff. It's really sexist.'

'Ai, there's no place in this coun'ry for right-wing idiots, Dove man,' Roy fulminated.

'You fucking Trots,' Dove snarled, raising his fist towards us.

The very next moment, without warning, Paulie shot out of the venue. He fled through the revolving doors. In a split-second he had vanished. There was barely a single frame 'after image'. He was off into the high-street. This was not to show solidarity with the working class and to fight the young Nazis. No, it was to hide out in the shopping centre.

Wellington was gone; as if he'd identified a long lost identical twin unexpectedly flown back to the UK from Australia, after a tragic separation at birth. I only got the most fleeting glimpse of the flaps of his jacket. For a few seconds the revolving doors were still turning, without any occupant.

'Tell Snot and his band that the gig is off,' Dove was saying.

'Mortal won't listen to any threats,' I said.

'British youth are sick of socialists.'

'You want another kickin'?' their drummer asked.

'May the best punks win,' I suggested. I was beginning to stammer. That happened. It made me sound frightened. Which I wasn't. Anyway, I wasn't frightened of Dove. Thermo-nuclear war maybe. The scrapheap, certainly.

The NF boys shifted on steel-capped boots.

'Away man, any more fightin' and intimidation… the socialist movement'll be weetin to fight you during tonight's gig,' Roy warned.

'Make it a date, Trot.'

'Stan wants his guitar back,' I said. 'That's right, don't be surprised… I know you nicked it from their dressing room… That's a special guitar. His uncle gave it to him.'

'What guitar?' Dove jeered.

'Not anybody can play that instrument. Be warned. It could fight back, if you plug it in.'

'What you talking about? *Shit*, Bottle.'

'Give it back!'

'Fuck off. I've got my guitar.'

'Away man, that doesn't belong to you… you fascist bas'tad.'

Dove scoffed. 'So property isn't theft any more, Trot?'

'Stan needs his guitar back.'

'Let the British people judge.'

'Another fool, Roy. He doesn't get it. Stan's the only lad who can handle that guitar,' I warned again.

'What's so fucking special about it? Just a bit of wood with metal strings, isn't it.'

'Away Bottle, what's happened to our Paulie mind?' Roy exclaimed, looking desperately from side to side.

38. Teenage Lobotomy

At last the doors of the Civic Hall were unlocked. The kids with advance tickets rushed inside, while the others formed a rough rowdy queue around the ticket office, looking for returns.

Early comers were in a hurry to get their drinks and to find the best places stage front. Downstairs was standing and upstairs was seated. The only snag was with getting there early was to endure a welcome speech from Councillor Stanley Fairbright. The politician made a direct grab at the town's youth vote, in preparation for upcoming council elections. As I said, in approving a music competition the council expected a local version of *New Faces*. They didn't understand the popular forces being unleashed. After so much hot air Fairbright had the task of deciding the running order. He tossed all the band names into a top-hat and drew each one out in turn. Mortal was announced last of all. We discussed if that would be an advantage or not. The biggest danger was offering them more time to fall out, against the clear positive.

Marty didn't believe that playing last was good. He felt that the judges' opinion would be clouded by alcohol and violence by then. Immediately he lodged an official appeal. This was on the grounds that *S&M* groups should not have to compete one after the other. Here was an independent pop entrepreneur (Gorran) up against the rock establishment (Starry). Marty was determined to make his presence known; he burnt more calories than an Olympic pentathlete. He succeeded in completely antagonising the members of the panel. The punk king let his passion get the better of him this time. He pushed his claim and raised the stakes by demanding a longer interval between sets. Apparently these tactics had some impact, as all the judges were sick of his malleable mug. They definitely got his number and marked his card, for good or bad.

The punk MC had some joy because Turbo Overdrive was moved to second slot. Unfortunately the judges wouldn't relent over Mortal. Snot and the lads would have to play the punks home. Viscous Kittens were allotted fifth, which gave more time for Paulie to get his act together. The other Kittens began to cross their fingers, that their star was aligned. But it was all in the lap of the gods.

The group to open up the Battle of the Bands was Amyl Exciters. We S&M punks didn't get much advance notice about their sound or style. This outfit was hard to ignore, as they swept into the venue with a posse of family, friends and supporters. We nervously eyed their confident progress, while noticing they'd brought a big following. They radiated an arrogant stars' attitude to the whole event, with plenty of attitude. This made the Nulton punks bristle. The band had settled into one of the venue's best dressing rooms too.

Marty got twitchy at mention of Amyl Exciters, because he'd caught them in a semi-final. They were the only group to turn me down for an interview. Being enigmatic was one of their tactics. It was true that we didn't know much about them. Marty said they had played gigs in Manchester and Newcastle, followed by a small review in *NME* (generally positive, apart from insults about their hair styles). Nulton's punk *eminence de grise* was in a mental flap, trying to work out some advance spoilers. He said they'd been out clubbing with Tony Wilson. Marty would do everything possible for his acts, but at television stations he still couldn't get past reception.

The band's stage line-up was unusual: three members stood behind a synthesiser each, a *Minimoog* and *Fairlight*s; the fourth operating a Linn drum machine and electronic percussion; producing a swirl of electronic, 'artificial' melodies, SFX and beats. Presumably they were influenced by early Kraftwerk – as it was – and other 'kraut rock' bands and electronica sounds. Beach Boys' style 'barber shop' harmonies were overlaid. You'd describe their sound as 'avant pop' before its time.

From the opening riff their entourage offered noisy appreciation. And you could feel the Exciters' fan club steadily growing. They played a short set of three songs – as allowed by the contest rules – and it was fifteen minutes of high tension for Marty; and for Les Phoenix. It was a future-looking accessible sound. The shock waves of their set definitely spread to other bands.

Don't go thinking this group was early Roxy (while Eno was still a member) or Berlin period Bowie. It was more Planet Earth than Space Oddity, mixing dance-styles, even disco, with heavy rock. They were blonde-rinsed muggers in zip-up jumpsuits. Harmonising such banalities as:

Pony Girl! Pony Girl!
You join the shopping world
Look phony girl, phony girl!

Red boots high
Communication to hire
Ignorant desire

Total bollocks, as Snot argued. Marty had seen Amyl play the *Green Man* and admitted that they'd improved – new sounds, songs and ideas. You might think he'd want to sign them. Especially while he was shaking in his pixie boots, worried that they could win. Sometimes he could be enthusiastic about gimmicky sounds, if he thought these were clever. For him a gimmick had to accompany good music. Marty had to be impressed by songs and sounds, and he wasn't delighted by Amyl Exciters. He wouldn't compromise or sell out on his tastes and judgements. And I don't reckon he was far wrong.

'Gord elp us Bottle, what kind of rinky dink bullshit sound is this?'

'They're definitely a bit superficial,' I agreed.

The advantage of playing first was to catch the judges sober, the disadvantage was to play to a half-full auditorium.

Even so the Exciters got a positive reaction. As the town's celebrity rock hack I couldn't write them off. Maybe they were a bit like Depeche Mode, a few years in advance. They were not as sharp and hooky as the Basildon lads. The washing bank of electronic chords anticipated Tubeway Army and Gary Numan (without the glum look).

Beautiful robots
Sex crazed despots
Shoot down imposters
Hard shiny lusters (lustres?)

Gorran was visibly relieved when they left (in fact everything Marty did was 'visible'). And he closed his ears to the cheers and calls for an encore. Luckily encores were not part of the rules either.

I cast my eyes along the judges. Disturbingly the EMI A&R man looked perky. Starry had roused himself, surprised by the first act, and waking up to potential talent in this hick town. There he was offering his views to his fellow judges. Even the normally wary Morton Treble, the *Record Shack* owner, was stirred to nod back. All the same, on the basis of his extensive punk record section, Morton wouldn't place Amyl at the top. I was confident he wouldn't even offer them free record tokens.

Unsurprisingly the owner of *Keith Smidgens' Keyboards* was most enthusiastic. The other judges were middle-aged rockists to a man. Their task was to scribble down impressions during performances. At the end of each set they consulted with one another, compared notes, until agreeing on a rough score. At the end of the entire competition, when every band had played a set, would they agree on final positions.

Amyl Exciters divided the panel. But there were a lot of groups yet to play, so which way would they go?

There was intense expectation, an atmosphere of tension and imminent violence. Inevitable when all the best punk bands were gigging on the same night for such a prize. Fans steadily crammed into the auditorium, expecting fireworks. There was a strong possibility, with revolutionary socialists, anarchists, soccer casuals and fascists tossed into the mix, that they wouldn't be disappointed.

Nothing beats the excitement of a good gig. Put behind all your daily cares and troubles, whatever they are. Put your heart, soul and body into the music and the bands you support. Feel part of a scene that is bigger than you; and nothing *without* you, the fan.

Join with all those lads and girls who are into the same groups. Hook up with people you have an affinity for. Get the hum of energy and chat inside the venue, as everybody waits for that inspirational racket to kick off. Enjoy the chance to socialise with your mates, rather than to be harried by your boss, or threatened by the bailiff or belittled by the YOP bloke. Take a break from the narrow-minded bloke at the Job Centre who bullies you into a shit job, and implies that you're lazy. All the bullies and scalds, too mean and selfish to acknowledge the dreams and aspirations of youth. Forget there's a great big hammer pointed towards the back of your head, for most of your life.

* * *

Turbo Overdrive was next up. Marty was glued to the bar like a coat of varnish. Apparently, while Turbo was rocking away, he was anxiously nodding, mouthing the lyrics (however dumb), and rapping his knuckles. If hard rock was never Marty's scene Rob definitely lit his fire. The top music manager was staring through the proscenium arch with love light in his eyes. He followed Rob and Spike's outrageous moves, totting up a potential score, like the trainer of a top ice dancer. Blind love gave them a chance in hell, and I wasn't going to be the snowball.

Rob Shaw was eye-catching and charismatic as a front man. Marty wasn't the only one besotted. Rob and the lead guitarist, Spike Murray (a heavily muscled, whiskered guy in a leather tank top) bounced off each other. They had a great stage rapport, despite legendary fist fights away from it. Clowning and camp routines got the crowd whipped up, and musically the melodic songs had full metal treatment. Spike went in for extended solos, in honour of his own guitar heroes. While he was absorbed in doing that, you might go outside and find an Indian restaurant on the high street, and still get back in time for his finale. In fact Spike put the band over time, and they were penalised. That most likely did for their chances.

Notwithstanding, I'd heard worse HM bands than TO. Victory would be against the odds. Frankly, if they did win this competition (and there were a handful of rockists on the panel) then I would volunteer for the vacuum factory, to be honest with you.

Gorran realised the band's deficiencies, while keeping faith and loyalty towards his boyfriend. The music magnate kept those doubts to his narrow chest and was hoping for the best. Anyway, the group was very popular with the Nulton heavy rock fraternity, male and female. Those lads had a great time for the price of their tickets. Turbo offered them a chance to practice air-guitar routines. The dust heads were piled up at the front, whisking their long hair in front of speaker towers, as the music rattled at crunching volume.

There weren't enough metal fans in the Civic Hall that night. Overall it was the year of punk.

39. Shock Tactics

While Rob and Spike were busy grandstanding, I wandered backstage to find out how Mortal was getting along (if that's the phrase). For a while Gina had been out of sonic range and began to trigger mental controversy. I wanted to make sure she didn't suffer the shake rattle and rolls again.

On my way along the back stage corridors, I picked up sounds of jubilation and hilarity coming from Amyl Exciters' dressing room. They were already having a bit of a party. The atmosphere with my friends was more subdued. That was understandable, as they had not yet played or decided on their set. Yet that Graffiti on walls and mirrors, of abusive slogans, both political and personal, didn't lift the mood. This didn't overly bother Stan because, as he pointed out, the Music Box's changing room wasn't exactly a suite at the Ritz either. Anyway Snot revelled in these punk conflicts and antagonisms. What most affected him was the loss of Luigi's guitar.

Without a word Steve Fenton dashed home to fetch his spare *Albanez*. This guitar was definitely very handy and good looking. Curious to try it, Snot hunched tinkering with finger holds. It couldn't replace Luigi's magical instrument. How could you ignore a guitar that had been played by Burton and touched by Presley? The Albanez was a beautiful replacement, even if the theft had left a crater in Stan's soul. But I'd a feeling that if he couldn't find the magic guitar, then the magic guitar would find him.

* * *

This was the definitive line up of Mortal Wound that played the final of the Battle of the Bands competition:

Stan Snot – lead guitar, backing vocals
Sour Cat – Rhythm gt, backing vcls and keyboards
Big Nut – vocals
Billy Urine – drums
Steve Fenton – bass

Yet, as I pushed into the room (by then crowded with mates of the band, partners and many hangers on) I didn't find Gina among them. There was some alcohol being passed around (with sweet smelling smokes) but not enough to satisfy Cat. Plus it was too noisy and crowded for her in a pre-gig situation. She couldn't endure that – she'd try to hide away some place. So I realised that our Sour Cat had performed her famous disappearing act, in search of musical obscurity. Whenever my back was turned, she'd get the sound of jangling nerves. Typically the rest of them just ignored the situation. Even though they depended on her as a vital band member, they assumed she'd somehow get back.

'Wake up, you lot. Why didn't you look out for Cat?' I objected.

It was hard to make myself noticed or to get heard. Snot's voice came out of the throng, amid is fan club. 'What are you fretting about now, Bottle?'

'What? Our Gina. D'you know where she is?'

'She's already got her Daddy. Let her go for her walkies. It's in her nature, Bottle, to deal with her demons… and she'll feel better for it… when she comes back… from her fucking adventures.'

Even if there was a twisted logic to that argument it was perilous.

'You been fucking smoking too much, Stan, or what?' I snapped back.

With a roll of the dark romantic eyes, a jerk of the bristly chin, Snot warned me off. Once more he focussed on finding something new. The world could burn, sometimes, as far as Snot was concerned.

'Fair play now, Bottle,' Billy put in, 'let Cat have a few jars to steady her nerves. She's probably gone to the foyer bar there. Don't give her such a *h-ard* time now. She'll join the rest of us lads later so!'

'After her temple hits the floor,' I argued.

'You need some nerve to play in this band.'

298

'She'll go an' crack 'er fuckin ed.'

'Don't go and get pessimistic, Nut.'

Big Nut was gargling to relieve his 'noodles'. At the same time his wife was using a small brush to re-apply glue to his Mohican.

'Don't blame me if it's a shambles,' I objected.

'This is rock 'n' roll, Bottle,' Snot informed me.

'Yeah, right, so you're relaxed? If anything happens to her… her parents are gonna sue you.'

'Poor little gel was out fuckin cold,' Nut recalled.

'Her parents are here tonight,' I warned. 'Marty got 'em a pair of tickets… he says they're watching from the second tier.'

'So they can drive her to the hospital,' Snot suggested.

'Glad you're so bloody concerned.'

'She's lyin on 'er feckin back somewhere lads… on the care-pet somewhere, as we speak now… so she is!'

'It's only fucking stage fright,' Stan argued.

That set me off spluttering with indignation. 'What? You don't have a gig… Or you don't have any chance of winning,' I argued, wound up. 'Not without our Gina!'

'*Gina this, Gina fucking that.* So don't hang about whining,' Stan argued, 'go and fucking get our canary back. This could be your chance, couldn't it?'

I still felt the heat. 'Right, so maybe I'll do that.'

'Start wid the foyers there,' Billy suggested. 'Yeah, she'll be around there now, Bottle mate. Yeah, look around them bars bay, if I was you now.'

'Buy her a drink,' Stan suggested.

Snot could definitely piss me off sometimes. No wonder that we used to fight over close games of *Subuteo* and 'War'.

* * *

As *Music Mail*'s 'latest celebrity columnist' I didn't have to worry about tuning an instrument. As the *S&M* roving fanzine reporter, I had licence to wander about.

On reaching the first level balcony, I found Roy with a bunch of his *SWP* comrades. Apart from enjoying the occasion, they were busy flogging copies of *Ob-scene* and other more radical publications. The Smith confirmed that Gina had stopped by; she had chatted and flicked through our fanzine. It was satisfying to know she'd been interested. Noticing my distress Roy tried to help. He thought she was heading towards the next floor, rickety on stilettos and rejecting numerous unwelcome advances along the way.

Without any time to waste, I darted off, Oxfam coattails flapping. Along the way there was an incident, which showed that she faced other dangers, more than the average hormonal lad. While I was heading to the third floor, pushing through crowds on the stairs, I came up against Mick Dove. He was getting psyched for his own set with his Dildo mates. Unfortunately he had more sinister ideas than just duffing me up again.

'If it ain't Nulton's famous music journalist,' he remarked.

'Yeah, yeah, well…'

'What you fucking doing?'

'You haven't returned to your Fatherland yet?'

'Don't be cheeky, guppy face,' he said, with a cold smirk.

'This is our country and we an't going nowhere,' added his bass player.

'Happy holidays!'

'How's that commie band you support?' Dove jeered.

'Rehearsing,' I said.

'What for?'

'Wait and hear.'

'How can they do that?'

'Talent will out,' I suggested.

'*Talent*, fucking talent,' he scoffed. 'If they try and play this gig, I promise … I fucking promise… they won't be leaving the building… not in one piece, any of 'em.'

'I'll pass on your message of support.'

He didn't worry me at all, although the drummer did. This lad was massive as a side of beef in the Co-op fridge, with about as much feeling in his body.

'If Snot plays this gig, the patriots are gonna crack his skull,' Dove warned.

I began to shoot side-looks, worried about finding Cat. 'Mortal gigs are always a riot.'

Dove looked me over with a forensic eye. 'What you doing anyway? Why aren't you back with that shit band… licking Stan's arse as normal?'

I was uneasy at disclosing the truth. 'Stretching my legs,' I said.

'Stretching your legs?' The pale eyes examined me with a sneer. 'Shouldn't you be watching the bands? Making some notes? So you can write those crap articles?'

'Just getting a feel for the atmosphere,' I told him.

'What you wandering around for? Someone missing?'

At this point I chose to notice Mick's new hairstyle. It was also a Mohican style crop, with red, white and blue dyed into it.

He noticed my glance. 'We're not ashamed of patriotism,' he snarled, in his low frequency way.

'Right. Well, definitely striking,' I said. Surely that would put him off my trail.

'As it happens, Bottle, I'm glad to find you,' Dove told me.

'Oh? Glad? I'm not interested in politics. Anyway, not half as much as you lads are.'

Dove took a step nearer. 'This isn't to do with politics.'

'Yeah, we wanted to find yer,' said the drummer. His only talent in life was for hitting things.

'We're looking for that girl in Snot's band. D'you know where she is?'

'*You*'re looking for her? Sour Cat?' I replied warily.

'Whatever she fucking calls herself. We're gonna ask her round the back. Then we're gonna jump her.'

'Jump her? What are you talking about?'

Dove set his jaw into a lock. 'We're gonna bang her. She's fit,' he leered. 'You can join in, if you want. We'll call a truce. Don't you want a bit? We'll all gonna take her after the show.'

Three of his mates came in and bustled around me, as if the cuts and bruises had never happened.

Dove's voice was down to a tense whisper. 'Don't think she'll run to the Old Bill. No, no, they never do. She'll be too ashamed to tell her own mother,' he told me, in his whispery voice.

I must have gaped in amazement. Even if Dove had form, as I remembered from college days, it was shocking. Certainly he didn't stop at shooting porno films, blackmail and robbery. In fact where would he stop?

* * *

The NF boys had all foyers covered, intending to pick her off. If I didn't take care, I'd just lead them to her. They were suspicious, knowing that Gina and I were friends. What I did to evade them was to slip back into the auditorium for a while.

When I got there – breathing more deeply - the next band on stage was Big Tits. They were a three piece militant lesbian punk group. They lived up to their name and felt no risk from Steel Dildo. Even before they'd got through the first song they had stripped off to the waist. The riotous behaviour which followed, and which fully tested Troy Cock's security staff, was predictable. Troy Boy's heavies waded into the mosh pit and began to drag out scores of over-enthusiastic youth trying to get on stage to express their lust.

By that point of the evening it was too late to pull the plug on the whole show. The organisers had already discussed the idea (we learnt) but realised it would spark an even bigger ruckus: the venue was packed, drink had been drunk, hormones and chemicals released.

I recognised our veteran MP for Nulton South, Ivor Handout, standing up in outrage from his VIP seat. That rarely happened in the House of Commons. The wife of the Lord Mayor – a bizarre mutation of Dame Edna Everidge, Elsie Tanner and Mary Whitehouse – was gagging into her ladies' handkerchief. Why did these people turn up to the event? What did they expect? Didn't they have any idea about the punk rock movement?

The buxom trio's opening tune 'Lesbian Laughs' reached a shrill climax. Most punk songs had the classic three minute pop single duration. Big Tits and Diana Ross and the Supremes had the same idea in that way. The lead singer (and terrible guitarist) Penny Tits was a big strapping girl with yellow haystack hair. As the crowd struggled to overcome screeches of feedback, Penny strutted to the stage edge and began to torment wild pogo-ing lads. The effect was total pandemonium.

Councillor Fairbright also got up and gesticulated towards the stage. This was beginning to resemble a 'standing ovation'. The show wasn't going according local government plans. The intended youth talent show (all too polite applause rounded off with a pointless judging competition) was turning into a nightmare. They'd unleashed the punk beast. Why hadn't they made a phone call to Grundy?

Faced with this shocking display of indecent punk mayhem the MP for Nulton North, sitting on a very slender majority, was equally 'gob smacked'. As I mentioned, all the local dignitaries, bigwigs and celebrities, had turned up for this concert, expecting a version of *Eurovision* or 'The Gang Show'. Instead they got the shock of their bloody lives.

Then again, maybe, Penny had just innocently *forgotten* to put on her knickers that day. If only she hadn't unzipped her bondage pants in the first place.

Penny later explained how she was trying to satirise stereotypes of femininity. She was sending up exploitation, debunking the 'phallic signifier'. That didn't go down well with VIPs on the night. The organisers and the Lord Mayor hadn't been on the same course as Penny – they hadn't done a module on Gender Studies at Nulton Arts.

Musically Big Tits made The Slits sound as tight as the Berliner Ensemble. As if a petrol lawnmower had blown up in someone's shed, they produced an incredible racket with catastrophic effects. And it went along to these priceless lyrics:

Scumbags 'a society
Enemies 'a propriety
Husbands' assassins
Enemies of sexists

Here we come, here we come
Watch out punk boys
We're the killer, killer, killer dykes
We're the killer, killer, killer dykes
(Killer Dykes)

Naturally there was uproar in the hall, and once again we made out ambulance sirens, bearing down on the place.

When the brawling and shouting had finally settled back down, the auditorium fell into a hum of astonishment and hilarity, as those remaining fans (sober enough) assessed the band's performance.

Anyway it would be something to tell the grandchildren about.

40. That's Entertainment

Exploiting his reputation as Nulton's big name music manager Marty swooped in to sign up Big Tits.

How could Tits ever impress Marty, you may wonder? During this period if any band failed to shock or amaze, it wasn't worth getting conscious in the morning. Soup Dragons, Wire, Pere Ubu, Television, became part his rock 'n' roll nervous system. Marty always had an eye for a genuine media event of his own making; a pop outrage to bring his bands to public attention. Big Tits – too smart for their social roles and too large for their bras – had potential to do that. So Gorran snapped them up on the G spot.

You only had to listen to Gorran talking about music, or to flick through his record collection or attend one of his 'CONTEMPTORY Music' or 'Pink Pants' disco nights to understand his instincts. The local maverick had reliable insights about pop music; which was, according to Brian Epstein, a mixture of music, performance and art. Or as Dave Crock used to put it:

'Marty boy, ee knows is moosic!'

The punk sage and I kept our distance from the assortment of thugs. Troy's security guys continued to eject rioters. These lads didn't put a dent into the Lord Mayor's limo, because it had long left its reserved space. No doubt our Right Worshipful was back at home, feet up with a brew, watching *That's Life* on telly.

Les Phoenix, hearing that *S&M* had got Big Tits on its books, was more outspoken about their appeal. The American eagle fixed us from his lofty nook in the rafters.

'Well, gee Marty, you shittin me over this group, man? Who are these freakin little chicks anyway?' he smirked. 'Shoot, these gels cairnt sing and, sure as hell man, they cairnt play. Shoot, this is the

305

worst group in this entire freakin English barn dance. How you gonna get these chicks to cut a hit rec'rd, baby?'

'Right, definitely, Big Tits is the tightest little girl group since Fanny down at the blinkin Ballroom. Fair play, I didn't have to think too hard about grabbing bloomin Big Tits.'

As we know, Phoenix's *Cadillac* was parked up at the kerb. Its engine was ticking over, the chauffeur (Vic from next door) was kept on high alert for Betsy Dandie's triumphant exit. Then Les would accompany her to a private party at Les' 'Roadhouse' as he insisted on calling his local. Next morning the Texan rock maestro would place that call to Benatar's people for better terms, including an upgraded dressing room with a hair dryer.

Phoenix's sequinned all-black body suit was worn in Presley's honour, to mark the legend's passing. The king was dead, long live the king. A few lads said he looked more like Alvin Stardust. That was unkind. They forgot how Les was one of the glittering rock celebrities in town.

'A friendly word of advice here, Marty baby. We've been in the moosic industry together now… *for how long is it*, Marty? Gee, its years man… and we know it's a tough industry to pitch to. You should know that by now… Shoot, it's all about the *matoo-er* adult market. Otherwise I was wastin my freakin time in Austin, man. If you're ever gonna get that big US break, you gotta find the big bucks and shift units.'

Marty ran fingers into the electrical atmosphere of his hair. 'Straight up Les mate, you couldn't have any more bloomin potential than these talented little girls in Big Tits.'

Betsy bustled over to our party and joined in. 'Hey, Marty, how yer doin man! I hear you signed em up? Fuckin Bit Tits! Why do you rate those dumb chicks?'

'Right, definitely, why do I blinkin rate 'em? No bullshit Betsy,' here he held the smile and began nodding in a visionary way, saying, 'this Big Tits outfit is the most exciting little kick-arse feminist punk group I've seen since this whole fucking punk phenomenon first kicked orf here in bloomin England.'

'Marty I'm surprised. You turned all fuckin hetero, man? What do you see in em gels? You of all people, man. They suck,' Betsy insisted, making a disgusted face. 'These gels can't even play their instruments.'

Gorran chose a disarming tack. 'Right, definitely Betsy, when does playing an instrument come into it? No bullshit, give em a chance to learn a few more chords and polish up their bloomin stage show first,' he insisted, fighting a battle with his rugged dentistry.

'What was that fuckin dope trying to achieve… taking her shirt off?' Dandie objected, with a dry laugh. 'Man, I was gonna ralph my fucking dinner. Yuck, what was all that about? Does she think she's gonna influence the judges that way?'

She had a fair point, though the rockist judges' tongues were hanging out into their beers.

With a thinly sardonic smile, Les Phoenix considered his rock rival's error. 'Sure Marty, you wanna listen to our Betsy here, cos how you gonna get these English chicks over in Freespring, Idaho or Catspaw, Ohio?'

'Right, definitely, same way I get 'em over in Nulton. Fair play, why should I want to worry about that, Les mate?' the pop guru said, twitching anxiously.

'If you can't break your artists past Salt Lake, Marty baby, you cairnt make it no place in the US of A.'

Les raised another tumbler of *Jack D*, savouring the warm fumes around the interior of his shark-fin nostrils.

'Straight up Les, the big plan's for Big Tits to grab one of those big blinkin prizes tonight, and get 'em up headlining in Duncehead by next weekend.'

The Lone Star CEO brought down the shadow of his hat brim. 'Shoot, if you ain't played LA, Marty man, you ain't even started in the biz,' Les argued. 'Period.'

'We're gonna blow that buncha losers from the hall,' Betsy promised.

'Right, definitely, these girls can be blinkin huge if they get some good fucking management behind them,' Gorran claimed.

'No bullshit Marty, you ain't got cat's chance in hell with these punk guys. You ain't gonna cut it, dealin your greasy acts in little ole England. Gee baby, you've got to start swingin in the States before the Day. It might sound like a hard pitch, but all my goddamn acts are getting past first base. Sooner or later we get to play freakin hard ball,' Les rumbled, squinting into the far horizon and savouring another mouthful.

'Right, definitely, Les mate, cos we're going to see about that won't we.'

'Jeez Marty, get real. Will you, man? You wanna find yourself a little gel with a big goddamn voice. And with *genu-wine star quorlity*.' Les was complacent under his Sunday chapel Stetson.

'Straight up, Les mate, England's where it's all blinkin happening at the moment. Fair play, they've passed the punk baton from fucking Alphabet City be now.'

'Sure thing, nobody rocks like Betsy and the boys,' Phoenix declared. 'Hell and she even looks freakin great!'

'I'm startin to feel sorry for these chickens,' Betsy joked.

'We're talkin big bucks, Marty, on the line for an extra show with Benatar at Birmin'ham,' Les boasted. 'You shoulda been at her last freakin show. No bull man, she brought the goddamn roof down on that freakin barn. That's what it feels like baby.'

'Right, definitely Les, if it gets us out the flat,' Marty commented.

'Sure,' Betsy put in, 'cos one day that little joint is gonna have a blue plaque above the door, showing everyone where Les Phoenix used to live.' The feisty Baltimore rocker came to her manager's defence on her stack heels.

Marty was keeping Mortal Wound's crisis secret from the Red Rooster boss. He turned to me, *Sotto Voce*, and suggested, 'Fair play, Bottle, what you doing hanging about here? Straight up, go and hop it, don't waste any more blinkin time on Les' hype. Get off and see if you can find Gina. *Gord elp us*, she'll go and crack her blinkin head again and it'll be fucking curtains for the bloomin lot of us.' He started shooing me away.

'Right, I'll do my best. I already searched the foyer bars. And Dove's looking for her too,' I warned.

Gorran gave a wince. 'Right, definitely, get off and find her then Bottle. No bullshit, before she burns another hole through her fucking stomach. Fair play, I can't chat up her blinkin parents again by the side of an 'ospital bed.'

'Okay man, so did you know John Lennon was raised in a council apartment?' Betsy declared.

Phoenix was gloating beneath the brim.

* * *

I slipped away in search of the AWOL punkette.

I came to re-join Roy at our *Ob-scene* stall. Apart from occupying the vanguard of the working-class, Smith had been joined by Sandra Gorran. The Trotskyite benefactor was flirting, awkwardly, with the media mogul's older sister. She resembled her charismatic brother a bit, although her features were tuned down, along with the personality. Our fanzine was continuing to fly from the table, not all of them nicked. Punks crowded around to flick through and so the piles of our fanzine began to dwindle. Local rock fans wanted to read about those groups taking part in the final of the Battle.

Roy had a fraternal glint, because, not only had he taken a shine to Sandra, but the *SWP* paper and other socialist publications were seriously shifting units as well.

'All right Smithy? How's it going, mate? Have you seen our Gina?'

'No marra, not for a while, like. Not since you last sauntered past mind.'

I was starting to pull my spiked hair out. 'The band's worried about her. She's missing.'

'Nothing new there, comrade.'

'She looked in a bit of a state,' Sandra said.

Sandra had an office job (not untypical for punks) which did not involve moonlighting in the music business like her brother – just on finals' night. Clearly she wasn't into the punk scene (either the music or fashion). She had no obvious taste for subversion, media outrage, record contracts or the other stuff.

'Which way'd she go?' I wanted to know.

'That way, comrade,' Roy pointed. In that pose he resembled a statue of Lenin.

'She could be slumped in a doorway,' I stressed. 'Swigging from a brown paper bag.'

'Away man, you think you've got problems with Gina mind. How'd you like to go and find Paulie for us and all?' Roy bemoaned the tom cat's erratic behaviour.

'You mean, he's not turned up yet?'

'*Nawh* man! It's a dreadful situ-ation mind. The Kittens are s'posed to be up on stage in aboot an hour like. The daft bas'tad promised us he'd be back here in time to plee.'

Roy's lively eyes began to pop and dart behind those thick smudged spectacle lenses. There was definitely another 'Paulie episode' in the making. He could almost relish it, apart from the fallout.

'Dove frightened him off,' I speculated.

'*Nawh*, that's not it, Bottle man. I don't reckon it's the fascists like. In my *opinion* the daft bugger's getting *cold feet* again… and about this *whoole* punk rock movement, mind.'

'Don't count him out yet,' I said. 'The chance of being a pop superstar will get the better of him.'

'Ai, well, his band are weetin… while that buffoon's coolin' his fuckin' heels at hoom, mind… primpin' up his curls like,' Roy complained, with a tremor of dread and resentment. He began to frisk himself for the inhaler, as the lungs stiffened. It wasn't in his jeans' pocket, so it had to be inside the jacket, didn't it. 'I know him well enough, man. He's changing his mind about bein' in a group. He won't be able to get away with this one, marra… Not if he lets that *group* doon again, mind.'

'Ego will get the better of him,' I suggested. 'Anyway, talking about letting your group down. I have to go and bring back Sour Cat. Sure she was off in this direction?'

I could easily visualise Paulie trying to forget all about a Battle of the Bands final and being Kittens' front man. He'd a talent for amnesia after losing all interest. He'd be hanging around the

Mansion, at that moment, enjoying having the whole place to himself, and waiting for the next big thing to come along. And the constant danger of coming second would play on his mind. Or maybe a girl had sparked his libido on the way home.

'To be entirely honest,' Herb admitted, 'we're getting desperate.'

Anna-kissed and he had the Civic Hall under surveillance, looking for their lost cub reporter. The crisis drew them out of the dressing room to prowl the venue, when we bumped in to each other.

'Any ideas where that dopey dip has got to? Can you help us?' Anna pleaded.

I had no new information for their Missing Person Report. We had to presume that Wellington was distracted. In fact only a Grammy award for best pop newcomer could tempt him back. Even then something different might turn up on the journey over, like a girl sat next to him on the plane or the offer of a starring movie role.

'Gina was in the Ladies,' Anna mentioned. 'I saw her in there… If you're looking.'

'What? You mean… in the toilets?'

'That's it. She was trying to retouch her lipstick but kept missing.'

'Right, so I'll wait for her to come out.'

'How she can miss that mouth of hers.?' Anna bitched.

I took the insult. 'She's the heart and soul of that band. Don't go bad-mouthing her. There's no way Mortal can win without her,' I told them.

'*Uh, huh*… She's the band wrecker.'

'At present we've lost our idiot of a singer,' Herb said, flouncing in a silk shirt and tossing his long, tinted fringe.

Wiggling their bottoms in contempt, they waltzed off along that balcony. David Attenborough had more chance of locating Paulie.

Any man will tell you how embarrassing it can be, to stroll by mistake into a ladies' public loo. To begin with I resorted to calling her name from outside. Contending with the background noise of crowds and music, it would be hard to get my voice heard from inside. It was like trying to whisper something into Beethoven's ear.

I had to change tactics; so I began to ask female patrons to enquire within on my behalf. Not surprisingly that got me some funny looks and a few negative comments. I was in danger of getting my neck wrung by one of them or by Crock Security. I looked a bit of a sight anyway after getting duffed up, with some fruity bruises.

Faced with such frustration, the only solution was to force a way in. After watching the movements of girls a bit, their coming and going, I got a sense of a rhythm; or the frequency of usage. So when the footfall dropped off – so to speak – I steeled my nerves and pushed inside.

The ladies' loo was better equipped than ours. It was a more pleasant environment in general (so I noted in wonder) with quality towels, soap products and electrical appliances. It had a prettier and more soothing colour scheme, as if disposing of body waste was poetic. For a few moments I was enchanted by a heavenly mood. But this wasn't the moment to apply a Barthesian reading of toilet architecture. No, that type of thinking would have to wait. This was the time and the place for direct action.

A few girls were hiding out in the stalls. I even got a hint of whimpering and breathing, as if they were afraid. This made it hard for me to find Mortal's backing vocalist. At opportune moments a girl'd burst out and make a dash for freedom. I was lucky one of them didn't bag me. New patrons strolled in, only to cop eyes on me and run away immediately. For me this was turning into a kind of dating nightmare. It was doing my confidence no good. It was the opposite of being a rock star, or watching an old movie of 'teen hysteria' run backwards. Within a few minutes I'd cleared the room.

Except, amidst this insane confusion, I noticed one of the cubicles remained bolted. Its door was clearly locked when I tried it.

Caution didn't operate, as I entered the next cubicle and shinned up the partition. Straining hard I put my chin over and looked down into the occupied one. Gina was slumped over the bowl there, staring into a pool of her own vomit. It had to be hers. Not a pretty sight, other than for Gina. I hauled myself all the way over – boots, overcoat and all – and dropped down to release the catch.

Cat was awkwardly positioned, so she'd jammed the door back. I was reluctant to move her, seeing the condition she was in. She was keeping a vodka bottle company – it was her favourite label – like a poor old vagrant in Nulton's main square at night. How did she get hold of a whole bottle? That wasn't the most relevant question. With my hands under her armpits, I managed to lift her up on to the famous stilettos, and to lead her out of there, before a Crock thug asked what I was doing.

Fortunately new entrants recognised an emergency. A pair of Goths conquered their panic attacks and came to our aid. If they felt comfortable around vampires and the undead they could definitely put up with Gina and me. Between us we lifted Gina up on her heels, with a few alarming slides, and out of that stall. It didn't take long before she threw up again. This time it was into a sink. So we had to clean her up a bit more. In the end she barely had any punk cosmetics. What a great night this was turning into!

How could she ever beat stage fright of this intensity? Why risk turning herself into one of those rock 'n' roll fatalities? What was the sense in turning into an *anonymous* rock casualty? What's the appeal of being a post-obit pin up on a teenager's bedroom wall? Best work at the *Co-op* than that, as I was doing.

Her condition didn't stand out in the context of a punk night. It looked like drunken camaraderie as we propped her up. But that didn't lessen my concern for her. It even put Mortal's success into the background. As Gina began to babble and ramble, the trouble was immediately obvious.

'I can't go up there tonight. No way. I'm not going to fucking perform.'

'All right, take it easy Gina. We'll get you walking first.'

'My parents are going to be here… *Watching* me. Oh shit. I can't believe this. What if it goes wrong? In front of all those people. If I make any mistakes?'

I was checking her pupils. 'Take some more deep breaths,' I suggested.

'Everybody's listening. Picking up wrong notes.'

'Punks don't hear bum notes,' I said. 'Or if they do… they like 'em!'

'Judging me. Waiting for me to go wrong.'

Was she kidding? After Big Tits performance?

'Oh no, Gina, we're all on your side. We're excited to see you… We want to win the record contract.'

'Don't put me on a stage. It's all stress and pressure. I was happy in there. I don't need this.'

'Don't worry.'

'Is that you Bottle? What you doing here? Take your hands off me!' she suggested.

'But you'll fall over,' I objected.

'Put me back!'

41. Paulie Takes an Early Bath

Gina and I staggered along the balcony, wrapped and tangled around each other. Even on that punk night we must have looked an interesting couple. I was a type of skinny beanpole and she was no waif. Then I propped her up into a plush seat and set about sobering her. To be honest I didn't think it was possible, without a clinic or some revolutionary new treatment. And I couldn't let her wander off again with the Dove of War ready to pounce.

Did Gina and rock 'n' roll really mix? Was that musical fusion anything other than a lethal cocktail?

If Sour Cat got into a music school and went on to become a professional musician, she'd need to face live audiences. Otherwise she would get nowhere in her profession; no more than a waiter afraid of busy restaurants, or an astronaut frightened of the dark. She had to beat those demons, one way or another (even her dad agreed on that). Going out to hear music on a Saturday night, or disco dancing with her mates, was a different type of musical appreciation. Maybe punk rock could still be the cure for her. That's why I tried to get her up on the podium – and not to return her home.

Cat began to respond to my excitable, stuttering chatter. The world looked like Queen's video of *Bohemian Rhapsody* through her eyes. We began to enthuse about Mortal and how exciting the music could be; the unique chemistry and adventure in the group. (Reluctantly we admitted) Stan was an amazing, gifted musician, probably the most charismatic performer we'd seen: even if he was number one awkward git. We agreed that his singing was shit though and we had to put a stop to that.

I recalled for her, the day when Snot – my spoiled introvert next door neighbour – came out into the street wearing that dustbin bag, with safety pin piercings. The punk scene had definitely moved on from those early days. The catwalks of the world were being influenced by then. Personally I still knew more about *C&A* than *Sex*. But we knew fashion was developing on the street. For the nation's young generations, forming bands was more popular than masturbation.

Gina and I began to talk about what interested us most. My sculpture was neglected, after I left college. But it was not forgotten. I hadn't thrown away my tools and chisels. I was eager to get back to it, when I got my hands on a decent block of stone – urban concrete wasn't suitable, even considering Rauschenberg. You might point out that she was too smashed to discuss the arts. She knew more about creativity than I did; obviously more about music. Though I found she was a great listener. Not only when she was off her head.

At first her voice was slurry and faraway. Gradually she returned to reality, whatever 'reality' might be. Lucky we didn't have to make another trip to the hospital.

In no hurry to return to the Mortal dressing room, she changed the topic:

'What's your opinion on John Travolta.? …as Tony in *Saturday Night Fever*? Travolta's got fantastic screen presence. He's real punk and that's obvious, Bottle. It's a middle finger to the dollar sign. He's got a great attitude, take my word for it. He's dynamite that lad.'

It wasn't exactly my scene. 'I reckon that's because you're out boogie-ing… at the *Hatter* on Saturday nights,' I said.

'Don't sneer Bottle, just because Travolta has a different hair style. Don't be put off because it has, you know, disco music. Don't you see my point?' Her eyes went to the middle and did something weird.

I shrugged and vowed to see it. Mostly I was glad she was more lucid.

'So if you didn't see *Fever*… did you see *Annie Hall*? Oh, I loved that movie. Diane's Keaton's character… and the big hats and long narrow skirts. I wish I could wear some of those on stage tonight.'

'For this gig? I'd like to see Snot's face,' I said.

'It's so fluid, punk fashion… the other girls would start copying me.'

'Yeah, I can see that.' Maybe she was pointing towards the abstraction of Cocteau Twins or even the drama of Kate Bush.

'If I get into music college I'll take up her style,' she said. Until her face darkened with anxiety. 'Assuming I get in to Leeds… which is a massive assumption. There are more auditions, you know.'

'Try to be more upbeat.' Immediately I realised how stupid that was comment was.

'You and Stan going to the *100 Club* this weekend?'

'*Yeah…* yeah, sure.' I tried to sound in control.

Gina was a fully briefed fan of Patti Smith. Not only could she quote the songs and poems, she also referred to articles in American magazines, like *Rolling Stone* and *Village Voice*. Of course this was bound to impress me. Unfortunately, even if I shared her tastes and interests, I didn't share her charm and good looks. If she was statuesque, I was like a gargoyle. Even worse, I stammered a bit and lacked confidence and experience. As soon as she sobered up – even around Christmas – she'd realise it.

* * *

A sustained rumble spilt from the auditorium. Gina and I sat together with our backs against the wall, so to speak, listening out. The noise originated from Betsy Dandie and the Screamers, with walls between us. We decided to return to the hall to catch the rest of her set. Obviously Les had instructed her to play heavy that night. It was a response to the judging panel's make up – or lack of any make-up. The Texan rock impresario told his starlet to adjust her amps from beef up her usual harmonious power-pop style.

Anyway, Betsy and the Screamers were going at full tilt, everything at max. It was their bid for a recording contract and stardom. A mix of Cat Woman and Dolly Parton, there was no sign of stage fright. A natural performer, Betsy strutted, prowled and seduced the boys. The Baltimore bombshell shook her guitar in the air, as she boiled like rice-in-a-bag in that leather body suit. Betsy was the equal to any strutting macho male rock star.

The Screamers were newly outfitted (leather pants and flowery shirts) wearing wrap-around shades like the sons of Gram Parsons. As usual they were having a laugh, mugging to the crowd (while being note perfect) grinding out Betsy's melodic numbers – hard rock with a power ballad to finish. The Screamers were obviously really going for it.

With a jolt, I knew they stood more than a bat out of hell's chance. Screamers and Turbo, Screamers and Mortal, Gorran and Phoenix, *Star Materials* and *Red Rooster*, this was a clash of the titans. Two juggernauts placed bumper to bumper, smoking and snorting. There was more than just pride and an Austin *Sunbeam* at stake.

* * *

Meanwhile, as this was going on, Roy Smith and Viscous Kittens were trying to get Paulie out of his comfort blanket. After fleeing the venue, he'd surely had time to prepare himself – to eat some tea, wax his bongos and change. Despite big prizes on offer, with the chance for global pop stardom, something else must have turned up.

Considering it an emergency, Roy went out to a phone box. With a pile of ten pence pieces ready to feed (Smithy was actually employed) he put a call back to the Mansion (he could now afford a home phone on his tax office salary). The effort was met with extended ringing (a harsh tone, like an alien getting its tooth drilled) until after numerous attempts, finally, somebody picked up. There was a delay, but the conversation went something like this:

'Paulie, man? Is it you? Are you there, comrade?'

There came a bewildered response. 'Roy? What's up, mate?' replied the cub reporter.

'Away man, what are you doing?'

'*Phew*, Roy, you sound worked up, mate.'

'What's the big idea, Paulie, runnin' *a-wee* like that man? What got into you, comrade? What the fuck you gonna do, when the actual revolution comes around mind?'

'What are you so wound up about now, Roy mate? You told me I oughta go home and get a bite to eat, before the gig started, didn't you? So that's what I've been doing.'

A noise of breathy irony and impatience filled Roy's earpiece.

'Away man, didn't you *nootice the tame*, comrade? You're expected back here to perform! What the hell are you doin' man? Draggin' your heeels, comrade, when yer grooop's weetin' far yer!'

'Come on, Roy, what are you getting bloody agitated about?'

'Paulie, wake up man, you're needed back here mind!' Smithy protested, beginning to steam up the call box.

'*Phoo*, I'm not sure how that's possible, Roy. Come off it, mate, you can't expect me to be back there at the Civic Hall in five minutes. Be bloody reasonable, will you, Roy mate.'

'*A*way Paulie man, I can't stand here and listen to this rubbish!'

Another pause. 'So what's the big hassle this time? Do they want me to come down there… to hold their hands, or what is it?'

This attitude provoked Roy to apoplectic fury. Sealed within a telephone box along the high street, with Paulie stubbornly at home, The Smith was beside himself. 'Ai man, this group a'yours been sittin' aboot for ages, worried sick. Wanderin' about the hall looking for you an all, comrade. *Nawh* Paulie, they can't fuckin wait any longer, comrade. You're scheduled to play next, man. We're all hangin' aboot the venue, comrade, wondering if you're gonna shoo up!'

'Come on, Roy mate, I already told you about that.'

Smithy almost choked with fury. Was there enough space to get to his inhaler in time? 'Told me *about what*, comrade? What the fuck did you tell me aboot, Paulie man?'

'I can't just turn up and start singing now, mate.'

'What the fuck are you doin' mind, wastin' yer time?' Roy demanded, shaking and squeezing the receiver to death.

'I told you, Roy mate. I got a lot on my plate at the moment.'

'Away man, there's hundreds of pee-ple in the hall, expecting 'em begin their set, comrade. So get your fucking arse down here, quick as you fucking can, Paulie man!'

Paulie's voice came back in a hush of shock. 'Have a bit of common sense, will you, Roy mate?' he appealed.

'Away, you daft bast'ad. Just get a move on will you.'

'*Phoo*, that's really dodgy. You want to sort out that anger of yours, mate,' Wellington suggested.

Hyper-ventilating, Roy rasped out some words. 'Away man, don't play the fucking buffoon t'night man!'

'What's the big hassle about this gig anyway?' Sounding bored and distracted, the idol was clearly losing interest. 'It's only a local band competition,' he chuckled. 'I don't see what their problem is. I'm not stopping them playing their gig, am I?'

'What are you doing, comrade, at this *moo-ment*, that's so fucking important… that you can't keep yer promise to your band… to come and play with 'em in the fucking final, like?'

'What am I doing? *At this very moment?* You really want to know that Roy?' he asked, with an ironic guffaw.

'Ai man, what are you doing *right now*?!'

'What do you think, Roy mate? It's been a long bloody day in the office. I'm taking a bath.'

'A *bath*?!'

'Yeah, a relaxing bath… I'm enjoying a bloody soak in the bath. What's your problem with that? After a bloody long day working at the office. I'm stood here with a towel round my waist, Roy… if you really want to know. I'm dripping on the bloody floor… while talking to you.'

'What the fuck are you doing…taking a bath at this time, marra… when there's a band comp'tition at the Civic Hall tonight? And yer grooop's wonderin' if they're *weestin'* their fuckin' time mind and should pack it all in, comrade?' he seethed.

Distorted noises of impatient amusement. 'Come on, Roy mate, some of us *have* to work. Some of us need to take a bath, mate. What's your problem with that, Roy mate?'

'Ai Paulie, you wanna know what my problem is, man?'

'Maybe *you* don't ever take a bath, Roy,' he commented.

'Away Paulie, you idiot!'

'I don't *need* this gig, to be honest with you.'

'You're the *vor-calist* Paulie comrade! You can't let them all down, man.'

'*Phoo*, come on Roy, one man doesn't make a bloody band!'

'Away man, you're the fuckin singer mind. You're the lad who writes all the songs… if you can call 'em fuckin' songs… What d'ya expect them to do at this teem man, if you don't shoo up? They're all fully dependin' on you, comrade!'

Smithy was wrestling for his inhaler, within the narrow confines of a public telephone box (piss filled and semi-vandalised).

'Be bloody fair, Roy mate, will you? I never made the band a firm promise.'

Smithy made sounds of strangulation. The flex might have been wound around his neck.

'I'll see how I feel Roy mate… after I've had my bath. This isn't going to stop the revolution, mate,' Wellington commented.

'What's that, Paulie man?!'

'The group know how to play my tunes,' he argued. 'Come on, Roy, I'll join them later if I can. They're not bloody *helpless*, mate. I'm not sure if I'm going to be free, to be honest with you, this evening,' he admitted.

'Away Paulie, don't play the fucking buffoon mind. Get yourself out of that bath and back here, man!'

42. Kittens Play and Dildo Stiff

Meanwhile, back in the dressing room, or aimlessly searching the building, the Kittens were getting disillusioned with Babylon. They'd no zest to play another set of instrumentals, to bore the bondage pants off everybody. Without a singer of some type – even Paulie – they had fat chance of impressing the judges.

The girls killed time by adjusting costumes and rehearsing harmonies. The musicians, such as Dennis, Anna and Herb, were frantic by then, looking for the bongo-playing beat-poet genius front man. They didn't understand that he'd probably found a new passion in life; which could have been anything, from market-gardening to tobogganing.

After all, even if the reporter was a 'complete buffoon' as The Smith would declare (at moments of crisis) the reporter was lead singer and songwriter. Roy didn't realise that Paulie put the Trotskyite revolution at risk. It was a mistake to recruit Wellington because – by accident or a mishap – Paulie would ruin the whole insurrectionary event.

Dennis Macdonald couldn't tolerate the situation with Wellington. There were minutes remaining, when Dennis rushed out and squeezed into seat of his beloved Fiat *Panda*.

Marty agreed generously to come to the Jamaican percussionist's aid. He lobbied the judging panel to give Kittens extra breathing space. Starry wanted thinking time to compare notes and to agree on the rough scores so far. More than this he had a splitting headache which needed time-out. Betsy and the boys alone were enough hard rock for one evening. But there was plenty of deafening noise yet to come.

The thing was, Smithy handed Dennis his set of keys for the Mansion. It was to be an authorised break-in. Anyway that wouldn't have put off the Caribbean style drummer. If he hadn't been given those keys he would have kicked our door off its oxidised hinges. We didn't want that because we already paid the 'bast'ad exploitative, class traitor landlord' enough rent money. It there was actual vandalism, we might have been evicted. And there was a shortage of affordable sub-standard accommodation, especially for a bunch of punks.

After letting himself in, stumbling around a dimly lit Mansion, Dennis picked out the super-sensitive warblings of Cat Stevens. These mellifluous strains came from the direction of our crummy bathroom, with sounds of plashing water. Paulie – resting up in the suds, reconsidering personal dreams and future ambitions – *really was taking a bath*. Apart from the thoughtfully romantic songwriting of Cat Stevens, issuing from a new tape-cassette machine, the cub reporter was completely alone. (He didn't dare to take a bath with a girl because the door catch was broken).

Dennis shoved the door in, reached forward and peeled Paulie's skinny arse away from the surface of the enamel, like a 2.99 sticker off a John Denver LP. Dennis lifted the cub reporter out of his (then) tepid bath, and stood him on a bathmat to drip dry. Normally the percussionist was a completely peaceful character. Not even a car-jacking by a bunch of Kingston gun runners, during a trip to his grandparents' house, had ruffled him. The situation with Paulie was entirely different.

'*Phoo*, Dennis, what you trying to achieve, mate?'

'Mek yourself decent Paulie man. We're off.'

'What are you playing at here? *Phoo*, this is really out of order.'

'Kittens got their big gig tonight… Di'n' you remember man, or what's hap'nin?' the percussionist fumed.

'This comes across as being a bit aggressive, Dennis mate,' Paulie suggested. 'I n I says there's no hassle.' He held eye-contract to avoid the truth that he was butt naked.

'There's our big gig down the 'all tonight. The audience's waitin for yer, Paulie man. Dincha remember? You're the voc'list boy.'

'All right, mate, I know about all that. No need to get heavy about it, is there.'

'Heavy?'

'Yes, mate, *heavy*… cos I haven't forgotten about the gig… You can let me rinse off this bloody shampoo, can't you?' he protested.

'Not this moment, Paulie man!'

'I was just gonna finish my bath, mate. I was just waiting for this song to finish. After that I was off to join you. What's your big problem with finding some inspiration, Dennis mate?'

There wasn't even time to pull out the plug, or to turn off his tape cassette. Wellington was lead outside, still wearing that towelling bathrobe. The drummer pushed his head down into the *Panda*'s passenger seat – as if he was under arrest. The lead Kitten was whisked back to the venue. Somehow he managed to grab his bongos on the way. The car shot back to the Civic Hall like a peanut gone the wrong way.

* * *

Soon rumours circulated that Paulie was at the venue. Jez Starry's paracetamols took effect and his fellow judges settled back for more rock chicks. The judges' glasses were refreshed when Viscous Kittens skipped out on stage. The crowd surged, grateful to get some music.

Herb started off the set with a pumping bass line. Soon Anna-kissed exercised her ham fist and Fiona was bashing a tambourine like Linda McCartney. The five Twinkle Sisters (Paulie changed their names again) flounced out in the druidical stage costumes. They stood around a shared mic. to close harmonise, along with eye catching dance routines, which had been rehearsed in bedrooms for weeks.

I'd read in back issues of *Blues & Roots* magazine about space and echo in dub treated reggae. Theory was put into practice, as Dennis gave the Kittens' sound mind-expanding rhythmic shape and momentum. The group had an awesome British-style reggae sound, thanks to Herb and him. Really it was Anna who gave the punk element, with her beginner's efforts. However smoothly or sweetly this came over, her garage-rock type of guitar style was jagged and discordant. For once she'd found her place in the band

and looked more comfortable. They were a tight unit making an exciting and unique soundscape, using roots, dub and lovers' rock styles.

In a terrifying blink Paulie wafted out to join them. There he was suddenly at stage front, twirling his robe, prancing and cavorting. Still sticky with unrinsed shampoo his silky curls were stuck up. He made a grab at the mic. and, pushing it under his button nose, began those peculiar muffled vocals. As I said, it sounded like a dirty phone call.

He performed to a hall packed out with various youth cults, while attired in the red towelling robe of course. Fortunately anything went during the punk period. For the punk crowd a bathroom garment was disconcerting – even weirder than X Ray Specs plastic costumes or Devo's plant pots on their heads. Amidst the violence and mayhem of punk, there was a sharp sense of humour. This saved the cub reporter from a musical lynching. I don't know what Starry made of this. At least the show wasn't as dull or as hopeless as he'd feared on the fast train.

Kittens played their best gig yet. Deep Jamaican sounds shook the hall, as if the Caribbean Sea itself was breaking around our boots. The group's British flavoured reggae mix was irresistible for dancing and swaying. The sound even predated the Ska revival, on labels such as *Two Tone* and *Go Feet!*: vibrant, brash, cynical, cool and political, as well as racially relaxed.

But however good Viscous Kittens sound was, nothing could disguise the cub reporter's gob smacking lyrics:

Walkin' down the mean streets
What do you see?
Cool Rasta dance man
Looks real sad like me

Walkin' down the mean streets
Shufflin' my little feet
The socialists n Indians
Facin' the same defeats

Walking down the mean streets
Strangled by suit n tie
I don't wanna work for the press boys
Man, I'd rather fucking die

Walk down those mean streets
Old ladies look so disappointed
Don't see any peace n harmony here, man
So what's the fucking point, mate?

If the audience could overlook the lyrics, they could lose themselves in the music. Viscous Kittens were taking us half way to Zion. All those rehearsal hours at Crock Sound paid off big time. Up to this point I was rooting for 'em. Herb and Dennis were Nulton's answer to Sly 'n' Robbie.

With such a great sound behind him Paulie stood a chance of winning. The Mortal posse began to discuss the horrible idea of a Wellington triumph. Even as we skanked to the poly-rhythms, we were getting nervous. There was the horror of Wellington gaining a fat recording contract; and projected to international pop fame, reinventing himself as the Peter Frampton of reggae tinged punk. Stan swore he'd never play the guitar again, if that happened.

* * *

The auditorium gradually settled, while the judges conferred.

Steel Dildo was next up. Despite their hard boy right-wing political message the group looked very nervous. Along with every other act, they understood that this was their one big chance. The stress of a big gig almost got the best of them.

Mick's hand was visibly shaking as he adjusted knobs on his amp. He must have noticed there were black, Asian and other faces in the audience that evening. How would that section of the audience react to him? Even if Dove didn't want to hide his message, he knew that it jeopardised his triumph of the will.

A hushed dread seemed to fall in the hall, as the Dildo guitarist and bassist attempted a tune up, now strutting and staring towards the floor as if they'd lost money.

Dildo was horned into nutcracker denims to a man – needlessly held up by pairs of braces. The beefy drummer wore a St. George's Cross tee-shirt with a swastika at the centre. Typically they'd stolen the Union flag, which was draped in front of his bass drum.

Dove and his mates took time-out to confront the hecklers, the spitters and projectile throwers. That didn't necessarily signify hostility, because it was part of the punk ritual. Already I heard Smithy and his SWP mates shouting rival slogans and threats, in the direction of the stage (you can guess the epithets).

'This's for patriotic youth!' Dove called out, pacing around. The only way to conquer his nerves was to begin to play.

Fights broke out at the first chord; terrifying whirlpools in the calmer sea of faces. Crock Security Officers jumped back in to join the fun.

Only, despite the shocking levels of violence, during Dildo's set (that battle had been planned) it was too late for the organisers to stop the competition.

The Dove of War was pogo-ing and throwing himself about the stage, like a V2 rocket. The band made a hard-core punk racket, which attacked your hair roots. Such youthful fury and frustration was the pure fuel of rock. They could have become a sharp three-piece, if they'd morphed into a Mod group. But they had no wish to become a local version of The Jam or even Secret Affair, under the influence of the Who and the Faces.

Despite such spiky adrenaline, I couldn't leave their politics aside. I generally kept to the back of the hall, getting that slimy sensation again, while trying to keep my reporter's notepad dry.

Jez Starry would never award Steel Dildo top gong. Snot pretended to savour the level of aggression. He claimed that this was all punk to him. Outrage, provocation, violence and hate – it was manna from hell. Snot refused to take anything in punk rock personally or too seriously; even when Dove targeted him and after the NF boys beat us up. Snot's attitude was shaken by the loss of his guitar.

He could still argue, 'Dildo are *really* nasty, see? No fucking sham with them. A lot of bands only fake it.'

'Found what you're looking for?' I snapped.

Snot's approval – albeit from a cynically safe distance – didn't convince. Marty was even more appalled by the spectacle.

'*Gord elp us* Bottle, what we got here? No bullshit, how do these little fucking Hitler herberts impress this lot of bloomin cauliflower eared judges? Fair play, how did such a bunch of stiff armed tossers get so far in the bloomin competition?'

Snot's anarchic admiration was quickly strangled off, as he noticed that Dove was posturing with Uncle Luigi's guitar. Dove had stolen it, as suspected, despite right wing protests. To think that this wonderful guitar had been handled by Elvis Presley and James Burton. What a miserable end it faced.

'I can't play no more,' Stan decided. 'Fucking never.'

'Don't blame you,' I replied.

Neo-Nazis were pogo-ing and moshing in front, and others continuing to fight with the left wing punks. Snot and I couldn't do much, except to observe in a depressed condition.

Like many a lad starting a band, Dove was self-taught and lacked technique. Strings didn't easily break on uncle Luigi's singular guitar, despite cack-handed treatment. In this way the strings of Luigi's magic guitar felt sharp and hot to Dove. Hotter and sharper, the harder he attacked.

Dove stopped for a while, trying to figure it out. He reached into the back pocket of his bum squeak jeans, to pull out a plectrum. Maybe that would fucking work. He thought it would protect his fingers. But the plectrum didn't give him any more joy. So he tossed it away in anger and decided to use his fingers again. It wasn't exactly strumming or picking. And this time he suffered a kick back from the strings – a shock.

Snot and I looked at each other in amazement. What in hell was going on here?

Pausing again, widening his stance, in a stronger posture, Dove slashed down. Mick was thrown backwards across the stage. He was off his soles, in a flash of light and smoke. And he landed with a thud on his spine.

Groggy, blinking in amazement, Dove crawled back to his knees, pushed himself up. There was going to be no surrender

– no sell out. However, the vocals had stopped. The other two had to clump along, without him. Maybe if you were in a prog rock band, that wouldn't be noticeable. When shouting out a two minute punk song, it left a gap.

'What the fuck is he up to? *With my guitar*?' Snot objected.

'What the fuck is your guitar up to with *him*?'

It was a spectacular thing to witness. I couldn't tear my eyes away. The crowd cheered, assuming these antics were part of the act. The judges were exchanging looks. Morton Treble was like a field mouse who'd seen a combine harvester trundling towards him.

Shaken, not deterred, Mick persevered. He tried to pick up the lyrics – a typically ugly rant. So eventually his hand makes contact with the strings of Luigi's guitar. With an alarming bang and flash, including a puff of smoke from an amp, Dove is jolted and tossed into the air once again. Wow. This was the most dramatic pogo of the punk era. Dove thudded down on the boards in a heap.

Only bass and drums continue, as he just lays there, crumpled, baffled, and badly winded. The guitar meanwhile has fallen free and looks undamaged. That guitar seemed to have a bigger ego than the musicians. Fans were whooping, thinking what a brilliant show. Only Dove, entirely stunned, really felt it.

The members of Dildo begin to glare at each other. In a crisis they turned accusingly on each other. They suspected each other of being the traitor – or saboteur. Dove groped for the mic. and, wobbly, confused, climbed back on to his boots. If he was shaky at the beginning, it was nothing on this. The band was going to make one more attempt to finish off their set.

Bass and drums kick in. They find their place in the song. They attack the chord with increased tempo. The performance is roughly back to normal. When Dove brings his fingers on strings, a burst of sparks shoots out from the neck of the guitar. With a blinding flash, dazzling the mosh pit for a few seconds, there is a further explosion, which ricochets into the dark atmosphere of the hall. This is more dramatic than the annual military show by the Territorials.

There are screams and signs of panic among the crowd. There is a pause in the mêlée of pogo-ing and fist fights. Some people try to scram, risking a stampede, thinking the whole place could go up. We can smell charcoal and sulphur, as smoke drifts across the hall.

The Dildo drummer and bassist abandon their leader. Dove refuses to admit defeat. There's no music now, just the leader's strangled vocals and painful shards of combatant guitar.

Mick Dove's red white and blue Mohican cut – which had attempted to set trends in fascist fashion – bursts into flames. Mick begins to scream and leap in panic. At last, in a desperate attempt to save himself, he tosses Uncle Luigi's guitar aside. He can't play that special guitar, which is fighting him so hard. So the instrument lifts, rises and floats and glides up into the rafters. Sparkling and spangling, the magical instrument comes down again to rest in Stan's hands.

This was amazing to witness and something you could not invent. Snot and his magic guitar were reunited.

The Civic Hall's head caretaker wandered out on stage. He was carrying a slopping bucket of water and poured it all over Mick's head. This seemed to douse the flames okay. Dove's 'patriotic' Mohican was reduced to a smouldering and charred stump.

Another ambulance was called. The NHS was free at the point of delivery. The organising councillors got into a huddle. Should the Battle be cancelled? They decided against it, fearing an even bigger riot that might spill out on to the high street and (worse) into the media. They knew there was an election in the air. There were prizes left to hand out and Jez Starry required his fee.

Roadies rushed on stage to prepare for the next band. Technicians had to repair equipment. Everyone in the hall needed to get their breath back. There was a bit of a delay as this went on. Lucky the event wasn't cancelled, in my critical view. Battle was to be resumed. Thank god for that.

43. Mortal Gets a Date

I returned to the Mortal dressing room for the latest scandal. The band had sent away family, friends and all hangers on (apart from me) trying to psyche itself up for the huge gig.

Fenton and Urine had the job of minding Gina for a while. She was sat about looking jittery and peaky, adjusting the guitar, having reapplied cosmetics and adjusted the stage outfit. Sour Cat didn't have her usual zip but she was on the mend. The Mortal manager was told that his starlet, in time-worn stereotypical rock style, had almost crashed out.

Snot argued it was best if she played the gig pissed. Amazing to think that he'd once penned a love song for this girl. Admittedly he only played it live once. Later on the ditty became a Mortal Wound obscurity. For me it was always his *Laughing Gnome*.

'Fire shootin' out the top of is fuckin 'ed.'

'All right, Nut, get over it. Will you?' Stan said.

'Right, definitely, what's all this, when you've got your big date with rock 'n' roll blinkin destiny?' Gorran warned them, checking off his paint spattering wrist piece. 'No bullshit Mortal, with all those fucking music biz big shots hanging about with check books open and blinkin pens at the ready. So, get in the picture and leave out all this nasty bloomin bitching.'

The punk supremo took to the centre of the floor, while the band members mostly changed and tuned, looking nervous and sheepish.

'Straight up, this is the moment of fucking truth for this amazing little blinkin punk group. No bullshit, listen up, cos when you hop up on that big fucking stage tonight, you gotta play the best bloomin set since Suicide blew 'em all away at the fucking Roxy,' the mogul urged.

'Or catch the bus back hom,' Stan said.

Gina snorted with repressed laughter.

'Straight up Snot, if you're gonna have any blinkin chance of winning that fucking record contract, you've got to make the Dolls sound like blinkin Smokey. No bullshit, like Smokey on a bloomin cruise liner,' Gorran argued.

'No pressure then,' Gina said.

'Don't fucking listen to him,' Snot advised.

'Right, definitely Snot, and all of you, we can't afford any more bloomin cock ups or even punch ups either. Fair play or Mortal Wound's going around the U bend like one of those blinkin submarines without a paddle,' their manager argued, pressing his palms against his heart.

'I'm only here for a riot,' Stan added.

One side of the rock guru's face was afflicted by an apparent savage tooth ache for a moment.

'Right, definitely Snot, that EMI bigwig thinks the kids in this town are always bloomin punching the lights out of each other. So, fair play, no more riot talk, when Starry's easy fucking pickings for any exciting little punk band playing out of their bloomin skins,' Marty urged, with his eyes pinging at the prospect.

Snot shrugged, grunted and returned his attention to the chord combination. But it was his way of showing commitment.

'No bullshit, I was chatting to my mate Jez earlier… straight up, sat up close together at the foyer bar… and he let me know, straight up, that he only wants to know if all this blinkin hype about Mortal's got any shred of fucking truth to it,' Marty explained.

'That's what e fuckin told yer?' Nutcase wondered.

'No bullshit, before he hands out that five album record contract to his blinkin favourites. Straight up, with the chance of getting David fucking Bowie behind the blinkin controls as executive producer.'

'For real?'

'Bowie isn't on that label,' Gina pointed out.

The punk sage gave a start and broadened his embrace. 'Right definitely Gina, what about it, that Bowie's not on the same blinkin label? Straight up, if that makes you feel blinkin better about throwing away your first million quid contract,' Marty objected, losing the wondrous grin.

'Marty's always ready to put his money where his mouth is,' I suggested.

'We know about that,' Stan said.

'No bullshit, if Mortal goes bloomin tits up tonight I won't be able to show my face in the blinkin Dragon for the rest of my life,' Marty objected.

Nutcase was the only one to be moved.

'Find another pub to drink in,' Gina suggested.

However, Marty's stream of hype and expectation was beginning to affect Gina. She's got that panicky look again.

Stan pulled on a mohair sweater, a pink one, that struck vividly against his olive skin and hacked black hair, green, red and blue tipped. 'Don't let the big cheese put you off. We'll camp it up and play loud. No fancy frilly keyboards either.'

Marty battled against those clamping facial muscles. The blocks of teeth came into view, rugged and recently chipped, like Stonehenge. The would-be reassuring leer only set off complex worry lines and late night grooves.

'No worries Marty. We wunt let yer down mate,' Nutcase assured him.

'Right definitely, no bullshit, this is the best blinkin little kick arse little rock band since Iggy was knee high to a fucking grass hopper. So, straight up, don't go and let us down by throwing all your fucking toys out of the pram.'

'Is that right now Marty?' Urine said, impressed.

Encouraged, Marty recovered an optimistic grin and worked it around the room at us.

'No bullshit Billy, don't go and play like a bunch of two thumbed fucking tossers tonight.'

'Ai, fair play now Marty bay, don't think it goes unappreciated,' Billy told him, whacking his cases.

Hope seemed to fill the dressing room, along with big inky palms and fingers and Gorran's halo of candyfloss hair.

'Cheers, Marty,' said Billy.

Nut spat into a cup. 'We'll do our fuckin best.'

* * *

Despite this inspiring speech, I had my doubts about Mortal's longevity. They had more cracks than in the ceilings of the Mansion. Gina and Stan's constant sniping only paused in front of an audience. That was rarely a winning recipe for any band. Gina did her best to make peace with Snot: she offered to transcribe his songs into musical notation. After that he might consider getting copywrite. Stan's eyes grew big at first, but after consulting his ego he turned her down.

When playing live together they merged and tensions vanished. The individuals became a group and the sound came together; as did the tunes. Magic happened.

He wouldn't tolerate her keyboard flourishes, accusing her of trying to copy Herbie Hancock. Snot would have to get over that.

But ultimately it was Snot's group.

* * *

Marty loped back to the auditorium, feeling more electrical tension than Wire, and offering some nuggets of advice at the judges' table.

I decided to tag along with the band as they finished their preparations. Rather than sitting on Marty's shoulder I opted for a backstage view of the gig.

The musicians picked up guitars, keyboards and drumsticks, and headed out towards the crowd. There was a lengthy nerve-jangling walk down long corridors towards the stage.

Even Stan was edgy this time, fiddling with the guitar strap and digging his fingers into his coarse, tinted hair. He knew what was at stake and had the will to win. It was as obscure as *Scott 3* though.

Nutcase turned out in his worn, paint splashed, work dungarees. Nut alone was capable of filling the proscenium arch. Sadly he didn't have access to Nulton Arts drama department's prop cupboard any more. No more bandages and buckets of fake blood.

Bassist Steve Fenton emerged in his ordinary clothes – what you'd later describe as 'smart casual' – in stark contrast to the others. It was a decent fashion tip – don't try to compete.

How was Gina going to cope? There was a charged atmosphere, following all those other bands. That infamous gig at Nulton Arts (so disastrous for Jon Whitmore) was the stuff of legend in town. Every punk in the county claimed to have been present. It was like those early gigs by the Pistols. All those lads had turned out to watch Mortal at the Battle final. They were even there to support them, wishing to hear what a Mortal debut album could potentially sound like.

'Break a leg,' I told Stan.

Snot cut a small, round-shouldered, phlegmatic figure, against backstage paraphernalia. He could have played a droll part in the Christmas panto, I reckon. So could we all. We were surrounded by ropes, pulleys, screens and props. Uncle Luigi's guitar was no prop. Stan clutched the special, if vintage, instrument tight. He knew that the guitar would protect him from loneliness, fear or uncertainty in life. I gazed at my friend with some awe and, maybe, a touch of envy, for that reason.

* * *

As I remember, Gina didn't lose the shakes. Her fibres were frayed by a powerful PA that pumped out Gorran's choice of records. There was a rowdy swell of bodies, the moment Stan was spotted in the wings. A packed hall of local youth – punks, skins, Mods, bikers, 'casuals' and the rest – fuelled by alcohol, drugs and adrenaline – were highly stoked. Cat was green and it wasn't her favourite colour. I found the situation alarming. And, even if I was taking notes for a *Music Mail* gig review, I wasn't a performer, just a spectator.

'You'll be great,' I assured her.

'I can't stop my hands trembling.'

'A bit of nerves is useful. It's natural,' I argued.

She pulled a face of affliction. 'Like dengue fever?'

'It'll wear off, when you start playing those keyboards.'

Sour Cat was getting a white-knuckle ride on the punk dragster.

'A drink would calm me down.'

'You're pulling my leg.'

She pulled a pleading face. 'Go and get one for me, will you, Bottle?'

'No, I won't… not anything alcoholic.'

'Why are you so mean to me?' she implored.

I noticed panic within the rings of grainy mascara. A mist of icy perspiration broke out over her forehead.

'Throw water over her,' Snot suggested, alerted.

'Take it easy so,' Billy assured, giving her shoulder a squeeze.

'Don't let her escape,' Stan ordered.

'They're all on your side,' I said.

Her beautiful new cherry coloured guitar hung heavy from her smooth shoulder.

'Concentrate on the music,' I suggested. 'Put those psychos out of mind.'

The creak of stage boards was like her nerves.

'What's bugging her?' Stan called.

'Nothing,' I replied.

'My dad can still come and collect me,' she suggested.

'Too fucking late for Daddy.'

'We all get nervous, dunt we,' Nut said.

'Cut out the bullshit, we're on soon,' Stan reminded us.

'You don't need me. You said so yourself,' Gina told him.

'She's a disaster,' Stan said flatly.

'Get a feckin grip Gina,' Billy advised. But he put his arm around her for a moment and gave her a one armed hug.

Shaking her head, stooped, 'I don't want to play punk rock,' she explained. 'I'm best on the piano.'

'Or in A&E.'

Crowd noise increased; levels of shouting and distortion rose. How did any of them have the guts?

'No other musician can take your place,' I said. 'You're essential. Nobody has your talent, Gina.'

'Fuck off Bottle. Save your lust for later.'

We took a step back from him.

The panicky black-ringed eyes widened at me. 'Where'd you get such confidence in me?' Gina asked. Her body language was shrunken.

'Definitely you're the heart and soul of this group.'

'Ah come on, Bottle, you're making me sound like Donna Summer.'

'Why not?'

She couldn't help sniggering at my solemnity. It was lightening her mood.

'I just feel totally isolated up there,' she admitted. 'There's just the bloody keyboard, grinning at me like Marty.'

At this moment I did something daring, or thoughtless. I gave her a hug. Not a comradely one-armed hug, as Billy had given her, but a full whole-hearted two armed hug. I wasn't hampered by carrying anything. I'd just got a reporter's note pad in my inside jacket pocket.

When I pulled away, 'What's that?' she said.

Then we stared at each other with the question and I kissed her. I felt the soft wrinkled warmth of her mouth.

Next moment the steward (charged with giving permission for bands to go on stage) checked off his stopwatch, looked down at his clipboard, and gave the cue. The band dashed on, finally all as one, with no chance to think or waver: Gina with them.

44. The Musical Gods

In characteristic nervy style Mortal went about plugging in, roughly getting into tune, while gesturing towards the sound mixer.

I was watching stage-left; next to the Swiss Alps: a panel of painted scenery left over from *The Sound of Music*.

Snot fiddled and twiddled with knobs and buttons; shuffling under the lights as the volatile cauldron bubbled. He had a couple of pedals going. Gina got into tune more quickly, eyes down, strumming and adjusting. She set up her keyboard and gave it a few guilty tickles. Nutcase began to pace alarmingly, emulating the restless soul of a warrior escaped from Valhalla. Billy clambered behind his kit, shook himself like a wet dog, flexed his muscles, adjusted the stool (as if he was going to sit at the bar all night) twirled his sticks and gave a few exploratory smacks.

Satisfied with technical preparations, giving a final thumbs up to the sound guy, Snot stepped into a dusty spot. As ever he cut a diminutive, awkward, tow-headed figure, trailing a lead. He tried not to flinch, or to pay much attention to the storm of spit, beer and plastic pots, immediately launched at him; although he dodged and kept a few paces away from the edge.

'We're touched by your love. We haven't seen each other for a while. Now I don't think I fucking want to,' he sneered, in Rotten's pantomime dame voice. 'What a bunch of horrible gutter snipes,' he continued. (He knew many of these lads from the *Dragon*). 'We thought you'd died of chart boredom. Now we're gonna fucking wake you up!'

Snot's opening chord reverberated like a circular saw through bricks and cables. It was left in the air, until Billy Urine came in on a fearsome roll. He kicked into that bass drum as if trying to knock a hole through walls. Fenton started up on bass and Gina to shadow on rhythm, holding back any flourishes – for later. Nut was pounding the boards from side to side, keeping in shadows at stage rear, a figure of torment. The giant shouter summoned his powers, waiting for Stan to give him a cue. Psyching himself up for a huge release of energy, he was getting inspiration from that mighty Mortal sound.

'Kill Your Social Worker' was instantly recognised by that rucking mob as a local punk favourite. Stan glided through the tune's three-chord pattern, allowing notes to reverberate; with only a slight anxiety over Nutcase's performance around him. Though 'Social Worker' was an early song, simpler to play, Sour Cat had to concentrate (she lacked rehearsal time). The old group chemistry began to flow (as I scribbled into my notepad). The band had that thunderous, unpredictable excitement. It was an incredible band. They made my neck hairs bristle like a forgotten paint brush.

Nutcase sprang into amazing pogo leaps, around the drums and keyboard. He was a huge out-of-control spring, projecting himself towards the front of the stage. Even some of the meatheads in that audience reeled back and gasped. Despite anxieties about his vocal cords, he delivered a terrifying opening high pitched wail. His singing made Kurt Cobain sound like Bing Crosby.

I'm so bored, so fuckin bored
I'm so repressed, depressed
I got out of bed to see her
Kill your social worker

Nutcase wasn't yet a rock god but he launched in that direction. Snot and Sour Cat maintained a fierce guitar backdrop. Anyway Stan wasn't in the habit of moving about on stage. He wasn't able to pogo or jump due to his leg and chest. Anyway that wasn't his role for the group. He was quiet and concentrated, an enigmatic presence, focusing on playing. There were moments when he even turned his back on the audience. There were moments when he *had* to.

Stan was never convinced about Fenton's playing. Later he'd coax Herb back into the group. He'd moan and accuse Steve of being stiff and mechanical, without personality. Fenton wasn't a Jah Wobble or obviously flamboyant or even, properly speaking, a punk. On the other hand he could really play and adapt to musical styles. Typically he'd stand rooted to the spot, staring blankly ahead, set next to Urine. Fenton was reliable in every way; he provided a strong pulse to Snot's erratic tunes. He reminded me of the glum one in Sparks – Ron Mael – a deadpan comical counterpoint. Except Steve's visual style wasn't a deliberate act.

'Social Worker' got a huge audience response. That A&R man from EMI should be wide awake again. When it was over the band looked at each other in euphoria and some relief. They hadn't played much lately and it could have been terrible. Barely pausing they cued up the next song, using eye contact to count the intro. This number went roughly to the tune of The Clash's 'White Riot' (a punk standard) and the lyrics were like this:

Cum, cum
Punk spunk, punk spunk,
When the kids wanna hump

Punk spunk, punk spunk,
Goin' through the night
The kingdom cums
Sup it up, sup it up!
Punk spunk, punk spunk!

Obviously this was one of Snot's shock songs. It came in a short savage burst. He'd penned it during a lunch break in the college refectory.

Mortal ran quickly into 'Stalin Was a Faker'. 'Stalin' had a dynamic snaking guitar line, the big achievement of Stan's bedroom practice. Snot could hit on the most amazing guitar riffs. And he got an incredibly smooth tone out of Luigi's guitar – even with this harsh material. Snot evoked guitar heroes who we pretended to sneer at – or claim we'd never heard! It probably saved us from his big ego. On the other hand, he'd say that was the whole idea of punk.

Snot pushed a button in the Central Nervous System. You could feel the strength of Hercules in his playing. Really, it felt miraculous. Yet he struck an improbable figure on stage; like I said, he barely moved, as if it was all too easy. Gina told me this was a sign of the best musicians – the stillness and an impression of withdrawal. That's why they'd be accused of aloofness or not caring about an audience. It was imposed on Stan by his disability and by his talent. No wonder we idolise such musicians, who inspire us so brilliantly. They don't only make us feel good, inspired, they give us a feeling of invincibility.

He wove a tale full of darkness and blinding lights, lulls and rumbles, love and revenge, hope and fear.

That's right, even this 'pigeon-chested' little bloke, Stan Snot, stooped under a mop of dyed curls, hardly bothering about the crazy crowd, and with the fickle power of the musical gods at his fingertips.

'Stalin' was one of my favourite Mortal Wound tracks. Roy and I had heard Stan repeating the riff over and over, while we had those broken springs up our arses watching the late movie. Repeat, repeat, start, re-start, until he got it dead right.

The lyrics were like this:

Stalin was a faker
Thought he was a dictator
Got all the lads he hated
Into the snowy wastes of Russia
Twiddled his moustaches
Giving out a thousand lashes

That Stalin was a faker
Kept all his people silent
Playing the old tyrant
Everyone knew old Stalin
Was nothing but a darlin'

Cos Stalin was a faker
On the stage of history
Comin' on the big dictator
To all the kids in Russia
Sent away his dissidents
The writers and the kulaks
To Siberian gulags

Even Solgynitzen
Wasn't makin' no sense
Cos everyone knew Stalin
Was nothin' but the darlin'

Cos Stalin was a faker
Came on the big dictator

Posed as a communist
For all the undertakers
He was the old twister
All the dirty work and firin'
Cos Stalin was just a darlin'

Gina put in her first keyboard figure, during the middle eight. She vamped it up for a few bars, having a monsters' ball. From time to time she checked Snot's reaction. Fortunately he chose to keep to himself. He was no fool, he realised how good she sounded and how it came over. She admitted to me that she was influenced by Nat Cole, Hank Jones, Herbie Hancock and emulated Diana Krall. Snot would rather have a fit than copy them. But it didn't matter, because it sounded great.

Meanwhile I checked the judges' table and she was definitely impressing. In fact she was knocking them out like King Daddy. As usual she gave Mortal another dimension. All those performance demons had run away through her fingers. Stage fright felt about as real as sea sickness. I hoped her parents were watching this, from the upper tier. There was a mass of happy punters out there. Mortal were so brilliant that night, even with the danger of missiles. Arguably it was an age of missiles, as the superpowers had hundreds of them pointing at our heads.

With barely a breath or adjustment, Mortal went into their last song. Jez Starry had to make his mind up. There was that recording contract and a major tour to hand over. After all this had driven the local music scene crazy for months on end, like a gold rush.

Billy marked the opening with a snare sound. Steve followed dependably on bass. Stan came tagged in for the next bar, cutting a swathe on his Uncle Luigi's guitar. Your eye went roving for the lead guitar, from the first notes. Gina started on rhythm before switching back to keyboards, even as Stan gave her a dirty look.

After an intro, quite long for a punk group, Nutcase threw himself into the first verse. He swiped the microphone as if he'd got Mick Dove around the throat.

> *Toast the rich, rich*
> *They've got the power*
> *They've got the poor*
> *An' they want more.*
>
> *So toast the rich, rich*
> *Enjoyin' their affluence*
> *Using their influence*
> *They got thru the squeeze*
> *Leading a life of leisure*
>
> *Toast the rich, rich*
> *They know how to use yer*
> *They only wanna please yer*
> *Manipulate and feed yer*
>
> *Toast the rich, rich*
> *They got 'emselves the fun*
> *Villas in the sun*
> *So never mind the scum!*

Snot's political ideas were a form of nihilism. Those nights of discussion, back at the mansion with The Smith and his SWP mates, clearly had some influence.

Suddenly, after pogo-ing ferociously, Nutcase put a boot through the stage boards. What happened? One moment he was springing about, and then the next he vanished beneath. There could hardly have been more anarchy and uproar in that hall, yet somehow the level went up. Only the tip of his green Mohican was showing above ground (or over the surface of the floorboards). It didn't move for a worryingly long time. Like a little privet hedge.

Meanwhile, even as their singer was underground, Mortal had the presence of mind to keep playing. Apparently, we realised afterwards, he'd gone down a faulty old 'trap door'. This device hadn't been utilised since a 1971 production of *Peter Pan*.

Eventually worry (and curiosity) got the better of the musicians. Stan and Gina needed to shuffle over to see where he had gone. Notably they didn't stop playing and singing, because they were determined to reach a finale. Hopefully the judges would think it was part of the act. There was always a chance that Nut would return, after recovering his senses.

Sure enough, after barely two dropped verses, Nutcase launched a comeback. Two huge hands emerged from the hole, followed by beefy forearms and elbows, after suffering Captain Hook treatment. Later we realised that Nut had been concussed. He couldn't remember much of the incident. His head felt worse than interrupted sleep with Little Nut.

There was a huge cheer, as the Mortal vocalist clambered back to his boots. Simply giving his face a rough rub, Nut was back jumping and launched into the song. Maybe some thought it was all part of the show, as when Mick had burst into flame, recreating the fall of the Third Reich.

Nutcase fired off the final verses:

Toast the rich, rich
They just help each other
They recognise one another
Deceive n smile n flatter

So toast the rich, rich
They got the wealth
They got the health
We're just the filth!

Roaring to the end, Nutcase didn't seem to notice that the old trapdoor still gaped. He threw himself into a perilous jig, and we half expected him to plunge again. Everybody held their breath, and maybe that was his idea. Luckily for Sandra and their young family there were no more accidents. Come Monday morning he'd be back plastering and painting ceilings.

So Mortal Wound, my favourite local band of all time, soared to a climax. The lighting rig had convulsions: spotlights crisscrossed into the hall, as if searching for bombers. The lighting technicians claimed that the system had just over-heated. We didn't believe that. Snot apparently floated a few feet into the air, as he played the final charmed notes.

After their set Mortal stood together at stage edge, very happy, enjoying a wildly enthusiastic audience response, as well as continuing to avoid projectiles.

To my mind it was nothing short of a triumph.

45. The Prize Ceremony

Mortal's set had concluded the entire Battle of the Bands contest. After Snot's final searing chord the judges had to put their heads together (in every possible sense). This was their vital time to agree on final scores and decide overall positions for the acts. The influential judges were Jez Starry, Keith from the keyboard shop and Morton Treble. And there were three rockers besides them, tanked up by then and struggling to kick their brains into gear.

During this waiting period, the local music talent were mixing on stage as edgily as bunches of poodles at Crufts.

After an interminable delay – which had emptied another brewery – judges agreed. Each group naturally thought *it* was the best since Presley had dyed his hair black, or a delta bluesman found a socket. As I took more notes I observed the array of big egos on display. There was more smugness there than dry ice at a Led Zep show. Egos inflated to the extent of 'Kiss Live' and artistic pretensions to the proportions of Pink Floyd's pig over Battersea power station. In fact they were almost as insufferable as a music journalist.

So we had the entire local punk glitterati of 1977 lined up in expectation. Betsy Dandie, Paulie, Snot, Anna-kissed, Herb, Bryan and Matty from Amyl Exciters, Rob and Spike from Turbo, Penny Tits from Big Tits and all the others. Only Mick Dove from Steel Dildo wasn't present because, obviously, he was wrapped up in bandages at the hospital.

Paulie Wellington was looking very happy and chummy, being most convinced about his victory. He was born for stardom and a centre-spread semi-nude photo-shoot for *Smash Hits*. Those staple marks along the navel were just a matter of time. Though, admittedly, he was still hanging around in his bathrobe.

In addition to a record deal, with a support slot on a major band tour, there were runners up prizes of equipment and recording time, even record tokens (courtesy of Morton Treble).

A short delay ensued, while the leader of the council made his way gradually on stage to join the artists. He was tasked with heading up and declaring the judges' verdict.

Councillor Hughie Fairbright was greeted by ironic applause, cat calls and hooting. Offended by this welcome the councillor darted stern looks, as he adjusted himself and the microphone. On the other hand, this wasn't the era of love and peace.

In a jiffy Jez Starry joined him, looking impossibly cool, as well as powerful and detached. Fairbright was acting in his capacity as chair of the sub-committee (b) of the committee of entertainment and youth – obviously 'b' stood for bollocks. Fairbright looked a lot like Eric Morecombe, except with a bit more hair and a total lack of warmth or humour. In fact Fairbright was the biggest 'straight man' to ever appear on that stage.

Of course the biggest laugh was really on Nulton rate payers.

There was a jarring visual contrast between the councillor and Jez Starry. Fairbright in his baggy brown suit like a public park exhibitionist: Starry in rock star designer gear – the tight black jeans and silky shirt. He was just back from a Caribbean recording session, where he was drinking mineral water with Jagger on a terrace. The councillor was Methodist teetotal.

Politicians *looked* like politicians in those days. Hughie Fairbright's prepared speech was grotesquely out of sync. The politicians had organised a well-meaning musical talent contest. But it had unwittingly tapped into the exploding punk scene. From their point of view, the evening had been as catastrophic as if the cub scouts had turned into the Khmer Rouge. The event would definitely get into the *Chronicle* for weeks. Paulie intended to write a gig review (for posterity) assuming he won as expected. Belly and Slapper were shrewd enough to send a more hardnosed reporter, to cover any potential crime and politics angle. Where did you start? Only the Crocks were safe, because if any negative stories appeared (about them or their businesses) they'd threaten to withdraw advertising.

'Is this microphone working properly? Can you all hear me, all you boys and girls out there?' Fairbright began. 'All right then. Good evening boys and girls,' he read from notes and a prompt sheet. 'Now then, I'm sure you're as eager as I am... to join me in commending tonight's demonstration of young musical...hum, er...*talent*. Yes, well. I'm very confident that you will join me in praising these young musicians... here in Nulton and Duncehead and all the villages adjoining,' he urged, to a wall of boorish jeers, booing and hilarity.

Brazening it out, Fairbright looked up and down from his papers. There was a seething mass of drunken, doped up, dazed and sweaty kids before him: like the grandchildren from hell. There was not a single cap and toggle in the place, as far as he could recall. No military uniforms, only the baffling uniforms of competing youth cultures. How did he agree to drop into this bear pit?

'Equally,' he persisted. 'I invite you, boys and girls, to condemn... yes, to utterly *condemn* the unsavoury exhibitions of foul language and physical violence that has been witnessed in this 'all tonight... not to talk about lewdly provocative behaviour... yes, indeed... that has been perpetrated by some young musicians performing here this evening.'

There was a crescendo.

Fairbright tried to moisten his lips; blinked out into dazzling lights. He tossed his shiny comb over and gave his paper a shake. Exploiting amplification he overrode the crowd's aggressive mockery.

'My fellow honourable councillors and myself have no doubt... no doubt *whatsoever*, I might stress... that the *vast majority* of young musicians have no sympathy for such yobbish antics... or for revolting displays of public nudity and confrontational behaviour,' he argued, checking off his audience, and loosening his jacket around the shoulders.

'I can inform you... I can inform you all now... *Yes, I heard what you said.!* I fully intend to write to the Chief Inspector to apologise for your behaviour here tonight... on behalf of the silent majority here tonight… And if anybody still at school or college I'll be sending a letter to your teachers,' he shouted at them, pointing out into the ruckus. 'And to apologise for all the foul and obscene behaviour, during this pop competition, which has so disgraced Nulton and Duncehead…and which so offended our Lord Mayor and his good lady wife… so they had no other options but to leave in their ceremonial car.

'We're not here to judge, but we didn't come for that!' he declared.

The turn of phrase was not appreciated. Fortunately for Fairbright most kids were too hammered. They were easy pickings for Crock Security.

'That's right, you lads don't like to hear the truth, do you! I'm certain that Mr Starry 'ere, up from the world famous EMI records in London… would endorse my strong words and back me up to 'ilt. There you are, you got it from the horse's mouth, of a music professional. Some of you lads think you're clever don't you. Let me tell you, you've making fools of yourselves. That's right… Any monkey with the wind up can shout foul language at decent people. Let me remind you, I'm an elected public official,' Hughie insisted.

In that awry neck tie, old suit and scuffed brown suede shoes, he was never going to set any fashion trends.

There was an exchange of views between him and Starry.

'Right then, so d'you want to hear the talent contest results or don't you? You wouldn't see such disgraceful antics from Hank Marvin and the Shadows. I can tell you they was one of the great rock and roll bands.' On this matter Snot and I could agree with him. 'What do you lot know about good music any roads? You can cut it out now! Or we'll get the police in. I don't care about any scandal. We'll have to deal with it. Now, I'm confident that our music executive, Mr Starry 'ere, would back me up on that point.'

Jez Starry shrugged and grinned, even though Hank was still paying for half his salary.

'If you 'aven't heard the Shadows, then you 'aven't heard classic guitar rock,' Fairbright argued. At this moment he was forced to dodge a flying pint pot – which he did with expertise. It went sailing past his head into the alpine backdrop. German lager was streaming down the side of a mountain. You hardly noticed him sway. So smoothly did his head twitch to the side. Only a politician with years of experience on the hustings could have pulled that one off.

Fairbright was frisking himself. 'Now, here's what you've all been waiting for… Yes, here they are. I'm looking for the results,' he stated. He moistened and worked his mouth. The next moment Starry had placed a gold envelope into his sweaty hands. The councillor began the process of opening this envelope, as if it had been lost in the post from Alaska. 'All right then, here we go, boys and girls… Just bear with me a moment. Who licked this blasted envelope?

'And the winner is!'

Starry leant across to stop him and to whisper instructions.

'I see… I see… I beg your pardons… So where is it.? What's this? In third place.? In third place… and winning themselves a block of ten sessions at Troy Crock Sound Recordings Studios, here in Nulton.

'It's Viscous Kittens!'

Even from the audience I could lip-read Paulie. '*Phew*, bloody dodgy. *Third?!* What's going on there, mate? That's a really dodgy decision.'

'Well done, boys and girls… well played!' Hughie shook the hands of the Kittens and Paulie's groupies in turn. Except that Paulie decided not to come forward to pick up. The stray cat immediately slipped off into the wings, in numb disbelief and disappointment. I just saw the whip of his cinch. Where next for him? We had to wonder.

'Now, let me arrange this other bit of paper here. Who was responsible for organising this envelope?' Fairbright fiercely challenged.

'Second place. *Betsy Dandie and the Creamers*!'

There needed to be a further intervention from Starry.

'*Screamers*. Sorry boys and girls, my mistake. Well, congratulations young lady. Well done. *Screamers*. Well I never. I really enjoyed that. First class rock and roll music. Just like mother used to make,' Fairbright praised, as Betsy and the band bounced forward.

'In second place you win vouchers worth up to a thousand pounds from Troy Crock Mail Order Music Services. Marvellous. And a ten pound record token from the *Record Shack*. Many congratulations, love.'

Betsy smiled widely, stoned by then, risking the edge of the stage. 'Cheers everyone!' she called out in her best British, holding up a punch of victory. Nevertheless Les Phoenix would be gutted. Vic the chauffeur had emptied the tank of his Cadillac. American rock stars and American rock impresarios just didn't come second. They'd prove it by phoning up Bonnie Tyler and asking her to do backing vocals on their debut album.

'*Pay attention Mr Starry… hold this for me, will you.?* Much obliged to you, sir. Now, it gives me great pleasure to be present here tonight… at the Nulton Civil 'All… on behalf of… of the sub-committee, bee, of the committee of entertainment and youth… as well as the steering group and as leader of the council and the majority group… and his Honour the Mayor and his good lady wife… to announce the winner of the first ever… Nulton Battle of the Bands competition. So here we go then.

'Right, this is it, and… just the ticket.' Fairbright turned the bit of paper from side to side, even upside down, in search of the pertinent information.

'Much obliged to you again, Mr Starry.'

He nudged Eric Morecombe spectacles back up his sweaty nose.

'I've got it. So the champions of the first Nulton Battle of the Bands contest… winning themselves a recording contract with EMI Records… Is that right, Mr Starry? So long as their material is strong enough… The winner of the contest is:

'Amyl Exciters!' the councillor declared.

Finally the leader of the council allowed himself a smile of relief.

Four toothy peroxide clones in jumpsuits (I was nothing but a balanced critic) gathered their prize from a beaming Jez Starry.

A large section of the crowd immediately began to chant Mortal's name in protest.

'Congratulations guys!' Starry praised. He was giving them a sample copy of a record contract, as well as a new winner's cup. What the fuck happened to that cup? 'See you guys at Abbey Road!' Starry called into the mic. with a big grin.

I couldn't avoid the dejected looks of Mortal Wound. Stan was trying not to give anything away. I had no trouble reading his coded body language and private thoughts. I didn't have to be Jacques Derrida.

'Thanks again Mr Starry. Come back next year will you! I hope you can agree with me… that, *on balance*, this inaugural contest has been a marvellous success story,' Fairbright argued.

There was nobody better for brazening it out.

Of course there was a hell of a scandal in the media. There never was a second official Battle of the Band competition. To be honest, we didn't need one because it couldn't be bettered.

'Have a safe trip home everybody,' Fairbright urged.

46. Paulie Moves His Bongos to London

So that was the end of the Battle; all the hype, rivalry and excitement of that summer were scattered and lost. There was a massive feeling of anti-climax for the musicians and it was a complete downer. There were more ruined egos in that room than smashed bottles at a Greek wedding (Stan's cousin's). Fortunately they had an after gig party to look forward to.

Mortal Wound wasn't in much better shape, as I put my face around their dressing room door. Stan was hunched away experimenting with Luigi's guitar; turned in on himself.

'Why the fuck should I be disappointed?' he said, snapping at me.

'Mortal're the punk band with a reputation around here. You're local favourite,' I argued.

He ignored me.

I was not deterred in my enthusiastic backing. 'Everybody wanted you to win. You played a cracking set.'

'It's just another gig for us, Bottle.'

'You were a shoe-in, Stan.'

'That's your critical opinion?' he put to me.

'Yeah. And the judges didn't even place you.'

'I expected fuck all from them,' he argued, twanging strings and squeezing the neck of his instrument. 'That's what you expect from the establishment. Then you're *not* disappointed… are *you*?'

'Mortal were awesome tonight. Don't tell me different.'

Nutcase was slumped into the corner opposite. Despite a regular weekly pay packet and the arrival of little Nut, he was looking morose. The giant punk cast a thousand yard stare; his Mohican was crestfallen (after the glue had melted). He was wringing those massive hands and cursing musical destiny.

'Those Amyl Exciters lads're good lookin' fuckers. Like fuckin male models,' he remarked. 'In a fuckin toothpaste advert or somefin. We cou'n't compete.'

There was no risk of Nutcase being cast in a toothpaste ad. He'd atonal features.

Like a snare drum Billy was trying to cheer things up. 'C'mon bays, why the long faces so? It wuz nuffin but a little set-back for us. So lads, there it is. This band's got a lot more feckin life in it yet. And we'd better *sta-art* thinkin ahead about our next feckin gig.'

'We've seen the sick face of the fucking pop future,' Snot argued, referring to the winners.

Nutcase looked over to him. 'What's that, Stan mate? What d'ya mean?'

'Music's coming out of a fucking aerosol can in future,' Snot argued.

'Feckin nobs!' Billy agreed.

'But they could really play those keyboards,' Gina unwisely added.

'Nice fuckin air cuts,' added Nut.

'Maybe they want another fucking keyboardist,' Snot told her.

She straightened up. 'What's that mean?'

'You only read fucking music, or what?'

'Don't pay any attention,' I advised. 'He's just temporarily bitter.'

'The Exciters' songs were interesting,' Cat persisted.

'Mindless and superficial lyrics,' disagreed Nulton's celebrity rock columnist.

She wouldn't be upstaged by a non-musician like me. 'No, I reckon there's a lot of irony in them.'

'Fucking ironing!' Snot cut back.

'They won, dint they?' Nutcase agreed, rubbing the shaved sides of his head.

'This isn't the time to be fair,' I argued.

'I an't been so down in me fuckin life,' Nut admitted.

'Ah, come on Nut, mate. Who gives a flying V?' Snot told him.

'Oh now, come on bays, we'll get over this, so we shall.'

'Mortal's the best group,' I insisted.

'Anyway we scared the shit out of that bloke… what was his fucking name?' Stan said. 'Fucking Starry?'

'I dunt fink e wanted another punk band,' Nutcase argued.

'We had too much attitude,' Gina said.

'The sound was ferocious,' I added.

'Yeah.'

'Wanker.'

'Nob.'

* * *

Snot had an acute ear for music. And he picked up a fresh note between Cat and me too. It wasn't only because I had to wipe her black lipstick off my cheek.

It had an instant cooling effect on our friendship. For a while our level of personal warmth was back to pre-punk levels. The plastic armies of Austro-Hungary began to move again on the Russian Imperial forces. Despite his hump and other physical problems, Snot had a way with the girls. Coming second was not familiar to him in any part of life; even if, off stage, Gina and he were frequently out of tune. And his parents had spoilt him savagely, so he was used to getting what he wanted. Snot had lost out with Sour Cat and in the Battle too; so the magic guitar was much easier to handle; and it belonged exclusively to him.

Gina agreed to go to see the Stranglers and the Damned in London with me. It had to be a date, or what else could you call it? All next week I was afraid she'd change her mind. I expected to get something negative over the grapevine. Perhaps she only agreed because of that bump to the head. She wanted to see The Jam with me the following week, there had to be something wrong with her mind. Of course it wouldn't last, but we *did* go out together a few times – we got some brilliant music in and had some great experiences.

That evening I was anxious that Gina would spot me as a nerd or a freak. For a long time I was suffering my own version of stage fright – off-stage fright. This terror glued my tongue to the roof of my mouth like loft insulation.

As for Snot, I didn't have much sympathy. He was constantly sniping at her, like John Lydon stuck in a lift with a tabloid journalist. He had more girls in awe than you could fit into a Pepsi commercial. So what was his big problem?

* * *

Not being stone hearted I agreed to buy Cat a drink. She deserved a relaxing tipple after that ordeal. So we found our way to the backstage artists' bar. Being eagerly anticipated by Nulton rockers the after-gig party was in full swing.

We made our way through the crush: musicians, entourages, friends, family, blaggers and liggers. I'd spotted Marty Gorran in his natural habitat. Phoenix was there, in a more subdued mood, pulling on a consolation Havana. He was less than impressed with that limey judging panel. Betsy and her Screamers were relaxed as ever – call it American optimism, or just a sense of proportion.

Les wasn't vindictive enough to demand Marty's car. The *S&M* chief was able pay back the loan in his own time. Not only were they good mates really but that Sunbeam was way too small for any Texan music magnate.

Amyl Exciters, we learnt, were not present. Jez 'Units' Starry had already whisked them away to the *Flamingo* for a celebration lig with crates of pink champagne ordered in. The freshly signed band were also being wined and dined courtesy of Dave Crock, as the detail of their recording contract was explained.

A bit later a flushed Roy dropped by with Cindy Gorran. 'Away Bottle comrade, we sold oo-ver two hun'red copies of the mag,' he told me.

'Good going,' I replied.

'Ai, the income'll pay for a second edition, marra, if you're int'rested.'

I thought about the idea. 'I'm in favour, if you reckon we'll find another six local bands to interview.'

'We'll do our best, Bottle man. All right, our Gina?'

'How's the revolution?'

'Ai, I'm in decent fettle at the moo-ment mind, thanks very

much. So how are you, comrade?'

'Fine fettle as well, thank you Roy,' she agreed.

'*Congrat-u-lations* marra, on that storming gig.'

'So you watched the band play? It was great, wasn't it? I really enjoyed it too.'

'That's good to *he-ar*, comrade, cos you played great tonight mind. There's no doot Gina man, Mortal's the best group by miles. What were those judges thinkin' of like? Don't worry marra, I've got them deaf bas'tads down in my little bo-ok,' Smithy pledged.

'I reckon they lost their critical faculties,' I added. They'd drunk enough beer to bring down a Led Zeppelin.

'We're not a big record company type of band,' Cat reflected.

'Away man, you're too fuckin good for those exploit-ative bas'tads.'

'That's what I told the others. But they'll all down hearted over it,' she shrugged.

'Away man, it's those fucking multi-national corp'rations!' Smithy rattled.

'We've got to live with them… If we want to make music,' Gina was saying.

'After the revolution we'll be makin' our *ooh-n* music, marra,' Roy explained. 'Ai, that's right, not just to make fat profits… for the ruling class mind. Without them bas'tads pullin' all the strings, comrades. Everybody'll get their fair chance mind,' he promised – brown eyes gleamed behind thick smudgy panes.

'Thanks for supporting us,' Gina said.

'Ai man, that Starry blork'll be one of the first lined up against the fucking wall, marra,' he promised, sticking the inhaler back into his mouth.

'That's turning into a long bloody wall,' I noticed: though the image of Starry against it was very appealing.

'Didn't they already build that wall?' Gina commented.

'Anyways marra, what are you two drinkin'?' Roy asked – ever generous.

The brewers and distillers were tolerable capitalist exploiters.

I turned down the offer of another pint. Two was my limit. As I mentioned, I was just waiting for the skinny Latte to arrive.

Of course it took another twenty years – except in those family operated Italian cafes in London.

'Changing the subject, lads. Where the hell's Paulie got to?' I wondered.

'Ai, don't even ask, comrade.'

'No? Well, I saw him slipping off… after Kittens were placed third.'

'Better than us,' Gina said. 'What's he complaining about?'

The Smith exhaled air of frustration. 'Ai man, but comin' third's not good enough for Welling'on, mind.'

'What's going on with that lad?' I bemoaned.

'Is Paulie all right? Do you think?' Gina asked.

Roy's whole physiognomy expressed disgust and weariness. 'Away man, the daft bugger's left his jab at the news-peeper this week. He's wanted to take his bongos to London. Wants to try his luck doon in the smurk,' Roy informed us, with a tremble of amazement and dread.

'Right, so he's moving out of the mansion?'

'Ai man, that's it now, cos he met these lads doon at the Electric Ballroom last week. Startin' their own band and he told 'em how he's a talented musician… and a lot of other bullshit. Now these lads believe him mind, and they want him to be their singer and play his bongos for 'em, marra!' Roy explained, amazed and appalled.

'That's the end of their group,' Gina predicted.

'Paulie's trying to reinvent himself… yet again,' I said.

'No more Viscous Kittens either.'

'Away Gina man, d'you think that lad's got any int'rest in music now? D'you think Paulie'll want to go and rehearse with 'em every week? Get down to the studio on time, comrade? Noooh! Away man, he's useless, a total *buffoon!*' Roy objected, struggling to breathe. Any hilarity over Wellington's antics had evaporated.

'What's Paulie going to work in London?' Gina considered.

'Away, I doon't have the fain'est idea, comrade. And at this moment, marra, I doont care!' he insisted.

'Can he look after himself?' I wondered.

The SWP man was agitated. 'Away man, your guess's as good as mine. I don't know what he'd told those lads down in London mind. They prob'ly think he's Ravi Shankar like,' Roy speculated, boggling behind the glasses.

'Paulie's off on his own planet,' Cat said.

'Ai man, he's fooked up this one now, hasn't he!'

'It's much safer for the Nulton music scene.'

'Away Bottle man, I can't be that lad's mother all the *tame*! See yer back at the mansion then, marra. I'll go and find our Cindy again, cos I offered to walk her hoom. Ai, it's gettin' dark like, and those fucking fascists are lurkin' aboot.'

At which he zipped up his parker, threw a proletarian knapsack over a shoulder and dashed off on his springy toes. Chronic asthma never stopped him moving quickly, at big demos or on other occasions.

'Paulie did make a bit of an arse of himself,' Gina mused, sipping her vodka and orange.

'That wouldn't bother him none.'

'All the same, Bottle, I feel sorry for him. Don't you?'

'I'm worried for him… just going off… to London like that. What the hell's he gonna do there. Apart from bashing his bloody bongos.'

'He's a bit helpless and lost that boy,' Gina mused.

I gave her a wary look.

'Almost too nice and innocent for this world, don't you think?'

Probably I had an expression of fear and disgust on my mug.

'What was he trying to pull in that bath robe?'

I could only shrug.

'Fucking Nora, *a bath robe*.'

'Yeah.'

47. Jacky la Costa *Introduces*

'The big record companies are sick of punk now,' Gina was arguing. Her head was clearing amazingly quickly.

'Depends on the band,' I suggested: propping an elbow against the wall, suddenly more self-confident, in a *man-of-the-world* posture. 'They wouldn't be sick of Mortal. If they heard you tonight, they'd snap you up.'

Cat gave a startled look. 'Snap us up? *Right*. They signed a few punk bands. Flavour of the month. They're afraid of missing something. Doesn't mean they *like* punk.'

'You got to be realistic,' I said.

'Realistic? That's for when you're dead,' she insisted.

'They're only in it for the profit. Like Roy said. What does he expect?'

'They'll be glad when this punk movement ends. So they can get back to blokes with blonde perms, singing about the fucking chicks.'

'I'm not changing my hair style. Not yet,' I assured her.

Cat grinned and touched it. She seemed to approve. 'We'd better enjoy this scene… while it's going on… cos people will talk about it years ahead. They'll be looking back. But this isn't nostalgia. It's happening.'

'Punk is necessary though, isn't it. A type of re-start for rock music and youth culture,' I argued.

'Yeah, right, we're got to enjoy this while it's going on. Maybe punk's just a moment,' she argued. 'Perhaps that moment has already gone.'

'That mad moment,' I said, sounding knowledgeable, milking my music critic celebrity. It seemed to work a bit of magic.

While Gina and I gassed about the future of rock 'n' roll, staring into the mirrorball, I became conscious – at the edge of my vision

– of a bloke ogling her. This character was standing about in a conflicted detached way. He was brooding around one of the bars, staring at Cat twitchily, as if smoke was bothering him. Finally he made his move across the 'artists bar' red carpet. *Just one evening with Gina* – I thought – *making a good impression with my music criticism and already the bloody romantic rivals come shoving me aside.* Probably she provoked a lot of blokes, with her natural wit, talent and beauty. It was highly likely. So if – by some miracle – we went out with each other, I'd better get used to that – buy myself a crash helmet and knuckleduster. We'd both land up in the General next time, unfortunately in single beds.

'Music and business doesn't always mix well,' Cat continued to riff – in her truthful yet confused way. She was always more coherent musically.

'Yeah, could be. Just a necessary marriage.' Unfortunate bed fellows, you could say.

'That's why they call our music the *avant-garde*.'

Any talk about the avant-garde was throwing me, as I was just catching up with Iggy, Devo and Patti Smith.

'Hey, how are you guys?' this bloke interrupted.

Sour Cat gazed sideways – as if cigarette smoke was beginning to bother her as well. She was still more interested in her musical argument. In fact she decided to continue with it.

'Is it Gina Watson?'

'Excuse me?'

'Jacky la Costa,' the bloke said.

'Yeah? So? If you didn't notice, we were talking.'

'Sure, but…'

La Costa was forty something years old. He resembled a cross between Burt Reynolds and Roy Orbison. He didn't allow an insinuating grin to drop from his older man's confident, dark walnut face.

'What you want? You saying you know me?'

'It's *Jacky la Costa*.'

'What's up?'

Jacky had a very rock 'n' roll slicked-back hair style, whisky brown eyes, peppery stubble and a penchant for a 'man in black' clothing style. The quiff wasn't a rug either, like Burt's or Roy's, although it was a bottled shade of raven black. His brand of handsome, charming self-assurance, put me on my guard. *This could be just my luck.*

'*Sour Cat*, right?'

She darted looks about the room, as if it could be someone else. Maybe she was just afraid her father was present (though her teetotal parents had gone home, delighted at her confident performance). She returned her gaze but refused to shake his hand. Jacky's tough tanned fingers poked out from a shirt cuff, broad and stiff as a cereal box. A few showy rocks knobbled his fingers too.

'Oh, sure, okay…'

'So am I expected to recognise you, or what?' she wondered. She was trying to place him; some tribute to Alvin Stardust? Kris Kristofferson?

'Sure, I'm feelin' your hook,' he told her strangely.

'What do you want?'

'It's no skin off my ass. But I'm Jacky la Costa, just the same, owner of a stable of leading independent record labels. Yeah, well, you might have read about me in the music papers every week,' Jacky suggested. 'Surely, not to worry Gina… Cos I've got a big roster of labels. The biggest is *Dick Discs*.'

Miss Cat finally got the reference. 'Oh yeah, I've definitely read about you in the music papers. I'd never expect to bump into you here.'

'There's a Battle of the Bands taking place. Didn't you hear?' he smirked.

'Something,' she replied.

'On a big music night like this,' I added.

'Surely, man. So you don't mind… if I join you guys?'

'Did you bring some carry outs,' she joked.

La Costa inserted his broad shoulders between Sour Cat and me.

'This is my mate, Paul Bottle. He edits a fanzine. It was on sale tonight. *Ob-scene*.'

'Sure, very entertaining,' Jacky said. 'Promises a lot!' He gave his inside jacket pocket a bash.

'You got a copy?'

'And he writes gig reviews for *Music Mail* too,' she explained.

'Oh right, sure. I was in the hall tonight and I really enjoyed your performance,' La Costa told her.

'The band? Ah, *thanks*. We did all right, with this gig.'

'Sure.'

'No big prize though!'

I was staring into La Costa's tufted ear hair at this point.

'Surely, you blew me away.'

'Mortal Wound isn't my band. I'm just a member,' Sour Cat explained.

'Sure. So how long have you been performing? You play the guitar well, you sing… *great*. Do you write your own songs?' The record mogul had an eager look.

'I'm not Burt Bacharach,' she teased.

'Right!'

Jacky's Cheshire cat grin crinkled his eyes. All the same he'd got a nervous thing going with his hand, as if he'd suffered too many drum tracks.

'You're a keyboardist too. Is that right?'

'That's what I can do. Only they don't like me doing keyboards. Stan writes most of the tunes, so far. Maybe I'll get the chance to contribute later on.'

'Right, Jacky, it's good to meet you… what's your interest in the band? What's your angle on this?' I asked.

Touching my elbow Jacky offered me a pitying 'leave this to me, son' smile. Background boy – that was my fate. 'You came over really damn well on stage, Gina. Talent, originality, presence. That's what I damn well got from you up there.'

Cat was thrilled with such an observation; keeping her previous fears a secret.

La Costa grinned, sighed, drew breath. He looked away and looked back again, as if Gina was a million dollars. Maybe she was that and more. 'I sure had a great time tonight. How could those pricks of judges fail to place you? I nearly jumped out of my fucking boots.' He ran his Gordian knuckles through that 'duck's arse' barnet. His quiff gleamed like a chunk of melting tar under the lights. 'Damn, how did they come to their decision?' Jacky said – still tapping – not breaking up his intensely narrow malty gaze.

Gina and I could only wince at the cold coffee of fate.

Jacky pulled out a twenty pack of cigarettes. 'Here. You like? Do you smoke?' he offered.

'Only after sex,' Cat told him.

He burst out laughing. 'Oh, yeah, really?'

'When it's any good.'

'Oh. At your age?' the leading independent record owner seemed shocked.

'I'm *seventeen*,' she retorted crossly.

'Oh.'

'And this isn't nineteen *fifty* seven.'

'Sure, right.'

I stared at my boots and rearranged the contact of the soles to the ground.

La Costa opted to abstain from smoking. Infact, just managing not to drop the pack, twirling and replacing them, awkwardly within the mature leather jacket.

'Who the hell was that bunch of jump suited clowns, Amyl Exciters anyway?' he declared.

'Is guitar music going out of fashion or what?' Cat replied.

'Total crap,' I said.

'That A&R guy knew damn all. It was the wrong damn call tonight.'

'We thought so.'

'Fuckin' typical, man.'

Cat was starting to warm to Jacky. His medley of tics was relaxing her. Perhaps being neurotic made him sympathetic towards music talent.

'Yeah and who was that clown, up there in his goddamn bath robe?' Jacky asked – his voice went to a croak.

'That would be Paulie,' she said.

Luckily Gina never got to smok in bed next to Paulie, after good sex.

'He's scrammed to London,' I explained. 'Took his bongos. Joining a group, a type of collective... or commune or something... calling th'emselves Rip Rig and Random.'

'Sure, that guy, who's singer with Viscous Kittens band, was it?'

'*Viscous*,' I said.

'Whatever, man. Stick or non-stick... I couldn't believe my fucking eyes... some guy stood up there in his bathrobe,' he recalled, shaking his head. 'Never seen nothing like that before.' I could hear the cigarettes in Jacky's voice, before and after sex.

'Right, but the rest of the group was good,' I argued.

'Surely. Then that trailer trash screecher coming second,' Jacky said. 'Give me strength.'

'Ah, c'm on, she wasn't too bad,' Gina said. 'I heard much worse. She's a good guitarist and her voice is powerful.'

'Surely, but you coulda tapped me over. I thought it hada be a damn mistake, when that politician muppet gave us the final order. Couldn't believe my damn ears. Even in that band you blew me away. You stood out. No damn doubt,' Jacky argued. The fingers of his right hand picked up a different time meanwhile.

'Right, so we got your opinion,' I said. 'So what do you gonna do for Mortal Wound?'

'Sure, I'll get back to the damn point of this... because I'm not going to overlook an original talent. It'd damn near kill me. I couldn't damn well live with myself afterwards!' he declared, hoarsely.

It was making Cat nervous. 'Well, right, so what about it?' the girl wondered.

'Sure, I'm going to offer you a record deal... that's what's about it!' The grooves and wrinkles around his malt flavoured eyes deepened.

Gina couldn't look unimpressed any more. She looked at Jacky la Costa as if he was Santa Claus with a sack of new records.

'Amazing. But I can't give you a postive reply... until I speak to the rest of the band.'

'Really, a deal!'

'*The rest of the band*? Why'd I want to speak to them for?' The face of experience creased like an old pommel horse.

'It's great, you know… that you want to offer us a deal, but you know… there's band democracy… we'll have to discuss this offer.'

It had never existed before. Stan was Mussollini. Yet I was impressed by her loyalty.

'The deal is for you, Gina, not for the others. *Dick Discs* is too big for those guys.'

Sour Cat and I exchanged looks.

'What's that? Too big for what?' she told him.

'Sure, I can offer you a copper-bottomed contract. We'll book you into our little studio in Hammersmith… with a leading producer. We'll get you reviewed, we'll get you on the damn radio. You can record all your own songs if you want to. After a couple of singles we'll release your LP… with the biggest publicity campaign since *Dick Discs* began,' he pledged.

Gina and I made efforts to recover from our shock. Or was she to be tempted into such a betrayal?

'Sure, because here in *Dick Discs* we have a massive reputation… And 'a better ear for music'. Sales last month were up to the level of *Stiff* and *Rough Trade*. We've got outstanding designers. Marketing and publicity are so damn hot, people get fired in the so-called major record companies. We got our *Gross Kunst* label over there in Berlin… to handle European distribution and copyright.'

'Trying to impress me or what?' Gina commented.

'No need to tell the others. Sure, we can't give you big money up front. I'm not going to argue *Dick Discs* is bigger than the majors. We don't have Abbey Road available,' he told her – laughing with frustration at her negative attitude.

'I don't care if you want to record me singing with strings,' Gina said. Her look came right out of the deep freeze. 'What are you trying to pull?'

'This is an honest interest, in your talent.'

'Nothing honest about it. You can't cherry pick one person out of our great little band.'

'It's a take it or damn well leave it offer,' he insisted – having lost that smile.

'Leave it. Otherwise, I know, you'll just kill it. You start picking and choosing with original personnel… the sound and the personality will go out of it. That's fatal. Whatever we've got… with Mortal… that's special. Do you get me?'

'You can't just dump Mortal like this. Not after how great they played tonight.'

The record boss took not a flicker of interest. 'Don't try to explain this business to me, son,' he said, grimly.

Gina narrowed her eyes – and I wouldn't want to be in such tight focus.

Jacky watched her estimation plummet. He took another sip of hard liquor and chuckled in a genial way. 'Sure. I understand where you're coming from. You're damn sweet and loyal. I can see that. But it isn't my job to do musicians any favours.'

'Excuse me, you don't have to do our band any favours.'

'Sure, but don't reject your big opportunity.'

'We come together or not at all.'

'Sure, but my job's to sell records. I need artists I can damn well promote. It's all about songs and image, man,' Jacky argued, up on his toes.

'Excuse me, but that's top quality bullshit.'

'Oh yeah? I'll never get kids to identify with a character like Stan Snot. The image is all wrong with that kid. He just doesn't look cool. I'm sorry.'

'It's been *fun* meeting you,' Gina told him.

'Surely, but you're not going to turn me down kid… are you?'

Gina gave a shrivelling look, accentuated by rings of black, like an owl from hell.

'Did the Pistols's talk upset you?' I asked.

'You're really going to spit on my damn boots?' La Costa marvelled.

'That's what the punks *do*,' Cat reminded him.

* * *

'What are you fucking hob-nobbing here about?' Stan demanded, shuffling over. The entire motley of Mortal came to join us. They still had that miserable aura of defeat.

'Recognise our lead guitarist?' Gina remarked. 'See any star potential?'

'What's that?' Snot wondered.

La Costa looked very embarrassed.

'I recognise Jacky La Costa, don't I?' Stan said.

'You did?'

'No double-take necessary.'

'*Dick Discs* is my favourite fucking label,' Snot enthused.

'Damn pleased to meet you all.'

'I'm totally in to Screamin Chickens,' he admitted.

La Costa was back grinning and gloating.

'I've got everything Septic Tank released on *Gross Kunst*.'

'Yeah, fuckin awesome. So when's the new Big Foot single out?' Nutcase asked.

'Next month,' the label boss informed them.

'Fuckin ace.'

'I got the tapes for their new EP last week.'

'So what's the chief of *Dick Discs* doing here in old Nulton town?' Snot wondered 'You wasn't here to watch that Battle of the Bands contest… otherwise known as the war of the losers, was you?'

'Sure, bang on.'

'Butlin's ballroom closed?' Stan said.

'What you fink Jacky, mate? Was we any good or what?' Nutcase enquired, wringing his giant hands.

'Fair play now, Jacky bay, we'd be happy to hear your opinion on us like,' Billy said. 'Fair play now, is there anythin' for us to feckin go on?'

'I don't believe it, Jacky La Costa from *Dick Discs*, here tonight, catching one of our gigs,' Stan said. It was so rare for him to show enthusiasm.

'Jacky heard us play, Stan. You caught Jacky and me in the middle of negotiations,' Gina said, averting her gaze, fluttering the killer-spider eyelashes.

'What fucking negotations?' Snot demanded.

'Gina, the big guy here is definitely out,' Jacky wheezed, behind his hand.

'You tell him that,' she retorted.

'What?' said Nutcase, looking between them.

The variegated bunch of punks were all confused.

'Sure, but I'd get more than I bargained for here,' Jacky told his protege.

'This is your lucky night,' Cat said.

Snot was very baffled. 'You going to explain this?'

Gina stared back at La Costa with mock bewilderment. 'Does this band have its record deal or what?'

Jacky laughed deeply and slowly, shaking his head.

'Since when did you negotiate record deals? I'm the leader of this band,' Stan reminded her.

'This isn't a solo act, this is a *group*,' I reminded him.

Stan glared as if I stole his toy tank again.

'Fair play, so what type of record deal we talking about here so, lads?'

'Mortal on *Dick Discs*?' said Stan. 'Or maybe some *Gross Kunst* EPs?'

'Sure… Stan… *Gina*… the rest of you guys… What I can offer you… What I can offer *Mortal Wound*… is a deal for two singles and an album… first up, right? Surely, if those first releases go well, man, we'll offer you a longer term deal. That's the best damn offer I'm throwing down on the table!' Jacky declared.

'I can't believe me ears,' Nutcase remarked, standing even taller.

'Cheers Jacky!' Billy told him, whacking the indie record boss's leather clad shoulder.

'Right, so what was the problem with me?' Snot said.

'Where you want to start?' Gina told him. She gave a tipsy laugh.

'How come I was tuning into something?' Stan objected.

'Tune out,' I told him.

'What you fucking talking about, Bottle?'

'Surely, no problem guys, cos I invite you all down to the *Dick Disc* office. Come and have a good damn look at our studio in

Hammersmith. I'm not gonna tell you *Dick Discs* is bigger than the majors. *Dick* is large enough to make an impact. We'll turn you into massive winners, straight down the damn line,' Jacky assured them.

'Cheers Jacky!' Nut declared.

'We'll draw up the damn contract, after you have a look at the studio. Do you guys have a manager yet? Right, so get the guy over here a. s. a. p. and I'll buy him a celebratory pint… and all of you guys!' he offered.

'Hello, *hello*. No bullshit, what's happening? Right, definitely, looks as if we got a proper blinkin big pow-wow going on here,' Gorran observed, descending. He turned an inquisitive grin around the grouping. 'Straight up lads, is there something wrong with my blinkin eyes or is this the big chief from bloomin *Dick Discs* stood before us?'

'One and the same, man,' Jacky informed him. 'And who might this guy be? Your manager?' he asked, turning to Gina.

'*Marty Gorran*, and I reckon you've already had your first blinkin introductions to the best little kick-arse punk band in the country. Fair play, and this side of the Sex Pistols' secret gig at Duncehead's fucking Ballroom last year,' Marty informed him.

'Yeah, sure, man…'

'*No doubt* Jacky mate, or I must be blinkin Tom Jones. No bullshit, I snapped 'em up first blinkin chance I got, knowing they'd make it up the singles chart quicker'n that Georgio bloomin Marauder on that fucking mini moog his.'

But no hype was necessary from the punk maestro at this stage. It looked as if Marty was about to lead the negotations and to strike his first gold disc. The next riot would be on a much bigger scale.

After striking a deal, cutting a first single, arranging the first big supporting tour, Mortal set off on the whole crazy, exciting music biz shebang.

Kyiv – July 16th, 2016

You may also enjoy...

NOAH'S HEART

'FRESH AND CLICHE-FREE'
- JILL DAWSON

NEIL ROWLAND

You may also enjoy...

THE CITY DEALER

NEIL ROWLAND

'...a real page turner – riveting'